# THE BENEFIT

## NICK MAYO

STEIN AND DAY/*Publishers*/New York

First published in 1980
Copyright © 1980 by Nick Mayo
All rights reserved
Designed by Louis Ditizio
Printed in the United States of America
Stein and Day/*Publishers*/Scarborough House
Briarcliff Manor, N.Y. 10510

Library of Congress Cataloging in Publication Data

Mayo, Nick.
  The benefit.

  I. Title.
PZ4.M47412Be [PS3563.A964]      813.'.5'4      79-65106
ISBN 0-8128-2679-5

*For my father, L.J.M.,*
*Who lived through most of it,*
*And for my very best friend*
*In all the world, F.M.N.,*
*To whom I owe, at least,*
*The rest of my life . . .*

# Acknowledgments

It is impossible, beyond my thanks, to repay my debt to Martin Baum, Edward and Mildred Lewis, Stanley and Betty Sheinbaum, Harold Heifetz, Fred Okrand, Pat Begalla, Alan Siegel, John G. Stratton, Ph.D., and Renni Browne for their invaluable assistance and support.

And to Sol Stein and Patricia Day, for the gift of their timely rescue and shelter, my gratitude and my love.

# Contents

"You have to shoot somebody, burn yourself alive, do something violent, in order to get any attention at all, however good your cause, however patient you have been, however well you have put your case. There is an absolute stone wall of indifference, all over the world."

–Arnold Toynbee (1889–1975)

*A funny thing happened on the way to the undertaker.*

*It was in all the newspapers, but the whole story never came out. If a scandal doesn't involve dirt in high places—like somebody's chicken-shit hand caught in the public till, or a congressman's secretary with her legs spread high in the air—it just doesn't rate first-class investigative coverage by the media.*

*So, except in Los Angeles—where it happened—this story was buried in the gutters of the back pages, next to the obits, where somebody thought it belonged. But the story still lives. Certain people, several millions of them, still talk about it as their one moment of glory . . . their noble scream.*

*The story needs to be told, all of it, with no holds barred to protect the guilty—or the innocent, who are rarely protected in any case. Who knows? Maybe it's not too late. Maybe somebody will do something.*

*Never mind who I am, or how I came to know these people. Or what they meant to me, or what I was to them. It is enough that I was there through the whole thing . . . before it started, and after it was all over.*

# 1

# THE MEETING

There is a little park, right in the middle of the City of the Angels, just behind the twenty-million-dollar Museum of Art, on fashionable Wilshire Boulevard. The land was deeded to Los Angeles County in 1915 by a crusty old land baron named Captain Allan Hancock, whose name it bears. But everybody around here just calls Hancock Park the La Brea Tar Pits.

About a million years ago, when the earth had cooled off from its flight through starry space and the polar ice caps had started to air-condition our little ball of mud, this park site was formed into a natural lowland bowl. Pleistocene rainstorms deposited water in great quantities, and the animals came in their turns to drink.

At dawn, there were the flocks of *Teratornis*, their giant wings beating the chill air. At midmorning, the herds of giant mastadon raised clouds of dust as they lumbered into the clearing of water holes. Then came pairs of giant ground sloth, gentle herbivores, who sniffed the fetid air as they slunk to the edge of the pond. Just before sunset, packs of great dire wolf arrived, snarling for position, as they circled the pools, finally taking their places to lap at the cool water. And last, through the blackness of the prehistoric night, came the predators. Prides of sabre-tooth cats, drinking in order of seniority, slaking their thirst after the kill.

These animals are all extinct. Too late, they learned that this oasis was a death trap. Just beneath the surface of the inviting water, the still-cooling subcrust of the earth slowly bubbled up a viscous petroleum substance, and nature here performed a slow and silent drama of death. The tarlike ooze sucked each unsuspecting animal victim down, holding fast against its futile struggle—until the animal sank deep enough to drown, died of starvation, or was set upon by the ever-waiting carnivores.

Now, a million years later, at the southwest corner of the little park, surrounded by a chain link fence, there is still a small stinking lake, an eerie vestige of the ice age, the oil still oozing to the surface. In the slimy water,

3

about twenty yards from shore, stands a huge concrete statue of a mastadon, his trunk and tusks reaching skyward, struggling painfully in vain as he is sucked down into the consuming mire. America is justly famous for its memorial monuments.

Some animals still frequent the park. The old ones of the very last species, *Homo sapiens*. For them, the county has here provided gently curving macadam walks, and long wooden benches, and large white waste cans, stenciled TRASH in red.

Here is where it all started. The plan had been festering for a long time, but here is where the desperate part began to take shape. Here is where the terrorists met on a bright and chilly January 1976 afternoon, while the others—who didn't believe what could be done—played checkers and pinochle and klabiash at the Senior Citizens' Center.

Stosh was the first of the conspirators to arrive, his overcoat collar buttoned tightly around his huge bull neck, his walking stick swinging at his side as he leaned forward against the cold wind. The stiff breeze flapped Stosh's coat at his knees and flattened the cheap fold-up card table he carried hard against his body.

Stanislaus Vlasic, a sixty-eight-year-old, six-and-a-half-foot Polish giant, had come to America at the end of World War I, after burying his young wife and infant boy, both of whom had died on the same day in the great influenza epidemic.

He came first to Pittsburgh, where he and his cousin Steve started a small ornamental iron shop, following the trade for which he was apprenticed as a boy in the old country. Steve worked on the outside, selling, and Stosh worked the fire and the tongs, shaping the black iron at the ringing anvil.

*Clang!-Clatt! Clang!-Clatt!* The exploding sparks carommed off the walls of the little shed as Stosh hammered and twisted the black ribbons of iron into window grates and grave enclosures and fancy front gates with designs of circles within circles and flowers and Greek keys and delicate, viney leaves. And soon the rich people who lived in the Heights were safe and secure behind the piked ornamental fences and the beautiful high gates, forged by Stosh Vlasic as he sweated and sang to the beat of his hot sledge and ball-peen. He was a powerful oak of a man then, his balloon arms larger than most men's legs. How he rejoiced in his youth and strength! Sometimes he would twist and curl the bands of iron *without* heat, laughing aloud as the metal turned to his will.

"You are only a dead mineral," he would shout, "and Stanislaus Vlasic is a man! A man from Cracow!" And as the black strand of iron twisted in his grip, squealing in metallic agreement, Stosh would toss his massive shaggy head back, his potato-face exploding with roaring laughter to the two-by-four rafters. And only he knew why he laughed. Only he knew how good

4

it made him feel to laugh in a new land. But that was then. And now is now.

Stosh stopped walking long enough to wipe the stinging tears from his old eyes with the sleeve of his coat. His eyes were watering much more these days, especially when he was out in a cold wind. He turned for a moment, putting his back to the wind. It had been warm a few days ago, when Louie Levine set the time and place for the secret meeting. Whatever the weather, the meeting would be today. They had put off the deadly business of this special day long enough.

Stosh turned and continued onward to the appointed place. When he reached the little lake, he placed his walking stick on a bench and set up the card table in front of three benches. He easily lifted the outer ends of the two end benches, swinging them to form a triangle around the table. To complete the conference room, Stosh placed a white trash can within the triangle.

A Neopolitan love song cut through the park air, the lilting tenor tones carried by the wind. It was Vito, of course, making his classic entrance, singing in Italian at the top of his lungs, as he pushed against the wind and the uphill grade of the path toward the meeting place.

His voice, still clear and strong at seventy-one, had that marinara mix of laughter and tears seemingly decreed by some ancient Roman god to be bred into all the men of Salerno. Caruso had it. So did Carlo Luchesi. And so did Vito Morelli. His arms and hands moving in tempo with the emotion of his song, his salt-and-pepper hair tousled by the wind, the stumpy tenor took his resolute little steps toward the lake of the mastadon.

Suddenly, two teenage boys on racing bikes came out of nowhere at full speed, their whirling spokes whining as they careened down the path toward their terrified victim. The song choked in the old man's throat. In this instant of panic, he knew it was too late to dodge, too late to do anything.

"*Dio mio!*" he grunted hoarsely, covering his face with his hands as he fell to the ground on his knees.

The two bikes zoomed by, the boys screaming in glee, pushing Vito's shoulders as they passed, knocking the old man over on his back in the dirt. Now for the part that was the most fun of all. They each reared up into a wheelie, circling their fallen pigeon in opposite orbits, taunting, taunting, one of the boys swinging a bike chain in an awful arc that clanked against the ground closer and closer to Vito.

"Hey, what's happenin', man? Can't you read English?"

"Yeah, ol' man. That sign says Keep Off the Grass."

Vito could only hold his hands and arms over his head. "Please, please, I di'n't do nothing to you, please!"

5

"Yeah? Well, we the park po-lice."

"Yeah, man, you lucky we don't report you!"

They howled with laughter as they raced around and around, closer and closer to Vito groveling on the ground, praying to his God in Italian, rolling from side to side as he tried to avoid the whirling chain.

Suddenly a torrent of Slavic obscenities came roaring down the path toward the torture scene. It was Stosh, his walking club held high above his head, hurtling down on them at top speed, screaming in a gutteral fury, "He-ey! Goddamn you son-of-a-bitchin' basta-ards!"

"Cut out!" yelled one of the young monsters, as he slapped his front wheel down on the ground and dug out in flight.

Too late for the boy with the chain. Stosh swung his club with all his might, slamming the rear wheel of the bike with a smash that lifted it right off the ground, sending bike and rider and chain flying. The boy tumbled in the air like a rag, then hit the ground with a thump, flat on his ass. He yelped in pain. Stosh started after him. The kid scrambled to his feet, ran to his fallen bike. Stosh beat him to it, grabbed the front wheel, and started to whirl the bike around and around. The frightened boy backed away, screeching, "No! No, man! No! No!"

Stosh was spinning faster and faster, the bike now parallel to the ground. The kid was holding his tailbone, whining in pain as Stosh grunted a mighty grunt and the bike sailed skyward, right over the kid's head, its wheels turning incongruously, the handlebars making a useless left turn in the air. Then it crashed to the hard ground with a metallic crunch, mangling every bone in its body, a pedal jumping up from the heap to find its own landing place a few feet away.

"Ha-aah!" The whole park could hear Stosh's scream of victory.

Sitting on the ground, where he had watched the flight of the bike, Vito applauded with childish delight. "Beautiful, beautiful! I never seen anything so beautiful in my whole goddamn life!"

The kid ran limping to his crumpled bike. Pressing his tailbone with one hand, he dragged his pile of junk with the other, cursing and whimpering to his companion, who waited at the safe edge of the park.

Stosh helped Vito to his feet and brushed him off. The two men walked toward the card table.

"Once more I save for you your life, little Vito."

"Okay, okay. But now you save it, whatta you gonna do with it?"

"I don't know. Maybe I can trade you in for couple hot pizzas."

"Show me the place. I'll trade myself in."

Vito sat down on a bench at the table. Stosh scanned the park for a sign of the others. "I go look out for rest of our bunch," he said. "Maybe more Hell's Angels in park looking for a little fun." Clinking the bike chain into his overcoat pocket, he lumbered down the path.

Vito reached into his coat pocket, extracting a box of playing cards.

6

Expertly, he shuffled the cards. His back to the wind so the cards would not scatter, he dealt out a tight solitaire set. He hit no aces the first time through the deck.

At the southeast corner of the park, a butterball of a woman wheeled a folding shopping basket onto the path. As she pushed her way toward the little lake, she looked to the right and to the left and behind, her eyes suspiciously sweeping the park.

It was Minnie Gold, zoftig of figure and spirit, her hair still a flaming red at sixty-eight, her ample buttocks blumping from left to right to left in a saucy rhythm as she waddled toward the meeting.

She was now a roly-poly two hundred pounder, but, oh, what Minnie Gold had been once upon a time—maybe fifty years and eighty pounds ago—costumed in shimmering ragtime red fringe and spike heels, her fantastic tits and ass moving in youthful abandon, her blue eyes dancing to the beat of the hoochy-koochy on the stage at Nick's Uptown! She couldn't even leave the club after the show until the bouncer had cleared a path through the Johnnies at the stage door so she could make it to her cab. And the club paid the taxi, too. But that was then.

Minnie spied Vito as he hunched over his cards at the table. Smiling in conspiracy with herself, she left the path and sneaked up behind him. He was just placing the fourth ace face up on the table.

"Aha! I caught you, Vito!"

"You caught me what? I seen you sneaking. . . . No woman ever caught me."

"Never mind! I caught you cheating, right at the beginning of the game. That's how you always win at the end."

"Big deal." Vito scoffed, jerking his chin at the shopping cart. "What is the *zuppa del giorno?*"

"Chicken, what else? But you will have to wait till everybody gets here. I'm not running a cafeteria."

Minnie dug down into the large bag in her shopping cart for a large thermos and a nest of paper cups, which she put on the table.

A trio of men, huffing and puffing, walked briskly toward the table. It was Stosh returning, with Louie and Oscar in tow.

"Look what I found!" Stosh shouted. "Louie Levine, our leader who got lost—und Oscar, the super Kraut!"

Oscar jabbed Stosh in the ribs with his cane. "I'll give you Kraut . . . Polack!"

Stosh frowned, wagging a huge warning forefinger. "Kraut is funny. Polack is not funny."

Louie Levine held up both his hands in a that's-enough gesture. "Never mind funny. And never mind lost. I was just checking the neighborhood to make sure no spies are hiding in the bushes while we are having the meeting."

7

They laughed aloud at Louie and his cloak-and-dagger precautions.

"Go ahead, laugh! But it's no joke," Louie said. "We came here today for a serious purpose. This is not a funny game. Vito, put the cards away. Minnie, pour the soup, already. Let's get started."

Minnie started to fill a paper cup, then stopped in midpour. "But we can't start yet. Abe's not here!"

Louie waved a never-mind palm at her. "Abe, Abe. Never mind Abe." Then, his eyebrows imitating Groucho Marx, "Besides, I thought you got rid of Abe."

"Don't be a smart aleck," Minnie said. "That's a private affair. Strictly personal!"

"Private, personal—nonsense!" Louie needled. "Everybody knows, for goodness sakes, why you and Abe got—" Louie was cut off by a pudgy hand clapped over his mouth.

"Don't be a loudmouth," Minnie warned.

"Take it easy," Louie complained, pulling away. "I told you, there are no spies in the park. I checked every bench. Only the same old parkees, and a few skinny birds—no stool pigeons." He chortled at his own shaggy bird joke.

"It's not funny, Louie," Minnie scolded. "You know what happens to the team of Silver and Gold if some fink from the Social Security would find out? Alcatraz!"

"Don't get upset, Minnie," said Oscar, hugging himself as he shivered. "It's too cold today here for the SS troops."

"Never mind too cold," she said angrily. "It will be a Siberian snow storm in Miami Beach on the day it will be too cold for them to spy on us! Don't you know they have a whole department of sneaks, opening up the mail boxes, and bugging up the telephones, and God knows what else? Read the papers. You think just because Tricky Dickie went to the beach, that all the Watergates are over?"

Louie put a hand to his head. "I'm sorry Minnie, darling. I didn't mean to start a federal case. I promise, I'll die with your secret. Wild horses wouldn't make me talk! Now, let's get the meeting started, already. Oscar you sit here and look out this way. Stosh, you here, to cover that direction. . . . You see somebody suspicious, you know what to do."

Stosh sat down, then jumped up immediately. "I see somebody—what do I do?"

"Where, where?"

They all looked in the direction of Stosh's tense stare.

"Behind hedge, way over there," Stosh pointed.

"Don't point!" Louie grabbed the big finger.

"It's only Abe!" Oscar said.

"It's my sunshine!" Minnie announced. "It's Abe!"

8

"Some sunshine boy!" Louie grunted. "Sit down, all of you. It's not somebody, it's only Abe."

They all watched as Abe Silver rounded the hedge in the distance, walking toward them in a rhythmic springy stride, his head held high, his arms swinging jaunty-jolly, like a drum major's.

"Only Abe, hah?" said Minnie. "My Abe is more of a somebody than anybody! Look at him, how proud he walks, like a young lion!"

Louie couldn't stand it. Love, spoken aloud, always embarrassed him, made him nervous. "Like an old alley cat, maybe. But a young lion?"

Vito Morelli knew what she was talking about. She was talking his language, the language of love. "Poor Louie! How can you see what Cleopatra sees in Julius Caesar? You got no romance in your soul."

"Ravioli!" Minnie said. "By you, he's Julius Caesar. By me, he's Mark Anthony!"

They were all laughing as Abe reached the meeting place. The dapper little man smiled graciously at his audience and punctuated his arrival with a couple of agile tap steps.

"How do ya like this? I must be hot today." he said. "I didn't even say anything funny yet—and already I'm getting belly laughs!"

"Sit down," Louie said, "and don't get excited about a comeback. Let's get the meeting started before we freeze."

"So, let me get my antifreeze," said Abe, detaching a paper cup from the nest.

Minnie poured it full of soup, lifting the thermos high in the air, then lowering it stylishly as the hot liquid filled the cup. "It should only warm your insides for a year!" she murmured, and gently touched her warm hand to Abe's cheek.

"G'wan!" Abe blushed. "As long as I got you, my insides will be plenty warm!"

"Aw, that's nice," Vito said. *"Dolce! Dolce!"*

Romeo and Juliet had finally overstepped Louie's limit. "That's positively it for the greatest love story ever told! Sit down—we're starting."

The sun was bright in the park now, cutting through the morning's damp overcast, shining down on the six old people huddled close around the card table. It was obvious that Louie Levine was indeed their leader in this enterprise, whatever it was. All eyes were on him as he cleared his throat to speak the terrible words they all knew must be spoken.

"Everybody knows the reason why we are here. The reason is, because we have tried *every decent way*. The letters, the petitions, the public hearings, the marches, the useless demonstrations. And what is the result? Nohing. Zero. It's like trying to put out a tenement fire with a cup of chicken soup. Our people are still hungry, humiliated . . . beggars on the street, digging in garbage cans behind the supermarkets, dying in the ghettos of the aged. What's the use of kidding ourselves? We are neglected by a heartless society. Deserted. Ignored. Despised . . . like lepers are despised."

Louie looked his special look around the table at his companions. They were all familiar with his style of rhetoric. Abe was nodding his head. Vito was shaking his. Minnie clicked her tongue in pity, as though Louie had been talking about a pogrom against victims in a far-off land. And Stosh stared grimly into his cup. Only Oscar, his eyes glazed, showed no emotion.

"So what is the answer?" Louie continued. "The answer is terrifying, my friends. Like others before us who have been betrayed, others who have felt the boiling frustration, the anger, the desperate need to survive in a world with no heart . . . like them, we, too, must become a gang! Gangsters. We, too, must perpetrate a major crime of violence!"

Vito grunted an involuntary grunt as though he had been punched in the belly.

"Yes!" Louie pressed on, his voice shaking with emotion. "There is no other choice. We must create a terrible event, a shocking event . . . so somebody will stop, look, and listen!"

For a long moment, as the significance of Louie's words sank in, none of the group could speak or even look at another.

Minnie broke the silence. "Louie, let me ask you. There is no other way?"

"No. You're asking me—I'm telling you. This is the only way left to us."

"What about Congressman What's-his-name?" asked Abe. "And the Western Conference on the Aged in July?"

Louie could control his anger no longer. "What the hell are you talking about? Congressman What's-his-name has been telling us that he cared about the old people before his last two elections. We went with him to his conferences. So what? He makes nice speeches, and nobody listens—not even him. Don't you understand? Congressman what's-his-name just wants to be *Senator* What's-his-name! He's not even trying so hard for our votes anymore. Somebody must've told him half the old people he asks for votes from in July are dead already by November, right?"

Once more, they were silenced by Louie's rhetoric. He looked at them, one by one, and recognized that desperate look of indecision he had seen on so many faces in his life. The fear a man feels of jumping into the dark waters, though the boat is afire and sinking under his feet.

"How many times more," Louie continued, "can you look into a coffin at an old woman, her face busted, killed on the street only because a hoodlum kid wanted her purse with some loose change in it, and her Medicare stamps? You, Abe—can you come again with me to the nursing homes, to see old friends lying in their own filth in beds that are changed only after they die?"

10

"No, Louie, please don't even talk about it," Abe said. "It made me so sick to my stomach, I couldn't sleep for weeks after."

"So what are we talking?" Louie asked, like a final statement.

"Louie, please," Minnie said. "We couldn't try one more time, the right way, at the Conference?"

"For what?" Louie snapped. "To get down on our knees in front of that big table one more time, to be humiliated in front of the microphones one more time? For a two-inch item on the back pages of the newspaper? Didn't we march already to the City Council, didn't we sign the petitions? Didn't we all try to tell our story the right way, like good little senior citizens? So what crime did we commit, that they don't listen to us? What crime did a nice old lady like Mrs. Emerson commit when she came with us to sit in with our signs at the Federal Building? How many more of our people can we watch drop dead of neglect, with nobody paying attention? It's a life not worth living, maybe, but don't you understand? *That's* a death with no meaning! You forgot already what we said to each other at the cemetery over Mrs. Emerson's grave, when they lowered her coffin into the ground?"

No one answered as Louie looked around the table to read their faces. Now he saw the look he was waiting for. The tragic nodding, the tightened lips, the tears filling their eyes as they remembered that bitter day at the county cemetery.

"Okay, my friends, this is it," he announced. "No more whining, no more growling, no more sitting up for a scrap of food. It's time right now to bite somebody on the ass!"

His people seemed suddenly to sit at attention. Their moment of truth had arrived, and they all knew it.

"So, now we will have our vote," Louie said. "Think it over careful before you answer. Because once you say you're with us, we will be depending on you for your part of the plan. And, God forbid, if you fail us, the whole plan will fail—and people could get killed, you understand? So . . . Abe?"

Abe hated to be first. Why did he have to be first? He stroked his neat little moustache and tried to read the other faces.

"Abe?"

Abe looked at Minnie, searching, so that she might really be the first to decide. Minnie didn't even breathe. Just smiled the special little smile he knew so well. He saw her answer.

"What can I say? If there is no other way . . ."

Louie knew how to run a meeting, how to move people his way. He was an organizer. He snapped his attention to Minnie, whose eyes told him she had expected to be next.

"You don't even have to ask me. I go where Abe goes." She put her hand on Abe's hand, and they became one hand.

"Vito?"

The little man had not stopped shaking his head the whole time. "I don't like it," he said, "but I see it's got to be. God help us."

"Stosh?"

"What crazy question to ask me! How could you do anything without Stanislaus Vlasic? One poof of wind, you all blow away! Of course! I am in the front!"

They all looked at Oscar for the last vote. His face was still expressionless, his eyes still glazed, as he spoke. "Long ago, in my country, I walked with the others to the cattle cars. Und into the camps. Many died—young und old alike. Millions. They were silent . . . obedient, like sheep. Without knowing, they volunteered for their own extermination. I was young then, und strong, also frightened enough to escape. Und I paid a price. I am too old now to run away, but I will not be led silently to the cars again. I go with you."

Louie slapped the table with the palm of his hand.

"Good." He reached into his overcoat pocket and extracted a large envelope, out of which he took a sheaf of folded papers. Reading the name at the top of each sheet, he passed them out to the conspirators, one by one. "This is the plan—the target, the schedule, and your individual attack assignments. Every little part of this plan must be carried out to the letter. Carefully, in secret, and precise in every detail. It has to be pulled off like clockwork, like D-day at Normandy."

Abe, who had read to the middle of his page, whistled in amazement. "Citizens' Bank?"

"*Shhhhh! Quiet!*" Louie hissed.

Abe lowered his voice. "Louie, this is some big show!"

Oscar was giggling, a ticklish Peter Lorre giggle. "On April Fool's Day! It's beautiful! But can we do it?"

"We can do it! I, Louie Levine, say we can do it—and that's a money-back guarantee!"

"Now, listen . . ." Louie lowered the volume of his voice to subconfidential, and they all strained forward to hear every word. "In the days to come, we will have to discuss our special event with each other many times, during the research, the preparations, the preliminary planning. When we talk about it, it should only be called *The Benefit*. Do you understand? THE BENEFIT."

Louie was smiling, for the first time. The others were humming the laughter of inner glee that feels so good, it doesn't have to be out loud.

Minnie raised her cup of chicken soup, standing for the toast. "To The Benefit! It will be a bee-ootiful affair!"

They all rose to join her, savoring the soup as though it were vintage champagne. And when the cups were emptied, they all knew the meeting was adjourned. Used cups were deposited in the white trash can, Vito folded up the card table, Stosh replaced the benches. Each member of the

12

attack team folded and pocketed a copy of the secret plan, and one by one they left the park, sauntering out just as though nothing special would happen on April Fools' Day.

Louie Levine was left alone at the site of his summit meeting. Slowly, he rose from the bench. He felt very tired. Drained. Maybe he would sleep good tonight, more than his usual four or five hours.

A child slipped out of her mother's grasp and ran to the chain link fence, her pudgy hands reaching up as high as she could. "Look, mommy, look! Look at the big elephant!" Her mother came running to her side.

Louie, too, looked out at the dying concrete mastadon, its trunk in a tortured reach for the sky, as though painfully trumpeting. Then he looked across Wilshire Boulevard at the beautiful modern buildings. His eyes swept upward, scanning the clean looming lines of a marble and glass structure. Up, up . . . forty stories high, to the top. To the huge sign, Mutual Benefit Life.

Louie Levine turned and slowly walked down the path and out of the La Brea Tar Pits, toward his furnished room.

# 2

# *LOUIE'S PLACE*

Louie jerked awake with a start, a fearful involuntary gasp still alive in his throat. He slapped his hand over his mouth as if to stifle the sound. He lay rigid on his bed, holding his breath as he listened in the dark. No sound of stirring came from the front part of his landlord's house, no sign that his nightmare had disturbed the family's slumber.

He sucked in a big breath and let out a moaning sigh. He sat up, swinging his feet to the floor. He was sweating a hot sweat, though the night was cold, and his head ached. He wiped the little pool of perspiration from the bottom of his neck with the blanket. He rubbed his eyes, trying to ease the pain behind them. He could see no sign of the dawn's light through his little stained-glass window. It was still the pitch black of the middle of the night.

That same goddamn nightmare again. He had thought it was gone. He had not dreamed about the strike riot for several years. And now again had come all the sights and sounds of that terrible day—the yellow chalk line, the screams of the surging crowd, the deafening *clack-clack* of the police horse hooves, the big animals charging into the milling strikers, knocking them down, the shrill whistles blowing, the teargas bombs exploding, men and women running around in circles, clutching their burning eyes, and then the sickening crunch of a cop's truncheon splitting his skull, and the sharp memory of the pain as he lay bleeding in the street; and later, the smell of his own urine as the police ambulance careened him to Bellevue, and the prison ward.

And now, again, the awful cacophony of that brutal day in 1928 still ringing in his head, Louie sat on the side of his bed, rocking back and forth, reciting the death list that only he could remember. Alphabetically, in a mournful, keening meter, he mumbled out the roster: "Esther Abromovitz—so young, only sixteen; James Chaote—he was studying nights to be a doctor; Lew Feinberg—a mensch . . . such a mensch!; Sean Gallagher—pimples, he still had; Mike Lotito—a voice like an angel; Rose Martoff—sewing to bring her sisters to America; Kathy O'Donnell and her

14

baby in her belly; Ilya Russikov—I didn't even know him; Johnny Sheridan—how that man made us laugh; Mario Tucci—fat Mario. Mmm. What a tailor!; Little Joe Tucci—he shouldn't even have been there that day; Karl Wolacek—so strong, so alive."

And then, the thirteenth name—"Brian McHale . . ."

The young cop the wild mob killed with his own horse before Louie could stop them. Again he sees his strikers pull the policeman down off his horse, the terrified horse rearing high, two men jerking down hard on the reins, the huge animal crashing down, his hooves crushing the cop lying in the street. The horse rears up again, and down once more. Louie sees the cop trying to roll out from under the flailing hooves, only to be beaten down again by a third striker and pushed back under the bucking beast. Louie snatches the reins out of their hands and runs with the horse, he and the horse both screaming with fright. The horse jerks loose and runs on, and Louie turns back to help the injured cop, lying in a pool of blood.

The cop is dead.

"Brian McHale."

Louie Levine, Garment Workers Union Local Number Six strike organizer, sees every martyred face. And then he cries, his frail shoulders heaving, rocking the bed as he sobs, almost silently. But the tears wash away the nightmare once again.

Exhausted, Louie lay back down on the bed, his eyes staring. His small stained-glass window was just starting to pinken with the first morning light, but he still couldn't make out the little angel holding high her golden cross. Light or dark, he knew that the leaded glass angel, looking down, could always see him. He had discussed that unfair advantage with the angel many times.

When he had first moved into the little back room he had planned to cover the window with an old plastic tablecloth. After all, wasn't it indecent for a Jew to be sharing the same room night and day with a kitschy Catholic cherub with wings?

For the first couple of days he had forgotten to buy the thumbtacks for the job. Then, as the daylight spilled into his room through the angel's feathery wings and her blue robe and yellow hair, Louie saw the beauty of it. And when he looked into the angel's blue eyes, smiling down on him with her sweet smile, Louie felt somehow that some new, secret someone cared about him, that after all these years, he no longer lived alone. The angel became his child, his dead wife, his long-lost little brother, his best friend. He shared his secrets with the angel, he told her of his fears, and of his last few hopes. But most of all, he quarreled with her constantly, heedlessly flirting with sacrilege. Why not? Wasn't he paying the rent? And what good was a roommate if you couldn't have a conversation?

"How come all the time you are looking down here at me? It excites you to see an old man naked? I'll go to St. Matthew's tomorrow and tell your

15

boss—he'll fire you on the spot! You know where fallen angels go, don't you? Sez you, he wouldn't listen—I'm one of his chosen people, don't forget. I can talk to him in his native tongue, kiddo!

"Go ahead—peek, peek! Yes, if you wanna know so bad, I'm circumcised. And before it became everyday automatic, too. By a rabbi, not an intern! You wanna talk status symbol—this is a status symbol! You're blushing? You don't wanna look? So turn around! Listen, this is *my* room. I'm sick and tired of always turning around when I get undressed! . . .

"Smiling. All the time smiling. Well, darling, tonight is not a night for smiling. Today was not a funny day out in the big, beautiful world. I fell down getting on the bus—the bus driver closed the door in my face and drove away. He couldn't wait for me to get up out of the gutter. He had his schedule to keep. I hope he gets where we are all going *very* soon. Never mind the other cheek—one cheek black and blue is enough! Your advice I don't need tonight. You wanna do something really nice for me, you'll light a special candle for the mailman—tomorrow is the first of the month. He catches the flu, or some dope fiend breaks his arm for him, then the substitute mailman doesn't bring my check until Monday. And if you noticed, I started my fasting today, already. Still smiling, hah? What's the use? Misery loves company, and that's the only reason you're not covered up! You're just another pretty face. You got no heart. . . .

"Who are you anyway? You got a name? Maybe you got a number? I got a number, little girl—a lotta numbers. A Social Security number, a Medicare number, a food stamp number, a bus pass number . . . each one longer than the one before. Don't worry, they got everything organized very good. I'm sure they're saving for me someplace a funeral number. Did you hear? Last month they passed the 'Right-to-Die' law. They can hardly wait for me to take advantage of my rights. Then they can use all my numbers for somebody else. Listen, sweetheart, if you're not going to tell me your name, I will give you a name. What are you? An Eyetalian angel, or Irish, or what? I think Eyetalian. I'll tell you what we'll do. We'll have a raffle. I'll put a bunch of Eyetalian names on little pieces of paper, then on Sunday morning I'll pick one out of a hat, we'll have a christening, and that will be your name. It just ain't nice to call an angel 'Hey, you!' . . .

At a certain time of the morning, at certain times of the year, the light of the rising sun richocheted from window to window at a special angle, so that as it struck Louie's angelic window, hundreds of magical little brilliant bursts of golden light bounced off the cross and the halo, twinkling through the angel's eyes and showering the walls and ceiling of the tiny room with a phantasmagoria of every color in the spectrum.

That morning of the tears was such a morning. Louie lay quietly in awe, watching the dazzling fan-shaped rays of reflected light, turning, turning, a

16

swirling concerto for the eye. The heavenly display lasted less than two minutes, and then the sun hurried on its arc to Santa Monica.

Feeling somehow renewed, Louie leaped to his own interpretation of this solar phenomenon as he got off his bed.

"Ah-h-h, Sophia, my beautiful Saint Sophia, do you see? The finger of God, pointing down right into my room! He has chosen Louie Levine to do great things today! You know, I *wondered* if he was at the meeting yesterday. I thought maybe it was too cold for him in the park, but he was there. How do ya like that? Can you imagine? God himself has put a blessing on The Benefit! And why not? Of course! . . . Isn't God a senior citizen? Listen, I don't have time to talk any more. I gotta get outa here and get busy on my assignments!"

Louie rushed through his toilet as he continued to talk to himself and his roommate.

". . . After all, mine is the most important job. The organizer. One piece by itself is nothing, but to put the pieces together is only a job for the leader. You hear, little girl? Your Louie is the leader! The research. The planning. The security. The diagrams. The communications systems. The attack schedule. These things are the heart and soul of a military operation." He stopped abruptly. "Oh, my God! April first is right around the corner—only nine weeks!"

Quickly, he put on his coat and headed for the door. Opening it, he turned back and looked up. "See you later, kiddo, You're all right—you keep me on my toes."

Then he locked his room, walked out the back door of the old stucco house and down the driveway to the street, toward the Senior Citizens' Center, to check on his troops.

# 3
# BUS STOP

The day was chilly and bright, and Minnie Gold was at her post. The early morning rush-hour traffic jerked and honked and chugged as it scrambled through the intersection of Beverly and Fairfax. Heavily loaded buses stopped at all four corners to pick up the half-awake passengers, who pushed each other toward the back.

Minnie took it all in and took it all down, as she sat on the bus stop bench, across the street from Citizens' Bank. Thousands of such wooden benches dot the bus stop corners of Los Angeles, and most of them, oddly enough, carry ads for funeral parlors. Minnie's bench advertised, in a tasteful Olde English scroll: *Sinai Hills Mortuary—Peace and Comfort—When the Time Comes.*

There she sat, as she had almost every day for the past month. The tools for her assignment were a small red notebook and the stub of a pencil, with which she surreptitiously made note of everything she saw as she stared across the street at the double front doors of Citizens' Bank.

Minnie logged every schedulable event that took place within range of her vision. The arrival and departure of the RTD buses, all four directions. The meter maid's rounds. The neighborhood black and white police car's cruising schedule. The punctual armored truck. The bank employees' lunch breaks. The gardener's hours for the care and feeding of the tropical plants in front of the bank. The janitorial service crew. The traffic signal timings. The bank guard's pre-opening entry procedures. And—most important—the daily employee arrivals and entry.

Minnie recorded every relevant movement, sitting big as life at one of the busiest intersections of the city, brazenly casing the Citizens' Bank—and nobody noticed.

Of course not. What is to notice? Just another little old lady with a shopping basket, lolling in the Fairfax sun, that's all. And this one was a ditty-hummer. As she wrote, she singsonged her notebook entries in a

18

barely audible tune that ran through her head, lapsing in and out of simple rhyme, speaking almost half the time . . .

*Mmmm-hmm-mmm-hmmm*
Watching the passing parade,
Looking at the notes I made.
Another day in high finance,
Planning for The Benefit dance.
Here's Brubaker, the bank guard.
Eight fifty-six by the Bulova.
It's cold so he's wearing his pullova.
Here come the tellers, the opening act is a trio:
Miss Opal Johnson, the fat girl from window number three-o,
And Henry P. McInnerny, head teller, window number six,
With his skinny blue tie, a hick from the sticks.
And Mio Yamaguchi, Safety Deposit Yamaguchi,
Immaculate, a regular Japanese doll.
This is a name a mouth can taste . . .
Mio Yamaguchi, *Mmm-mmm*, good!
Now Henry is clicking the door with a dime.
Brubaker sees them—now he's unlocking the door.
Sa-ay! I never noticed that before . . .
He unlocked with his *left* hand.
Aha! His six-shooter is also on his left.
Brubaker is positively a *lefty!*
He's locking again with the left hand . . . eight fifty-nine.

"You see, Minnie, like Louie says, 'You can look and look—and you'll see nothing, unless, at the same time you are looking, you are watching!'

". . . Here comes the executive car pool, exactly at nine,
Mr. Slack, the VP from the Mortgages and Trust Deeds,
Mr. Barnes, the assistant VP, who will never be the VP
And now, *Ta-ta-ta-ta-ta-ta-ta-ta-hh!* . . .
The Fairfax branch manager, Mr. Harley Wilson, the Third.
After you, Mr. Wilson, the Third. After you, Mr. Slack.
And then Mr. Barnes, keeping his place—in the back.
Brubaker is locking. Nine oh one.
And here comes the contingent from the inner city . . .
The Washingtons, Sidney and Lowina—no relationship . . .
Ha-ha, not on the premises.
What a beauty—a regular Lena Horne.
Lowina's through the door,
That takes care of windows Number One and Four.

19

Also, Number Five, Floyd Davis, the skyscraper.
And here he comes running, the wild dresser, Jesse Williams,
Window Number Two. Such a head of hair—like an
African lion!
Window Number Seven? Miss Hotsy-Totsy . . .
Still on vacation.
Again, Brubaker is locking—Hey, wait a minute, Lefty!
Here is Betty Lundy, late again, with the coffee and Danish.
Nine oh three. Oy, is she gonna have a big baby!
It could even be two maybe!
How long can she secretary, for goodness' sakes?—

The bearded young man who had just sat down on the bench next to
Minnie was startled by her question.

"I beg your pardon, ma'am?"

Minnie suddenly realized that her concern for Betty Lundy's pregnancy
had been too audible.

"Oh, I'm sorry—I wasn't talking to anybody. Pay no attention. I'm just an
old lady. I talk to myself sometimes."

The young man smiled gently. "Hey, that's okay. I'm young, and I talk to
myself, too."

The eastbound Number Four bus ground to a stop at the bench, its
airbrakes hissing, a few passengers spilling out. Minnie shouted over the
noise, "I know, I know! Who else will listen?"

The young man got on the bus, turning back as he winked broadly at
Minnie, "Ri-ight!"

The bus growled its gears and pulled away from the curb. Minnie sang
her entry. "The nine o'clock Number Four bus is right on time—exactly
seven minutes late."

"Here comes the tricycle motorcycle, every hour, ten after the hour.
Perfect. What an artist! She never misses a tire. Hm-mm! Blue. The chalk
is blue today. Okay. Blue on Tuesday. Tuesday—that's right. No Brinks on
Tuesday, so this means the morning show is over, and the spy can come in
from the cold."

Minnie closed her little red book and got up from the bench. The bench
was empty now, and she spoke to it freely. "Listen, you are a very nice
bench. Not comfortable, but in a perfect place. Don't worry—when my
time comes you'll get my business. But right now, if I move my fanny, I just
got time to get home and change clothes for my yoga class at the Senile
Citizens' Center."

And with that, Minnie blump-blumped down the street, wagging her
shopping cart behind her.

20

# 4
# HOCK SHOP

Oscar Stein had already acquired and checked off most of the equipment on his list: three hundred feet of number twelve copper wire, twelve rescue flares and caps, the black powder, the bottles and kerosene for the Molotov cocktails, forty feet of steel cable and a crimper for Vito, wire cutters, link chain, heavy rope, locks, and a small, deadly arsenal of souvenirs from a half-forgotten war. All scrounged from secondhand stores and hock shops, no questions asked. All reassembled and secretly put into working order for a necessary new civil war.

The only item he had failed to come up with was probably the most important—a blasting detonator. But he had already started to make one himself. It wouldn't be fancy, but it would do the job, if he was careful.

With The Benefit only a month away, Oscar continued searching for extra equipment that might come in handy. No telling what kind of weapons they might need in an emergency during The Benefit. He limped around for miles every day, swinging his short left leg, the built-up sole and heel on that shoe clop-clopping on the sidewalk as he covered every garage sale and rummaged every pawn shop in the area.

The old man aroused no suspicion as he made his nefarious rounds. Why would he? Nobody pays attention to old people. Nobody. Not even other old people.

Oscar stood looking into the front window of a pawn shop, admiring a beautiful French mantel clock. Six pink marble columns supported a carved Greek capitol over the enameled clock face. A muscular bronze figure stood gracefully poised to strike the hour chime. The heavy brass pendulum was finely engraved with a scrolled family monogram. It hung vertical and still, but Oscar could just imagine the pendulum swinging, the latticed hands sweeping past the cobalt blue Roman numerals, the bronze figure turning and striking the bell with his mallet. He almost heard the rich tone of the chime, and he felt a small rushing thrill in his stomach.

That's the way it was with Oscar and clocks. It was understandable. Until

21

Hitler instituted his ultimate solution for the fatherland, Oscar had been a master clockmaker for the century-old firm of Boehm and Boehm of Hamburg, clockbuilders nonpareil. To this day, their magnificent time-pieces grace the tops of many of Europe's town halls, and their mantel clocks are exhibited in the finest museum collections of the world.

As a young man, Oscar had personally built the famous three-tiered onyx mantel clock Adolf Hitler had given to Benito Mussolini in undying friendship. And, on the day Benito and his Clara hung by their heels, swinging upside down in a bloody Milan gas station, the sword-shaped pendulum of Oscar's clock was still swinging its geometric arc on the great fireplace mantel in Mussolini's villa outside Rome. The following morning, the rampaging partisans smashed it to bits, along with everything else, as they ransacked Il Duce's villa. And Oscar was so happy when he heard about it, he danced a jig.

Oscar nodded appreciatively at the clock in the window and couldn't help saying it aloud, "*Schön . . . sehr schön!*"

He walked into the hock shop and toward the back, where they kept the guns in locked glass counters. The long-haired clerk was in the middle of haggling with two young black men, over a red electric guitar.

"That's it, man," the clerk said. "I knocked it down five. that's it.

"Yeah, man," said the taller of the two, "you knockin' it *to* us, that's what you knockin' it."

The clerk drew himself up to his full height. "Look, my man," he said, "this is a first-class guitar with a second-class price tag. A hundred and forty-five—take it or leave it." He turned away abruptly, walking to Oscar, who was concentrating on an article in the glass counter. "Yes, sir?"

The two men headed toward the front of the shop, disgusted. "We leavin' it, turkey," the short one announced, slamming the door on the way out.

The clerk noticed Oscar's hearing aid and raised his voice to loud. "Can I help you, sir?"

Oscar winced and pointed to the article that attracted him. "I would like to see this . . . this pineapple piece. Yes, that one."

The man pulled the hand grenade out of the counter and set it up on top of the glass. "This? This is a World War II grenade."

"Oh-h, yes . . ." Oscar said, in his most innocent tone. "I see it is, now."

"It's disarmed, of course. No pin, no powder."

Oscar raised his considerable eyebrows.

"I should hope so!" he said. "What would I do with a live grenade?"

"Maybe start World War III!" the young man said.

"Yeh, yeh. Very funny," Oscar said. "Only I think you have lost count."

"Huh?"

"Never mind. How much is it?"

The clerk consulted the small tag. "Eighteen dollars, old man."

Oscar fiddled with his hearing aid.

22

"Thirteen dollars with the discount?"

"What discount?"

Oscar tapped the little speaker box on his chest. "I'm sure I heard you say you are having a five-dollar-off sale today."

"Oh, yeah—very good," the clerk said. "I always knew you deaf old people could hear what you *wanted* to hear. I can't knock it down five, but . . . I'll give it to you for fifteen."

"Give? When you give, you *give*. For nothing."

"Yeah, well, that's just an expression. I'll *sell* it to you for fifteen."

Again, Oscar fiddled with the volume knob of his negotiating tool.

"A what . . .?"

The clerk was losing patience. "An expression. A way of talking, you know?"

Oscar's blank look was outrageous.

"Look, old man," the clerk said, "you can have it for fourteen, and that's it!"

"Fourteen?" Oscar smiled sweetly. "I'll take it for fourteen."

"I knew damn well you heard the fifteen," the clerk muttered.

Oscar's face reclouded on cue. "What? . . . I can't hear you."

"Never mind," the clerk said, writing the receipt.

Oscar counted out the money and held the grenade up to the light. "It is probably not worth it, but . . . you know, it's really a beautiful thing."

The clerk pulled out a paper bag from under the counter. "What is?"

"A pineapple," said Oscar, beaming. "A pineapple is a beautiful thing."

He put the grenade in the paper bag and left the hock shop. As soon as he was out of sight, he removed the earpiece of the useless hearing aid, dropped it into his pocket, and walked on down the street toward the Senior Citizens' Center, carrying his beautiful pineapple.

# 5

# WRECKING YARD

The big shaggy yellow dog started to bark his toothless warning as soon as Stosh shuffled onto the dirt of the wrecking yard. It wasn't a Hey-what-are-you-doing-on-my-master's-property bark. The mangy old pooch had given up on that bark years ago. It was more of a Hello-big-man-you-ain't-been-here-in-a-long-time bark. His grizzly old master rocked in his rocking chair and watched Stosh approach the porch of the wrecking yard shed.

Stosh laughed, putting his big foot out toward the dog. "Here, dog, take bite from Stosh's leg. You won't like it. Very tough meat—no fat."

"Hey, don't feed my dog no Polack meat. He don't eat nothin' but Amurrican dog food. He's got a very patriotic constitution, git me?"

"Ha-ha!" Stosh said. "Imported leg of Pole too good for your dog. Only serve in finest restaurants!"

"How the hell are ya, Polack? Where ya bin?"

"I'm okay. I been busy, very busy. Now, I come to do business. You got magneto switch for my '52 Ford pickup?"

"Magneto switch? That's electrical. I get no call for those."

"What you mean, 'no call'? I am calling. What kind auto wrecking yard you are, no magneto switch?"

The old man laughed and scratched his stubbly gray beard. "You kill me, Stanislaus! You been here seventy- 'leven times and scrounged seventy-'leven parts for that old tin can of yours—and it still ain't never moved from the curb. That pickup died a long time ago. Why'n'cha let me haul it in here an' give it a decent funeral?"

"No, no!" Stosh shook his big head emphatically. "My truck not dead—very sick, but not dead! Just because old, not mean ready for bury, no, mister! I find right parts, I fix. I gotta fix very quick. Now. Got big job for truck."

"Job?" Griz asked, amused. "What kinda job kin you an' that ol' truck git done, anyhow?"

"Uh-h, big job . . . haul trash for big name movie actor, Beverly Hills."

24

"Oh, yeah—who?"

"Aw-ww, I forget name. But I remember house, big house. I go next week. Important job."

"Yep, sounds like mighty important trash to me, all right," the old Griz laughed. "Well, you're the only Polack customer I got, so I gotta take care o' ya. Tell ya whatcha do—you climb back into that northeast corner. There are a coupla wrecked pickups back in there. You might could find what you need, but you're gonna have to dig it out for yourself." He jerked a thumb toward his dirty yellow dog, sleeping on the rug at his feet. "My staff is dog tired, right now."

"What kind bargain price I pay, to dig out myself?"

Griz was in a generous mood. "For you? The best price goin'." He gestured a zero.

"Hey, old man, you run best damn wrecking yard in whole L.A.!" Stosh headed off for the corner of the lot. "You got also best damn dog in city!" he yelled back over his shoulder.

Then the giant gleefully clambered up the heap of discarded heaps, like a ten-year-old boy conquering a pile of construction gravel.

As he pulled himself up from the top of one rusting wreck to the next, he saw something that stopped him cold.

There, near the top of a pile of crushed autos, lay the mangled remains of a high-powered, late model car, its roof bashed in, the seats burned out, and the front grill pushed back almost to the steering wheel.

And still clinging eerily to the hood ornament, there were red-white-and-blue streamers and pompoms waving in the breeze. "Just Married" was painted on the crumpled doors, and tin cans still hung wired to the rear bumper.

Quick tears came to Stosh's eyes as he remembered his cousin Steve and his wife Rini during his first year with them in this country. Then the memory of that first neighborhood Polish wedding flooded in on him.

Stosh had not wanted to go to the affair, but Steve had teased and badgered, and even bought Stosh a new white shirt. The largest he could find. And a new black tie.

"How can I go at night to be with people?" Stosh argued. "I am greenhorn. A man who knows only how to pound iron. I do not yet even know to talk the language. I would feel like big fool!"

"No!" shouted Steve, "I am the fool! Why else did I spend good money to buy a shirt and a tie for a big rock?"

Rini stepped between them. "Wait, wait, Steve! Shouting only closes the ears." Gently she combed through Stosh's hair with her fingers, as he sat on the bed looking up into her soft eyes. "Stanislaus, sweet mountain, don't you understand? They are all greenhorns. They will all have new shirts. We are all new here, walking a new path, living a new life."

Then, like the sun rising, his face broke into a glowing smile, every wrinkle laughing its own laugh. Stanislaus Vlasic rose to his feet, looking down at his only two friends.

"I will go!" he shouted. "What the hell—I will go!"


The Polish-American Social Club was upstairs, each of the five windows facing the street proudly boasting one of the five words beautifully block-lettered in gold, edged with red. It was one large loft room with a hardwood floor, an enclosed office and kitchen space in one corner. Red-white-and-blue crepe paper streamers were tented from the walls to the center of the painted tin ceiling, and spiralled around the many wooden posts that supported the roof. The patriotic motif was carried through to the long buffet and punch table along one wall, the streamers basted as a border to the linen tablecloth. The heady odors of Polish cuisine steamed into the room from the hot stoves long before the guests were due to arrive, and three young women were busily setting the tables with the mismatch of the neighborhood's best chinaware.

The wedding had taken place in the church across the street. The moon-faced bride wore her grandmother's once-white lace wedding gown, let out in panels of taffeta to accommodate her heroic figure. The groom wore a tight rented tuxedo, which was, somehow, even skinnier than he was. They were the only ones in the half-filled chapel who were dressed formally. The family and friends wore dark, neat clothes—nice, but not formal. It was not expected.

The priest performed the ceremony in Polish, intoning the litany in a loud and ringing voice as though he wanted the whole world to know that he was this day cementing a union that only God could put asunder. Members of the joining families sat stiffly in the pews and smiled and clucked and nodded and sniffled and craned their necks so that they might hear every word, see every expression of the bride and groom. And then, it was over. The string bean and the cabbage were pronounced man and wife—and their bouncing babies would be American citizens.

The happily dazed newlyweds stumbled up the aisle and ran from the church, across the street to the rest rooms of the social club to change their clothes for the grand wedding reception, as the onlookers threw rice and groats.

The wedding party spilled out of the church, regathering on the sidewalk to stall and gossip—the men with the men, looking at their shoes, the women with the women, pulling at their dresses.

The groom, now in his plain suit, stood at the open American window with his buxom bride, finally plumped into her party dress. "We're ready!" he shouted to the crowd below. "Come up—orchestra is here!"

The accordion-and-saxophone band played loud and joyful Polish music for the sweating couples who moved across the floor in rhythms of their

26

own, sliding and spinning and hopping together as they danced in carefree celebration.

The platters on the serving table, heaped high with bigos and ham and kielbasa and paprikash, were replaced again and again. Dozens of clear bottles of homemade raisin wine were emptied at an astonishing rate, as each male member of the two merging families proposed his own homely wedding toast to fruitful union and long life.

The Poles, unlike the Irish, never organize much fun at funerals and wakes, but they eat and drink the hell out of a wedding. And afterward, at home, each man is inspired to outdo himself as he heroically thrusts into his eager, willing wife in ritual commemoration of their own nuptial night, no matter how long ago that was. The big Polish beds bounce and sway and creak and knock against the walls, and the giggles and groans and *oh-h, oh-hhs* echo through the neighborhood night like a victorious Paderewski symphony, and the angels sing.

Stosh stood in a corner of the room, watching Steve and Rini sliding and spinning their way around the dance floor. How like a single body they were! Their upraised hands were pressed together, her breasts barely touched his chest in a constant tingling pressure, their eyes were locked in a trance, totally excluding the rest of the world.

Stosh could barely stand the pain and beauty of watching them. He turned away, flushed, swallowed the half-glass of wine he had in his hand, and headed for the exit door, longing for the feel of the cool night air.

As he circled the room to reach the stairway, the swinging kitchen door suddenly opened hard, bashing him flush in the face. Down went Stosh. Down went a fully loaded tray of dishes, with a deafening clatter. And down went the bearer of the tray, skidding and tumbling head over heels in a somersault which, somehow, landed her astride Stosh, who was lying belly up, his battered nose gushing blood.

Stosh looked up at his shapely passenger, seated prettily on his belt buckle, her hair in disheveled ringlets falling every which way, her green eyes frightened wide open. She did not move.

Katya looked down at the mountain she and the kitchen door had leveled, his blood staining his new white shirt, his eyes looking up at her in disbelief, thunderstruck by a direct hit to his soul. He could not move.

This moment was suspended in time as the truth and meaning of the collision struck home. His angel. Special delivery. From above, no doubt of it. Destiny, accompanied by the appropriate drumroll of crashing crockery and the gonging bell in Stosh's head. Stanislaus Vlasic was knocked flat by Katya Mazewski—and everybody in the room knew it. Kismetski.

Two months later the bans were posted, and three months after that, Stanislaus and Katya took each other to have and to hold, in the same little church, in sickness and in health, welded together by the same priest, for

27

richer for poorer, the same witnesses assembled. . . . Their big bed rocked and the angles sang, till death would them part.

Stosh shook himself out of his reverie and climbed up to stand on the very top of his pile of wrecked cars.

There, as he looked down, near the bottom of a stack across the aisle, was a '52 Ford pickup, exactly like his. The hood was missing, and he could clearly see the metal housing of the magneto switch he needed.

He pulled his big screwdriver out of his rear pocket, threw it across the drive to the bottom of that stack to mark the place, and started to climb down.

28

# 6

# *SILVER AND GOLD*

Their whole lives together were proudly exhibited on the walls of their one-room efficiency apartment (*Shhh!—Minnie's* apartment). The walls were covered with framed posters and window cards and pictures, and even a one-sheet advertising the appearances of the vaudeville team of Silver and Gold. Yellowing smash reviews of their act, appropriately underlined, formed a veritable atlas of the Bijous and Orpheums and Lyrics and Rialtos and Strands and Palaces and Majestics and Lyceums of the eastern United States during its heyday of vaudeville and burlesque.

The posters were a compendium of the art of theatrical flackery, circa 1920: 3 SHOWS A DAY 3, ON STAGE! IN PERSON! 8 HEADLINE ACTS 8, DIRECT FROM NEW YORK'S HIPPODROME, NAUGHTY BUT NICE! NEW COSTUMES! NEW SONGS! NEW JOKES! THE LATEST HOLLYWOOD MOVING PICTURE—GLORIA SWANSON IN "MALE AND FEMALE," DIRECTED BY CECIL BLOUNT DeMILLE! AND PROFESSOR SABATINI AT THE GIANT WURLITZER ORGAN. EXTRA BONUS! KENO FOLLOWING SECOND SHOW! PRIZES GALORE!

There were eight-by-ten glossies of Minnie and Abe doing their act. Dancing cheek to cheek. Abe, pushing Minnie on a flowered swing. Minnie and Abe in a ballroom dancing pose, a deep slicker-dip, her tiny glittering foot kicked gracefully up behind. There were pictures of Minnie and Abe with biggy celebrities, too. Like Jenny Grossinger, Henny Youngman, young Irving Berlin (autographed), Georgie Jessel, Ted Lewis, Julian Eltinge, even Al Jolson (the back of his head), and Mickey Katz. And, of course, in a gilt frame that set it apart from all the rest, their formal wedding picture, cutting the cake. It was inscribed "Silver and Gold, Jumping To Our Happy Conclusion, Leap Year Day, 1924."

Hanging from the ceiling, in a corner of the room, was a braided red velvet rope. And dangling from the braids were several hundred keys and tags, souvenirs from the Waldorf in Baltimore, the Plaza in Scranton, the

Grand Hotel in Cedar Rapids, the Ponce de Leon in Miami, the Brevvoort in Indianapolis, the Savoy in Rochester, the Chesterfield in Philadelphia, the Deshler-Wallick in Columbus, the Milner in Peoria, the Fort Des Moines, the Pittsburger . . . just name the town. They never stayed in anything less than a B hotel. Never. After all, Silver and Gold were almost headliners on every bill they played.

But that was another life. Before "September Song." Before change of life. Before arthritis. Before constipation. Before Social Security.

Minnie was trying her best to hurry changing her clothes, but chubby elbows, hips, and knees kept bumping the confines of the tiny dressing area behind the Murphy bed. Abe sat on the bed, busily sewing on a funny-looking furry object. Every time he passed the needle through the object, he would ouch a small ouch, signifying a finger pricking. From behind the Murphy bed, he heard Minnie singsong.

"The thim-bull . . . my darling dummy, the thim-bull."

"The thim-bull don't fit the right fin-gerr!" he singsonged back.

"You are using the wrong fin-gerr!"

"Oh, boy, what a straight line."

"Never mind! I'm almost ready—are you almost ready?"

"What do you mean? Ready to go, or ready to 'you-know'?"

The only thing Minnie's body was programmed for this morning was yoga. "Don't be fresh with me! Ready to go. Besides, I know when you're ready to 'you-know'."

"Is that so? Well, they don't call me quick-Silver for nothing!"

"Only I call you quick-Silver, and I know why!"

The blow was low, but Abe knew she was only teasing. The fact was, he had been feeling horny quite a lot lately. "I got big news for you," he announced. "Since you became a divorcée, I'm ready to 'you-know' a lot more than you know."

"Ha-ha! The retired comedian refuses to retire."

Minnie came out of the dressing area and into the main room. She had changed into a tight bright red leotard, her red hair little-girled in braids with two small bows. Abe did not look up. When two people live together for that many years, they don't look up unless somebody blows a bugle.

"Ta-da-ahh!"

She was posing right in front of him, one foot pointed in front of the other, her hips pushed provocatively forward, one hand sexy on a hip, the other behind her head. Abe looked up.

"What is that outfit? You look like a naked fire truck!"

"Oh, yeah, smarty? This, for your information, is my new yogi leotard, two-ninety-nine on sale at Rafkin's."

"I'm not seeing what I'm seeing," Abe said, shaking his head. "Tell me I'm not seeing."

30

"I'm wearing, you're seeing, sweetie."

"Listen, I'm not so sure I want my ex-wife parading around at the Senior Citizens' Center dressed like a Playboy bunny. There are some *junior* seniors there, you know."

"Yes, and I know exactly which ones they are!"

"Oh, you do, hah?"

"Yes, I do, hah. But, my darling lover, always rememm-berr . . ." It was a song cue, of course. Her voice smiled with the joyful last chorus of the exit number from their act,

> This Silver and Gold
> Will never break up,
> 'Cause after we fight,
> We love to make up.

As always, Abe took his cue, joining in,

> (And how!)
> We're forever a team,
> Our love is two-fold,
> Like coffee and car-eam,
> It's Silver and Gold!

Then Abe, with his solo line,

> This Sterling Silver
> Will never grow cold,

Then Minnie again,

> This Gold is antique,
> But never too old,

Then in harmony, cheek to cheek, on creaky, bended knees,

> Our love's uncontrolled,
> We are body and souled,
> Gold and Silver,
> Si-ilver and Go-old!

The song ended with the same affectionate kiss they'd exchanged for fifty years, and graceful bows to tumultuous applause from the Murphy bed.

"Okay, already. No encore," Abe said, slapping her on the fanny. "I'm ready to go. The last wig is finished. Put something over your body, and let's get going. I'm late for the game."

"All right, all right! Don't order me around like I was your wife. I got my makeup on and my hair fixed. All I gotta do is go behind Mr. Murphy and throw on my overgarment."

Minnie went back into the dressing area; Abe stuffed the fuzzy objects into a large shopping bag. But he just couldn't resist. Retrieving one of the wigs, he put it on his head. Now a pair of large dark glasses. He sneaked up on the mirror, then quickly popped up to look. He burst into an uproar of laughter.

"What is so funny ha-ha?" asked Minnie, bending to tie a shoe.

"Wait, you'll see."

Abe lifted the Murphy bed to its standing position.

"Abe, don't you dare! . . ." She had anticipated the catastrophe, as it was happening. "Abe! A-abe!—"

Totally unmindful of the logistics of time and space, Abe revolved the bed into its hideaway position. The back of the bed thumped Minnie in the rump, shoving her hopping out into the main room, a shoelace still clutched in one hand. Still off balance, Minnie caught sight of Abe in the mod wig and glasses. Her laughter was an avalanche, knocking her off her feet and flopping her onto the couch, where she continued to shake in a howling fit.

"Oh, that is funny ha-ha! That is the funniest ha-ha thing I ever saw in my whole life."

"Please, please!" said Abe. "A little respect for my disguise. I didn't laugh out loud at you in your Santa Claus suit."

"My yogi outfit may be a giggle, but you . . . you . . . you are an outrageous HA-HA!"

"Never mind," Abe said. "Like Louie says, the only way we're gonna be able to pull this thing off, is with surprise. So who would be afraid of an old man with a gun? This wig takes fifteen, twenty years off. Who knows, maybe some young chicken will give a look!"

"Dreamer! The only chicken you can handle is in a bowl of warm soup. Your chicken plucking days are over—just ask the little red hen."

"Yeah? Well, just don't let my age confuse you, little red hen. I'm still a rooster—cock-a-doodle-doo!"

"Yeah, yeah, the rooster what useter! So, have you got the front door key, cock-a-doodle?"

"Yeah, we got no back door." Abe slapped his leg for the three thousandth time, and deposited his wig in the bag with the rest.

"Are you sure?" she asked. "Got your bus pass?"

"I got my pass, I got my key—step on the gas, and follow me!"

"Listen to this, I married a regular Longfellow!"

"Correction," said Abe, picking up the bag. "You *divorced* a regular Longfellow."

32

Minnie opened the door. "Can I help it? "After forty-nine years you don't turn me on unless you are a bachelor?"

"How do ya like this?" Abe leered. "Are you sure we have to leave the apartment right this minute?"

"Make your exit, Silver." She jerked her head toward the open door. "And no tricks—you saw my outfit!"

Abe raised both hands innocently as he passed Minnie with an adept hip move, forcing her to flinch with a reverse bump.

"Cock-a-doodle-doo-oo!" said the rooster to the hen.

As always, Minnie came out of the front door of the apartment house alone, while Abe waited on the inside stairway for the signal. Minnie looked up and down the street both ways, then over her shoulder, to Abe, "Olly-olly-oxen-free!"

Abe came down the last few steps and out onto the front walk. Minnie slipped her hand through Abe's waiting arm, and together, in perfect step, Silver and Gold walked toward the bus stop, to wait for the Number Four bus to the Senior Citizens' Center.

# 7

# THE CENTER

The Senior Citizens' Center is a substantial modern building situated close to the Fairfax shopping area and the high low-rent district inhabited by many of the aged, halt, and needy of Los Angeles. It was built exclusively for them out of public funds and private profit motive, thanks to Mayor Sam Yorty. The bronze plaque bolted to the front of the building tells everyone whom to thank. It is only seven handrailed steps up from the street level and a half a block from the bus stop, and it boasts all the institutional facilities any group of elders could ever long for, as they live out their last days in a sweet and gentle geriatric Disneyland.

The Center is a noisy, busy place. Comings and meetings and goings. Greetings and arguments and laughter. Canes and crutches and blue-white hair. European accents shouted at deaf ears. Cigar smoke and coughing and spitting. Ceaseless shuffling and the arthritic choreography of waving arms and hands. A buzzing swirl of the anger and the energy and the desperation of living in advanced age.

Vito Morelli hurried up the front steps of the Center. He was late for the game. As he reached the lobby, he was frozen by a loud argument at the tour desk. It was Ida Katz, the killer, versus poor Cantor, behind the counter.

Vito was definitely allergic to Ida Katz. She was always cornering him to invite him over to her place to taste her juicy version of *lasagne al forno Piemontese*. Just like she had made for her dear departed husband, who had given it four stars, and he oughta know, because he was half Italian. Vito knew what she meant when she looked him up and down, and it gave him the heebie-jeebies.

He quickly turned his back to the fray, hurriedly skirting the desk. Ida Katz's loud voice still grated in his ear as he headed for the card room.

"Please, Mister Cantor! Don't give me again the business with the sign!"

Pointing was not enough for Ida Katz. Now Cantor was reading *and* pointing, to every word on the hand-lettered sign over the desk. "You are

34

responsible for arranging tour partners. . . . The 'you' means *you*—it does not mean *me*."

"Is it my fault Mrs. Segal fell down getting off the Number Seven bus to the beach and tore her ligament? You got our deposit for the Las Vegas tour for two and a half months. We were the first couple to sign up!"

"Please, Mrs. Katz, give me a break! I didn't push her off the bus, either. It's not my fault or your fault—it's the *rules*. And *they* make the rules, I don't. My only job is to inflict them on the members. Go find another lady—you still got two weeks."

"Go find! You hear what he says?" She was engaging Mrs. Bernstein to take her side. Two against one could be the end of Cantor. "Where will I find a partner who is compatible in two weeks?"

"Listen, Ida," said Mrs. Bernstein, "why don't you make yourself a partner with Mr. Adler, he's a single. Maybe *he* would be compatible."

"*Shhhh!* Harriet! You oughta be ashamed to suggest such a thing!"

"Why? What's so terrible?" asked Mrs. Berstein, unashamed. "He's an old man. What could he do?"

"What could he do? He could do his best, that's what he could do!" And Ida Katz about-faced in a huff toward the card room, as Cantor sighed in relief.


Louie was dealing the cards at the pinochle table in the corner. He looked up at the big clock on the wall and shook his head. "It's almost 11:30. Still no Silver."

"You are surprised?" Oscar was arranging his hand. "He won a dollar forty from us on Monday, he is not too anxious to give back."

"Don't worry," Louie said, "he'll be here. Today is the day he delivers his first homework for The Benefit. *Shhhh!*" Louie had suddenly noticed Mrs. Katz and Mrs. Bernstein approaching the table.

"Good morning, Mr. Levine, Mr. Stein, Mr. Vlasic." Ida Katz turned toward Vito. "And *buon giorno, Signore Morelli.*"

The men nodded, or grunted, or neither. The women just stood there like two trees, taken root.

Louie Levine was a plain talker. "The bus don't stop here, ladies."

"The bus, Mr. Levine?"

"The bus, Mrs. Katz." Louie jerked his thumb in the direction of the big game room. "They are just passing out the bingo cards, ladies. Don't be late."

Water off a duck's back. Ida Katz zeroed in on Vito.

"Mr. Morelli," she purred, "I didn't notice your name on the Las Vegas list."

Vito winced. "Play, play!" He grunted, as if the bidding would make Ida Katz disappear.

"Ha-Ha-Ha!" Stosh roared. "You hear, little Vito? Nice lady is look for your name on list!"

Vito held his cards high, trying to cover his red face. "I don't go to Las Vegas," he blurted out. "I ain't no gambler."

The men at the table spluttered with suppressed laughter.

Ida Katz was undaunted. "Who knows, maybe you'll change your mind, Mr. Morelli."

"Yes, you still have two weeks," Mrs. Bernstein said, up-and-downing her eyebrows as Vito sank even deeper into his chair.

"So, *arrivederci*, Mr. Morelli," Ida Katz said.

Vito cleared his throat loudly to say nothing.

"*Ciao* for now, Signore!" Ida Katz pulled Mrs. Bernstein toward the bingo room, smiling back over her shoulder all the way.

As soon as they were out of sight, Louie and Stosh bombarded poor Vito with a barrage of slaps on the back and pokes in the ribs.

"Oh, boy, Vito," Louie said, grinning lasciviously. "Has that Ida Katz got her eye on your Eyetalian sausage!"

"Ya," Oscar snickered. "Also your spicy meatballs!"

"*Marron!* I don't even look at that stupid woman!" Vito said. "What'sa matter with her? Enough! I come here to play cards. Play!"

"So play," Louie said. "It's *your* play, if you can get your mind off Ida Pussy Katz!"

"It's not so funny, Levine, I'm telling you!" Vito looked at his cards. "I pass."

"Good idea to pass, little Vito," Stosh said. "You couldn't do for her what she wants, anyhow."

"And you, big Stosh? What could *you* do for her?"

"The same, little Vito." Stosh smiled. "I pass, too."

Oscar studied his cards, rearranged them, shook his head woefully, and rearranged them again. "*Hmph-hmph-hmph!*" he groaned, and then, "*tsk, tsk, tsk.*"

"Enough with the Beethoven symphony," Louie said. "Play pinochle!"

"'Play pinochle,' he says! Deal cards instead of trash," Oscar complained, "und I'll play pinochle. What can I do? I pass. Everybody passes to you, Levine. You can get the hand dirt cheap."

Louie smiled and bowed from the neck. "Thank you for the bargain, Mr. Stein. Spades."

The game of pinochle has not changed in the twenty-four hundred years since it was invented by an ancient pre-Russian, in a cave situated in the district of Paskudnyackia, deep in Siberia. After the four players are dealt their hands and have made their bids, they play out their cards, one by one in turn, punctuating their plays with clockwise grunts or groans or gloating cackles, clearly indicating which team has taken each trick. There are losers and there are winners. The winners are always brilliant clairvoyants and accomplished tacticians. The losers are divided into two distinct types: The one with the loud voice during the point-totaling is a fine pinochle player who had the previous hand all figured out. His partner—and this is the ancient law, carbon-dated back to the cave—is invariably a schmuck.

Louie snorted or growled at every card Stosh played. At the end of the hand, he slapped his last card down so hard the table rattled. "Whatta ya coming out with your clubs for?" he hollered. "If you don't open clubs, I know you got clubs, so why come out with clubs?"

"Well, uh, you opened spades," Stosh stammered, "so . . . so I don't know—"

"Of course you don't know, schmuck! I had a singleton club. I could get to you in diamonds, but once you come out clubs and take my singleton club, I can never get back to you!"

"You're lucky you had the ace, Louie," Vito gloated. "I had six spades."

Stosh looked from face to face. "But I was, uh—"

"You was making a stupid play, that's what you was uh! If you came back a heart or a trump, then I know you got clubs. By the way, schmuck, how many clubs did you have?"

"Four," Stosh admitted.

"Four!" Louie shouted. "That's a fortune, if I know it, schmuck!"

"Take it easy, Levine," Oscar said. "You'll hurt his feelings."

"You worry about his feelings," Louie snapped. "When he's *my* partner, I worry about my money!"

Vito, looking across the card room, spotted Abe, wending his way through the crowded room to the table.

"Look who's here" said Louie. "The gay divorcée!"

"What kinda teamwork is this?" Abe asked. "Here I am, working my fingers to the bone over a hot needle and thread, while you bums sit around all day playing penny pinochle."

"Never mind what we're doing," Louie countered. "You're a half an hour late. You bring your homework?"

"Wait till you see—they're beautiful," Abe said, showing the shopping bag. "Guaranteed to chop off twenty-five years a man!"

"*Shhhh!* You crazy?" Louie said. "How many times I have to tell you people?"

He scanned the room, then leaned forward to whisper. "Now, listen carefully. I will only chew my cabbage once. Abe and I go first. We'll be in the last booth. Keep the cards going. The score don't count, no money changes hands today—"

"But we got you on a bagel," Vito objected. "Forty-two points—"

"Big deal!" Louie said. "This is more important! Now, Abe and I are in the men's room. One by one, very casual, you come in, try on, go out, come back to the game. Then the next man. In and out, no conversation. Understand?"

The four men nodded.

"I'll take the shopping bag," Louie told Abe, getting up. "Count to three slow, check on Cantor in the lobby, then follow me."

Louie left the table, sauntering toward the hall to the men's room. Abe started to count aloud, *"Uno . . . dos . . . trés."* Then, out of the side of his mouth, *"Hasta la vista, Señores.* Deal the cards."

Abe headed for the lobby, walking nonchalantly and whistling "Makin' Whoopee," his favorite whistling tune. He could make that song sound so sad, or gay like a trilling bird, or even like the score for a mystery movie, tremulous and scary. He could make Eddie Cantor smile, wherever he is. That Abe Silver was some fancy whistler.

He poked his nose around the corner into the noisy lobby, just as Cantor was answering the desk phone.

"Hello, Senior Citizens', Fairfax Branch. . . . Who? . . ."

Abe started toward the men's room.

"Oh, Mr. Mandel, the birthday boy? . . . Person-to-person?"

Abe turned back quickly at the mention of the name, and saw Cantor's face redden.

"No, he's not here. . . . When do I expect him? Well, who is the party calling from Chicago, Operator? . . . Oh-hh, *also* Mr. Mandel? . . . Usually? Yes, but not today. . . . Yes, I am sure. Ask your party if he will talk to me. . . . Yes, I know, you *told* me person-to-person, but—whatta ya mean shouting? I only wanna make sure you hear me! . . . Listen, Operator, I'm trying to tell you—it's too late to take a message, too *late* for person-to-person. Today is Wednesday—Emanuel Mandel died Monday morning, a couple of days *ahead* of his birthday! You tell your party, *Mister* Mandel, if he wants any more information about his father, he should call his landlady. If he doesn't have the number, I can look it up for him. . . . All right . . . yes . . . good-bye."

Cantor hung up the phone. "A son," he muttered.

A few minutes later, in the men's room, four pants legs and four shoes could be seen under the door of the last booth. If a stranger came in this might attract attention. But where else could the gang try on their wigs? In the ladies room?

"No, goddamn it!" Louie hissed. "I won't do it, and that's all!"

"Listen, Louie," Abe whispered, "you told us yourself—we are each responsible for the planning and security of our own jobs. On April Fool's Day, you will be the big cheese, but today, when it comes to the disguises, I am the boss! So just do what I tell you!"

"All right, Abe, all right. I'll do it, but I'm gonna feel like a schlemiel."

"Maybe you'd feel better if somebody walked in here right now and saw both of us in this toilet booth? Now, gimme your hand and help me up!"

"My hand—?"

38

Suddenly, only two legs and two shoes could be seen under the door. Then, all at once, Louie's pants flopped down onto his shoes. No reason for suspicion now, should an old pisser happen in to answer his bladder call—they were just another old guy sitting on the toilet.

"Turn around," Abe whispered.

Louie did as he was told, his pants and shoes making a hundred-and-eighty-degree spin to face the toilet bowl in a seemingly astonishing contortion.

Inside the booth, Abe stood carefully astride the toilet seat, ducking down just enough so that he could not be seen over the partition. He turned a wig in his hands, finding the front.

"Oh, boy," whispered Abe, looking down at Louie. "Could I blackmail you right now, sweetie!"

"Come on, already, will you!" Louie growled.

Abe placed the curly mod wig on Louie's head, pulling it snugly down into place. Louie's knees buckled slightly at the tug.

Abe leaned back to view his handiwork. "Well? How does it feel?"

"How does it feel? It feels like a hot shower cap. How does it look?"

"Perfect," Abe said, beaming. "Makes you look just like a young Paul Muni."

"It's that good, hah?"

"Take it from me, the little ol' wigmaker. You could pick up any forty-two-year-old girl on the street—easy!"


Meanwhile, back at the pinochle table, Vito got up from his chair. "'Scuse me, gents. I gotta go to the gent's."

"But Louie said one at a time," Stosh said.

"He didn't say I couldn't go, if I *hadda* go, did he?"

Vito set out down the hall to the men's room. Just as he approached the door, an elderly sprinter, one hand fumbling at his pants zipper, shouldered Vito aside and pushed inside. Vito decided to pass the men's room, pretending that it had never been his destination. His urge to pass water had curiously dissipated, anyway. Damn it, he had been waiting for the feeling all morning. He walked into the lobby, posting himself in a position to watch down the hall.

Inside the last booth, Louie and Abe were whispering.

"Whozat?"

"*Shhh!*"

The old gent, just starting to pee, swiveled his head at the sound, spraying the side of the urinal and his pants in the process. He saw that the slow-closing door to the men's room was just finishing its *sh-shh*ing of the disinfectant spray mechanism attached to the hinge. Content that he was in private with his privates, he finished his tinkle with a quiet, heartfelt groan of pleasure and relief. The final squeeze, the last two little shakes, a slow zip, and the old man headed for the bank of sinks.

Cautiously, Abe straightened up to peek over the enclosure door. Ducking back down, his mouth right at Louie's ear, he whispered, "He's not one of ours."

At the end of the hallway, Vito could wait no longer. The pressing tickle had returned. He walked briskly toward the men's room to keep his postponed appointment with the urinal.

It was predictable, of course. God works in wondrous ways at the Senior Citizens' Center. Vito was just passing the ladies' room, when Ida Katz breezed recklessly out of that door, bumping him against the opposite wall. Startled by the sudden collision, three drops of pee escaped before he could control it.

Ida Katz was instantly the Fairfax belle. "Oh, Mr. Morelli, fancy bunking into you here!" She simpered. "Ships passing in the night, isn't it!"

"Oh, Mrs. uh. . . . I'm sorry, Mrs. uh. . . ."

"Katz. Ida Katz. You remember?"

"Yeah, Katz" Vito whirled to escape her.

"Mr. Morelli!" She stopped him with a hand on his arm. "You can feel free any time to call me Ida."

"That's, uh . . . okay, Mrs. uh. . . . Somebody's waiting for me! I mean, I gotta go!" Vito shot through the men's room door and across the room to the urinals, cursing in Italian.

"Nu—brief encounter." Ida Katz shrugged, smiled a bittersweet smile, and headed back into Bingo.

"It's Vito," Abe whispered.

"I told him one at a time!" Louie hissed back.

Vito stood arched at the urinal, enjoying the blissful sensation of release. The interloper who had preempted Vito's earlier entrance had not quite finished with his toilet. Bending close to the mirror, he systematically wet the few strands of hair on his head, then combed and, carefully patted each one into place across the bald expanse. A long and frowning look, turning profile. Another pat. Another look. Finally satisfied, he pocketed his comb and left the rest room.

"Why the hell doesn't Vito come in here?" Louie asked.

Abe peeked over the booth door once again. "He's busy taking a leak," he explained.

Vito flushed the urinal and turned on a tap at the sinks.

"Now what's he doing?"

Abe didn't even bother to peek. "He's washing his hands, of course, like his mama taught him."

"Yeah?" said Louie. "Who taught him to piss on his hands in the first place?"

Vito tossed his used paper towel into the waste can and turned to the last booth. The sight of Louie's shoes and dropped pants stopped him cold. "Louie," he whispered to the pants under the door, "should I go out and come back later?"

In response, the booth door was suddenly jerked open, a grasping hand shot out, and Vito was jerked roughly inside by his coat lapels.

Louie slapped a hand over Vito's mouth. "Make even one little squawk, and you won't be able to swallow spaghetti for a month, you dumb guinea!"

Vito's eyes darted from Louie's face to his wig, to his boxer shorts, to Abe, standing on the toilet with his forefinger held urgently to his pursed lips.

"Let him go, Louie," Abe said. "He'll be quiet."

Vito nodded and glumphed emphatically under Louie's hand, and Louie released him. Vito took a free breath, and a new look at Louie and his curly wig. "Oh, you're beautiful, Louie!" he whispered. "You look just like Mario Lanza, God rest his soul and his beautiful voice!"

"Not like Paul Muni?" Louie asked, disappointed.

"Paul Muni? Never. Mario Lanza—exactly."

"Never mind," Louie said. "What the hell took you so long?"

"I don't know what you talk about. It didn't take me no longer than usual. None of us pee like we useta, y'know."

"Funny, very funny," Louie said, pulling the wig off his head and handing it to Abe. "Here, it fits me all right. It doesn't matter how it looks—Muni, Lanza, what's the difference?"

"Oh, there's a big difference," Vito insisted.

"Come on!" Louie pushed Vito out of his way and pulled up his pants. "I'm going back to the game. Hurry up in here. The bingo will be over pretty soon, and this room will get very popular all of a sudden." With that he opened the booth door and quickly made his exit from the men's room.

"Turn around and drop your pants, Vito."

Vito looked up at Abe quizzically. "Why? I don't have to, I just—"

"What if somebody comes in, dummy?"

All at once, the meaning of the recent scene that he had been pulled into dawned on Vito. "Oh-hh. That's why Louie . . ."

A pair of Italian pants dropped to the floor with a clang of a pocketful of keys.

41

# 8

# SHUFFLEBOARD AND YOGA

Grace Lotis was the yoga instructor. That was her honest-to-God name. She was a Greek girl, and her figure was a sculptor's dream. Every smooth curve of her body was a snaky arch, leading the eye on to the next sinuous curve, from her artfully arched foot to her lovely, long, Nefertiti neck. Her hair was shiny black, and the leather thong she tied around it at the back let it hang nearly to her waist, where it swayed sensuously as she walked her gliding walk.

Grace Lotis had studied yoga under Richard Heckinger, who had that "Yoga For Life" show on TV, and for a while she was one of the two girls in tight leotards who demonstrated the yoga postures on camera. She was the one who did all the advanced exercises—not the one that out-of-town salesmen jerked off to as they watched late at night in their hotel rooms. That was the one with the big tits, who did the easy exercises for beginners. Then, when Yogi Heckinger came on with a stronger interest in her yoni than in her yoga, Grace decided it was time to go out on her own. Now she was teaching one night a week at UCLA, a couple of days a week at the playgrounds, and every Wednesday afternoon at the Senior Citizens' Center.

The large open room is used on Saturdays for modern dance and self-defense classes, too, so it has the mirror and dance bar all along one wall. Senior citizen students pay fifty cents for each class and, to Honor Thy Father and Thy Mother, the county of Los Angeles chips in the other buck to pay for the instructors.

The weekly yoga class was by far the most popular class of all, filling the room to capacity with wall-to-wall bodies, all because Grace had a special way with these women. She didn't just teach the yoga disciplines in the usual formal, cool, Oriental manner. After all, she was Greek. She covered the serenity aspects during the body exercises, of course, but Grace understood that the human body is not mainly a vessel of tranquillity and inner calm. She knew that the healthy body is mainly fire. Churning in full

42

blaze, or smoldering quietly, but fire nonetheless. And she knew that these old women needed to be put back in touch with the feel of the fire within their bodies, even more than they needed a temporary sense of inner peace.

And so, at the beginning of each yoga class, Grace would introduce the day's routine in a slightly off-color way. She tickled the ladies with her gentle obscenities. She shocked them a little—and she got their minds and bodies fired up. They would giggle at her harmless vulgarities, oooh-ing and ah-ing and aha-ing and oh-my-goodness-ing. She was the Lenny Bruce of yoga, and they loved it.

"All right ladies, if you can't quite make the Sukhasana posture, it's okay. Just sit there in a semi. Even a half a semi is okay. Spines straight, chins high, relaxed. Good. Now, today, we're going to start a series of exercises in Hatha Yoga that are especially good for the tits."

Snickers. Giggles. Blushes.

"You notice I do not call them breasts. Breasts are for feeding babies, and you've all done as much of that as you are going to. Tits are for holding up. And sticking out. And feeling—even if you have to feel them yourself."

Raucous laughter. Oh-my-mys.

"There's nothing wrong with that. I do it all the time—it feels good!" And with that, she put her hands on her tits, squeezing them gently.

Little gurgles. Tee-hee-hees. Tsk-tsks.

"All right," Grace said. "All those who think it doesn't feel good, raise your hands—I dare you!"

No hands.

"Of course, she continued. "That's what we're all supposed to feel—good. Not just when we're young, but all of our lives. Greta Garbo feels good. That's right, Greta Garbo has followed the yoga disciplines for many years. She is over seventy now, and when she walks down East Fifty-Second Street, her head is held high, her arms and legs are as firm as they were when she was forty, her ass is tight, and her tits are sticking out and pointing up to the sun! And I can tell you that young men on the street fall all over themselves trying to keep up with her, just to watch her body move and to dream of being alo-one with Garbo. Now, are we ready to try to be like Garbo?"

Wild applause! Excited shrieks!

"All right, ladies. I love your enthusiasm, but now it's time to calm down and get started with our two postures for today: Bhujangasana, The Cobra—and Salabhasana, The Locust. And, of course, we will do The Sponge in between—Savasana—which allows you to fully relax from your labors, and to feel all the lovely life energy flowing into your body through every pore, rejuvenating every muscle and every tingling nerve."

Minnie Gold and Kate MacAfee lay side by side in their leotards, puffing and straining on their little mats as they tried their damnedest to assume

43

the postures. And during The Sponge, they would gossip, *sotto voce*. Today, Minnie would try for her first convert.

"All right, ladies, roll over on your stomachs, foreheads on the mat. . . . Now, place the palms of your hands flat on the floor, as close to your shoulders as you can. . . ."

On Wednesday afternoons at the Center, shuffleboard is very popular, too. The shuffleboard decks are outside, just across a narrow flagstone walk from the yoga room, with its floor-to-ceiling windows, and the men fight to get their tournament reservations in early. And if they aren't on a team, they are sure to be in the gallery, sitting on tiered benches and staring right through the Senior Citizen Superbowl Shuffleboard Championships and through the large windows at Grace and her yoga ladies, as they move their bodies to a slow steady count on the floor. The men can't hear the instructions, they can only see the bodies turning and arching and stretching and squirming in a dreamy slow motion. Hearing would only be distracting.

". . . Slowly . . . slowly . . . pushing steadily . . . seven . . . arching up . . . and up . . . nine . . . keep your buttocks muscles tight . . . eleven . . . head moving up and back, slowly . . . thirteen . . . elbows almost straight, now . . . feel each vertebra . . . rolling . . . arching . . . sixteen . . . now ease your hips off the floor, if you can . . . and hold . . ."

The Wednesday afternoon tension was terrific. Big colored plastic disks swooshed down the length of the concrete shuffleboard deck, clicking and clacking opposing disks out of the way. *Swoo-oosh, crack-crack! Swoo-oosh, click-clack!* And the competitors didn't miss a single trick—of the shuffleboard competition, or the prick-teasing body show through the window. The loud whoops and hollers were for the shuffleboard shots, and the quiet appreciative grunts were for the yoga. Is evvree-bodee ha-appee?

". . . Thirteen . . . keep your buttocks tight, feel the tingle . . . fifteen . . . almost down, tits almost touching . . . eighteen . . . keep your chin up till the last . . . twenty . . . now, forehead slowly to the mat, and slowly exhale. . . . You were all lovely cobras, ladies . . . lovely. Didn't that feel good?"

It did make them feel good. It made them feel so good to touch, even briefly, the warm memory that their bodies were once young and healthy and desirable to someone. And sometimes, when they lie on their backs, moving their legs up and down and apart to the slow counted cadence, each woman is young for a little while, and she remembers the face of her long-ago man. And his touch, and maybe even his words. But the women never tell each other about that.

"All right, my sexy cobras, you've earned a little rest. Savasana . . . roll over onto your backs . . . slowly . . . arms at your sides, palms up . . . now you are all sponges. Close your eyes . . . feel every pore in your body open up . . . inhale slowly, taking in all the energies from the atmosphere around you . . . exhale, slowly . . ."

44

Grace's sponges are not supposed to talk. They are only supposed to lie there with their pores open, inhaling and exhaling. But it was impossible for Minnie Gold to be an obedient sponge. What good is breathing in, if you can't talk on the way out? Minnie did not believe in wasting breath.

"Try it!" Minnie urged her sister sponge as they lay at the back of the class, "Whatta ya got to lose?"

Kate MacAfee was shocked. "If I even suggested such a thing as that to Mac, he would scream a stream of bloody murder you could hear all the way to Belfast."

Minnie lowered her voice. "Yeah, but would he holler when the extra sixty-two dollars came in on the first of every month?"

"Indeed he would. Oh, yes, I know my Mac. I can hear the cursin' now. He'd call me a sixty-two-dollar-prostitute, he would."

"What's so terrible?" Minnie reasoned. "If your ex-husband is your only customer, he should consider it a very nice compliment."

"But it's a mortal sin," Kate said.

"Big deal. Listen, only a mortal *can* commit a sin," Minnie said. "Besides, it's such a nice sin, I can't begin to tell you!"

"No, I don't think you understand," Kate said patiently. "If Mac and I were divorced, we'd both be excommunicated from the church!"

"Tell me, is that worse than being excommunicated from life? Listen, you think Abe and I enjoyed a divorce after forty-nine years of a beautiful married life? Of course not. One more year, we would have made the golden anniversary."

Kate shook her head in sympathy, but the big question was burning the inside of her mouth. "But how could you have done it? In the Lord's name—what were the grounds for divorce after forty-nine years?"

"What else?" Minnie asked, "Irreconcilable differences."

"After forty-nine years? What in heaven's name were they?"

"Simple," Minnie said. "The difference . . . is between what the Social Security gives an old married couple to live on, and the amount we need to survive. Irreconcilable."

"Ah, now *that's* clear as a bell, that is."

"Now we are single," Minnie continued, "we get sixty-two dollars extra a month. We sneak around a little, and we live in your mortal sin—and my Abe is a single swinger with new life, you wouldn't believe it!"

"Ah, Mrs. Silver, sure you're one of a kind!" Kate said.

Minnie never could take a compliment. "Nonsense. We do what we have to do, that's all," she said. "There's an old saying, 'When you got nothing but lemons—you better learn to make lemonade.'"

Kate nodded, smiling. "If only we could live according to all the nice old sayings. Sure, it would be a better world to live in."

"Don't kid yourself," Minnie said. "A saying is just a saying . . . but a doing is a doing! You know what I mean, Mrs. MacAfee?"

"I, uh, think so, Mrs. Silver. But I'm not sure . . . I'm just not sure. . . ."

Minnie looked at her yoga mate and realized, sadly, that she could never effect even the smallest conversion on this sweet and docile Irish woman. "Kate, darling, let me put it this way," she said. "Anybody who ever did anything worthwhile in this world, did it right in the middle of not being sure!"

As though on cue, Grace Lotis gently tinkled her little temple bell, and the yoga class was over.

The sound of the bell pierced the window, as it did every Wednesday, at the opening and closing of the class. And play was abruptly suspended at the shuffleboard deck by unspoken agreement, as it was every Wednesday. And the men stood in long gray lines, leaning on their cues or with hands in pockets, to watch the women get to their feet and file slowly out of the yoga room. And the women, on parade, did their best imitation of Grace walking, their stomachs sucked in, their tits held as high as thrown-back shoulders and gravity would allow, as they did every Wednesday.

Wednesday was a not-such-a-bad-day at the Senior Citizens' Center.

46

# 9

# THE MEDIA MAN

Saturday was a good day for calling the television and radio stations. The weekend staff would be more likely to give Louie any information he wanted. Very few higher-ups would be around to ask if such information was allowed to be given out. But before he could leave his room for his sidewalk office, Louie had to finish his daily check on his gang's research work-in-progress.

He sat bent over his table, filling in the last of the vehicle schedule notes on the big bank intersection chart. Minnie had done a thorough job, and Louie was proud of her. He was proud of every member of his attack team for the good work they had accomplished toward The Benefit during the past two months. They were right on schedule. A-OK, and counting down to April first.

He sat back and looked down at the chart with great satisfaction. Stretching his kinked back muscles into an arch, he glanced at his Union wristwatch with a start.

"Oh, my God, little girl, it's nearly nine-thirty. Okay, okay—by *your* God also, it's nearly nine-thirty. I'm usually hitting the street by seven sharp, they could set a clock by me."

He got up from the chair, retrieved the red and white striped plastic table cloth from his bed, and methodically replaced it, covering table and chart. Then, he got down on his knees, and ducking under the table, he retaped the table cloth to the bottom of the table. Very carefully, he inserted a paper match in the folds of the plastic, so that if the cloth were removed in his absence, the telltale match would fall to the floor.

He rose from the floor and tugged at the tablecloth gently. It was solidly stuck. He looked underneath the table once more, to check the match. His little sentry was still hanging there.

Turning to his clothes closet, he put on his scratchy plaid wool jacket and his Dodger baseball cap. Reaching up to the closet shelf, he took down a cardboard box of dried prunes. He slipped his hand into the box and extracted a handful of prunes, popping one into his mouth and the rest in his pocket.

A shadow seemed to cross the angel's face.

"Don't worry, sweetheart, I'm only gonna eat one at a time, during the whole day."

He shot the prune pit out of his mouth with a two-point thwunk into the empty wastebasket. Again he reached into the prune box. This time he took out a small spiral notebook, and, opening a shirt button, carefully slipped it under his shirt. He rebuttoned it, took a quick look around the room for a last-minute check, and headed for the door.

"Have a good day, bright eyes. I'll see you in shul."

He locked his door, and hit the street.

A little after twelve o'clock, Louie began to feel the hunger pangs, but he wasn't ready to quit the phone booth yet. He still had almost an hour to get the sixty-cent federal discount lunch at the church. He preferred the heavy breaded cutlet a little soggy, anyway. It was easier to chew.

Louie stood in the phone booth and flipped the pages of his little notebook back to review his progress so far. The KFI page was full. NBC–TV? No luck. "I'm sorry, sir, we're simply not permitted to supply that sort of information over the telephone. If you would like to write a letter stating your request . . ." At that point, Louie had hung up in disgust.

KFWB. The whole news team, and their schedules.

KNX. A couple of names. Not enough yet.

KPFK. Oh, boy, that was a good one. The news director himself got on the phone. He asked Louie to be sure to call him direct, ask for him personally if he had any information concerning an act of civil disobedience that Louie hinted at. He even gave Louie his home number.

KABC. The switchboard operator was so new and so dumb, she sounded like a recorded message: "I'm sorry, sir, there's no one in the newsroom at this time, you'll have to call back Monday for that information. I'm sorry, sir, there's no one in—" Louie hung up on her, too.

Now, he was up to the CBS–TV page. This one would be a little special. Louie dropped a dime into the coin slot and dialed the number listed in his little book. As the number rang, he was staring out of the booth window and across Fairfax Avenue, right at CBS Television City. His eyes swept the length of the big black modern building and fixed on the stark white CBS logo.

"I'm looking you straight in the eye, Walter Cronkite," he said.

"CBS Television."

"Hello, CBS? Connect me with the news department, please. . . ."

Louie hated the telephone. All his life, he hated the telephone. It was frustrating not be able to look at a person when he talked to them. Not to see the tilt of someone's head, to see hands move, to know for sure that they were really paying attention.

"Newsroom, Machado." The voice was crisp, efficient.

"Hello, is this the news department? To whom am I speaking, please? . . . Aha, Mrs. Machado . . . Oh, I'm sorry, *Ms*. Machado . . . I would like to talk to to a newsman, please. . . . Oh, I see, you are a news*person*. . . . Well, I would like to talk, please, to the *head* newsperson. . . . I see. . . . If he *was* in the office, what would his name be? . . . Listen, lady, what if I wanted to report a riot? . . . No, no, there is no riot right now. But if—*if* the time comes, I am a witness at a riot, who would I ask for at CBS, to report it to the head newsperson? . . . George Van Wick. Thank you very much, Ms. Machado, you are a very nice person. And thank you for your advice about the police. Give my best regards to Walter Cronkite. . . ."

Louie hung up, shaking his head in amazement at the woman's idiotic suggestion. "Why the hell would I call the police department to come to my riot?" Then, on second thought, "Wait a minute! Listen lady, maybe you gave me a good idea."

He made the new entry on the CBS–TV page of his little book. "CBS News, George Van Wick. Oh-hh, yeah. . . . Six o'clock news, the guy who cries when the Dodgers lose and smiles when he's reporting on the bus strike."

Louie slapped his little book shut on George Van Wick and slipped it back under his shirt. Peering out of the booth, he checked the sidewalk both ways. Then he took a handkerchief out of his jacket and carefully stuffed about half of it into the coin-return box. He fished around in his pants pocket for his last dime, dropped it into the slot, and dialed 0.

She answered on the first ring. A miracle.

"Operator . . ."

"Listen, Operator, I just put in a dime, and I got a wrong number!" Louie's voice bristled with outrage.

"What number did you dial, sir?" Ma Bell was patient, polite.

"It was a very easy number, OL1-2345. Positively, I dialed it right. Some Japanese lady answered."

"What is the number of your coin telephone, sir?"

"Just a minute. . . . "Louie squinted up at the dial. "The number here is 645-9116."

He heard the electrical impulse as the operator activated the coin-return mechanism—automatic telephone company procedure, before asking for the address of the wronged caller. At least a dozen coins tumbled down the chute into Louie's handkerchief. Jackpot.

"Was your coin returned, sir?" She thought she heard a jingle.

Louie was fumbling with his handkerchief full of change, and fighting back his urge to burst out laughing. He turned on all the indignation he could muster, shouting into the phone, "Of course not! How could you give me my dime back? The Japanese lady used up my dime!"

"I'm sorry, sir. If you will give me your name and address, we will be happy to mail you a check for ten cents."

Louie was jamming the handkerchief of coins into his pocket. "No, I don't have time. I gotta go—here comes my bus" He slammed the phone back onto the cradle. There was hardly enough room for the wide grin that spread across his face.

Louie reached into his pocket, shook the handkerchief gently to free the coins, then he drew it from his pocket and wiped the sweat from his neck. It was hot work doing business with the networks and the telephone company.

This particular public telephone often suffered from a fairly common malfunction. It did not collect coins when they were first deposited; it simply held them at the midrange level. Nor did they drop into the big collection box, as they are supposed to do, when the caller was connected with his number. But, upon electronic request from the operator, all the coins thus stored from previous calls were magically released into the coin-return scoop at once. A one-armed Santa Claus on Fairfax Avenue.

Funny thing, this telephone had been out of order in this way for about three months this time. And nobody had been good enough to report the trouble.

Louie opened the phone booth door and stepped out onto the sidewalk. One hand in his pocket, his baseball cap set at a rakish angle, he jingled his coins quietly as he strolled toward the Church of the Holy Breaded Cutlet.

# 10

# SUNDAY SOCIAL

The men all shaved on Sundays.

Sunday was Social Day at the Senior Citizens' Center, and almost every ambulatory member showed up for the festivities. Entertainment, not religion, was the opiate of the people here. On Sunday, the Social Committee arranged for a lecture or a travelogue film or a tea dance or a concert. Sometimes there was even a play put on by one of the local colleges.

Senior citizens are a great audience—except for a few geriatric eccentricities. They love good music, especially good singing. But sometimes, it puts some of them to sleep. And when they sleep, they snore. Or fart. The men, mostly. It's not really the noise made by the flatulant that disturbs the performance in progress; it's the shifting of the folding chairs following the misdemeanor.

This audience loves good dancing. Especially when somebody else is doing it, on stage. Tap dancing is their favorite. But sometimes the dust that is raised makes some of them sneeze. Not quiet constrained sneezes, but full-out catarrhal explosions that rock the hall.

But most of all, they love dramatics. A thoughtful play, a cast of well drawn characters clashing in good argument, and this audience goes mad with pleasure. They choose sides. They identify with the actors, taking part in the performance vocally by shouting encouragements, or warnings, or disapprovals, or congratulations.

Last year, a performance of *Who's Afraid of Virginia Woolf?* provoked a fist fight in the audience, right in the middle of the second act. Henry Hoover called the wife a "lousy two-bit whore" out loud, and Lew Hyman pushed him off his chair onto the floor. By the time they were pulled apart, Hoover had a bloody nose and Hyman's upper denture had been smashed under Hoover's heavy foot. The two men still don't speak to each other.

Two Sundays before The Benefit, Patty Lewis and Benny Lessey were scheduled to appear on stage at the Center for a record-breaking third

51

return engagement. The members adored Patty's pert way with her comedy songs, and they never tired of bowlegged Benny and his copyrighted zany popcorn *shtick*, the little white puffs flying up into the air from every conceivable angle as he and Patty danced and sang together. They were terrific.

And they were always ready to perform for free for the deserted people— the ones in hospitals or prisons or old age homes. But Patty had been rushed to Mount Sinai in mid week, where the doctors found the terrible evidence of the Big C. She was never to come out of the hospital, and the popcorn would never fly again.

Joe Glass, chairman extraordinaire of the Social Committee, and veteran Master of Ceremonies, had tried his damnedest to replace Patty and Benny, but Florence Henderson was taping "Hollywood Squares" that Sunday, Shari Lewis and Lambchop had a gig at Magic Mountain, and he couldn't even get through to Jack Carter. So Joe had put together an all-member all-star show.

The large room was packed, as usual. The table at the back had its usual platter of day-old sponge cake, and the coffee brewing, and the hot water for tea, waiting. And out in the lobby, as usual, Louie Levine sat at his card table with his collection box for *The Voice of the Aged*.

Louie never watched the show. He hated shows. And movies. And even TV, except for the news. "A show? Who needs a show?" he liked to say, sourly. "Life is not *enough* of a show for you?" Nobody ever argued the point with him.

The audience sat entranced, or at least attentive, as Mrs. Hansen, a six-foot woman of heroic hourglass proportions, corseted to within an inch of her life, stood planted at the mike, rendering *Un Bel Dí* in a piercing soprano which threatened mass eardrum puncture at any note. Her hands, clasped tightly in front of her waist, seemed to squeeze each shrieking tone out through her pursed lips in ever sharper distortions of the published score.

At last, heaving with unbridled emotion, Mrs. Hansen murdered the last few bars of her aria, putting poor Puccini out of his turning misery with a punishing fortissimo flourish.

Joe Glass came running out on stage, clapping his hands in an attempt to clear his inner ear as Mrs. Hansen bowed her considerable bosom to the generous arthritic applause from the most tolerant audience who ever bent ass to folding chair. Glass continued to milk the applause for all it was worth. Then, at long last, Mrs. Hansen lumbered off the stage; her head held high, as though in triumph at the Met.

"Wasn't she sensational?" Joe Glass gushed. "It doesn't really matter that I couldn't get for us today a famous comedian or a TV singer for our show— our own members are as talented as any performers in the whole entertainment world, right?"

52

"Big deal!" Mrs. Bernstein said to Ida Katz. "A fat old Swedish lady, trying to make like a young Japanese geisha girl, singing in Italian!"

Stosh reached forward and tapped Vito on the shoulder. "How you like *that* for singing, little Vito?"

Vito turned around in his seat. "You call that a voice? That ain't no voice, that's an ambulance!" Stosh roared with laughter, slapping Vito on the back.

"All right." Glass tapped his finger on the microphone. "If I can have the undivided attention of all the members of this lucky audience . . . it is my great pleasure now to introduce—no question about it—the stars of our show! It was not an easy job, but yours truly talked them into coming out of retirement, and coming back together again—!"

The audience erupted into a loud buzzing and scattered applause. Glass continued to speak, shouting over the noise. "No, no! Don't get me wrong—just to appear on stage together, doing their act, that's all!"

The audience groaned "Aw-ww!" and quieted down.

"You all know the story. So to make a long story short, here together on our stage today, for the first time since the divorce became final, ladies and gentlemen . . . and, I ask you, if Sonny and Cher can do it, why can't they?"

Applause. Cheers. Laughter. Stamping. More applause.

"That's right, folks, we are all grown-up, groovy people here! So without any further ado, I introduce to you—direct from their smash engagement at the world-famous Grossinger's Hotel, in 1946—the one and only, both of them . . . Silver and Gold!"

The kid at the piano sailed into the time worn intro, and Minnie and Abe strutted onstage to a warm welcoming applause. They were costumed in the crisp and cool summer whites of the thirties, Abe with a rakish straw boater and bent rattan cane, Minnie with a flowered tulle chapeau and shouldering a cute parasol. They looked great.

Their opening number was "Easter Parade." Of course. And they transported the audience to a Fifth Avenue Sunday in a flash as they scissor-stepped back and forth across the stage, Abe expertly twirling his cane, and Minnie coyly spinning her parasol.

They *were* a parade. And their audience joined them with foot-tapping and finger-snapping and tongue-clicking, volunteering their little fanfares of enjoyment in accompaniment to the carefree song of long ago.

The first chorus was a gentle up-tempo schmaltzy reminiscence, warm and bouncy and gay, as they skipped lightly down the sunny avenue. The second chorus was the mandatory waltz-clog soft-shoe, and when the piano stopped for the breaks, their tippy-tappy feet remembered every tricky *tap-a-diddle-tap-a-diddle-tap-a-diddle-sh-hhh*.

In the last chorus, they interpolated Berlin's original lyrics, written long before his new words would make the song a smash hit in *As*

53

*Thousands Cheer* on Broadway: "Smile and show your dimple, It's really very simple . . ."

After the refrain, they ricocheted into a double-time march tempo for their fancy ride-out finish. Two false endings, then all the way across stage, marching fast in close-order drill, with Minnie right against Abe's back as they walked offstage as a single person.

Then came Minnie's bit, as she backed onstage. Holding onto the stage-right curtain, she kicked her little foot back. Then, she stuck her fanny out suggestively. The impish wink, the big smile, the cute little hop and she was gone with a swish of her skirt.

The audience creaked to their feet, thundering with wild applause. Silver and Gold took no chances. Their first number had to be big, BIG! Clifton Webb and Marilyn Miller couldn't have touched them with this number—not with this crowd, not on this day. They were called back with screams of "More! More!" "Encore, much more!"

And they stayed back. For over an hour, they sang, they danced, they did two-liners, they did impressions—Chaplin—Mae West—Fibber McGee and Mollie, would you believe? They even did a series of dirty jokes titled "Sex in the Seventies, in the Seventies."

. . . "Jake, you want I should *loan* you the two dollars?"

. . . "If I woulda known *this*, I coulda saved Eleanor Roosevelt!"

. . . "How was I able to make love to *three* women in different parts of town all in *one* night, at age seventy-one? Simple—I got a ten-speed bicycle!"

And the audience roared with laughter. Everyone there knew the punch lines when they heard them—but they had long ago forgotten the beginnings of the stories, so it was as though Minnie and Abe were premiering a brand new comedy act.

They were terrific. A once-in-a-lifetime performance to remember, for whatever was left of a lifetime. And, for the people in that room, the memory of Silver and Gold would never tarnish.

The audience would have kept them on for another hour, but it was almost six o'clock, and they had to clear the hall by seven on Sundays, right after coffee. Also, Louie needed some time for his collections for The Benefit—*Shhhh!*—for *The Voice of the Aged*.

The crowd sat hushed, waiting for Minnie and Abe's closing number. They stood center stage, smiling softly at each other. Slowly, Abe put his right hand around Minnie's waist, barely touching the small of her back. She rested her right hand lightly on his left, as she looked up at him adoringly. The fingers of her left hand were softly caressing the back of his neck, as they started to dance in their own dream. Were their feet really touching the floor? They seemed to be floating, floating, as they waltzed slowly around, and around, gliding, gliding, in graceful twirling circles to the soul-haunting melody of "The Anniversary Song"—what else? And out

54

in front, the folding chairs creaked softly as the entire assembly swayed slowly back and forth in waltz tempo with the dancing couple, honoring the fiftieth anniversary of Abe Silver and Minnie Gold.

Then, as they danced, Abe began to sing. Softly, at first . . . "Oh-h, how we danced . . . on the night we were wed . . ." His rich baritone rose gradually in volume and intensity . . . "We vowed our true love, though a word wasn't said . . ." By that time, every eye in the place was brimming with tears . . . "We'd find that our love is unaltered by time . . ." The emotion in that room at that moment was an overflowing tide . . . "My darling, I love you so-oo . . ."

It was a wipe out. Silver and Gold were upstage center, dipping the final tender loving dip. And Abe was kissing Minnie kissing Abe, their bodies pressed together in that lifelong perfect fit.

The audience was tearing the place apart. On their feet, screaming, and stamping the floor with their chairs and their feet and their canes. Mere applause was completely covered by the sound of the other, louder noises, as the ovation went on and on.

Abe twirled Minnie back and forth in front of him in curtsy after curtsy. Minnie threw kiss after kiss—*Mw-ahh! Mw-ahh! Mw-ahh!* And the audience suddenly realized from whom Dinah had borrowed her TV trademark. They could have had *fifty* curtain calls if someone had been working the curtain.

Joe Glass knew that there was no way he could get the crowd to settle down simply by asking. So, during the endless bows, he ran out to the reception counter and grabbed the little counter bell. He was back with it now, *ting-ting-ting*ing it into the mike. "Ladies and gentlemen, if there *are* any ladies and gentlemen on the premises . . . I have yet an announcement!" At last, the crowd came down off their orgasmic high and paid poor Glass a modicum of attention. "Well, ladies and gentlemen, that is our show for today, and I'm sure you will agree with me that no finer show was seen today anywhere in the city of Los Angeles!" They gave him all the applause they had left, which was a mere ripple. "If you liked the show as much as you yelled you did, don't forget to stop at Louie Levine's table in the lobby. Remember, your donations pay for the sponge cake and coffee . . . but, more important, for *The Voice of the Aged*. If you do not donate for the Voice, we will *not* be heard! Go have coffee, and go put money in the box. Thank you very mu—"

The sound system abruptly died with a squeal of feedback, and the buzzing audience shuffled noisily toward the coffee table and the exits. They came out into the lobby in a frazzle. Women were still wiping tears away with their handkerchiefs, the men mostly blowing their noses.

Louie sat at his table—almost directly in front of the main exit door, so nobody could miss him. There he sat, doing the breast stroke as he directed the traffic flow of potential contributors. "Keep moving around the table, please. I only wanna see *paying* customers. Absolutely no pledges! Nobody signs the Honor Roll for less than a dollar! The cheapskates keep moving, please! You know who you are!"

A line had formed in front of the table, and people were dropping coins and an occasional bill into the open cigar box marked The Voice of the Aged. One by one they picked up the mimeographed two-fold monthly newsletter that Louie edited and mailed out.

*The Voice of the Aged* made the troubled pages of any metropolitan newspaper look like a comic strip. No flowery language. No reportorial jargon. Just the facts:

—Mrs. Mae Dunphy, dead at 71. County Hospital. Cause of death: Concussion, broken cheekbone, shattered sternum, internal injuries. Beaten on her doorstep, during daylight mugging by three young thugs. Robbed of purse containing loose change and Medicare stamps for February. Beloved wife of Ian Dunphy, member. Hometown: Donegal, Ireland.

—Mrs. Alexandrine Herrmann, dead at 70. Cause of death: Suicide. In her room. Sleeping pill overdose. Confined to her wheelchair for many years, she took her life when the County Department of Social Services abruptly terminated her monthly homemaker assistance payment. Her suicide note, found clutched in her hand: "I do not wish to take my own life, but see no other alternative. I am disabled, but could manage with homemaker assistance. With my intelligence and background and so much to live for, for me to have to go into a poor nursing home would only mean further torture and slow death." A quote from Chris Cooper, Deputy Regional Service Administrator: "I'm very sorry she committed suicide. Our action was right." Widow of John Herrmann. Hometown: Minneapolis, Minn.

\*\*\* Write to Morrie \*\*\* Write to Morrie \*\*\* Write to Morrie \*\*\* Morris Weintraub, Ward 303, L.A. County Hospital. Our popular Morrie, snappy dresser and 1973 Intermediate Shuffleboard Champ, would like to hear from some of you members while he's recuperating from his recent surgery. No flowers, please! Morrie says: "They stink up the whole room!" He also says he doesn't need more than one lung to beat you bums when he gets out! Good luck, Morrie! Keep your hands off those nurses!

—Mrs. Frieda "Fritzie" Cohen, dead at 82. Cause of death: Toxic poisoning. In her apartment. Our Jack Cantor discovered Fritzie's body by going to her residence after she had not come to the Center for a week. Jack said: "It's the first time she ever missed three Bingo nights in

56

a row." The traces of the poison, found by Dr. Noguchi during the autopsy, came from a half-eaten can of Hi-Vita cat food Fritzie got at Thriftyway Market on Melrose. Members—pass by Thriftyway! Steal someplace else. Widow of Benjamin "Bitsy" Cohen, late member. Hometown: Linz, Austria.

Always plenty of hard news to fill the four pages of *The Voice of the Aged*. But most people who are not old, do not want to read about old. Old is creepy. Also, it's a well known fact that regional administrators and councilmen and mayors and congressmen and governors and senators just never ever get old—so somebody else will have to find the cure for the common old.

The Liberation Army of Louie Levine, maybe.

The line at Louie's collection table was thinning out, but he kept up his famous pitch. "Remember—a nickel can't even buy a pickle! Only a dollar can make a holler!" Louie was busy helping an old lady sign the Honor Roll when big Henry Hoover stepped up to the table and stuck a dollar bill under Louie's nose. As soon as he took hold of the bill, Louie felt that the donor was holding tight to the other end. He looked up, annoyed. "Oh, it's the vacuum cleaner!" Louie let go of the bill.

"Come on, Levine," Hoover said. "One more time—where is all this money goin'?"

"Keep moving. You're holding up the line . . . Next?"

Hoover stood his ground.

"What is it with you, Hoover?" Louie asked. "Every week the same question. What do you think, I'm keeping a chippy?"

"Ha, ha. I just want to know *where* this money is gettin' us heard, that's all."

Louie looked up his nose at Hoover, "Don't worry. We will be heard. Everyplace your committee can get in," Louie said. "The City council, the Old Age Security Office, Social Security . . ."

The lady standing in line behind Hoover stuck her little bird beak around his elbow, and joined the inquisition. "But Mister Levine, you *been* to all those places. Do they ever listen?"

Louie paused for a moment. "Mostly, they *don't* listen, to tell you the honest-to-God truth. But . . . your committee has come up with a brand new approach. It's called *affirmative action!* Also, we got a new place to go, where they will hafta listen to us!"

"Yeah? Where?" Hoover again, the nonbeliever.

"Never mind—*that* is classified information. But mark my words down—this time the voice of the aged will be heard. This time, the whole world will hear us! You got my personal guarantee!"

"Is that a fact, Levine?" Hoover asked with a new respect, impressed by something in Louie's voice.

Louie answered his question with a question. "Did Moses lead a parade?"

It took a second to sink in. Then, Hoover slapped his leg and said, "Levine, you shoulda been a country preacher, I swear! You know somethin'? I see a new look in your eye. Tell you what—this week, I'm not gonna ask for fifty cents change!"

With that, he dropped the dollar bill into the box.

"Hoover, you're all right!" Louie said grandly. "Step right up and sign the Honor Roll. I take back every rotten thing I ever said about your FBI—may it only rest in peace!"

Hoover signed the Honor Roll, picked up his copy of *The Voice of the Aged*, and, shaking a go-get-'em fist at Louie, said, "Go get 'em, tiger!"

"Oh-hh, yeah," Louie said softly as Hoover walked away. "This time, we'll get 'em. You can *bank* on it!"

The little stream of contributors ran dry, and Louie counted up the take in the cigar box. $31.25.

Not bad. Musta been a pretty good show tonight, he thought to himself. Let's see . . . current balance in the fund, $46.80. Jeez, is that all? It takes money to run a benefit. So that makes . . . five, zero, carry the one, eight, seven . . . seventy-eight bucks, and a nickel. Coffee and stuff for next Sunday, about eight bucks, that leaves seventy. Paper and stencils for mimeographing the April issue of *The Voice*, one thousand copies this time—will run about twenty-five bucks, give or take a dollar. That's not counting postage. But it's not gonna be mailed out this April Fools'—it's gonna be *handed* out—person to person! Looking them straight in the eye! So, that leaves forty-five bucks. Perfect. Oscar needs twenty-three ninety-five, plus tax, for the architect's tapeless Measure-Master at Keuffel and Essner's. That leaves about twenty bucks, and we still have another collection day left before the first.

Louie put the collection money into a white business envelope, folded it in half, and put it in his inside coat pocket. Then he pushed the card table up against the wall, placed the empty cigar box on the lobby counter, and walked out of the Senior Citizens' Center, smiling a $31.25 smile.

# 11

# THE GETAWAY TRUCK

The Benefit was only a week away.

B-day minus seven, and there were still a multitude of things left to be done. The pickup truck. The final bank measurements. The detention system. Complete staff ID. Siege-support food supply. Gas masks. At least one more gun. More ammunition. And much more dynamite.

Sunday was the go/no-go deadline. If everything wasn't in first-class assault status by Sunday, Louie said they would have to postpone. They had come too far to risk a failure now. Or somebody getting hurt. Or killed.

"Try again!" The yell came from under the pickup truck, parked at the rear of the old gas station. Oscar turned the key in the ignition. *Grr-uh–grr–uh–grr-uh!* Some vital piece of the poor old truck engine was trying desperately to fulfill its function, but lacked the stamina or the connection to succeed.

"Okay, Oscar—stop!" Stosh shouted again from under the vehicle.

Oscar turned the key off and took his foot off the accelerator. A loud grunt. Then another. Then a harsh metallic tapping. Then, "Goddamn! Goddamn!"

"What happened?" Oscar called down to the two huge feet sticking out from under the truck.

"I bang finger!" Stosh complained. "Try to tighten damn gas line. Don't drive away!"

Oscar chuckled one chuck, then sat patiently at the wheel of the dead truck, waiting for the next command while the Polish grunts and curses continued to rumble under him. Looking out the open car window, his eye was caught by a long thin red line on the ground which seemed to be moving, pulsating along its entire length. Then he saw it was a column of ants, playing follow-the-leader in two endless lines, disappearing down through a cracked eruption in the oil-stained macadam topping. It was an ant hill, where no ant hill should be, established by the tiny insects right through the thick paving.

Oscar watched, fascinated, as the busy red ants hurried in steady streams to and from the tiny hole which marked their underground domain. Almost every ant heading for the hill was carrying a burden, held high overhead, that was many times its own size. In a sparser line, ants would emerge from the hill, moving quickly along, directly toward the oncoming traffic. The worker ants in the two opposing streams engaged in a peculiar social ritual. They would pause, but only for an instant, gently bump each other's noses, then pass by quickly, each to his urgent destination.

Oscar had never before observed this eccentric phenomenon. He was mesmerized. Were they greeting each other? Were they communicating?

"Hey, Oscar! Goddamn, you go to sleep? You don't hear me holler?"

Oscar snapped out of his musings. "Ya, Stosh! *Was ist?* You want me to try again?"

"No, goddamn, I want you to fly over ocean! Yes! Try again!"

Oscar dutifully turned the ignition key. *Grr-uh–grr-uh–grr-uh!* By now they had both learned the language of the battery and the starter motor and the flywheel. Once again, the machine's message was clearly grated out— *Grr-uh–grr-uh–grr-uh! Will-not–can-not–start-up!*

"Okay! Okay! Enough! Goddamn!"

Oscar turned off the key, shrugging, and turned his attention back to the ant hill.

"Goddamn . . . you stubborn piece of iron, you! Arr-gghh!"

Suddenly Oscar felt the truck start to move. He quickly reached down and pulled back hard on the emergency brake. The truck was still moving.

"You think you gonna beat Stanislaus Vlasic?" Stosh was roaring with rage, and all at once, Oscar realized that the truck was not moving forward, it was bouncing—bouncing to the rhythm of the mountainous anger of the giant Pole, who was pushing upward with all his furious strength on the truck's frame, over and over again, shouting out his frustration. "You are nothing! A box of stupid bolts! I am a man from Cracow, by God! Vlasic from Cracow!"

"Stosh! Stop, stop!" Oscar screamed, as his head hit the roof of the cab, "You're killing me! Sto-o-p! Please, Stosh!" The bouncing subsided and stopped. Both men exhaled in relief, as though they had just been involved in an accident in which no lives were lost.

Stosh slid out from under the pickup and rose stiffly to his feet. "I sorry I get mad und bounce you, Oscar. I no can help. Nothing makes me mad like machine—not even woman!"

Oscar looked at the sweating giant, and understood. "So? What are we going to do, Mister Mechanic?"

The big man leaned on the pickup, which bent to his weight. "Goddamn, I don't know . . ."

"We better tell Louie," Oscar said.

"Tell Louie what?"

60

"That we have no transportation to Citizens' Bank on Thursday," Oscar said. "He *must* be told."

"What he will do? Take pickup truck out of his pocket?"

"I don't know what he will do. I only know it is getting hotter und hotter out here, und I know I am getting sick und tired of turning this key to listen to this . . ."

The motor turned over and started the instant Oscar turned the key. Stosh stepped back from the pickup in wonder. Oscar finished his sentence with a new meaning: " . . . this noise! This beautiful noise!"

The two men beamed at each other as the pickup jiggled with its first movement in years. Stosh opened the pickup door. "Move over, Mister Watchmaker."

Oscar slid over. "Come right in, Mister Mechanic!"

Stosh got into the cab and put his hands proudly on the steering wheel, his chin pointing high, as though the putt-putting pile of junk were a new Lincoln Continental.

"You see, Oscar, sometimes when you get good and goddamn mad— something very good can happen!"

They both knew what he was talking about. Stosh revved the motor. *Vrr-rr-rrm–Vrr-rr-rrm–Vrr-rr-rrm!*

# 12

# *INSIDE-JOB*

Minnie's motor was running, too, as she waddled into Citizens' Bank, pushing her folded shopping basket ahead of her. The uniformed bank guard glanced at her as she passed through the front door, and Minnie gave him her nicest how-do-you-do nod. As she walked deliberately in a straight line, along the row of executive desks, toward the back of the bank, she seemed to be aimlessly scanning, left and right, perhaps looking for a directional sign. Nonsense. Purely a diversionary tactic.

Pushing her basket, she quietly sang her little tune to herself, committing the pertinent lyric to memory:

> The desks are sitting on the left,
> The tellers are sitting on the right . . .
> TV in the corner way up high,
> Vault in the back all locked up tight . . .

Minnie reached the far left corner of the large room and stood just to the side of the mortgage window, against the counter. Rectangular coordinate number one. She shot a quick glance over her shoulder to check the guard's position. He was at the front door. Good guard.

She turned her right palm over, on the handle of her shopping basket, revealing for only an instant, the round-faced meter attached to the handle. Oscar had done a beautiful job, replacing one of the basket's wheels with the calibrated wheel of the architect's tapeless measure, and snaking the cable through the hollow metal leg up to the meter under Minnie's hand.

Minnie pushed the restart button on the meter, snapping the needle back to zero, and headed for one of the big center tables, singing her ditty:

> Seven inches, eighty-two feet . . .
> One more side, and it'll be complete . . .

62

Reaching the table, she took her little red book out of her purse, and made her entries. Scanning down the line of tellers' windows, she sang as she wrote:

One-two-three-four-five-six-seven . . .
Windows in the money heaven.
Seven inches, eighty-two feet . . .
April first will be so sweet—

"Can I help you ma'am?"

Minnie almost dropped her purse.

It was Brubaker, the bank guard, who had sneaked up behind her and was now smiling his official silly smile at her.

"What? . . . Oh, no!" She snapped her notebook shut. "I don't think you could help me. Thank you kindly, anyways."

"You're welcome," he said, as he stood there with his hands clasped behind him, rotating his head around the bank.

Minnie clearly did not appreciate his guardian presence. She had a difficult task to accomplish, and he wasn't making it any easier. She would have to chase him.

"You make me feel very protected, Mr. Bank Guard, you know what I mean?" she said. "With your uniform, and your gun, I feel really safe, you know?"

"Oh, really? Well, I'm here mostly just to help the customers," Brubaker said, "for their convenience."

"I see, thank you," Minnie said. He didn't move. Minnie leaned close to him. "You do your job good. You are a very convenient bank guard."

"Thank you, ma'am. You have your account with us?"

"Me, an account?" Minnie laughed. "No. But my uncle, he has an account. *He* keeps his money here."

"Your uncle?"

"Of course, my Uncle Sam!" Minnie took her Social Security check from her purse and waved it at him. "And I give your bank all my business. Like clockwork, every month, I cash my Social Security right here."

Brubaker nodded blankly.

"You see, I cash near the end of the month," Minnie went on. "I manage to stay a month ahead, for the funeral."

"The funeral?" Brubaker asked, eerily. "What funeral?"

"*My* funeral, of course!" Minnie said, brightly. "You think I'm gonna let the Social Security buy me a pine box? Not on your life!"

Now she had him. He was shifting uncomfortably, from flat foot to flat foot.

"I see," he said. "Well, if you, uh, need any help . . ." His offer trailed off as he backed away.

"Oh, yes, I'll let you know," Minnie said, "but I know my way around this bank pretty good, thank you very much."

"You're very welcome," said Brubaker, now in full retreat.

"It was very nice socializing with you!" said Minnie as she watched him driven all the way to the front door.

Positive that he would show no further interest in her unless she pulled a machine gun out of her purse, Minnie calmly returned to rectangular coordinate number one. Methodically, she pressed the restart button and pushed her measuring basket across the width of the bank to the tellers' counter. Coordinate number two. Checking the meter for this measurement, she made the entry in her notebook. She looked again at the meter, smiling in admiration. "Oscar, you are more than a fine watchmaker," she informed the meter. "You are a genius. A regular genius!"

Minnie closed her book and wheeled down the red velvet-roped aisle to window number seven. At the moment, the buxom blonde teller was occupied with a ritual adjustment. Two fingers slipped quickly under the bra. A little tug on the left one, pulling toward the center. Now the right. Now a short poof of cool breath blown down the cleavage. That's better. Will they ever invent a proper lift-and-squeeze bra for a poor girl with a 40D bust?

The teller with the tits looked up and noticed Minnie waiting. "Good morning," she said, motioning. "How are you this morning?"

"How am I?" Minnie shrugged, putting her check on the counter. "How should I be? I'm an old lady, I have aches and pains. But today, I'm better."

"That's good," said Big Tits, as though she cared. "Sign here."

"Yesterday," Minnie said as she endorsed her check, "my arthritis hurt me so much, every joint. My hands, my legs, my back. But today the sun came out, and my check came in, and the pain went away."

"Have you seen a doctor about it?"

"What doctor? They get enough Medicare stamps to cash in without Minnie Gold, believe me! I cure myself!"

"Really?" asked the teller. "How?"

"How?" Minnie echoed. "How else? With anger! An old person's body only has room for one or the other—pain or anger. You get angry enough, the pain goes away. You feel sorry for yourself, it hurts you everyplace in your body!"

"I'll have to remember that," the young woman said, counting out the cash.

Minnie smiled as she picked up her money. "Believe me, young lady, you *wouldn't* remember. There are things in life that we each have to learn for ourselves. Sometimes even when it's too late, already."

The teller smiled vacantly. "Okay, have a nice day, now."

"So far, knock wood, it's a very nice day," Minnie ventured, putting her cash into her purse, next to the little red notebook. "I'll see you next month, Miss, uh . . ." she read the small nameplate, "Miss St. Clair."

Minnie rolled her shopping basket happily toward the front door. "Angela St. Clair," she said to herself. "The bazooms don't fit the brassiere, and the name don't fit the bazooms!"

Minnie smiled her farewell to the bank guard, then sailed out of the bank feeling like a kid with a straight-A report card. She checked the time as she waited on the corner for the DON'T WALK light to change, so she could cross Fairfax Avenue. Almost time for the "pass" in front of Dave's Deli. And Louie was never late.

As she reached the opposite curb, she looked up the block. "How do you like that?" she said aloud, "he's already there! Walking back and forth, like he's waiting in the delivery room for his first baby boy. Your Mata Hari is on her way, Levine. Don't get your bowels in an uproar!"

Nobody heard her, of course. In this neighborhood, people are too busy listening to themselves.

Louie saw Minnie. Minnie saw Louie seeing Minnie. He stopped his pacing and stiffly took up his position to the right of the deli entrance, his newspaper folded under his arm. No telltale sign of recognition passed between them as Minnie wheeled past Louie and pulled open the glass door to the deli.

Suddenly a woman even fatter than Minnie tried to push her way out onto the sidewalk. The deli entrance was simply never designed to handle this kind of dual jumbo action. *Squoosh-oooF-splat!* The massive collision immediately dislodged the full bag of groceries flying from the fat lady's arms, sending a big glass jar of gefilte fish smashing to the sidewalk. Minnie's shopping basket overturned and her purse slid off her arm, spilling its contents right out on the sidewalk at Louie's feet.

The two women scrambled to retrieve their bouncing belongings. Louie quickly stooped to help Minnie pick up the mountain of junk that had burst out of her purse, deftly tucking her little red notebook into his folded newspaper and under his arm.

A skinny old man with a quick cane made a fancy hockey move and saved one of the rolling fishballs from falling off the curb. Smiling victoriously, he fetched the fishball back to the fat lady, who raised her hands in horror, screwed up her face and hollered "Feh!" as loud as she could at the man. The poor little good Samaritan quickly retreated to the curb, dropping the fish ball into its guttery grave.

"I'm sorry I bunked into you," the fatter lady said.

"Oh, no, no," Minnie apologized, snapping her purse shut. "It was all my fault! Out is *first*. In should wait until out gets out, and *then* in can go in! I wouldn't let you take the blame!"

"What's the difference whose fault?" said the fat lady, "as long as nobody fell down and broke anything—a kneecap, an ankle. After all, gefilte fish is only gefilte fish." There was no arguing the wisdom of this pronouncement.

"You're absolutely one hundred percent right!" Minnie agreed, and went into the deli.

The absolutely right fat lady made a careful detour around the broken jar of gefilte fish and hurried away as though it had been someone else's messy accident.

By this time, Louie was more than a block away, strolling along, his folded paper under his arm. They hadn't planned it quite that way, but Alfred Hitchcock could not have devised a more perfect covert public pass of the top secret fruits of Minnie's undercover assignment.

# 13

# CHECK AND DOUBLE-CHECK

Louie sat hunched over his little table, Minnie's red notebook in his hand, the quarter-inch-scale floor plan of Citizens' Bank spread open before him in the early morning light. Matching. Comparing. Double-checking. Measuring.

The sun bounced a prismatic finger of blue and yellow light through the angel's robe and across the large drawing. Louie looked up.

"Well, well! Good morning, little girl! I thought you was gonna sleep the whole day away. Even eternity has a limit, you know. You waste one minute, you never get it back. You gotta stay ready for the come-and-get-it day—and that big day is coming soon, for both of us."

He turned a page of Minnie's book, checking a number. Then, using his large metal rule, he carefully verified the most important measurement on the floor plan.

"From the safety deposit box counter to the gate of the vault, seventy-eight feet. Another ten feet, each end, for the slack—ninety-eight. So-oo, we need a hundred feet number twelve duplex. And we got—"

He referred to Oscar's list of acquired supplies, running his finger slowly down the page.

". . . Wire, wire. Yes, here . . . a hundred and twenty-five feet. Plenty. Beautiful." He made a red-pencil X next to the word "wire" on his countdown sheet. Now for the master list.

"Pay attention, sleepy head, this is the final checkup. First, the schedules." He ticked off the alphabetical items. "The armored truck—check. The buses—check. Employee arrivals—check. The gardeners—check. Janitor crew—check. The metermaid—check. Neighborhood squad car—check. Traffic signals—check. Nothing missing. Perfect! The schedules are a hundred percent. Gorgeous! Next, the telephone list. . . ." He referred to a little black looseleaf. "The newspapers—yes. The LAPD—yes. I got your number, Chief Davis, your private number! The radio stations—yes. The Social Security office—oh, yes. And, last but not least, the TV news—all three networks, and four local channels. What a communications directory! This time, little girl, the voice of the aged will be heard loud and clear!"

A passing cloud blotted out the sunlight, darkening Louie's little room for a moment. Again he looked up to his angel. "Don't go away, sweetheart, I'm just getting to the best part. My special job. The PRO. The Planning, the Research, and the Organization. Without the PRO, the whole Benefit will be a flop!"

Louie carefully arranged five stacks of papers across the table, like a fan. He placed his master planning list in the center, lined up his colored pencils in a row beside it, and rubbed his palms together in anticipation.

"Now. Now we shall see if the Liberation Army of Louie Levine is ready for the invasion! A for Air-conditioning equipment location . . . Oh, yes, in Minnie's bible . . . aha! Wall panel between the rest rooms. Right here."

He drew in the appropriate red box on the floor plan. "Pure gold. You hear? That Minnie is pure Gold!" No laughter from the angel. "You don't like that one, hah? I never told you I was funny. Only smart!"

He continued down his master list, cross-verifying each item with the status reports from the members of his team. "B for binoculars—got 'em. C for cable—Vito's got the cable. And the handcuffs. Chain and rope. Stosh—got 'em. Cocktail mix for Mr. Molotov? Oscar—yes. Conference room—about eighteen feet by 'I don't know,' she says. *Hmph!* East to west, far left corner of the bank . . . here."

He marked a blue rectangle on the floor plan. "Twelve-foot fancy conference table . . . fourteen comfy chairs, she says! Perfect for the party! No letter D. E for Employees ID. ID? Minnie's got the whole family, leave it to her! Explosives—Oscar's got the gunpowder, and the caps. One grenade. No blaster. Dammit, still no blaster!"

Angrily, he scrawled a battle memo across his master list, biting off the words as he wrote. "'Oscar. Still no blaster? Is this any way to run a benefit? Make it, steal it—but *get* it!' . . . F for first aid kit—got it. God forbid we should have to use it. Food—got the order in at *Dave's Deli.* G for guns. Yes, my dear, the terrible guns. Guns . . . four guns, seventy-five rounds. We gotta have at least one more, Oscar. One more. H . . . I . . . J . . . K . . . Keys. Vito's machine—simple, no charge. L . . . M . . . N . . . O . . . Operation Benefit, four-phase rehearsal, Wednesday in the park—if we are really ready. Portable radio—ah, we got it. Attaboy, Abe. Q . . . R . . . S for shaving cream—right now!"

Louie got up, went to his medicine chest above the sink, and took out a push-button can of shaving cream. He brought it back to the table and set it on top of the floor plan.

"No use taking chances—I'll shave with soap till Thursday. The sign. Sign, sign, sign . . . no sign. That's very important, the danger sign. We'll have to make it ourselves. Abe. That's a good job for Abe. T for tools. Stosh.

That's a good one! He says, with the tools he's got he could take down the Brooklyn Bridge! Transportation—got it. He's a Polish prince, that Stosh. U for uniforms—we got two, and Lefty Brubaker will loan us the other one. V . . . W for wigs—we got the stupid wigs.

"Well, that's it, my darling. We don't need anything that begins with X-Y-Z, so that, as they say, is the whole enchilada! Two or three things are missing yet, but I *think* we are ready. As ready as six old cockers will ever be to change the world a little. And maybe—with a little luck, and the help of your boss, maybe—the world will not be ready for *us* on April Fools' Day! Listen, sweetheart, I'm not kidding—this is at least a two-God job! So you'll put in a good word, right? Today is Sunday, but it doesn't have to be today. Just any time before Thursday. And don't talk with any in-betweens. I'm giving you plenty of time to get through personally to your big boss."

Louie carefully secured his briefing materials, taping his little paper match under the table for the last time. He pocketed the list of incomplete items, opened the door, then turned back and pointed his finger up at his little stained-glass friend.

"You thought I would leave you out, hah? Not on your life! You are my guardian angel, for God's sakes, and now—you have your assignment for The Benefit, too. Don't let me down, sweetheart."

He locked his door quietly and hit the street, walking briskly toward the Center, his head held high, like a young man of fifty.

# 14

# VITO'S PLACE

Hardly anybody knew that Vito lived there, because it was against the law to live in a garage with no kitchen or toilet facilities. But that's also why the rent was so cheap—only seventy a month, no utilities. A hot plate was all the kitchen he needed, for strong morning coffee. And the back door of the house, where he had bathroom privileges, was only a few feet away, well within the range of Vito's bladder. Only rainy mornings caused problems, when the tickle to pee started even before he awoke. On such mornings, he didn't even bother to take advantage of his privilege. A good-sized open knothole in the big front door of the garage and a well-drained driveway took care of this little necessity of life.

Vito was very happy living in this place, really. He had it fixed up pretty nice—even a kitchen curtain at the window.

The converted garage still had the big wooden workbench along one side, with power tool receptacles above it and a strong steel vise bolted through one end. Vito's antique Yale-Towne handcrank key-cutter stood proudly as the centerpiece of the work bench, its polished brass fittings shining brightly. The little precision machine had been handmade by a fine Yale craftsman in Stamford, Connecticut in 1923, and Vito had carried it with him wherever he lived for over fifty years. It was his most prized and least common possession.

Most of the people at the Center knew that Vito was an underground locksmith, and though he still only charged fifty cents a key, he managed to make a few illicit dollars every month to augment his Social Security dole and to support the only active vice he had left. Cigars. One key—one cigar.

Everybody loved Vito. Everybody hated his cigars—and told him so . . . often. But cigar smokers have thick hides, and the more the complainers complained, it seemed, the more Vito enjoyed his cheap cigar. Bigotry breeds righteous revolt. Nobody could win an argument with Vito about his cigar . . . Nobody. "A rose is a rose is a rose," he used to say, sarcastically.

"That crazy woman don't know what she's talkin' about—but a cigar is a cigar is a CIGAR! Capish?"

Nobody knew what Vito was talking about when he said that, so they didn't even try to debate the point with him. But every once in a while, at the pinochle table, Louie would get so full of cigar smoke from Vito's exhaust that he'd get annoyed enough to respond to the statement. "Listen to this! The Pope has spoken!" he would say. And Vito would puff, and smile, and blow his smoke up out of the corner of his pursed lips in a long, tapering gray jet of contented defiance. Then he would look at each player, one by one, very slowly, around the table. And then he would puff, and smile—and blow again. Capish?

Monday night. B-day minus two, and Vito was soaking wet with sweat, his cigar stub clenched between his teeth so hard he could hardly curse. "Sombitch!" he grunted. "Marron!" But the swearing didn't help at all. The big crimping pliers kept slipping off the metal collars, and the three-eighths-inch steel cable kept springing open, slithering from around the little work table and blinga-dinging onto the floor.

Vito stood holding the big crimping tool, breathing hard through his clenched teeth and around his cigar butt as he stared balefully at his enemies. The length of cable on the floor, the wooden table, and the last collar he had tried—which had ricocheted into the corner of the garage.

"What's going on here, anyways?" he asked them. "I guess you don't know who you foolin' around with. You gonna do like Vito wants you to do, sooner or later. Ma! So why not sooner?"

He bent over and picked up the cable for another try. Then, he noticed something about the tabletop. It had developed two rough grooves, filed into the opposite edges by the raspy cable, where he had tried again and again to cinch and attach the stubborn steel snake around the table.

All at once, Vito smacked his forehead hard with the butt of his palm. "Tony! No pushada-trunk, dummy! Use your dumb head—not you fat ass. Stupido! So simple!"

He went to the tool rack above his work bench, brought back a small crosscut saw, and started sawing at the two worn grooves in the tabletop. "Okay, you guys . . . you wanna coupla notches? No big deal, you gotta coupla notches!"

He wrapped the cable around the table once more, fitting it down into the two freshly cut opposing notches. "There you are, you big beautiful fettucini. Here's a nice new collar for your pretty neck. . . . Then, Vito slides you tail through. . . . Hold still, I gotcha! Gotta pull you nice and snug. Now . . . one good hard squeeze, and you gonna be together forever! You hear me? Forever!"

Vito squeezed the two steel handles of the crimping tool together with all his stocky might. Pressing, grunting, pressing. At last, he released the tension on the big tool and stood back to admire his handiwork. He tested the joint by lifting the taut cable, raising the table right off the floor. No slippage. The cable was as securely crimped together as if it had been done at the factory. No man could pull this joint apart, and when two or three more steel collars were cinched on, twenty men couldn't do it. Only a pair of giant wire cutters.

Vito started to sing. Not real words, just syllables. To a finiculee-finiculah kind of melody with a happy upbeat.

*"Bee-yah-pah-pah-pah-babababa-peeyah-yah! Babababa-babom-bah!"*

He was the piccolo and the trombone, the French horn and the tuba, the tiny triangle and the big bass drum. He almost skipped around the garage as he sang and set about the vital test procedures for his newly invented Morelli Detention System.

Kneeling at the foot of his bed, he unlocked a metal foot locker. He dug through the junk to the bottom, finally unearthing a pair of handcuffs and a small new padlock. Seated at the table, he slipped the padlock through the center chain link of the handcuffs and around the steel cable, snapping the lock shut. Carefully, he put the padlock key and the tiny key for the cuffs on the table. Now, one by one he slipped his wrists into the handcuffs and clicked them shut, squeezing them closed to his wrist size.

"Gotcha, Capone" he whispered. "You goin' to Alcatraz!" Vito exerted pressure on the cuffs, pulling them apart as hard as he could. They didn't budge. Then he pulled back, testing the stretch of the cable slack. It held fast in the deep notches, no matter how hard he tried to dislodge it.

Then, he got up, and sliding the cuffs down to one end—where the cable went over the edge and under the table—he jerked both his arms down hard, whacking the padlock into the notch. The lock suddenly blumped through the notch with the power of his jerk, sending the two little keys hopping off the table and *plang-tanging* onto the floor in separate directions. The cable snapped back into the deep V of the notch, and Vito found himself on his knees under the table. He sat down on the floor, spitting his dead cigar butt across the garage in disgust. "That's using your ass, dummy," he grunted.

After a momentary survey of his awkward situation, he started to pull the table along, inching himself toward one of the keys on the floor, which had landed near the door. Just as he reached the key, there was a knock at the door. *Bop-bop-bop!*

Right above his head. Eleven o'clock at night, a knock at his door. Who could it be? His landlord? An inspector from the zoning commission? A thief in the night?

He sat rigid, hardly breathing. If he stayed silent, maybe whoever it was would go away.

Another knock, louder. *BOP-BOP-BOP-BOP!* Mother of Jesus! A noise

72

like that could wake the people in the house. Or the next door neighbor's goddamn dog, and *he'd* wake everybody in the county.

"Who's there?" Vito whispered hoarsely.

"It's us!" Abe whispered back. "Minnie and Abe!"

"You'll have to wait a minute. I'm tied up."

"You're what?" Minnie asked.

With some difficulty, Vito tilted the small table so that it stood on edge on his lap, allowing his hands to reach the floor. But the tabletop now shielded his view completely from where he had spotted the key. He tried desperately to stretch his neck around the edge of the table to see the fallen key. Impossible. The cable was too snug.

*BOP-BOP-BOP-BOP-BOP-BOP!*

"Come on, open up!" Abe said. "It's freezing out here!"

"Quiet! It'll take me a minute—I'm on the floor!" Vito grunted as he struggled with the table, trying to move forward, toward where he had seen the little key.

"Whatta you got, a woman in there?"

"Very funny!" said Vito, who had finally worked himself far enough so that the key was right at his crotch. Straining against the cable, he managed to pick it up, sweating as if he were in a steam bath.

He let the table thump forward onto its legs and then its other edge, as he struggled to his feet.

"What's going on in there for goodness' sakes?" Minnie asked.

"You'll see, you'll see in a minute! Wait, I'm coming, but don't touch the door whatever you do!"

Pulling the table over as close to the door as cuffs and cable would allow, Vito bent over, stretched his neck for all he was worth, and took hold of the inside door latch gingerly, with his dentures. Rotating his head clockwise, he carefully turned the little oval knob until the lock clicked to the open position. He straightened up with a little groan of relief, then whispered through the door. "Abe?"

"No, *not* Abe—it's Jack Frost! Open up, for God's sakes!"

"Now, wait a minute, Abe! You gotta listen, and do like I say. . . . Are you listening?"

"I got a choice?"

"Now, when I say 'Okay'—you open the door very careful, come in, and close the door quick behind you. But you *gotta* wait till I say 'Okay.' . . . Okay?"

A pause from the other side of the door. Then, "Vito . . . this is a silly game, eleven o'clock at night, Vito."

"It's no game, Abe, I swear! Please! Wait till I say 'Okay'!"

Dragging the table again, Vito positioned himself to the left of the door. Then, contorting his whole body, he craned his neck sideways, straining,

73

reaching for the light switch with his nose. His eyes slowly crossed, and his nose came closer and closer to the toggle.

Contact. One quick, deliberate nod downward, a click, and the room was blacked out with the speed of light.

"Vito!" said Minnie. "The lights went out!"

"I know, I know!" said Vito, wiggling his nose. "Just a second, now!" In the pitch darkness he backed up, cautiously dragging the table back from the door.

It was written in the stars.

"Jesus Christ!—*Arghh!*" There was a simultaneous crash as Vito fell backward over a chair, collapsing in a bruised heap under the *galump-umping* table, the familiar sound of the caromming key *ring-a-ting-tinging* in his ears.

"Vito, Vito, you all right?" asked Minnie.

Vito just sat there for a moment, his chin pressed heavily down against his chest, held there by the weight of the table on his head.

"I'm okay," he muttered. "Okay."

Nothing happened.

"Abe . . . I said 'Okay.'"

The door opened slowly, creaking on its hinges, and the two shadowy figures entered the room. Vito could hear the squeaky little wheels of Minnie's shopping basket come to a halt. The three silhouettes were cast in silent concrete.

"Abe."

"Yeah, Vito?"

"You can close the door now, Abe."

"Oh, yeah!" Abe shut the door. "Now what do I do?"

"Now, you put on the light. The switch is on the left."

Abe fumbled around, feeling the wall until his fingers found the toggle switch. He flipped the light on. Minnie and Abe looked around the room, baffled. No Vito.

"I'm down here."

Minnie bent over in the direction of the pitiful whimper. Abe kneeled. There Vito sat, flat on his ass, under the table, held prisoner by his own ingenuity, an expertly joined steel cable, and a sturdy pair of dime-store handcuffs.

Minnie and Abe stared at Vito. Vito stared back at Minnie and Abe.

"I dare yez to say something funny," said the man under the table.

Minnie and Abe slowly circled the hapless little Italian, examining him in wonder, as if they had just paid their quarter to get a close look at the Wild Man from Borneo.

"What are you, Houdini?" Abe asked finally.

"No, no!" said Minnie. "Can't you see? The Prisoner of Zenda!"

"My dear Mr. and Mrs. Whoever-you-are," Vito said, firmly in control despite his ridiculous position, "you are both wonderful artistes. You

74

understand music and lit-ature, maybe. But you don't have no appreciation for mechanical genius!"

"Izzat so?" Minnie asked.

"*Ma,* sure! You're the first people in the world to get a look at Vito Morelli's patented hostage control system!"

"You don't say!" said Abe, impressed.

"Didn'cha just hear me say?"

"It's very, very nice," said Minnie, feigning a yawn. "Let's go, Abe, I think Leonardo DaVinci wants to be alone with his invention."

"I think you're right," Abe agreed, and they both made a quick move toward the door.

"Don't you dare!" Vito almost shouted. "You can't leave me here like this! Please, Minnie . . . Abe!"

Minnie and Abe turned back, looking down at Vito, who looked up with the pleading eyes of a basset hound.

"What do you think, Abe?" Minnie asked. "Have we got a coupla minutes?"

Abe checked his watch.

"Please, Abe . . ." Vito said.

Abe always was a lousy straight man. He broke up and they started to laugh. First it was him and Minnie, only giggling at first. Then Vito, laughing at himself in his stupid predicament. Their laughter grew louder, until they were all convulsed, holding their sides and coughing from the strain of their hilarity.

"*Shhhh!* We gonna break my lease!" Vito whispered hoarsely.

"Vito, if you only coulda seen your face." Abe snorted, trying to catch his breath.

"Oh, Oh, Oh!" Minnie gasped, fighting to recover.

"You really got me good" Vito said. "Now get me outa this thing."

"Yeah, how?" Abe asked, and they were all laughing again.

Vito directed Abe to the keys. Soon the cuffs were off and the mechanical genius was on his feet, mopping the sweat off his face and neck with a towel.

Abe studied Vito's invention with true appreciation. "Hey, Vito, this is a real winner!"

"You telling me?" Vito asked, rubbing his wrists.

"Do they hurt on the wrists?" asked Minnie.

"Naw, they're adjustable." Vito demonstrated the cuffs. "Big wrist, little wrist."

"Where did you get these?" asked Abe.

"Woolworth's. Two-fifty, in the toy department. Genu-wine Kojaks. I got a dozen and a half."

"They sell these to *children* in the five-and-dime store?" Minnie asked. "Little children?"

"You be surprised what they sell to kids these days" Vito said. "I hadda go to a coupla different stores, four-five different times, so nobody'd get wise."

"Are they strong enough?" Abe asked.

Vito gave him a funny look. "Whatta ya think I was doin' on the floor, kiddin' around?"

"Lemme see," Abe said, picking up the open cuffs. He tested them, pulling them apart, hard. "I just can't believe it. These are *toys?*"

"That's right," Vito said.

"They are terrible toys," said Abe, shaking his head. "What if the wrong kids gotta hold of these?"

Vito and Minnie looked at Abe incredulously.

"What if the wrong *kids* . . .?" Minnie asked pointedly.

"Okay, okay," said Abe, getting it, "but I still don't stand corrected."

"All right, already," said Minnie. "Enough with your five-and-ten toys, Vito. We got a surprise, too!"

Out of her shopping basket, Minnie lifted a large paper bag containing an object of some bulk, which she set carefully on the table. "Wait'll you see *this* fancy piece of machinery, Vito! But first, is the door locked?"

Vito checked the door. *Click.* "Now it's locked."

With great ceremony, her fingers dancing stylishly in midair, Minnie peeled back the tape strips that held the big bag closed. Then she reached down into the bag. "*Ta-dah!* Just feast your eyes on *this* work of art, Morelli!"

As though it were a rabbit out of a hat, she pulled out an old-fashioned maplewood blasting box, perfectly intact, plunger and all, and set it on the table in all its rich-grained glory.

"*Mamma mia!*" Vito threw the Italian kiss, both hands exploding from his mouth. "*Mmm-Mmm!* Where didja find this?"

"Would you believe," said Abe, "a crappy garage sale on Third Street."

"No kidding!"

"Vito, you shoulda been there!" Abe said. "Minnie spots this thing on one of the tables, way at the back of the driveway. I didn't even know what it was, so—"

"—So Abe," Minnie said, "Abe is trying to pull me *away* from it all the time. He didn't even know how much he was helping me out!"

"Leave it to Minnie!" Abe continued. "She says to the man, 'And what is the asking price on this scratched up antique lamp base, my good man?' And the guy says, 'This ain't no lamp base, lady. This is an old blasting box, like they used to use for blowing up the dynamite for making highways and such.'"

"Can you imagine?" Minnie said. "He tells me exactly what I only think I know!"

76

Vito was trying his best to follow the narrative, swiveling his head back and forth as if he were watching ping-pong.

"So Minnie says, 'Highways and such? I'm sorry but to me, it's an obvious out-of-style lamp base in need of repair. How much you asking?'"

"So wait'll you hear this!" Minnie took over again. "So the man says, 'It's marked twenty-five dollars on the bottom.' 'Twenty-five dollars?' I say, 'But this was when you were selling it to builders, to build highways, and such. I'm just an individual homemaker. I gotta spend money for a lamp shade, and wiring, and a plug, and—'"

"So, to make a long story short," Abe said, "the guy hollers uncle, and throws up his hands just to get her to shut up, and he lets her have it for seven-fifty!"

"Seven-fifty!" Vito lifted the box carefully and carried it to his work bench. "You stole the man blind!" He turned on the work light above his bench, revolving the box three hundred and sixty degrees. "'Atlas Blasting Co. 1936,'" he read off the handsome brass plate, "'12 volt, D.C. Pat. Pending.' What a beauty! All brass fittings. . . . This must be worth over a hundred dollars, at least!"

"Yeah?" said Minnie, "maybe I oughta make a lamp!"

"You crazy?" Vito said, unscrewing the back cover of the box. "This was the only thing missing. Louie was beginning to think we'd have to pull it off without the bomb. Wait'll he sees!"

Vito had the back off the box and was looking at the inside under the light. "Look at this—it's hardly even dusty inside! A little rust, only. All I gotta do is file the points, Oscar gets the battery, and The Benefit will be some blow-out!"

Abe moved to the bench to fondle the box affectionately. "You gotta hand it to Levine," he said. "This time, the voice of the aged could really be heard around the world!"

He took hold of the plunger handle with both hands, carefully, almost in slow motion.

"Are you listening, world?" he asked quietly.

Then, with an eerie look on his face, Abe suddenly plunged the blaster handle smack down to the hilt, and in a drawn-out, chilling whisper that seemed to echo, he said, *"BOO-OOM!!"*

# 15

# THE GIFT

Vito sang his way down the block from the bus stop. His step was springy, and his spirits were high as a kite. His homework was a hundred percent—and with two days still to go! He could hardly wait to make his report.

But just as he approached the Center, Vito was brought up short by a large flock of pecking pigeons on the sidewalk. He stopped and leaned against the building. He knew at once that he would just have to wait. Nobody walked through her birds until her paper bag was empty. Nobody.

There she was, Old Lady Kahn, right out in front of the Senior Citizens' Center, throwing little pieces of stale bread onto the sidewalk to her pigeons—fifty or sixty of them, pecking at the crumbs and each other, and flapping, and *coo-coo*ing, and shitting, and completely blocking off the steps to the Center.

Cantor had told her a thousand times, goddamn it, not to do that anymore. He even threatened to have her membership revoked. Who the hell did she think had to sweep the pigeon shit off the sidewalk after it dried? He, Cantor, of course—and it never dried, goddamn it.

Old Lady Kahn was almost totally deaf, and cataracts covered both her eyes almost completely. Despite these minor infirmities, she probably saw Cantor, and probably even heard him. But she was not about to take orders from a kid like Cantor, for goodness' sakes. He was only sixty-eight. Old Lady Kahn was—well, nobody knew exactly how old she was. Some people said she was in her nineties. But Gustav Dichter, before he died last year at ninety-six, told somebody that he had known her late husband in the old country, and he swore that she was way over a hundred—and Gus never told a lie in his life. "Life is too short to even learn the whole *truth*, for God's sake!" he used to say. "So why fool around trying to keep track of a lotta lousy lies!"

Funny thing, by the way, about *how* Gus died. Cantor opened up the Center one Monday morning and found Gus, dressed in his best pressed suit, freshly shaved, and completely dead, just sitting on a folding chair in

78

the big room, looking up at the stage with a blissful smile on his face.

Cantor was probably right, the way he finally figured it out. Sunday, the night before, Joe Glass had put on a pretty good show for the folks. They had a mandolin orchestra from Boyle Heights that played some great Slavic music, and the woman who sang with them must have sung songs in a dozen languages, reaching everybody in the house in their own native tongues by the time the night was over. Then, to top the evening off, Leo Fuchs did about forty-five minutes worth of his ancient ethnic stories, half-and-half English and Yiddish. Cantor remembered clearly seeing Gus laughing his head off at every punch line. Leo Fuchs is no Myron Cohen, but he sure hit Gus Dichter's funny bone that night.

When the show was over, everybody had coffee and cake, or tea and cake, and finally everybody went home. Everybody but Gus. Nobody noticed Gus, still sitting in his chair, still looking up at the stage as if Fuchs was still standing at the microphone. Old Gus Dichter died laughing at Leo Fuchs, and nobody noticed, that's all. The undertaker couldn't have asked for a sweeter open-casket smile.

"Dirty Harry" Haldeman spread the story that he saw Tillie Fields going down on old Gus during the show when the lights were off—and *that's* why he was still smiling when Cantor found his body. Everybody knew that was a lie. Number one, that would never have killed old Gus. Number two, he wouldn't have been looking up at the stage, no matter how funny Leo Fuchs was.

But then, nothing is sacred to "Dirty Harry"—not even his own death. He's actually got it in his will that when he dies, he wants to be cremated and he wants his ashes to be flushed down the ladies' room toilet at the Center. Honest to God. Harry say he believes in a certain kind of life after death, and that way he can enjoy looking up at his favorite sight for an eternity to come.

Vito was still standing there, leaning against the building with several other people, waiting for Old Lady Kahn to finish feeding breakfast to her pigeons so he could go inside to meet Louie and the others.

Just then, a big mangy-looking dog loped around the corner, licking his chops at the prospect of grabbing off a pigeon or two. Old Lady Kahn moved toward him like a lion-tamer, poking her three-legged aluminum walking stick at him. "Don't you dare disturb my birdies, you dirty dog, you!" she croaked. "Shoo! Go find a cat to chase! You hear me? Get out of here—I'm warning you!"

When old ladies talk to animals, they somehow understand, and it didn't take the dirty old dog long to figure out that the tirade and the cane were meant to do him no good if he hung around. He beat a hasty tail-down retreat, back the way he came.

Cantor, who had a moment earlier come out of the front door, all worked up to do battle once again, suddenly thought better of it, put his tail down like the dog, and went back inside.

At last the bag was empty. The pigeons squabbled over the last few crumbs and were aloft as quickly as they had all gathered at the rattle of the old lady's paper bag. She watched the last pigeon take off, flying up to join his buddy on a telephone wire across the street, and then she turned toward the steps of the Center.

That was the signal. Everybody could go in now.

Struck by some unusual feeling of gallantry, Vito walked over as the old lady took her first step up the stairs, taking hold of her elbow to help her up. The instant she felt his hand, she jerked her arm away.

"What are you doing?" she demanded. "Get away from me! What do you think, I'm decrepit?"

"But, Mrs. Kahn, I was—"

"I don't need your help up the steps!" she screamed. "Who asked you? All I need is leave me alone! Why can't people leave people alone? Take a hike for yourself!"

Old Lady Kahn was nearly deaf and nearly blind and nearly crippled, but if there was something she was *not* nearly—it was mute. Everybody knew she could burn the hair right out of your ears when she really got worked up. She had even been known to hit people with that cane of hers if they didn't get out of her way fast enough when she was under full sail.

Vito vaulted up the steps two at a time, escaping into the safety of the Center, the old witch's ungrateful invective still twisting in his ears. The legs are the first to go, he mused—but the tongue is the last.

As he hurried through the lobby, he heard someone yelling his name.

"Hey, Morelli!" It was Cantor. "I got a package for you here."

Vito U-turned back to the counter. "A package? Not for me!"

Cantor read the address on the package in his hand. "You *Signore* Vito Morelli or ain't you?"

"*Signore*—? What are you talking about, Cantor? Nobody calls me 'Signore,' and nobody sends me packages!"

"Not till today, *Signore*." Cantor winked, holding the parcel out. "And I just love the pink ink!"

"Must be a mistake," Vito said. "Return it to the sender."

"No can do, *Signore*. No return address."

"No ret—? Lemme see that." Vito took the package and looked at it curiously. He turned it over. Then over again. It was addressed to him, all right—no return address—a dollar-thirty in stamps—wrapped and taped very neatly—Beverly Hills postmark. He shook it, listening. No clue. Who the hell would be sending him a package at the Center? And what was inside?

Goddamn it, only one way to find out. He walked back to the men's room and went inside. All clear. He walked over to the last sink, pulled out a paper towel and dried the edge of the sink. Then, using it as a work table, he proceeded to open the package.

With his pocket knife, Vito meticulously performed surgery on the parcel, slitting through the tape only, so as not to cut or tear any of the brown wrapping paper. When all the tape had been cut, he carefully unfolded the brown paper.

Who the hell was Dunhill? The second wrapping was a fancy slick black paper, with Dunhill printed all over it, in gold. Oh, yeah, probably the store it came from. But what the hell do they sell at Dunhill, and who the hell would be sending him anything they sell at Dunhill? Vito performed the same delicate operation on the fancy paper and flipped it off the box.

Jee-zus Christ! Cigars. Not just any cigars, but a double box of fifty Monte Cristo Especiale Deluxe cigars! Holy Mother of God! Vito hadn't even seen a Monte Cristo cigar since Castro grew a beard and back-packed into the hills with his little brother! This box had to cost somebody a fortune! But *who*, somebody?

Vito levered his knife under each of the two little brads that held the top of the box closed. The small nails came out of the soft balsa wood easily. He opened the box.

There it was—the Dunhill gift card. Vito read the handwritten pink message: "Happy Birthday, *Signore* Morelli! I know that some people I know object to your smoking cigars while you are in their presence. However, for your information, I happen to *love* watching you! You smoke them with such elegant style! (over) . . ."

Vito turned the card over. More writing. ". . . Just like a regular Italian count, or something! Besides, you know what they say about a man who smokes cigars! Ha. Ha. (I happen to believe it, too!) You can park your cigar in my ashtray, anytime! So—Enjoy! Enjoy! . . . Yours truly, A mysterious admirer from afar."

Vito looked up from the card, and looked at himself in the big mirror. His mouth was turned down, his eyes set in a hooded look that could have killed his own reflection.

Mysterious? Shit! The best present he ever received in his whole life, and he couldn't accept it—not even one sucking puff!

"*Fon-gool!*," he moaned, "she gives me an offer I gotta refuse! . . . Okay, Vito, what'd ya do?" he asked his mirror-image. "What'd ya do to make that woman chase after you? . . . C'mon, you musta done *somethin'*! . . . Oh-h, yeah, maybe that picnic in Griffith Park, when you got stinkin' on that vino and you sang for all the people. . . . But why should *that* do it? I sang, that's all. . . . Who you trying to kid, Goomba? You was singin' right at her all night. . . . Yeah, but Jeez, I couldn't help it! . . . There she was, sittin' up on that picnic table, with her legs spread wide open. How could I sing lookin' anywheres else?

81

*Vo-la-re* . . . oh, oh!
*Can-ta-re* . . . oh, oh, oh, oh!
*Nel blu, di-pin-to di blu* . . .
*Fe-li-ce de sta-re las-sù* . . .

His head was tilted just like Sinatra's, his hands expressing the schmaltzy emotions of the song, as he bent the phrase-ending notes just right. . . . "*Vo-la-re*, oh, oh—"

The door suddenly squealed open and Joe Glass came sailing into the men's room with a pained expression on his face. Vito choked off a high note so fast he almost pulled a ligament in his vocal chords as he grabbed at his box and wrappings.

"Not bad, Morelli," said Glass. "Maybe we oughta get you to sing for us some Sunday night."

"Forget it!" said Vito, fumbling with the papers. "I only sing for myself—in the can."

"I wish a few of our headliners stuck to that rule," said Glass, as he walked into a booth and dropped the toilet seat with a bang.

Vito turned his attention back to his gift package. Fifty Monte Cristo Especiale Deluxes! The crème de la crème of the Cuban cigarmaker's art. His mouth began to salivate at the sensuous aroma that wafted up out of the box. Gently, he took one cigar out of the box and rolled it back and forth between his fingers, pressing it lovingly, as though it were the tender nipple of a woman's warm, round breast. It felt soft, but springy and moist inside—the perfect promise of fantastic flavor. He raised the cigar to his nostrils, deeply inhaling the heady fragrance. Ah-hhh!

Glass grunted out a loud resonant fart from inside his booth, and Vito was torn rudely from his heavenly Cuban reverie. He realized, in a tragic flash, what he must do.

He replaced the cigar and the card in the box, reinserted the two little nails, and carefully resealed the parcel precisely as it had been wrapped by his mysterious admirer. He held the box tenderly, grieving, as though it were a tiny coffin. Then, all at once, his pent up anger and frustration exploded.

"Aw-ww—shit!" Vito yelled, shaking the box furiously.

"What the hell do you think I'm trying to do?" Glass asked.

Vito was not amused. He took a long deadly look at Glass's shoes under the booth door. "Glass," he said grimly, "I wish for you Sicilian diarrhea—all sauce, no lasagna!"

"Why would you wish on me a curse like that?" But all Glass heard in response was the long *Shh-hhh* of the door closing.

As Vito turned the corner at the end of the hall, he saw a group of people, mostly women, just being let into one of the classrooms. It was the special

82

self-defense class for the elderly, sponsored and instructed by the Los Angeles Police Department.

And there she was, at the back of the small crowd—his mysterious admirer, Ida Katz, batting her eyelashes at him.

Vito stopped in his tracks, suspended . . . encased in jello. The box under his arm felt like a piano.

Ida Katz was beaming her mysterious admiration from afar, all the way down the length of the hall.

He tried to move—backward—sideways—about-face would be good. But his will was disconnected from his moving parts.

The rest were inside now, and she had to go in with the others. She smiled wistfully, waved a coy hanky at him, and disappeared into the classroom.

Vito's knees were weak; his palms were sweaty; his eyes were blurry. He leaned against the hallway wall for a moment, to collect himself. Then he walked unsteadily toward the card room.

As he passed the classroom, he looked at the neatly lettered sign on the door: Learn To Attack Your Attacker. That's a good idea, Vito thought, but I'd never get away with it.

"It's about time, Morelli," said Louie as Vito reached the pinochle table. "Maybe we shoulda baked a cake!"

"Sorry I'm late. I got . . . held up." Vito sat down, putting the box on his lap, trying to slide it under the table as he scooted forward. It wouldn't fit.

"Whatta ya got there, Vito?" Stosh asked.

"Hm? Oh, just a package. What'd I miss?"

"We all see it's a package," Abe said. "What's *in* the package, Vito?"

"Whatta ya mean, what's *in* the package? What's in your pants?"

"We all know what's in my pants, Vito, but we don't all know what's in your package."

"Well, y'aint *gonna* know, either."

"It's not so nice to keep secrets from your best friends, Vito," said Oscar. "If I had a package, I would gladly—"

"Yeah? Well, go get yourself a package, and maybe I'll trade you some secrets! What the hell is this today, anyway—everybody-get-on-Vito Day?"

"Don't you know what today is, Vito?" asked Abe.

"Yeah, Tuesday. So what?"

"I'll tell you so what!" said Abe, grandly waving an important finger in the air. "Today's Tuesday is different from all the other Tuesdays in the year!" Then, his finger poking Vito in the chest, "Today's Tuesday is your birthday! Happy birthday, Vito."

"Ja! *Felice, felice!*" said Oscar, slapping him on the back.

"Happy birthday, little Vito!" Stosh chimed in, crunching him with a birthday bear hug.

"Come on, you guys," Vito said. "Cut it out!"

"You think we could be nice to you on your birthday?" asked Louie, punching his arm. Vito tried in vain to protect himself from their good wishes, as they back-slapped him and poked him and tickled him and pummeled him with happy birthdays from all sides, until his secret package was at last dislodged and fell to the floor.

Abe snatched it up, holding it over his head, yelling, "I got it, I got it!"

"Open up!" Stosh said, leaning two hands and two hundred and seventy pounds down on Vito's shoulders, helping him to remain seated.

"Yeah, let's see what's in it!" Louie said.

"Abe! Come on, Abe, I'm warning you! You open that box, there's gonna be trouble! It'sa no funny no more, I'm tellin' you!"

They all heard the tone of his voice and they all realized that it was *not* funny any longer.

Abe handed him his parcel. "We were just kidding you, for your birthday, Morelli."

Vito put the box back on his lap. "Yeah, I know, I know," he said, almost calm again. "How'd you guys find out about my birthday, anyways?"

"Oh, a little birdie told us," said Louie.

"Yeah? What little birdie?"

No one answered him.

"Maybe it wasn't no little birdie," Vito said. "Maybe it was a little kitty-cat, huh?"

"Ja, could be," said Oscar. "Could be pussy-Katz."

"Yeah, that'sa what I thought. What'sa matter with that woman? She's crazy!"

"She crazy for you, little Vito!" said Stosh.

"Yeah? Well, I ain't interested!"

"Listen, Vito, she's not just one of the paupers around here, y'know," Louie said. "Her last husband left her a good life insurance payoff, when he cashed in his chips. She's got her own one-bedroom apartment in the La Brea Towers, carpets wall-to-wall, good plastic on all the furniture, and everything. She's got no children, she keeps herself nice—you could do a lot worse than Ida Katz around here, y'know what I mean?"

"I don't wanna do worse, I don't wanna do better! I don't wanna do nothin' with nobody. *Capish?*"

"Listen, Vito," said Louie, "we're your friends. We just don't want to see you pass up a good thing, that's all. What'll it hurt? Be nice to her. She'll take you up to her cozy apartment, you'll watch a little TV together, quiet, nice. She'll cook for you a well-done rump roast—"

"And from what I been told," said Abe, "Ida Katz knows how to roast a rump *well done*, y' know what I mean?"

"I don't want my rump roasted by no Ida Katz!" said Vito.

"Then," Louie went on with the rendezvous, "she'll pour you a little vino into a crystal glass—"

84

"Und then," Oscar chimed in with violins, "she will turn on the soft music on the stereo, und change herself into a hostess gown, und then she will light the pink candles—"

"Yeah, and then she'll look at me with her little pink eyes!" Vito sneered. "Come on, you guys, get off my back. I want a matchmaker, I'll look ina yellow pages."

"Wait a minute, wait a minute!" said Louie. "I think I know, maybe, what's *wrong* here." He leaned toward Vito and lowered his voice. "Listen to me, Vito, y' know this woman is a woman of the world—married three times. She's a woman of experience. I mean . . . if you're afraid, maybe, you wouldn't be able to, uh, to *do* for her, you don't have to worry. If you're a little bit rusty—she knows all about it. She'll help you out."

"Help me out? I don't even want her to be there!"

"But Vito—it's her apartment," Stosh argued.

"I don't care!" Vito shouted. "Wherever the hell I am, I don't want her to be, goddamn it! *Capish?*"

"All right, all right," Louie said, holding up a pair of palms. "Let's lay off him. When the blood's not hot, the horse won't trot, that's all."

"Now you got it," Vito said, "Finally, jeez!"

"Too bad, Vito," Stosh said, sadly. "I was having good time with you in her apartment."

"Yeah, too bad," Vito said, closing the subject.

Louie tapped the table top with a serious finger. "All right, enough monkey business, already. Let's get the important business started. Where's Minnie, Abe?"

"She told you," Abe said, "she was going to the special self-defense class this morning. She oughta be out in about half an hour."

Louie made a sour face.

"It's all right, Levine, you can start," Oscar said. "We all know for sure that Minnie has already finished her work, except the rehearsal tomorrow. She'll catch up."

"Yeah," said Louie, looking at Oscar. "I wish everybody did their job like Minnie, we would have the gas masks now."

"Everybody can only do their best, Levine," Oscar said, a little edgy. "I was able to complete my entire assignment, except the gas masks."

"The extra gun?" asked Louie.

Oscar nodded.

"Ammunition?"

"Of course, ammunition."

"Then would you tell us," Louie said, quietly, "—and don't get excited— what happened with the gas masks?"

"It is impossible," said Oscar. "Simple respirators with paper filters would cost us more than one hundred fifty dollars, und they would only keep the dust out, *not* tear gas. Real antismoke equipment, with oxygen support, costs three hundred dollars each unit—times six—figure it out yourself. We will *not* have gas masks."

They all looked to Louie for his reaction. He took a moment to study each worried face. "So . . . we go without masks," he decreed.

"You really think they would use gas on us?" Abe asked.

"Yes, I do."

"Even with hostages?" Vito asked. "Innocent people?"

"Even with hostages," Louie answered flatly. "It's all up to the man in charge on the scene. If he thinks he needs it, he'll use it. They have done it before."

"Maybe this time, they won't use," Stosh said.

"Yeah, maybe," said Louie.

Suddenly, they were startled by a piercing shrill noise that screamed through the Center.

Louie shot up out of his chair. "What the hell is that?"

"Take it easy," said Abe. "That's just the whistles from the self-defense class. They teach them how to blow a whistle in the mugger's ear."

Louie sat back down. "This is self-defense?"

All the students in the self-defense class were holding their ears.

"Sergeant, Sergeant!" Minnie shouted. "We'll blow a whistle like this at a purse-snatcher, we'll puncture an eardrum!"

"I'm sorry it sounded so loud, folks," said Sergeant Ryan. "It's just that we're inside, and it reverberates. But we've got to make sure that when you blow these police whistles, you blow them good and loud—loud enough to frighten your attacker off, or to attract help. Remember, ladies and gentlemen, you senior citizens are the prime target of street attacks, because the street criminal knows that you are not ready for him. He also believes that you are helpless. That's why Chief Davis of the LAPD has instituted this program, to give you this special training so you can protect yourselves."

As Sergeant Ryan spoke, he posed. Powerful arms akimbo, hammer fists planted at his thirty-inch waist, his chest an expanded barrel. A step forward, a step back, moving on the two muscular pillars that were his legs as though he were about to charge through a brick wall.

"Now, once again," he was saying, "Three things are going to insure your safety on the streets. *One*, vigilance—be aware that you are the target. *Two*, preparedness—you must learn these techniques of self-defense, and learn them well. And *three* —the most important—lack of fear. . . . You must not permit yourself to be frozen with fear during an attack, because if you are afraid, your assailant will know it, and then—you're dead."

New tricks for old dogs. Just two or three sessions of basic training in the techniques of guerrilla street warfare, and they would be transformed. On feet crippled and tired with age, on swollen ankles, with stiff backs and frail arms, hard of hearing and seeing and walking—but now newly armed with

86

Chief Davis's crash mayhem course and a shiny police whistle—this intrepid new battalion of the aged would surely be able to avenge every mugging and purse-snatching and rape and beating and murder that was ever perpetrated on them and their peers as they tried to survive the twilight of their years. And the one simple thing they had to remember was . . . *not to be afraid*.

"Okay, folks," Ryan went on, "let's go through a couple of the basic skills again. Mr. Cantor, come up front here, and you and I will demonstrate the front punch."

Cantor moved to the front of the class.

"Okay, Mr. Cantor," Ryan said, flexing his knees and raising his arms to karate stance, "I'm your assailant, and I'm coming at you from the front. Now, remember—the heel of your hand, upward and hard, right to the nose! That's the most vulnerable part of your attacker."

"I know another part," Cantor said.

"So do I," Ryan said. "Okay, Mr. Cantor—here I come. Are you ready?"

"Yeah, but will the hoodlum ask me that? That's the question!"

Ryan made his move to grab Cantor by the throat. Cantor lunged forward between Ryan's arms, flailing his open palm at Ryan's face. Ryan snatched Cantor's wrist into the vise of his right hand as his left hand grasped Cantor's throat gently but firmly, holding the old man helpless. The short violent game was over. Attacker 1, Victim 0.

"Okay class," Ryan said. "As you saw, Mr. Cantor's defense was not very effective. Remember, you're only going to get one chance to discourage your attacker, so you must be quick and accurate, and you must deliver your blow with all your strength. A weak punch or jab or kick will only make him angry, and then he'll probably hurt you in addition to robbing you. . . . All right, Mr. Cantor—let's try it again."

One by one, Sergeant Ryan took the class through all the terrible tactics listed on the blackboard—the front nose punch, the cane jab, the arm bite, the ear bite, the shin kick, the eye stab. The poor criminal had a list of vulnerabilities as long as an old man's broken arm. No doubt about it, the victim had the upper hand.

"Okay, now for the last move on the board, and one of your most effective tactics—the foot stomp—a very useful response when you are attacked from behind. I'd like to have a woman to help me demonstrate this time. You— the redheaded lady with the scarf around her neck?"

He was pointing at Minnie, who was shaking her head *No*.

"Come on, come on," Ryan beckoned. "We can't learn to protect ourselves without practice."

"So let somebody else go up and practice. I'll watch, I'll learn," Minnie said.

"Go on up, Minnie!" said Mrs. Bernstein. "Show him you can dance rings around him!"

Everyone laughed.

"Come on, Minnie," Ryan said, "we only have about fifteen minutes left, and I want to be sure you've all had a turn up here."

"All right," Minnie said, walking toward him. "But I'm warning you, I'm a very powerful person, so if you try to rape me, I'm liable to send you to the hospital with very serious injuries!"

Ryan laughed. "I'll try to protect myself at all times. Now, your attacker has come up behind you—"

"Why behind? I turned around?"

"No," Ryan said, "he jumped out from behind a bush."

"That dirty sneak!"

"Right, Minnie," Ryan continued. "That dirty sneak is going to try to bear hug you from behind. Now watch carefully—this is what I want you to do. Raise your right leg up. Higher. That's it! Now, with the back of your heel, feel his shin. Feel it? Once you feel your heel touching his shin, you just stomp down on his foot, *hard*, with all your strength and all your weight. It only takes about fourteen pounds of pressure to break a man's toes. And an attacker who has just had his foot broken by a good hard stomping is definitely a discouraged attacker. All right, Minnie, now I'm going to grab you hard this time, and I want to see you really stomp down hard, like you really mean it."

"Listen, Sergeant, I don't wanna hurt you . . ."

"You can't hurt me. I've got my shin and shoe guard on. See? So don't worry, just stomp away with all your might! . . . Okay, I'm behind you. And now—I grab!"

Ryan grabbed Minnie in a bear hug from behind. Minnie raised her right leg high and stomped down with all her considerable weight, thwacking the heavy plastic foot guard with a resounding wallop.

"All right! Excellent!" Ryan was hopping around on one foot. "I can see that no street criminal is going to take advantage of you. No, ma'am!"

The class was applauding Minnie's demonstration.

"Oh, I'm sorry," Minnie said, concerned. "Did I hurt you?"

"No, honestly," Ryan assured her. "It just smarts a little. It goes with the job. You can't teach self-defense without getting a few little bumps and bruises. I'm used to it."

"I feel so bad!" Minnie said.

"It's okay, really! Now, for the last tactic, the oldest and most paralyzing of all—no, stay up here, Minnie—" He took hold of her arm.

"No, I did enough," she said, backing away.

"This is the very last one," Ryan insisted. "It'll only take a minute. Now, I want you to face me, Minnie. A little closer . . . that's it. Now, class, we realize that you senior citizens are not as strong or as agile as you once were, and that some of you are not very accurate, especially with your arms and hands, to properly inflict the necessary damaging facial hits. But as Minnie just showed us, *everybody* can kick, and kick with power. Now, this

88

tactic is not listed on the blackboard with the others. It's simply called 'knee-lift to the groin.' Most people—"

"Knee-lift to the what?" Minnie asked, horrified.

"To the groin. Right here," Ryan said, showing her where. "Now, this is not as simple a move as most people think it is. You must be in the proper position before you try to deliver the blow . . ."

Minnie felt the back of her neck getting hot and clammy.

"You must not have your feet laterally even with his," Ryan went on. "If you are naturally right-footed, as most people are, move slightly to your left, so that your right knee will be sure to come up right between his legs. If you are going to lift your left knee, move slightly to your *right*, of course. Be sure you are standing close enough to your attacker so that it will be a telling blow. And one more important thing before we demonstrate . . ."

Oh, God, Minnie thought, he's going to ask *me* to demonstrate.

". . . Do *not* try to gauge the height of his groin. Just lift your knee sharply—and *hard* . . . as *high* as you can! Now, Minnie, I want to assure you that you cannot hurt me—I'm wearing a special padded steel cup like the professional football players wear. See?" he said, knocking on the cup with his knuckles.

Every man in the room flinched at the sound.

"Now, which knee are you going to kick with?"

"No knee," Minnie said. "I'm not gonna kick."

"Why not?" Ryan smiled incongruously.

"Because I can't," Minnie said. *"That's* why not."

"Minnie, I told you—you can't *possibly* hurt me."

"I know . . . I know . . ." She was finding it hard to speak.

"But don't you realize, this man is probably armed with a knife or a gun? Also, chances are he's high on dope—and extremely dangerous."

Minnie tried to swallow. "It doesn't matter," she gulped out. "I just couldn't do it."

"Why not, Minnie? This man is trying to snatch your purse, or stab you, or rape you."

"I know, I know!" she shouted, starting to shake all over.

Ryan took hold of her shoulders. "But that doesn't make any sense. He's an armed criminal, a vicious animal, don't you understand? If you don't kick him in the groin, right now, he may kill you!"

"No, no!" she shouted hysterically. "I don't care! I couldn't kick him there—not there!"

"But why not?" Ryan shouted, almost shaking her.

Minnie stiffened, frozen into an eerie calm. Slowly, she backed out of Ryan's grasp. Then she stopped and took a breath. "I'll tell you why not," she struggled, in a halting voice. "I know . . . no matter what the man is trying to do to me, I couldn't kick him there. Not there, because . . . don't you understand? Because . . . it's a holy place. That's why."

Then, Minnie turned on her heels and marched out of the self-defense class, slamming the door behind her on the silence in the room.


Louie Levine never believed anything that was told him just once. He had to have confirmation. If he didn't see a shadow, the sun was not shining. If a second witness could not be found, the event simply had not taken place.

"Tell me the truth," Louie asked Abe earnestly. "You saw it. Will it work?"

"I'm telling you, Louie—like a charm! If Minnie and I don't come over to his place, Vito would still be attached to the table, flat on his ass."

"Und I saw it also, when I went to pick up the blasting box," said Oscar. "Vito's detention system is a fine piece of work. First-class."

"I hope so," Louie said. "That's all we need, is a bunch of loose hostages running around!"

"Ain't gonna be no loose hostages, pal," Vito said.

"Aha! Here comes Minnie," Abe said. "I told you she would be through soon."

They all looked up as Minnie approached the card table. Vito popped up out of his chair. "The class is over, huh, Minnie?"

"Not yet," she said. "Just for *me*."

"Whatsa matter, you flunked outa the class?" Louie asked.

"Yes," she said quietly. "I flunked outa the class."

"Whatta ya mean, you flunked?"

"Wait a minute, wait a minute," Abe said, getting up. "I smell a herring here. What's the matter, doll?"

"Nothing, nothing," she said, shaking her head.

"Listen, sweetheart, I know when a nothing is a something with my Minnie." Abe put his arm around her shoulder, like a warm comforter. "Come, we'll take a little walk, you'll tell Abe all about it. We'll be back," he said to Louie.

Minnie leaned her head onto Abe's shoulder as they walked away from the men at the table and out of the card room to the outside patio.

"What's going on?" Louie asked. "Any of you know what's going on?"

"I dunno," Vito said fidgeting. "But I gotta go!"

"You gotta go where?" asked Louie.

"I gotta *go*," Vito repeated. "I gotta . . . see a frienda mine. A man about a dog, you know what I mean?"

The men all stared at him blankly.

"Whatsa matter with you people? You no speaka da English?"

With that Vito tucked his package under his arm and walked briskly out of the card room.

"Where the hell's everybody going, anyway?" Louie complained. "I thought this was supposed to be a meeting!"

90

Oscar and Stosh looked at each other, offended.

"What do you mean when you say everybody?" Oscar asked.

"Yeah," Stosh said, "what you think—we nobody?"

Louie groaned and put his head down into his hands.

"Shut up and deal the cards," he said.

Vito peeked around the corner and down the hall. All clear. The classroom door was still closed. Walking almost on tiptoe, he sneaked up and bent his ear to the door to listen. The voice was barely audible, but he heard Ryan talking.

"Okay, folks, one more time!" And suddenly thirty police whistles shrieked out an earsplitting whine that sent Vito jumping back from the door, wincing with inner ear pain. He ran like hell to the other end of the hall, where he waited until he heard a short burst of applause. The classroom door opened, and the noisy crowd spilled out of the room.

Sergeant Ryan, head and shoulders taller than his elders, quickly moved through the group and out into the lobby. He had two more Senior Citizens' divisions to train that afternoon. Vito watched the new crimebusters disperse, identifying each face.

There. There she was. Walking out into the hallway with two other women—Ida Katz, the mysterious, Ida, with her own fancy apartment, Ida, the rump roaster, Ida, from afar, coming-hither, toward him, and smiling that certain smile.

Vito stood leaning against the wall, his fingernails digging into his sweaty palms. He would need luck—a lotta luck—to pull this off. He hated to do what he had to do—but it was his move now. Vito smiled back at Ida Katz— a warm and knowing smile, forced and false, almost a maybe-I-go-to-Las Vegas smile, and his face hurt with it.

Ida Katz caught his smile with a shiver of joy. Her shoulders gave a little wiggle-waggle, then she fluttered her Maybellines like a humming bird gaining altitude.

Vito watched the display and groaned under his breath through the strain of his smile.

The three women were now adjacent to the door. Now! It would have to happen right now, this instant, or he'd be out of luck. He'd have to face her in a public place, or—Oh, thank God! It happened. Just like he hoped it would.

The women took a sharp right turn into the ladies' restroom, Ida last in, tossing Vito a parting leer over her shoulder.

Vito stood watch, counting the entrances and exits, into and out of both restrooms, side by side. Ryan's army was certainly in need of considerable relief—men and women, in and out, in and out, as Vito counted and tried to keep track.

At last, the men's room was cleared. Only Ida Katz and her two friends still occupied the ladies' room.

Why the hell do they take so much longer than we do? Vito wondered as he waited.

There! They're coming out! Not Ida—only the other two. She's still in there—alone!

The two women whispered to each other, giggled at Vito, then turned around and walked away toward the lobby.

He was lucking out, but he had to move fast now. He ran down the hall to the ladies' room, checking over his shoulder to make sure nobody would see him do this shameful thing. All clear.

Vito slipped stealthily through the outer door and into the ladies' room. He found himself in a short vestibule, in front of another door. Carefully, he pushed the inner door open about three inches, wide enough for his nose and one eye.

He couldn't see anything. He couldn't hear anything. Was she still in there? Had he somehow missed her coming out?

He sneaked the door open another inch. Still no sighting, still no sound. He felt a drop of sweat roll down his back. He had to make a move—do something—anything. He cleared his throat. It was a baritone sound.

"Who's there?" asked a startled voice. "Is that the janitor?"

Vito couldn't speak.

"There is someone using the facilities in here, for goodness' sakes!" Ida Katz said angrily. "Don't you even *warn* a person?"

Vito opened the door wider. It was a reflex to locate the source of the voice. Jesus Christ! There she was, sitting in one of the booths. He saw her shoes under the door, and her pants hanging at her ankles. Goddamn it! He thought he would catch her at the sinks, not sitting on the toilet.

But in that flash of a thousand mixed-up thoughts, he still knew he had to go through with it. He cleared his throat again. "It's not the janitor, Mrs. Katz," he said, fighting the quaver in his voice. "It is Vito Morelli!"

"Mr. Morelli! What are you—?"

"Wait, wait, Mrs. Katz!" said Vito, squatting down to talk to her shoes. "I didn't come in here to peek at you, or nothin'. I just gotta say somethin' to you."

"Can't you say it to me someplace else, Mr. Morelli?"

"No, no. I gotta say it to you alone, and this is the only place we can be alone."

"But Mr. Mor—"

"Shut up, please, Mrs. Katz, and just listen!" Vito's eyes were tightly closed. "Since my wife died, 1958, I never wanted nobody else around to say hello and good-bye, y'understand? You're prob'ly a nice lady, but it ain't my birthday—and besides, I ain't on the market. That's all I gotta say! *Capish?* Here!" Vito opened his eyes and slid the box of cigars across the tile floor toward her booth, like a shuffleboard shot. The box skidded to a

92

smacking halt between Ida's black oxfords, right under her drooping drawers. Bullseye!

Ida gasped, grabbing the crotch of her underwear as if the cigar box were a camera about to snap a picture.

"Thanks, anyways," said Vito, and slipped out through the door into the hallway. He leaned in a heap against the wall, sweating buckets, gulping in air, and trying to round up enough saliva in his mouth to swallow. It was very hard work, the boys against the girls.

After a moment, his heartbeat and his breathing had returned to a normal thump and wheeze, and he started walking down the hall toward the card room, a free man again.

It was only then that he felt the sinking anguish for his terrible and tragic loss.

"*Holy Mother of God!*" he said aloud, smacking a palm to his forehead. "A whole fuckin' double box of Monte Cristo Especiale Deluxe cigars! Jesus! Happy Birthday, Vito!"

Minnie and Abe were back at the table when Vito rejoined the group, and Minnie was in the middle of her report. Vito pulled over another chair and sat down.

"I got the whole wardrobe picked out," Minnie was saying. "All bright colors, so everybody can see."

"You are positive everybody can see you from where you got them standing?" Louie asked.

"Positively positive—I checked every spot."

"I'm still number one, Minnie, right?" Vito asked.

"Right. You are number one, the same as Louie, but you are the yellow delicatessen bandana."

"That'sa me—number one," said Vito, "and that's my favorite color, yellow. Just like sunny Italy!"

"It better not be your favorite color when you get to the front door!" Abe said.

"Are you kidding?" Vito asked. "You're lookin' at a man ain't scared of nothin' or nobody in this world!"

"Boys, boys!" Minnie said. "Can I please finish up my report? I gotta get home and get ready for the social worker, so we won't lose the twenty dollars cleaning money."

"They want to take cleaning money away?" Stosh asked.

"Do I know what they want?" Minnie asked. "*They* don't know what they want! Every time a new social worker gets assigned to me, they gotta come to see in person that I can't bend down to clean under the bed. So every time, I gotta hide Abe's clothes away in the big trunk in the cellar, and make sure there is plenty of dust under the bed and the bureau, and then—

when the government spy comes—I go into my can't-bend-down act."

"Yeah, yeah, very interesting," Louie said. "Now can we—"

"To tell you the truth," Abe cut in, "I think the word-of-mouth got around the Social Security office, and now Minnie's act is a smash hit. They figure it's worth an extra twenty dollars a month, just to come every once in a while and see Minnie try to bend over!"

"You better be careful, big boy," Minnie warned him. "You make too much fun of my bend-over, I can put your whole wardrobe in the ash can while I'm at it!"

"Come on," Louie said. "Abe, Minnie—please!"

"You know, there used to be a very funny act in vaudeville," Abe went on. "This man by the name of Don Williams, out of Cleveland, I think, he had this big dumb-looking cocker spaniel dog—"

"Levine, can't you stop him?" Oscar pleaded.

"No, wait, wait!" Abe continued. ". . . And every time he told this dog to do some stupid easy trick, like climb up two steps, this dumb dog would just—"

"Into the ash can, I'm telling you!" said Minnie.

"Why, why?" Abe asked. "What'd I say? I didn't say anything wrong."

Minnie was standing and gathering up her things. "What'd you say? You compared me to a dog act, that's what you said! *A dog act!*"

"But, Minnie—"

"Besides," she shouted, rising to her full five foot two, "his name was Bob, not Don—*Bob* Williams! And he came from Akron, Ohio—not Cleveland! And the dog was not a cocker spaniel, dummy, the dog was a *setter!* That's what made the whole act so funny—get it? A setter!"

Abe just stood there like a post.

"I'm going home," Minnie announced. "To take care of *your* clothes, and the Social Security lady!"

She turned to make a quick exit, and Louie grabbed her by the arm. "Minnie, Minnie!" he said urgently. "You won't forget tomorrow, in the park, two o'clock?"

Minnie gave him her special look reserved for dumb questions.

"What am I—crazy?" she asked. "You think I'm gonna let you people take a chance with *my life*, without a rehearsal? She strode out of the card room, looking like she could bend over or do a hand spring, a cartwheel, or anything else she wanted to do, any time she wanted to do it.

Abe just stood there, watching her leave.

"Abe?"

He was still standing in his own little fog.

"Abe!"

"Yeah, Vito?" Abe said, coming out of it, slowly.

"What did the dog do, when the guy told him to climb up the steps?"

94

"What? . . . Oh, he just sat there. That's all."

"Didn't move?" asked Vito. "Just sat there? What the hell was so funny about that?"

"He just *sat* there," Abe said. "A *setter*. And he just *sat*. Why didn't *I* think of that, all these years?"

"You mean he didn't do no tricks?" Stosh asked.

"He didn't do a single trick, he didn't move a muscle. No matter what the guy told him to do . . . he just *sat*."

"Und the audience thought that was funny?" Oscar asked.

"Hilarious," Abe said, and started to laugh quietly to himself.

All three men shook their heads, not a smile among them. Then Louie rapped on the table. "Abe, will you sit down, please? You'll drive us all crazy with your Minnie and your show business. I forgot, already, where we were in the meeting."

"My turn," said Oscar, taking out his list. "Like I told you, I have everything except the gas masks."

"Wait a minute," said Louie. "Lemme get to your page. . . . Wire?"

"Wire," Oscar nodded.

"Skinned, both ends?"

"Of course both ends!"

"Don't get your water hot," Louie said. "I gotta ask! Now, how about the chocolate cake?"

"We have a cake almost twelve pounds," said Oscar.

"Is that enough?"

Oscar smiled wryly. "Twelve pounds is enough to move this building across the street. In small pieces, of course."

"Don't joke!" Stosh said. "Maybe we won't need use it. Pray to God we don't need!"

Louie looked at the big man. "Please, Stosh, you gotta understand. Even if we don't use it—we gotta use it."

"Okay, Louie," Stosh said slowly, "I trust you. You say we gotta use, I believe, I do anything you tell me."

Louie put his hand on Stosh's forearm and smiled up at him. "I know, Stosh. I know you will." He turned back to Oscar. "How about the safety deposit boxes?"

"We got two," Oscar said. "Und they are perfect! Big ones. One on each side of the room, und both high up—couldn't be better."

"And the stuff for them?" Louie asked. "The melting stuff—what is it?"

"Thermite. I got for each box almost a pound."

"Only a pound? That's enough?"

"Oh, boy!" said Oscar, his eyes shooting upward.

"How about the whatta ya call it, the blasting box?"

"Perfect," said Oscar.

"You tested it?"

"With a light bulb only."

"What happened?" Louie asked.

"Exactly what is supposed to happen," Oscar said patiently. "When I pushed the plunger down, the light bulb went on—bingo!"

"This is a test?" Louie asked.

"You didn't want me to blow up the cake for the test, did you?"

"No, but when the time comes—"

"Ahh! When the time comes—the cake also will light up, bingo!"

"I believe you, Oscar," Louie said. Then he flipped the page. "Okay, how about the sign, Abe?"

"The sign is beautiful. A work of art! Hooks and everything. We only have to get it to the pickup."

"Oh, yeah," Louie said. "When are you gonna get all the stuff together, Stosh?"

"We do tonight," Stosh said, "after gets very dark. Vito and me, we go everyplace, get everything."

"How about the pickup truck? It's running okay?"

"Sure! Me and Oscar, we fix. Goddamn pickup runs like new Cadillac! Hah, Oscar?" Oscar's face showed no trace of enthusiasm.

"How about gas? Got plenty of gas?"

"He-ey, Louie, you know what's wrong witchyou?" Vito said. "What's wrong witchyou is, you don't think nobody besides you's got'ny brains. We are gonna fill the tank before we make the pickups tonight, so's we don't have to go into no lit up gas station with all the stuff in the backa the truck, get what I mean?"

Louie nodded. "Morelli, my friend, most of the time you drive me nuts with your monkey business and your Eyetalian singing, but you know what?" He tap-tapped the side of his nose with his finger. "You got brains, *paisano!*"

Vito smiled and joined him in the gesture, tapping his own nose, pinning on his own medal. "You bet your Palestine ass, Levine!" he said.

# 16
# A MONTH WITH 31 DAYS

Most old people here haunt their mailboxes. They picket them. They open them twice, three times, every day . . . waiting, hoping for a letter from the outside world—from a niece in Camden, from an old friend who still lives in the old neighborhood in Pittsubrgh, or from a distant relative—like a son in Chicago.

The gray groups of gossiping women stand in sunlit little knots in front of their seedy apartment houses, waiting for the mailman, who is always late. The men usually come later, when the coast clears of women—one at a time, sneaking up on the mailbox—a quick open, a quick peek, a quick stick-it-in-the-pocket—if there is anything there.

Each, a private life. A life almost lived out. Leaning against the winds of time as they shuffle toward the grave and the maybe beyond. A destination *certain* requires no transport. Only waiting. And so, they wait. For the dawn. For the bus. For the cafeteria tray. For the monthly Medicare book. And most of all, for the mail.

March thirty-first. A month with thirty-one days is an eternity for the old people who wait. Maybe the gold check will come from the Alabama Computer Center one day early. Maybe.

It has happened. In November of 1971, over ten thousand California Social Security recipients received their checks one day early by mistake—for twenty-one of them, just one day before the mortality rate caught up with them. Checks were cashed, and two-dollar loans were repaid, and rents and gas and electric bills were paid, and groceries were bought, and part of a chicken was eaten for dinner that night. And then, the next day, these twenty-one old people died, giving no prior notice—cheating the United States government out of their dole for the whole month, and getting away with it, Scot-free.

So . . . they wait. Especially near the first. They wait.

But not Louie Levine. Louie does not wait. He hates his mailbox. In the crisp early morning he leaves his four walls, and as he passes the metal box posted between the sidewalk and the curb—he spits his first defiance of the day at the bottom of the wooden post.

"What will you bring me today, box? A nice mistake maybe, from the computer?—with three extra zeros, I could move into a Beverly Hills mansion? The Irish Sweepstakes, maybe, picked my number? The telephone company will send me all their extra dimes? Never mind, don't do me any favors! You just stand there and stay empty. Don't bring me any surprises tonight. Anything you bring me, I don't need—except on the first of the month, sweetheart! But don't fail me then, you hear me?"

Then, to drive home his point, he gives the post a swift, unaffectionate kick. The mailbox will have a heart attack from waiting, maybe, but not Louie Levine.

The day was cool, and somehow getting cooler. Louie felt chilled as he walked the eight long blocks to Dave's delicatessen. Maybe he should walk back to his room for his heavy wool sweater, before it was time for the rehearsal in the park. He entered Dave's and walked to the rear of the take-out counter. He didn't ring the little bell, or try to get the attention of the counterman. It wasn't Murray, so he waited.

He looked aimlessly through the glass display case at the rows of whitefish and smoked cod. He glanced at the stainless steel pans of new-mounded chopped chicken liver and creamed herring. The tantalizing garlicky perfume of just-warming pastrami and corned beef reached his nose from the steam tables behind the counter, and a rush of saliva filled his mouth. The irony of it always infuriated him. The only reflex he possessed that was still as sharp as an eighteen-year-old's—and it had to be a coupla stupid little glands in his goddamn mouth!

Just then Murray came out of the back carrying two heaping pans, one of freshly made cream cheese and one of Dave's special potato salad. He set them into the empty spaces in the display case and winked broadly at Louie.

"Hello, stranger. You're a little early today."

"I got a big day, today," said Louie.

"Oh, yeah?" Murray said. "You are organizing our waitresses not to spill matzo-ball soup on the patrons, or what?"

"No, no," Louie said, "the waitresses are already organized—to *spill* the soup. I wouldn't interfere with their union. No, I am working on the big world—out there," and he jerked his thumb toward the street.

"Is that all?" Murray asked. "Well, if you're gonna take on the whole world, you will need some powerful fuel to keep up your strength. What'll it be?"

"To tell you the truth," Louie said, fingering the few coins in his pocket, "I don't feel very hungry, today. Maybe a little end of salami, that's all. Not too big."

Murray shot a quick glance around the deli and took two salami ends out of the case. One was about two inches long, and the other about six inches. He put the shorter one on the scale.

"That'll be twenty-eight cents, sir," he announced loudly. "Will that be all, sir?"

"Yes, thank you. That's fine."

Murray quickly popped both salami ends into a paper bag, following them with a half-dozen rye bread heels from the tray of freshly sliced loaves.

"What do you think?" Murray asked as he stapled the bag shut. "You think it'll rain today?"

"Who knows?" Louie said, taking the bag and the twenty-eight-cent sales check. "It doesn't matter. I wouldn't melt."

"Come in again, sir," said Murray.

"Oh, I'll come in again, don't worry," Louie said. "It's a pleasure doing business with you!"

Murray gave him a wink, and Louie walked toward the cash register.

Louie had the agenda of his whole day carefully planned. A brisk walk through the park. A nice quiet lunch in the Rodin garden of the County Museum of Art. A water fountain chaser, to settle the salami and rye. A leisurely tour of the giant statues, running his hands over the massive bronze limbs of Rodin's women. Then standing, as motionless as they were, looking up into their deep eyes for a long time . . . while the light changed . . . and the shadows moved . . . and the eyes followed him.

Louie never felt any closer to God than when he stood small before the sculptures of Rodin. Strange soul fellows, Louie Levine and Auguste Rodin. Well, why not?

Then, the meeting. The very last meeting before The Benefit. The last chance to check the equipment, the assignments, the timing, the signals. The last chance to make sure that his gang was ready to do this terrible thing that they must do tomorrow. Tomorrow they would not be talking about it. They would be doing it.

After the meeting, he would go home and make his own private final arrangements. He would pile his life into neat little stacks, with well organized notes attached to each pile. Who should get what if tomorrow was to be his last day. And he would write some other things down. Not important things. Just for himself, he would write them. A last clearing of the heart. No epitaph. And yet, if strangers were to read what he wrote, so be it.

Louie Levine had lived among strangers all of his life, anyway. So what?

# 17

# FINAL BRIEFING

The shaggy lion of March was still hanging around Los Angeles, quietly growling his distant thunder from off the California coast. The sky over the La Brea Tar Pits grew dark and sullen, as glowering clouds gathered in threatening black masses above the heads of the six conspirators huddled around their card table near the little lake in the park.

A chill wind blowing in from the sea bent the tall hedges, fluttered the new leaves on the tall trees, and tugged at Louie's large diagram of the bank intersection, which was spread out on the card table for the rehearsal.

This part was Minnie's show. The rehearsal for the hit. Like a tough drill sergeant with a bunch of green recruits, she barked them through the invasion schedule and the signals and the assignments. The only distraction to the final plotting of B-Day was the chocolate Sara Lee cheesecake that waited on a corner of the diagram, a cigar stuck in its center. Whether Vito liked it or not, a celebration of his birthday was the cover for the last briefing of The Benefit.

"All right, one more time," said Minnie, like a wedding photographer, "to make sure for sure we got everything memorized cold."

"Do we have to go through the whole *megillah* again?" Abe pleaded. "We almost had it perfect last time!"

"Yeah—almost! How would you like to *almost* make it into the bank tomorrow?"

Abe didn't dare answer back.

"All right, from the beginning," Minnie continued. "Louie? It is seven o'clock, A.M."

"I'm the yellow drugstore bandana," Louie said, "and I—"

"Point, point!" Minnie reminded him. It was her only chance to order Louie around.

"I'm sorry, I forgot," Louie said, pointing at the drugstore on the diagram. "I am the yellow drugstore bandana, here, and I'm number one."

"Good," said Minnie. "Vito?"

100

"I'm also number one," Vito said, pointing to the chart. "And I am the delicatessen bandana, here."

"And who has the gun?"

"I got the gun," Louie said. "I told you, Oscar gave it to me last night."

"Just making sure," Minnie said. "It's on my check list, here. Now, what is the first thing with Brubaker?"

"I know—the thumb, the thumb," Louie said.

"The *left* thumb," Minnie corrected him.

"Yes, yes, the left thumb. I won't forget."

"You better not," she warned him. "Stosh, your turn."

"Okay—I am green shawl, at pickup truck."

"And where is the pickup truck?"

"You know damn well where is pickup," Stosh said. "Where I parked fifteen minutes ago—on Fairfax, next to bank. Here!" His pointing finger nearly went through the table.

"And what you do first thing when you get out of pickup?" Minnie imitated him.

"I know, I know," Stosh said, like a kid tired of saying his catechism. "The dime in parking meter."

"He knows, he knows," Minnie said, patting him on the back. "What a smart Polack we got here!"

"Polack is not funny joke, Minnie," Stosh said.

Minnie smiled warmly. "Of course not, Stoshele. A Polack—is a necessity of life! Oscar?"

"I am the light green sweater," Oscar said. "Und I am *also* in the pickup. By this time, we have already my equipment dolly on the sidewalk. Stosh has my gun. I have the pineapple."

"Perfect," Minnie said, "always perfect, Oscar. Abe?"

"I am the shoe by the dime store," Abe said. "Why do I have to be a stupid shoe?"

"Will you stop, already?" Minnie scolded. "What else can I take off—my brassiere?"

"Now you're talking my language, cutie!" Abe said, doing his Groucho leer.

"You are a dirty old man, you know that?" Minnie said.

"Let me tell you something, sweetheart. A *clean* old man, is a *dead* old man!"

Vito suddenly broke into song, singing "Happy Birthday." The others joined in immediately, as they all noticed a strolling couple coming up the path toward the table. The sextet sang three repeat choruses of "Happy Birthday, dear Vi-to," their voices blending like peanut butter and ketchup, until the couple had safely passed.

"I'm getting tired of that song," Abe said.

"How do ya think I feel?" said Vito.

"Now listen, Abe," Minnie said, continuing right where she left off. "You are the shoe, and that's that. And remember, don't walk too fast—I have to get the shoe back on."

"All right, all right. But how about the gun?"

"I told you before, Abe, I will have the gun," Minnie said. "You would shoot a big toe off. You remember Coney Island, don't you?"

"Coney Island?" Vito asked.

"Yeah, Coney Island, on the boardwalk," Minnie giggled. "Big shot Tom Mix, here . . . he is trying to impress me at the shooting gallery. He breaks eight Mae West prize dolls on the shelf, misses the target altogether. The man almost hit him over the head with the gun!"

"Never mind," Abe said over their laughter. "I hit my real target later that night, at the Half-Moon Hotel—remember, Minnie?" And he slapped her on the rump.

"You think I could forget that night?" she asked, suddenly sweet seventeen. "An innocent young girl does not forget *that* night!"

"Please, please," Oscar moaned, "with all due respect to the honeymoon, we came here to rehearse the plan of attack. I am getting very cold, und it looks like it will rain on us if we don't finish up soon!"

They all looked up at the blackening sky and saw the fresh sea wind pushing the dark clouds into each other. Sometimes, in Los Angeles, this seething black quilt of clouds blowing across the basin brings rain, and sometimes it doesn't.

"Ain't gonna rain," said Vito, like an expert. "Naw! In San Bernardino, maybe—but not L.A."

"Somebody ask you for the weather report?" Louie barked. "Come on, Minnie, let's keep moving."

"My part is finished," Minnie announced. "Everybody is inside the bank. *You* are the big boss now."

"Right," Louie said, assuming command.

"Louie," Stosh's face suddenly clouded over. "What we do if somebody comes in and knows us, who we are?"

"Don't worry about it. Nobody will recognize us in Citizens' Bank on the first of the month—not with our wigs on, and never on The Day of the Eagle."

It was a neat answer, but Stosh was not convinced.

"Okay, Louie . . . but what we do if somebody *does?*"

"I'm telling you, nobody *will!*" said Louie, annoyed. "You ever look at a bank teller on the first of the month, with your check in your hand?"

Stosh looked back at him blankly.

"Well, well?"

"Wait, wait . . . I think about it."

"Don't bother thinking, Stosh, your brain will get a rupture. Take it from me—*nobody* looks at the teller on the first of the month. We stand in line,

102

and we look at our shoes, that's what we look at. Then we look at that miserable money when they count it out, and then we look for the *door* to get out quick, that's all!"

"I think you right, Louie," said Stosh. "Nobody looks."

"Bet your ass I'm right! So . . . all right, already. We all know our parts, and everybody knows who's who." Slowly, watching his own hands move, Louie folded his master check list and put it in his pocket.

"Okay, all of you," he said, "no more make believe. Tomorrow is the real thing. We will all be in our places on the corner, Johnny-on-the-spot, at eight-thirty sharp—*On the dot*—not one second after! Everybody got that?"

All five nodded emphatically.

"I got it, Louie," Stosh assured him, separately.

"Good." He looked from one face to another. "One more thing." he said, holding up a finger, "the most important thing. There is no way I can set for sure an exact plan for after we open. You all know what you are supposed to do, but nobody knows exactly what might happen. So you all have to watch *me* with one eye while you do your jobs like you would watch the orchestra leader if you played the violin. Remember—there will be lives at stake! In between every move you make, give me a look. I will let you know when we clear the bank and go into Phase Three. You all know your jobs good for that. Anybody got questions?"

"Yes, I got a question," Vito said. "Can we cut the cake now? It's gettin' dusty."

"You know what?" Louie said. "I got an answer." Turning to Minnie, he smiled and said, "Let 'em eat cake!"

Vito grabbed the cigar out of the center of the cheesecake. "Aw, Minnie," he groaned, "you stuck the wrong end into the cake!"

"You expect *me* to know which is the right end?" Minnie asked as she started to cut the cake.

"Any woman don't know the right end of a cigar," Vito grumbled, "don't know the right enda nothin'!" He tried to lick the chocolate and cream cheese off the business end of his cigar.

"Here," Minnie said, "wrap your mouth around your piece of cake, birthday boy."

"Happy birthday to you, happy birthday to you . . ."

Stosh started the song off, leading the rest of the off-key brigade into the song, while Vito sat trying to light his gummy cigar.

"Happy birthday, dear Vi-to, Happy Birthday to you!"

"I'll tell you somethin'," Vito said, "This is the longest goddamn birthday I ever had in my whole goddamn life!"

As if God had overheard his name twice taken in vain, the sky suddenly opened and the rain came drizzling down, sending the gang into a panicky scramble to gather up their things, gulping their pieces of cheesecake and swallowing their coffee, as the drizzle quickly turned into a roaring torrent.

103

"Hey, Louie!" Abe yelled above the noise of the pelting rain. "What the hell do we do if it rains like this tomorrow morning?"

They all heard the question, and they all stopped to hear Louie's answer.

"What do we do?" Louie hollered. "We get wet, that's what we do! You all hear me? Rain or shine—*The Benefit is tomorrow!*"

God added an ominous clap of rolling thunder, and they all ran frantically for cover, scattering in different directions as the soggy remaining half of the chocolate cheesecake was blown off the bench by a strong wet gust, flipping *Happy Bir*— upside down in the mud.

Louie was still shouting to them at the top of his lungs, turning as he ran, "Rain or shine! You all hear me? *Rain or shine!*"

# 18

# LONG NIGHT'S JOURNEY

Louie stood at the window in his room, looking up at the sky for a star, the moon, anything that might indicate a hint of tomorrow's weather. It had stopped raining a while ago, just after he had gotten home, but that was no clue. Not in Los Angeles.

He could see nothing, only blackness. He shivered. It was cold in the room, expecially near the window, and he was still chilled through to the bone, even after his warm bath.

He never could take a really hot bath. He had tried that only once, when he first moved into the little back room. And when his landlord came home a while later and found that the hot water had run out, he ordered Louie into the main part of the house, and there was all hell to pay.

Louis knew damn well that he hadn't depleted the hot water that evening. The landlord's husky thirty-five-year-old daughter Florence, back home to live after her divorce, had followed him into the bathroom they shared, and through the thin wall Louie had heard the water running into the tub for over half an hour—and he knew *exactly* what was going on.

At first, he heard only a light trickling, and a quiet gentle sloshing and swooshing. Then he heard her throaty humming, and the water gurgling and lapping, then her low moaning as she moved against the fluttering flow, groaning ohh-hh. . . . And Louie touched himself as he listened, close to the wall, to her hot, selfish pleasure, and he closed his eyes and wet his lips, picturing her big back arched, her big tits bobbing, her legs spread wide open, her feet high up on the white tile, as he heard the falling stream turned a quarter-turn ticklier, ahh-hh. . . . And he was hard now, the hot waterfall gushing now, his robe open. His hand was moving, sliding in tempo with her steamy ah-hhs and oh-hhs. . . . And she was rocking, bucking against the thick hot stream oh-hh. . . . Then he heard the whimpering of a name, and his head was spinning, and *he* was that name, moving in her, shoving deep into her, thrusting, pounding, ah-hh. . . . And he heard her panting, now, oh, yes, yes, yes, oh-hhh, now. . . . Then a sudden tight silence, hanging, hanging. . . . Then, over the water still rushing he heard her slow deep groan of release ohh-hh. . . . Louie came hot and wet into his robe, and the water was cut off.

The old man opened his eyes and fell back on the bed, breathing hard, his waning pulse still throbbing in his hand. Then, through a hazy fog, he heard the whirlpooling water spinning its song down into the tub drain.

After a moment, he heard her start to sing, softly crooning as she dried herself, "People . . . People who need people . . ." A sweet accompaniment for Louie as he wiped himself off. He could wash the old robe. Or throw it away. It was worth it.

But later that same night, she sat at the dining room table at Louie's arraignment, like a hanging judge, glowering at him as if he was dirt. Her eyes were cold and hard, and she shook her head reproachfully while her father bawled the hell out of Louie for using all the hot water. Threatened to kick him out if he ever did that again. And she just sat there, and didn't say a thing.

Louie read her icy frown, and he knew that she knew that he knew. But she didn't say one word to defend him. The bitch, no longer in heat, just sat there and watched Louie squirm as he suffered the brunt of her father's anger.

But Louie never let on. He just stood there with a dry mouth and took the humiliating harangue, shifting back and forth from one foot to the other like a petty thief.

And when his landlord stopped screaming at him, Louie apologized. He promised never to do it again. . . . He hadn't realized. . . . He would bathe only twice a week. . . .

He liked the little room. It was in the heart of his village, and the rent was right. And there was his angel, Sophia—how could he leave her?

Besides, every time an Old Age Security recipient changes his address, they send a goddamn social worker out to inspect the new dump, to ask a thousand stupid questions to make sure the pathetic old remnant hasn't inherited a million bucks from someone, thereby disqualifying himself from the dole. And he didn't want to go through that again.

He would find a way to get even with the bitch. He would fix her wagon, leave it to him. Maybe piss a little into her mouthwash bottle. Or on her hairbrush. It would serve her right for what she had done to him.

It didn't take Louie long to think of a way to get his revenge. It was simple, and perfect. Louie watched and waited. Then, about a month later, Florence took over the bathtub just after he had finished, the bathroom still warm and moist with a man's odors. She was singing softly to herself, and Louie knew that this was it.

He heard the tub filling, as she opened and closed the medicine chest, preparing her bath oils. He heard the toilet flush. Then, the loud splashing sound into the tub stopped. He could almost feel the warm water creeping up her legs as she slowly stepped into the tub. Then he heard her sigh with the pleasure of her warm wet submersion. Steathily, he stepped up onto his kitchen chair, close to the wall.

He listened. Soon he heard the familiar tinkling trickle from the bathtub spout, and he knew he was about to get his revenge. He waited. Yes, now she was turning the hot water tap open, little by teasing little, twisting the knob, increasing the diddling flow of fluid. . . . And still he waited. Waited until he heard her low humming sounds . . . until the water was a rippling gulfstream, and he heard her moaning, groaning ohh-hs and ahh-hs . . . until he knew she was twisting hard against the hot gushing stream, and he heard her panting ohh . . . ohh . . .

Then, from high above his head, Louie dropped the dozen heavy books crashing to his linoleum floor, reverberating like a shot from an elephant gun.

He heard a stifled little scream, and the sounds of watery thrashing from the bathroom came to an abrupt halt.

Knowing he had her undivided attention, he started to cough. He coughed a loud and grating old man's cough, hacking far down his throat to bring up the deep phlegm. Then he spat the stuff loudly into a paper bag, and blew his nose thoroughly, for good measure. He would have farted if he could.

She turned the tap off, and he heard the water swirling out of the tub. But he heard no singing. She quickly dried herself and left the bathroom, slamming the door behind her.

Louie smiled to himself all the while he was picking up his books. And the dirty water nymph *never* followed him into the bathroom again.


No moon. No stars. Not even the lights of an airplane. No clue about tomorrow's weather. Louie shivered again and moved away from the window, cursing.

"Goddamn it! We check a thousand little details, nobody thinks to find out the weather report! Well, I'll tell ya the truth, Sophele, I got nobody to blame but myself. I'm the leader. It's my responsibility. And if one of us gets killed tomorrow, that'll be my fault, too . . ."

The little pan of water on the hot plate started to sizzle, and Louie switched it off. He put the soggy tea bag into his cup and poured the boiling water in, lifting the string of the bag up and down, hoping to extract just one more cup of weak tea from the tired old bag. He tried one more squeeze of the blackening half-lemon, but the little pulpy teeth at the edge of the cut lemon had long since given up the last of their juice. It was a typical last-day-of-the-month cup of tea.

Louie walked to his clothes closet and reached into a coat pocket for an envelope of sugar. He tore it open and emptied it into his cup. What the hell, Dave's Deli didn't count the little packets they kept on their lunch counter. And after all, wasn't he a steady customer?

Louie snapped his fingers and jumped up out of his chair. "Hey, maybe they put today's *Times* in the trash already!"

Quietly, he opened his door and peered out on the back porch. The big yellow plastic refuse container stood next to the back door. He walked out and looked into it. The paper was there all right, but the garbage from the landlord's family dinner was on top. "Dirty bitch," Louie muttered. "She knows goddamn well I buy my paper here." He scraped the foul-smelling sauce off the paper with an empty can, as best he could, and brought the paper back in to his table.

"Weather, weather . . . yeah, here, Part Three, page fifteen." He turned the damp pages to the weather page and hunched over to read.

"How do ya like that? They got the death notices on the same page with the weather reports!—Are you listening? These dead people have to know what the weather will be tomorrow?"

He couldn't help it. He was running his finger down the column. "'Johnson . . . Kaufman . . . Kimura . . . LaRue . . . Lerner . . . Levine—' Levine, Louis? . . . 'Levine, Louis, beloved husband of Esther, loving father of Malcolm Lewis and Rhoda Schneider, devoted brother of Isadore and David, cherished grandfather of seven. Services Friday, 1:00 P.M., Home of Peace Mausoleum.' . . . *Hmph!* . . . Well, rest in peace, Louie Levine."

All at once, Louie started to laugh, uncontrollably, as if he had just heard the funniest joke of his life. "Ah-hahahahahahh! Woe is me! Hahahahahahh! I *died* the day before yesterday, and it wasn't me! Hahahahahh! You hear that?—One Louie Levine had to die that day, and they didn't pick this one! Hallelujah! I lost the raffle again! Hahahahahahahahh!"

Then, he stopped laughing, and looked at his namesake's obituary again. "Hmm-mm. 'Beloved . . . Cherished' Sure! How much you wanna bet?"

Louie tapped his finger on the obit. "Listen to me, Levine—you're prob'ly better off, I'm telling you." He looked back to the weather report.

"'Southland forecast, Los Angeles . . . night and morning low clouds and fog, variable cloudiness today and Thursday. Fifty per cent chance of rain Thursday.' Dammit! Fifty-fifty is lousy odds for tomorrow, little girl. Aw, what am I talking? The whole thing is a gamble, for God's sake! He spins the big wheel in the sky just like Major Bowes: 'Round and round it goes—where it stops nobody knows.' So one day it stops at *that* Louie Levine, and the next day—it'll stop at *this* one."

Louie drank the last swallow of near tea and got up from the table. He dropped the dead tea bag splatting into his waste basket, picked up the half lemon skin, putting it to his mouth to get a last tart taste. Then he thwunked it into the basket.

"You know what I forgot?" he suddenly remembered. "I'm so anxious to get inside, outa the rain, I ran right past the mailbox. Don't go away, little girl, I'll be right back."

He put his overcoat on over his bathrobe, kicked his slippers off, slipped his feet into his wet shoes, and started out the door. Something made him change his mind, and he came back into the room.

"Am I crazy? It's dark already, I can't go out there alone!"

He pulled open the bottom drawer of his dresser and reached for his hammer. He stopped in midreach, and, lifting his battered old briefcase, he took hold of the gun. He straightened up, holding the cheap gun gingerly.

Suddenly, he saw himself in the mirror, his image pointing the gun back at him, and he felt a wave of revulsion. "So, Mister Big Shot, is *this* the way you're gonna go? Like a hoodlum, full of holes on the street?" He turned toward the door, then stopped again. "What the hell am I thinking? Somebody catches me outside with this thing *tonight*, and it's goodbye Benefit *tomorrow!*" He replaced the gun in its hiding place, and grabbed the hammer.

The air was chilly and damp as Louie walked toward the mailbox at the curb, swinging the hammer at his side. He looked up again, scanning all the sky he could see. There was no moon, no stars shining in the cold sky. "Fifty-fifty rain tomorrow," he muttered.

He checked the wet sidewalk both ways, and took a tight grip on the hammer handle just as a big kid came scooting along on a skateboard. Louie stepped back, waiting until the boy passed; then he crossed the sidewalk and opened the mailbox. Sure enough, there were three pieces of mail for him, and one was a large, slick envelope. He closed the box and walked back into the house, to his room.

"Mail, we got mail, sweetheart!" he announced to Sophia. "Somebody in the world knows I'm still alive and kicking!" He put the mail on the table, hung his coat up, kicked his wet shoes off, and stepped into his slippers. Then he carried his shoes to the hotplate, flicked the switch on low, and placed them on the element.

"Don't forget to remind me to take them off before I go to sleep," he said to Sophia. "You remember what happened last time!"

He sat at the table and spread his mail out in a fan.

"Looka this—forty-six cents! Somebody spent forty-six cents to send a pauper a piece of junk mail!" He slit the large envelope open, reading the return address aloud. *"Playboy?* What kind of joke is this?"

He pulled out the large color brochure and unfolded the center-fold-sized advertisement. He stared at the outrageous big tits sticking straight out from the smiling blonde bunny—both girl and tits seemingly oblivious to the laws of gravity.

"No, sir," Louie shook his head solemnly. "These are no joke! Listen to this: 'Here are just *two* reasons you'll live the good life and love it as a key-holder to our new Century City Playboy Club. Newly arrived on the West Coast from our Chicago hutch, our Playmate for all seasons, Bunny Amanda McCoy, will make your every entertainment dream come true! Join the

Playboy Club now, and get your key to the swinging life for only twenty-five dollars!' . . . That's all? 'Come on in, and let Mandy take care of you—she's the real McCoy!' . . . Take care of me? With her equipment, she could *kill* me just trying to do me a *favor!* It's gotta be a mistake."

He checked the envelope again. "No mistake—right name, right address. Wrong person, that's all. Oh, boy, did somebody give the *Playboy* the finger with a mailing list!" And Louie burst into laughter again. "Hahahahahahh! Listen, are you paying attention?—*The Los Angeles Times* is burying me six feet under, and the *Playboy* thinks I am just ready to start living it up!"

He looked at the color blowup again, his eyes shifting back and forth admiringly from nipple to nipple, dizzying himself momentarily. Finally, he turned her over, tits down, onto the table. "Sorry, Mandy—Social Security can't afford the real mcCoy!"

Louie gave the other two pieces of mail a sour look. "I don't even know why I'm opening them up. I know what they are, my dear, and they ain't Valentines. Ah, what the hell—the coffin's open, you gotta look in! This one's gotta be first—these people got seniority with me. Over the years, they must've spent over a hundred dollars on postage alone, just to get my business!"

He slit the envelope open, spilling the contents of the mailer out onto the table. "And no matter where I move, they always come up with my new address. These people really care!"

He held the brochure up for Sophia to see. "Look, here's a picture of your boss. What a beautiful marble statue, isn't it? They got always very pretty pictures, the Forest Lawn pamphlets. Looka this, a little lake with fountains, and white swans, and trees, and green grass, and nice flowers—I can hardly wait! 'Forest Lawn—The only true memorial park. Beauty that comforts. All funeral arrangements are provided completely within our sacred grounds, a final resting place of beauty and dignity for the dear departed.' Yeah? What about the *undeparted?* Where does somebody keep the beauty and dignity for *them?* 'Our mortuary, flower shop, churches, mausoleum, and cemetery are all available in one quiet, secluded place to honor the departed loved one.' You see how *nice* they make it for you, when you're dead? How nice, how beautiful, how peaceful? That's the catch, Sophele—*only* when you're dead!"

Louie turned his chair to face the stained-glass angel more directly. He looked up into her eyes and felt a bitter sadness welling up in him.

"I'll tell you a little story. You got a minute? I know I'm talking a lot tonight, but . . . well, I ain't sleepy yet, and I don't wanna scare you, but who knows? Maybe we won't be talking like this after tomorrow. . . .

"Anyways, when I was young and new in this country I was in the labor movement, you know? I was a union organizer for the I.W.W., the

Industrial Workers of the World, and we were fighting the bosses to form trade unions, fighting to change the inhuman working conditions in the factories and sweatshops, and to get for the poor worker a living wage in this land of plenty, and decent hours, and better safety, and so on.

"But the bosses wouldn't give in so easy, and Big Bill Haywood, the leader of the I.W.W., told us how hard we would have to fight, and how long, and he warned us that many lives would be lost in the struggle against industrial slavery.

"Don't worry, I'm coming to the point of my story, it's just around the corner. They were trying to organize unions in the needle trades, and there was talk of a strike for a fifty-two-hour week, when all of a sudden there was a terrible fire at the Triangle Shirtwaist Factory. One hundred and forty-six people were killed in that fire, mostly women and young girls. Can you imagine? Trapped like rats! And the whole nightmare only took eighteen minutes! You know why? Because the doors were all *locked from the outside!* The bosses, they locked the factory doors during working hours to keep the union organizers *outside* and the workers *inside,* see?

"Most of them burned to death at their machines, and many were killed jumping out the windows from the ninth and tenth floor to the street. There were no fire escapes at Triangle, only sewing machines.

"Afterwards, there was an investigation of the firetrap. *Always afterwards.* The mayor and the fire commissioner promised that steps would be taken, new safety regulations, and so on, so that a terrible tragedy like this could never happen again.

"But these kinda promises come easy to politicians on the hot spot, and they didn't fool labor leaders like Sidney Hillman and Big Bill Haywood. They called a memorial mass meeting for the fire victims in Washington Square. There was a white coffin up on the platform with all the names of the dead written on it, and thousands of people wearing black arm bands stood in a cold drizzle to hear the speeches and the prayers. One by one, the labor leaders got up to talk, calling the fire a crime against humanity, and they demanded the right to form official labor unions to bargain with management so that, once and for all, the violence and the killing of the labor wars could come to an end.

"Then Big Bill Haywood got up to speak, and with a voice as big as *he* was, he called the fire a murder—*a mass murder,* perpetrated by the industrial bosses on a bunch of unorganized ignorant immigrants who were too weak to protect themselves!

"All of a sudden, the crowd got outa control, people were running and screaming, fights broke out between the mourners and police, and it turned into a regular riot. The cops and goons attacked the platform with their clubs, and they pulled Bill Haywood down and took him to jail with blood all over his face.

111

"But I'll never forget a poem he recited to us that day before they knocked him down. I'll remember it until the day I die, and it went like this:

Though they promise you a Heaven,
Though they frighten you with Hell,
They won't do a damn thing for you,
Till you're Dead, Dead, Dead.

It doesn't rhyme, sweetheart, but think it over . . . he was right. He was right then, and he's *still* right. It's like Walter Cronkite says: 'That's the way it is, that's all!'"

Louie got up out of his chair and started to pace, circling his little table like a stiff old cat. Then he stopped and flopped a never-mind hand at his angel. "Aw, what am I bending your ear with my yesterday . . .?"

Louie's throat was dry. And his eyes were burning, starting to tear. Little by little, he was tiring himself. Wearing himself down so he could sleep. Just sleep, without dreaming, on this night when he was afraid to sleep.

He sat down and opened the last envelope. "Whatta we got here?" he asked, as he pulled out a picture of a boat. "Here's a new one, I'm on their list! 'The Neptune Society. Complete 'Cremation Service.' Tell me the truth, Sophele, isn't this fun? I'll bet you never knew what we have to go through before we get to be where you are, hah? 'The dignified alternative,' it says. 'No embalming, no cosmetology, no grave, no casket, no limousines, no tombstone or other extras.' Sounds like a nothing funeral to me.

The Neptune Society performs a tasteful and orderly disposition of the decedent after cremation. The Society is simply notified as soon as death has occurred, and is able immediately to begin its service, avoiding all unnecessary costs and preoccupation with the dead body. The body is transported discreetly to our repository, where it is held until the death certificate is signed. A cremation permit is secured and the deceased is taken directly to a state-licensed crematory. Disposition of the cremated remains takes place exactly as specified by you on the enclosed application. Usually, this is done by dissemination at sea, in undisturbed tranquillity. Almost every evening, one of the graceful Neptune Yachts slips quietly out to sea, sailing westward to the three-mile limit. All engines are stilled as the anchor is dropped, and the ship's crew assembles on deck. The Captain orders the flag lowered to half mast, then the Captain or a clergyman reads a brief service as the cremated remains are gently scattered into the calm waters . . .

"Isn't that beautiful, Sophele? Doesn't that sound peaceful? And I never been on a yacht before, either. How much does this barbecue and boat ride

112

cost? Oh, yeah, here . . . 'Disposition of the deceased by the Neptune Society costs only $255, a fraction of the cost of conventional funerals.' Well, you gotta give 'em credit. They know exactly what the Social Security will go for—$255, no matter how much you weigh! . . . 'Simply fill out enclosed authorization forms for membership. Rates, which are payable only once, are: Individual, $15, Couples, $25 . . .' How do ya like that? You get a discount if you bring along a date! Well, maybe for a boat ride, I could get somebody to go with me!"

Louie sat staring at the color picture of the Neptune Yacht, heading westward toward his sunset, the flag at half-mast, the glassy sea reflecting the last of the sun's orange light, the hazy horizon sky glowing warm and serene in the background.

He was dead tired now. Talked out. Empty. Wearily, he got to his feet. He picked up the pile of mail in both hands, staring at it for a moment, then he held it out to his angel. "You see, little girl? You didn't believe me when I told you what an important person I was, hah? You see how they fight over my body?"

Then he rolled the stack of mail into a cylinder, slowly twisting . . . twisting the papers and gritting his teeth, harder and harder, his face flushing with new anger. At last, when he could turn them no tighter, he said to them, "Take me off your list. Forget about me. I died a long time ago."

He thwunked the stick of junk mail into the waste basket on top of the dead tea bag and the squeezed-out lemon; then he turned off the hot plate and the light, and fell on his bed, exhausted.

About three o'clock in the morning, a crack of thunder shocked Louie out of a deep, tense sleep. He sat upright with a start, not sure at first where he was. For an instant, he thought someone had slammed his door. Then a sudden white flash of spring lightning, followed by another smack of thunder, made him realize where and when and who he was.

He cursed under his breath as he heard the pelting rain on the roof and outside on the driveway. He swung his feet to the floor and walked to the window to watch the rain peppering the concrete, the big drops bouncing up off the ground like water boiling in a pot.

He walked back and sat on his bed, staring at the window as he listened to the steady downpour. "Goddamn it!" he muttered.

Another zap of lightning bleached the room with a flash, and in that instant, Louie saw Sophia looking down at him. She was a silvery-white apparition, an avenging angel with a cold blue light flashing from her eyes.

She was blacked out now, but he knew exactly where she was. "What are you, with the Social Security?" he demanded. "You're working for the FBI? What kind of traitor are you? I thought you were my best friend, that I could trust you with my life! I gave you one job, *one simple job*. I didn't ask

113

He should cure my arthritis—only to keep the rain away for one more day, for God sakes! *One more special day.*"

Louie shivered and pulled the covers up around his shoulders. His eyes were accustomed to the dark now, and he could just make out the angel's silhouette. "Listen, I told you—this is something we *have* to do! It's the only way. We can't turn the other cheek anymore, we are black-and-blue from the slapping around already, can't you understand? Why do you aggravate me?"

The old man sat there on his bed in the dark, clenching and unclenching his fists, punishing the pain in his fingers, listening to the rain, and thinking about tomorrow, fearing tomorrow.

Then it suddenly dawned on him. "My God, it's today! There *are* no tomorrows anymore—just one big today! You hear me, little girl? It's too late to back out now. We reached our limit, and we gotta go through with it, that's all! You think old people *don't have their limits?*"

He sat very still. He sensed no debate from the angel.

"A-ah, what's the use! What the hell am I arguing with a stupid piece of glass? I shoulda covered you up a long time ago, you're nothing but a troublemaker for me! Listen, you just hang onto your little cross, and I'll do what I have to do, that's all!"

Louie put on his slippers and his robe. Reaching out, he switched on the light and walked to his book shelf. Slowly, he ran his eyes over the titles, remembering the pleasures of them, every word in every book. He had devoured them like a starving man, stuffed himself with them; every morsel had been tasted, chewed double, consumed, and burned to become a part of him . . . and he had never felt full, never. Always hungry for more.

But books cost money, like all other food, so for many years Louie had gone without a good steak, without caviar, and without books. He spent many afternoons in the public library, of course, but that wasn't the same— not the same as choosing one book from all the other thousands in the shop, and carrying it home in the book store bag, and putting it proudly on the shelf, next to the bookend, where he could make love to it anytime he wanted to. The public library was too public. He couldn't underline a passage. He couldn't read a piece of prose aloud, and shout, "My God, how this man can write!" or "How do ya like that? He's talking to *me*—right to *me*, he's talking!" or "Here is a man! I'm only thinking it, feeling it, but *he*—He's *writing* it! In black and white for the whole world to see—for as long as the world has eyes!"

These were the Gods of Louie Levine. The men who could write, And Louie valued his communion with them above all else. Gastric digestibles were only necessary incidentals. These books were his true food, his bread.

Tenderly, he ran his fingers along the line of books, caressing them, one by one. Then he started to take them down off the shelf, three or four at a

114

time, and stacking them on his table. His possessions. His estate, to be divided and distributed among his heirs. *Exodus* and *John Brown's Body* and *The World of Sholom Aleichem* and *J'Accuse* and *Dun't Esk* and *The Wall*. These, he piled in one stack. *Man's Fate* and *Mein Kampf* and *The Descent of Man* and *Das Kapital* and *The Old Man and the Sea* and *The Lower Depths* and *Remembrance of Things Past* and *Les Misérables,* he put on another stack.

He reached out for *The Count of Monte Cristo*—then he whirled around and slammed the book down on the table.

"What am I, crazy? What the hell am I doing? I got nothing to leave—I got nobody to leave to! Here you are, little girl! They're all yours. If I don't come back from tomorrow, *you* inherit a first-class library! Some Mexican ambulance driver will get my bus pass and my Medicare stamps, some coroner will get my gold wedding ring, and that's the end of the reading of the Will, that's all!"

Louie sat motionless at the table, holding his ring finger with his right hand, staring down at his ring. He looked at how his finger had grown big around the broad gold wedding band, holding it fast for a lifetime. Slowly, he twisted the ring around on his finger. He stared at his initials, L.J.L., cut deeply in a graceful scroll on top. Then his lips moved to the words of the inscription on the inside of the gold band. He had not taken the ring off his finger for over thirty years, he couldn't have. But he could see the fine engraving hidden on the inside, as clearly as he could see his dead wife's face—in his inner eye, where all things of true worth are truly perceived.

*"I will love you longer than my life."*

A rush of flooding memories engulfed him. Page after page of sepia snapshots riffled through his mind like a penny-arcade show, spinning him around and around and back over the years of his life.

He remembered his mother and his father and his brother, and the house of his birth, and the laughing snows and wooden sleds and hot black bread of his childhood. He felt rough mittens and tall grass and running and rolling over and over down a distant autumn hill. He saw the long beard of his grandfather and the tears shining in the eyes of his mother.

He saw again the bloody pogrom in his village, the houses burning, and the hiding cellar, and Grischa the gentile boy who didn't have to be there; the agonizing screams at the cemetery, and the woman throwing herself into the open grave of her husband, and the anger of Moses on the face of the rabbi, and the empty mud-rutted roads after.

He remembered the benches on the provision wagons and the train jerking through Austria to the port of Bremen, and the big German boat with its tiered wooden steerage bunks, and the smell of manure and the babel of a thousand frightened people, and the singing the first day out, and the babies crying, and the rancid food on tin plates, and the burning disinfectant rubbed into his hair, and the lice anyway, and the heaving sleepless sickness of the sea. He felt again the coins that must not jingle sewn into his jacket, and the big yellow tag hanging from his coat button, and the rope tied around his wrist to his bundle, and the itch of his boy beard. Then he remembered the shouting cheers and the sight of the huge statue of the lady with her book and her torch, then the long crushing line on the Customs Wharf in the misty rain outside the red brick buildings of Ellis Island.

He remembered shivering in the nude while the immigration doctors prodded and poked, peering into his eyes and ears and throat as he tried to keep watch on his bundle of clothes heaped on the cement floor, and the mysterious marks they made on his yellow tag as they pushed him along from line to line, clutching his bundle and his fears as tight to himself as he could.

He remembered the cold doctor's cold finger, poking up hard as he flinched and coughed left and coughed right, until finally he was pushed through a doorway with a blue sign that said Entry. He didn't know what that word meant then.

He remembered the commotion at the door. They were pulling a struggling young girl through the doorway to his line. She couldn't have been more than fifteen or sixteen years old, and she wore a yellow tag, too. She was crying hysterically, trying to fight her way back into the women's examination room, waving her arms and screaming, "*Meine Schwester! Meine Schwester! Meine Schwester-rr!*" The husky matron shoving the girl yelled, "Trachoma! Trachoma! *Verstehen Sie nicht?* Trachoma in America *ist verboten!*" The girl only screamed louder, "*Meine Schwester-rr!*" A big customs guard ran over to control the unruly immigrant girl. "*Hier, Hier!*" he shouted at her, grabbing her arms roughly and pointing to the end of Louie's line. "*Schnell, schnell! Und still! Sehr still!*"

They dragged her to the line. The guard made a quick loop of Louie's rope around the girl's wrist and barked an order, "*Du! Ihr vorsicht! Verstehen Sie? Sie ist allein. Vorsicht!*" Louie nodded obediently and the guard marched away. The yellow tags understood the German commands at Ellis Island.

The girl had stopped her fighting, but not her crying. She stood behind Louie in line, her head down, her shoulders shaking convulsively, clutching her coat collar to her neck, sobbing uncontrollably for the loss of her sister.

Louie slowly unlooped the rope, freeing her wrist. Then gently, he put his arms around her, murmuring, "Shah-shah, shah," as he patted her back. She sobbed quietly in his arms while the line moved on ahead of them.

116

"*Achtung!*" a guard yelled at them, "*Vorwärts, vorwärts! Mach schnell!*"

The girl looked up at Louie, and he looked down into her dark eyes brimming over with tears of grief . . . and gratitude. It was Sarah. Louie had found Sarah. And Sarah had found him.

And from that moment on, it was Sarah. During the two weeks of quarantine, they were with each other day and night, talking and laughing and learning each other's faces and fears and dreams . . . hands holding hands tightly, so tightly . . . breathing each other's breath . . . huddling close together against an uncertain new life in a strange new world. Louie and Sarah. Sarah and Louie. Together alone, lost and found, standing in the doorway marked Entry.

"Sarah . . . Sarah . . ."

The old man was speaking her name aloud, chanting her name, her name, the sweetest sound to ever come from his mouth, and he was smiling with the taste of it.

"Sarah . . . Sarah . . ."

Then all at once, the silence snapped Louie back as he realized that he was no longer hearing the sound of the rain. He looked up at the angel, her colors just brightening with the dawn. The long frightening night had passed and the rain had stopped.

"Sophele, Sophele," he said fervently, putting his hands together in grateful prayer. "My guardian angel, I knew you wouldn't let me down! Yes, it's a fact—every new dawn is a true miracle. And the dark night before is only a fraud!"

Quickly, methodically, he replaced his books on the shelf, a stack at a time, and started for the bathroom to get ready for The Benefit.

Within fifteen minutes he had shaved, put on a neat white shirt, blue tie, and gray suit, shined his shoes, and was putting on his overcoat. He opened the bottom dresser drawer and took out the old briefcase. He put his wig into the case and picked up the gun. He checked the safety, and put the gun into the case.

"Ready or not," he said, "here we come."

A passing cloud darkened the room. He looked up at the angel. "Don't be scared, little girl. I think everything will be all right. Listen, I never had a bad day on a day I had a good bowel movement!"

Just then, the rising sun sprayed its sparkling bright light through the angel and onto the walls of Louie's room. Louie smiled warmly. "That's better," he said, "*That's* the sunny smile I like to see on my Saint Sophia. See you in church, kiddo!"

And he was out the door.

# 19

# APRIL FOOLS' DAY

They met in the middle of the block, promptly at dawn. Mutt and Jeff. Oscar and Stosh. Their silent greeting consisted of quick shivering nods, and they sneaked down the alley toward the back of the gas station, where the camper pickup truck was parked. Suddenly, two cats came screaming out from under the truck, one chasing the other in zigzag leaps right across their path. Both men hit the ground.

Slowly, they started to get back up on their feet. Oscar suddenly stiffened and grabbed Stosh by the arm, pulling him down again.

"What is wrong?" Stosh whispered.

"Somebody . . . is in the truck. Look!"

Stosh raised up on one knee. Sure enough, he saw a man sleeping in the pickup, his tousled head leaning against the window on the passenger side. "Dirty sonofabitchin' bum! We get him out, come!"

"Wait a minute, Stosh! We must be careful. He could wake up the whole neighborhood."

"How we be careful? We just kick him out, drive away!"

"No, no, if we wake him up und scare him—he hollers, it's all over for us!"

"So? What we do?"

"*This* is what we do," Oscar said. "You go quiet to the driver's side, I sneak up to *his* side. When I say 'Go!' I open his door und push him inside. You open your door und quick start the motor. . . . We will take him with us, then we will let him out, away from here, before we go to the bank."

"Good. Okay! Pray to God pickup starts for me—before he yell bloody murder."

"Don't worry." Oscar said. "I will have my hand over his mouth, he will be lucky even to breathe! Get your keys ready."

Stosh reached into his pocket and took out the truck keys, holding them up. Oscar nodded and cautiously waved Stosh toward the pickup. Bending low, the two men sneaked silently to their preplanned positions. Oscar

118

looked under the truck and saw that Stosh's feet were in place, on the other side. He took a big breath. "Go!"

Stosh opened his door and slipped quickly behind the wheel. At the same time, Oscar jerked his door open. He grabbed the trespasser as he started to fall out, slapped his right hand over the man's mouth and pushed him roughly back into the truck. Something fell from the man's lap to the floor with a loud thump as Stosh turned the ignition key and stomped on the gas.

*Grrr-uh–grr-uh–grr-uh! Grr-uh–grr-uh–grr-uh!*

"Goddamn-goddamn!"

Oscar looked down on the floor at the fallen object, and saw a silm paper bag, the neck of an open wine bottle protruding.

*Grr-uh–grr-uh–grr-uh!*

"Goddamn! Oscar, you smell gas?"

"No, not gasoline!" Oscar made a face. "This man drank a whole bottle of wine in here before he passed out!"

The wino's full weight leaned heavily on Oscar as he held him tightly, his left arm around the man's neck. The truck reeked with the stench of cheap wine processed by the wasted organs of the unconscious derelict.

*Grr-uh–grr-uh–grr-uh!*

Stosh's head dropped to his chest in disgust.

"Try again, please!" Oscar pleaded. "I can't hold him forever—und I think I will be sick!"

"I can't! She's flooded, goddamn it!"

"It couldn't be!" Oscar argued. "Try! Try again!"

*Grr-uh–grr-uh!*

"Goddamn!"

*Grr-uh–grr-uh!*

"Goddamn!

*Grr-uh–grr-uh–grr-uh!*

Suddenly, Stosh started to bounce up and down on the seat as hard as he could, still turning the key and stepping on the gas. The engine was grinding—*grr-uh–grr-uh!*—and Stosh was bouncing—*bonk-a-bonk!* And each time the mountain came crashing down in the seat, Oscar and his drunken charge were propelled up off the seat like clowns on a trampoline, Oscar grunting with each bouncing impact.

*Grr-uh–grr-uh–grr-uh!*

*Bonk-a-bonk!*

"Ugh!"

"Goddamn!"

"Stop, stop!" Oscar begged. "Please, you will wake him!"

"If he ain't awake by now, he's dead." Stosh growled.

*Grr-uh–grr-uh–grr-uh!*

*Bonk-a-bonk!*

"Ugh!"

119

All of the sudden, the motor turned over and started, jiggling the pickup with its new song, *Umpititit!—Umpititit!—Umpititit!* Stosh gunned the motor.

*Vrr-rrr-rrrm! Vrrrr-rrrr-rrrr-rrm!*

"Bee-ootiful!" Stosh grinned. "She had little muscatel hangover, that's all!"

"Very funny!" Oscar said. "Out, out! Let's get out of here!"

Stosh backed the pickup away from the parking barrier, shifted into low gear, and careened out of the gas station onto the nearly empty morning street.

The centrifugal force of the sharp left turn was too much—the wino's full dead weight slammed into Oscar, crushing him against the door and forcing him to release his grip from around the man's neck. The vagrant's body folded into a fetal blob and plopped to the floor on top of Oscar's feet.

They both knew immediately that the man was dead, had been dead all along.

"The man is dead," Oscar announced.

"Goddamn! I thought so," Stosh said. "He didn't put up no fight. What we do now, Oscar?"

"Just a minute. Give me a moment to think. You drive! Keep your eyes on the road!"

"What you mean, think? We only few blocks from bank. I find place to pull over, we dump him out.

"Right on Beverly Boulevard? Are you crazy?"

"No! I turn onto side street!"

"No, no! We can't do that, *Dummkopf!* Someone sees us—everything is *kaput!*"

"So, Oscar, What we do?"

"Red light!" Oscar screamed.

Stosh slammed on the brakes, skidding halfway into the crosswalk. "Hell with red light! What we do with him?"

"Simple," Oscar said. "We take him with us."

"Into bank?"

"No, not into the bank, Stosh," Oscar said, grinning. "He will wait outside for us in the pickup. He will *watch* our truck."

The signal changed. Stosh stared at Oscar.

"You crazy," he said simply.

"Green light," Oscar said, pointing.

Stosh stepped on the gas. The motor coughed twice and died. The two men looked at each other. Stosh turned the key. Nothing. No *grr-uh*, nothing. He turned the key again. Nothing—except a bluish smoke and a new acrid odor, wafting into the cab from the motor, mixing with the aroma of dead muscatel.

"The battery?" Oscar asked weakly.

120

"No. Not battery."

"What, then?"

"I don't know. But is bad."

"*How* bad?" Oscar asked, knowing how bad.

"I afraid to find out," Stosh said hopelessly.

"*Gott in Himmel!* What will happen to us? What will happen to Louie and the others? They are depending on us."

Oscar was shaking like a leaf.

Stosh laid his big hand on the little man's shoulder. "Take it easy. Move over to wheel. You steer truck, I push back to curb." He got out of the pickup and walked to the front.

Oscar pulled his feet from under the dead man and slid under the wheel, shuddering as he looked down at the puffed and battered face, which he now saw for the first time. He looked quickly away and turned the wheel, as Stosh pushed the pickup backward to the curb with one hand, waving the oncoming traffic around their truck with the other. The tires hit the curb and Oscar set the brake. "*Gott, Gott!*" he moaned, his head in his hands. "*Bitte, bitte, Gott!*"

Stosh opened the hood of the pickup and bent to the motor. The strong smell of melted Bakelite immediately led him to the problem. He pulled the distributor cap off and looked inside. It was a molten mass of copper and insulation, fused together into a mangled lump. He threw the cap at the crippled engine in disgust and came back to the driver's side of the cab.

"Move over," he said, opening the door.

Oscar slid over obediently, holding his feet up off the floor—because now, if he let his feet down, they would have to rest on the dead man's chest. "So? What is wrong with the motor?"

Stosh didn't even look at Oscar. He just looked straight ahead toward Citizens' Bank, eight blocks away, and shook his big head slowly. "Distributor burn out. Pickup truck is dead." Stosh looked down at the crumpled body on the floor. "He is dead . . . we are dead. Goddamn!"

The two men sat motionless, staring straight ahead, as though they were encased in aspic. The signals changed and the morning traffic roared past them. A stray dog wandered up to the pickup and lifted his leg, pissing on the front tire. Neither man made a move to shoo the dog away.

Oscar's legs were tiring. Gingerly, he shoveled his feet under the dead man's shoulder, resting them on the floor. He took out his antique pocket watch and snapped open the case.

"It's half past seven," he announced, as the watch tinkled "*Ach! du lieber Augustine, Augustine*".

Stosh said nothing.

"Seven-thirty," Oscar repeated, snapping his watch shut.

"I no ask for time," Stosh snapped. "Shut up."

"I know," said Oscar. "Time asks for *us*."

The signal changed to red. Suddenly, a fancy florist's van came to a screeching, skidding stop into the crosswalk. The rear doors of the van flapped open, and a huge carnation funeral spray and several vases full of gladioli tumbled out onto the street, exploding white pieces of crockery all over the place. A car following behind swerved crazily to the left, barely missing the flying flowers, and continued right through the red light.

The tall, skinny, blond driver flew out of the van in a flaming fury, running back to the fallen spray, cursing a pink streak of sibilant obscenities.

"Suck-suck-suck! I *told* that ugly Arab faggot that stupid raffia string wouldn't hold those silly doors," he screamed to the world. "I'm going to get his brown ass fired this time, see if I don't!"

He was gathering up the crumpled metal easel stand that served as support for the fallen spray of flowers, and kicking angrily at pieces of the smashed vases, the shards bouncing off the curb as he tried to clear the street.

Suddenly Stosh poked Oscar with his elbow. "Follow me!" he ordered. "Get tape—big tape!"

Stosh jumped out of the pickup and ran toward the angry driver. "Hey! We help you!"

"That's okay, mister, I can manage," the young man said.

"No, what the hell! We help you. You could get hurt out here." Stosh started picking up the fallen flowers.

Oscar came limping out of the pickup, the tape bulging his coat pocket as he started motioning the oncoming traffic around the two men stooping to retrieve the fallen funeral garden. Within three or four changes of the traffic signal, Stosh and the young man had scooped up all the flowers and the big spray and had stuffed them back into the hold of the van.

"These stupid doors are still not going to close," the young man hissed. "I *told* Vincent I should have taken the big truck for this load. The service is at one o'clock. Shit, I'll never make it!"

"Okay, take it easy," Stosh said. "You and me, we push hard, we close doors."

The young man pushed hard on his door. Stosh grunted but hardly pushed—and, of course, the doors would not close.

The traffic was building up behind the van, and drivers were honking impatiently as they tried to switch lanes to go around. A swarthy truck driver, struggling as he turned the wheel of his fully loaded ten-ton semi and trailer, yelled out the window of his cab, "Where the hell do you think you are, you stupid fairy?—In the Rose Parade?"

"Blow it out your ass, greaseball!" the young man shouted back.

A chorus of honking horns from the backed-up traffic obliterated the truck driver's cursing as he pulled away.

"Quick!" Stosh shouted over the din. "You drive around corner. We got

122

tape—we tape doors together." He pushed the young man toward the cab of his van. the young man got in, started the van, and made a right turn into the side street, with Stosh and Oscar running after him.

As the van pulled to the curb, Stosh grabbed Oscar's arm, tightly. "We do same trick!" he said urgently.

"What?"

"Same as dead man!"

Stosh ran to the van before the young man could get out, as Oscar ran limping to the other side, understanding all at once what the two-inch adhesive tape was for.

"I hope your tape will—"

The young man opened his door.

Stosh pulled the door fully open, jerking it out of the young man's grasp, then he shoved him roughly back onto the seat, flat on his back. Oscar was already in on his side, pinning the young man by the shoulders, pressing down on him with all his frail weight.

"What are you old farts—?"

Stosh clamped a sudden giant hand over the young man's mouth, shutting off his voice and most of his breath as he leaned his full two hundred and eighty pounds on top of him. The young man was writhing, his eyes popping with fright.

"You listen!" Stosh commanded. "We no hurt you!"

"*Blmph-Umphmph!*" the young man said.

"We have to take your truck for few hours," Stosh said, his face close to his flattened victim's face. "We *need* it—very important!"

The young man suddenly surged up, lifting a knee hard under Stosh, trying to kick him in the balls.

"No, no! Not nice!" Stosh grabbed for the man's legs with his free hand, never letting go of his face.

"*Shh-hhh!*" Oscar warned. "Someone will hear you!"

Stosh clamped his lips shut tight, choking back his grunts, as he struggled to contain the young man's thrashing legs. At last, he managed to lock a firm scissors-grip around his opponent's legs and pin his arms behind him. Still the prisoner persisted in bucking with all his might to get loose, or attract somebody's attention to his attack. Miraculously, no traffic had come down the side street during the struggle.

"Come around with tape," Stosh ordered. "Quick!"

Oscar scrambled out and ran around to the driver's side.

"Tape feet together! I hold!"

Oscar quickly wrapped the wide adhesive tape around and around the man's ankles.

"Make tight, tight!" Stosh said.

"It's tight!" Oscar said, stopping.

"More, more!"

"We will need tape later!" Oscar objected.

"Hell with later! We need tape now!"

Oscar wrapped three more times around, until the young man's socks were almost covered above his suede desert boots.

"Okay," Stosh said. "Push feet inside."

Oscar tore the tape free and shoved at the trussed feet to push them inside the cab. But the victim refused to cooperate, stiffening his legs for all he was worth, *blmphing* and *umphing* as he fought like a cat to keep his bound feet outside the van.

"I can't get them inside," Oscar complained. "He won't let me!"

"Push hard—he will let you. Watch!" Stosh poked a stiff giant forefinger hard into the young man's groin, a scant inch above his penis. The reflex was dramatic. The young man coiled into a fetal ball with a suddenness that catapulted Oscar off balance, right into the van. Stosh pulled the man's body over to the passenger side, his hand still wrapped tightly around his victim's mouth.

"Good boy," Stosh praised the young man, leaning down almost nose to nose with him. "You no fight no more! You no make noise, either—or else I use all my fingers—like *this*, you know?" Stosh held up a ham of a fist, and the young man nodded enthusiastically.

Oscar slammed the door, started the engine, and turned right into the empty alley behind the row of shops, pulling into a parking place in the middle of the block.

The young man lay very still, his eyes darting back and forth above Stosh's big hand as he tried to anticipate what was going to happen to him next.

Stosh looked down at him, smiling like a visiting uncle. "Listen, boy," he said "we not stealing truck, understand? We only borrowing."

"*Blmph-Blumph!*"

"You never learn nothing when you talk," Stosh scolded, "only when you listen! We need truck very important! You find out later—maybe you understand."

"Quickly, Stosh," Oscar urged. "It is coming up eight o'clock!"

"Okay, okay! Now we have to tie you up, and keep you quiet," Stosh informed his captive. "You know that, hah?"

The young man nodded as much as Stosh's grip would permit.

"Okay. I gonna let loose your arms. I no want hurt you, but you try something—I get plenty mad, you know what I mean?"

Again, the captive nodded docilely.

Stosh released his arms. "Okay. Now put hands together, slow, just like for praying."

The young man obeyed, his long fingers coming together in fearful prayer.

124

"That's nice boy!" Stosh said warmly. "You smart fella."

Oscar moved in to wrap the tape around the man's wrists, but it was already too late. With a mighty lurch, the young man swacked his arms outward and jerked his head loose out of Stosh's grip.

"Help! Help! He-elp!"

Their terrified captive had his mouth wide open, screaming bloodcurdling murder as loud as he could, rolling from side to side to avoid recapture, as Stosh grabbed desperately for the man's head.

"No, no! Please!" Oscar whispered hoarsely, "no noise!"

"Help He-elp me, somebody—!"

Stosh clamped his Polish vise together with a crunch, one huge hand under the young man's chin, the other on top of his head. His hapless prisoner was lucky to get his tongue out of the way before it was guillotined by his teeth, as they came gnashing together with all the force of Stosh's might.

"Bad boy!" Stosh said, as Oscar looked out in all directions. He saw no sign of anyone in the area. Oscar waggled a naughty-naughty finger at the prisoner.

"Listen, young man," he said, "we are trying to be nice to you, under very desperate circumstances. What do you want to do? Get us into trouble for God sakes?"

"Trbl? Uminulotuftrbl, too, y'know!" the young man whined through his clenched teeth.

Oscar shook his head impatiently. "No, no! *You will keep quiet,* und I will see to this!" Moving quickly, he tore two lengths of tape off the roll and stuck them to the back of the seat for a moment. Then he reached over the back of the seat and into a large bucket of cut flowers. With one hand he took hold of three or four stems of snapdragons. With the other, starting at the bottom of the stalks and pulling his tightened fist upward, he shucked off a heaping handful of blossoms. Catching them in both hands, he turned back to the young man, who whimpered pitifully from under Stosh's hand.

"What you do, Oscar?" Stosh asked.

"I show you," Oscar said. "You release his chin, but hold his head still, und I will feed him breakfast. Then, a few times around with tape—und he will not be able to make a sound for several hours!"

Stosh looked with admiration at his partner in crime. "Oscar, you *something!*"

Oscar smiled modestly and nodded. "Yes, I know. Ready now?"

"Ready."

Stosh quickly released his hold, switching his hands immediately to the sides of the young man's head and holding it immobile, as he crunched the heels of his hands together against the young man's temples, almost causing concussion.

125

"Oww-ww!"

Oscar stuffed the handful of flowers into the man's mouth. "Eat! Eat it all!"

The man's cheeks were puffed out like a blowfish. Oscar grabbed his lips, pinching them together hard, so he could neither spit out, chew, nor swallow. "Now, Stosh!" he ordered. "Hold his mouth closed!"

Stosh switched his hands back to his former headlock, holding the man's jaws shut tight.

Oscar grabbed a length of tape, holding it outstretched as he approached the young man's mouth. In a final defiance, the young man pursed his lips out as far as he could, trying to affect the adhesion of the tape as it headed for his mouth. Oscar looked down at him, flabbergasted at his stubborn resistance. "Tell me, young man, you would like to hold your lips in this position for a whole day?"

For a moment, the young man returned Oscar's steady gaze, his blue eyes ablaze with bravado. Then, all at once, his lips melted into an accommodating zipper over his double mouthful of snapdragon salad, and, moaning an unmistakable sigh of submission, he lay still, simply waiting for the tape to be applied.

Oscar placed the tape strip hard against the man's bulging mouth and around the back of his head, where he overlapped the tape. "It will not be so terrible," he told the young man. "I lived once for three days in the Black Forest on a diet of berries und flowers. They are good for you—no constipation!"

In a matter of seconds, Oscar had completed his job. He almost felt sorry for the young man. "After a while, the saliva will come back to your mouth, und you will be able, maybe, to chew and swallow a little at a time, the flowers. But chew very carefully," he counseled, "in case there are bugs, you know?"

The young driver winced under the adhesive. There he lay, bound from head to foot, resigned to the dubious distinction of being the very first of his persuasion ever to be raped in broad daylight by two senior citizens. Tears of frustration and self-pity filled his eyes.

"All right, Stosh," Oscar said, "now we must hide him."

"Hide? Where?"

"In the back!" Oscar jerked his thumb. "Under the flowers!"

"Okay! Wait, I move." Stosh turned and stood on his knees on the seat. Then, leaning over, he breast-stroked a quick clearing in the forest of funeral flowers, spilling water from buckets and crushing leaves and blooms in his careless wake.

Having cleared space to receive the body of their captive, Stosh turned back, grabbing the mummified young man by his armpits while Oscar took hold of the back of his knees. With one easy heave, they dumped him onto the wet floor in the middle of his once-beautiful cargo.

126

"Quick, now," Oscar said. "We must get tools und coveralls und wigs."

"Right!" Stosh started the van. "I drive around block to pickup."

He turned the corner onto Beverly and pulled up at the curb right behind the dead pickup truck. It was still the only vehicle parked on the block. The coast was clear. Both men got out of the van.

"Act natural," said Oscar. "Do not look around you."

Stosh opened the rear doors of his pickup, and together the two men lifted out the heavy tool dolly, dropping it to the street. Oscar reached into the truck and pulled out the cardboard box containing the coveralls and wigs. He slammed the doors shut and carried the box to the rear of the van while Stosh wheeled the loaded dolly.

Neither man could bear to look into the front seat of the pickup.

A hundred cars must have whizzed past on the busy boulevard while the two criminals transferred their munitions and other apparatus from one truck—which contained a dead man—to another, which contained a bound kidnap victim.

But nobody passing by really paid any attention. Who cares what two ancient farts are doing on Beverly Boulevard early in the morning, moving stuff from one truck to another?

Stosh opened the van doors. Suddenly, the big funeral spray jumped out at him with a whooshing force, hitting him on the chest as it fell to the street.

"Hey, goddamn!"

Their rebellious captive, trussed up though he was, had straightened his legs with enough kicking power to propel the stand of carnations out through the open doors. And now he was making the only kind of vocal sound he could make without choking on his mouthful of snapdragons.

"*Mmmph! Mmmph! Mmmph!*"

"Such a foolish young man," Oscar said, shaking his head.

Stosh stepped over the fallen spray and up into the bed of the van. He leaned over the young man. "I tell you something, kid—last time, I tell you! One more noise I hear—one *little noise*—I got big hammer, I hit you on top of head—hard! You no make noise for week—maybe never! You understand?" The hostage nodded emphatically, and silently. Stosh pushed a wall of flowers onto him, clearing the doorway for the tool dolly, and the two men lifted the dolly into the van. Oscar put the big box into the front seat.

"No room for big stand flowers," Stosh said.

"It is not a problem," Oscar said calmly. "I will put the funeral into your pickup."

Oscar lifted the big spray and carried it around to the passenger door of the truck, opened the door, and looked in at the body of the vagrant wino on the floor. The smell of stale cheap wine and urine nauseated him, but Oscar somehow seemed held there, by the pathetic sight of that piece of

127

human flotsam, his wiry gray hair a frazzled halo hinted with red, his battered and discolored face almost smiling, his filthy raincoat wrapped around him in death like a bitter shroud of pain and neglect.

Oscar, the poor man's only mourner, shook his head sadly, keening at the death of a life he never knew. Then, gently, he lay the expensive carnation spray on top of the dead man's body. He straightened the wide red satin ribbon with the silver letters pasted on, "Rest In Peace."

"Yes, peace. Rest in peace, whoever you were, my friend," Oscar whispered. "If only you had died for a better cause." Then he slammed the door on the coffin and walked to the van.

Stosh was already half into his coveralls, struggling to get his arm into the second sleeve. Oscar helped him find the sleeve hole, and proceeded to pull his own coveralls on over his clothes. Stosh zipped up his zipper and reached into the box for his wig.

"Oscar, we have to wear wigs?"

"Yes, we have to."

"Why, Oscar, why?"

"Because everybody else will be wearing theirs, that's why!"

"Aw-w, goddamn!" Stosh pulled on his wig and looked at Oscar for his re-action. Oscar met his challenging stare without the slightest change of expression.

"Why you don't laugh?" he asked Oscar.

"I don't laugh, because I cannot laugh," Oscar said. "We are late, Stosh— go!" And he pulled on his own wig, looking straight ahead.

Stosh started the van and zoomed away from the curb into the flow of traffic toward the bank, eight blocks away.

Eight blocks away, Louie Levine was pacing the sidewalk in front of the drugstore across from Citizens' Bank. About-face. Wearing out his wrist-watch with his incessant time checks. Buttoning and unbottoning his top overcoat button. About-face. Patting the gun in his pocket to make sure it was still there. Looking east on Beverly. And north on Fairfax. And even higher north, to a God he didn't altogether believe in. About-face.

From their assigned positions, the others watched him, as he paced back and forth. He was furious. Fuming out loud. About-face.

"A Polack and a Kraut. I knew I couldn't trust them! It's eight thirty-two! Three months work down the toilet! I'll get my hands on 'em, I'll kill 'em both!"

He wrung two imaginary deserving necks in quick succession with his bare hands, twisting them viciously as though they were chickens and dumping his phantom throttled victims into the gutter. Then he grated his throat harshly, bringing up an angry oyster of phlegm, and spat it out noisily into the gutter after them. About-face.

"So whose fault? My fault. I picked April Fool's Day, and I picked a

128

coupla first-class fools, that's all. So? What could I expect to find at the Senior Citizen's Center—the U.S. Marines?"

About-face. Unbutton the button. Pat the gun in the pocket. Look at the watch. Look east. Look north. Kick the telephone pole. About-face.

Watching Louie from his position in front of the dime store, Abe thought, "He's going crazy. The big organizer! Everything worked out to the minute, like a Swiss railroad—only we're all waiting at the station, and there's no train!"

Abe checked his watch. "Eight thirty-five, for goodness sakes! Doesn't he know they're not coming? We're all out here freezing our balls off, and Stosh's pickup is broken down somewhere. We'll have to cancel the show, that's all! Ha-ha! Give back the money at the box office. Look at him. Now he's talking to himself. Maybe I can get him to look at me."

Abe waved his hands madly above his head, crossing and uncrossing them like a football referee. Louie saw the frantic signal and stopped pacing for a moment, furious at the public display. Abe spread his palms upward and outward from his waist, his eyebrows shooting up, his chin jerking upward in a long-distance *nu?* Louie sent a scathing look back across the street at him, shaking his head angrily and waving his palms downward.

"Oh, God, that's right," Abe remembered. "We're not supposed to *know* anybody until we get inside the bank." He looked away quickly, pretending not to be acquainted with the man he had just signaled.

Vito watched the two of them from his position in front of Dave's Deli. "Enougha this shit!" he said to himself, "I'm gonna go talk to our leader— find out what's goin' on here!" He waved across to Louie, his hand scribing an agitated clockwise circle high in the air.

"That's all I need," Louie said aloud. "Now little Sicily's got his bowels in an uproar!"

Vito pointed at himself with two little jerks of his thumb, and then across at Louie as he set out to break security by crossing the street. Louie shook his head violently back and forth, motioning Vito back with two pushing no-no palms. Vito shrugged peevishly, whisked the back of his hand under his chin at Louie, and turned back to his assigned position.

Fairfax body language. Unconcealed, bigger-than-ordinary-life gestures of intercourse. Urgent pantomimes of conspriacy on the public corners of a busy intersection. But only the participants were aware of the exchanges. Their wild and waving antics didn't rate a single sidelong glance from the passing pedestria at the corner of Fairfax and Beverly. It's a mind-your-own-business world, isn't it?

Eight thirty-eight. Louie looked kitty-corner across the intersection, checking Minnie's termperature as she sat at her place on the bus stop bench. He saw no sign of the jitters. She wasn't even looking at him—or at her watch. She was intently scanning the streets, in all four directions, looking for the overdue pickup truck. She knew, as they all knew, that if

Stosh and Oscar didn't arrive with the tools and the explosives in the next five or six minutes—The Benefit was dead.

A bus squealed to a stop at Minnie's bench to pick up a lone passenger. Minnie ducked around the back of the bus, so as not to lose sight of the two curb parking spaces at the side of the bank. The bus pulled away, and Minnie saw that one parking space had already been filled by a big chicken truck. The driver was unloading his fattened feathery passengers into the kosher butcher shop, swinging them by their feet, three in each hand, as they squawked their heads off.

Minnie wondered what Abe's reaction would be if her hearty hot chicken soup squawked like that when she poured it into his bowl. He would never drink it again as long as he lived, that's what he would do. She giggled at the thought and looked fondly across the street at her Abe, his new mirrored dark glasses flashing little rays of sunlight as he shook his head at her.

Another rush hour bus blocked Minnie's view momentarily as it pulled to the curb. Minnie again ducked around the bus—and saw to her horror that a fancy golden van had pulled in behind the chicken truck, at the only remaining parking meter. She gasped and rose to her feet as though she had just seen a terrible accident. She stared in panic at the scrolled black lettering across the rear doors, Les Fleurs de Vincente.

Minnie flashed a look across at Louie, who had also seen the van and was slapping his forhead in a fit of frustration. Suddenly, as they watched, the van doors opened, and two blue-coveralled men, one small and one huge, jumped down onto the street, lifting a heavy metal tool dolly down after them.

"My God," Minnie said aloud, "it's a miracle! Somebody gave them a ride to the bank!"

Stosh gave Louie a big nodding wink across the street. Louie stood stunned in his tracks, as Oscar slammed the two doors shut. Abe put his hand to his mouth to keep from bursting out with nervous laughter. Vito, seeing the reactions on the other three corners but unable to see around the bank corner to the van, started heading west to see what the hell they were all staring at. Louie recovered from his shock just in time to wave Vito sharply back to his place.

Stosh and Oscar lifted the dolly up onto the sidewalk.

"Well?" Oscar asked, looking up at his big partner.

"Well what? We're here." Stosh said.

"The dime in the meter," Oscar said.

"Oh! Yeah, yeah!" Stosh plunged a hand into his pocket, held the coin proudly aloft for Louie and Minnie to see, and deposited it ceremoniously into the parking meter.

"Very good, Stanislaus," Oscar said.

130

"Hey, Oscar," Stosh said, "why dime is so important, anyhow? Van belong to florist, ja? *He* has to pay parking ticket!"

Oscar put both his hands on Stosh's arms and said, "Please, Stosh, no more conversation. I have already a headache. You just watch Minnie."

"Okay, Oscar."

Minnie looked at her watch, feeling the familiar butterflies starting to flutter their opening night wings in her stomach. It was a good feeling—exciting. Good butterflies, good show. Minnie could always tell the difference between the friendly butterflies and the heebie-jeebies.

She checked the corners. Everybody ready. Each standing at his entrance, waiting for his cue. Waiting to play his part in the show of his life. Maybe the last part he would ever play.

Minnie checked her watch again, then looked at the big glass front doors of Citizens' Bank across the street. "Come on, Brubaker," she said aloud. "It's a quarter to nine. Raise the curtain, already!"

At that instant, as though he were a puppet Minnie had strings attached to, Brubaker, the bank guard, raised the shades on the glass doors, and the show was underway.

Minnie nodded her head three times, and her confederates knew at once that the bank was about to be opened to employees and to The Benefit.

Fourteen minutes to nine. The intersection was beginning to growl louder now, like an angry living thing, moving to nine o'clock like a speeded up time-lapse film sequence; each bus swallowing more people, belching more people out; more cars and trucks stacking up at each stop light; shopkeepers rasping open the metal grates in front of their stores; teenagers shouting and laughing as they ran to their sleepy first class at Fairfax High; a Southern California Gas Company jackhammer crew exploding into their *rat-tat-tat* digging in the middle of the block, forcing the westbound traffic into a horn-honking single lane; and the CBS pages, out on the chilly balcony of the Television City building, barking directions at a noisy studio audience of out-of-towners shuffling into Studio Forty-One to see the new quiz show "Boys Against The Girls."

None of this frenetic activity distracted Minnie Gold from her assignment. She saw every move, checked every passing face as she sat on her bus stop bench, searching like a hawk for the arrival of her first target.

And *there he was*, getting off the bus—Jesse Williams, window number two, with the wild Afro. He was turning, offering his hand to a woman getting off—Fat Opal Johnson, window number three, in her buttercup number with the high waist. And right after her, Mio Yamaguchi, the Safety Deposit Japanese doll.

"Bee-ootiful!" Minnie said to herself, "Three in one." Rising to her feet, she looked up at the morning sky. "Please, God," she prayed, "it should

131

only go good—break a leg!" Then she whipped off her yellow bandana and sat down.

Louie nodded pointedly to Minnie, slipped his hand into the pocket with the gun, and quickly joined the trio at the curb as they waited for the traffic signal to change. Vito saw the bandana signal too, and headed briskly toward the bank.

The signal changed to Walk, and Louie-Paul Muni walked abreast of the three bank employees as they crossed the street.

Eleven minutes to nine. They all reached the front doors of the bank at the same time, Louie and Vito half turning their backs as Brubaker saw the familiar trio of employees and knelt to unlock the glass doors, urged on by Jesse.

"Hurry up, man! Jesse's got to be the first one inside this morning!"

The floor lock snapped open, and Brubaker rose, pulling the big door back. As the door opened, Louie turned and firmly shoved Jesse inside, while Vito pushed the two young women from behind, propelling them through the doorway and right into the astounded bank guard.

"Hey, wha—?"

"*Shhhh!* Quiet! You," Louie barked, jerking his gun at the guard, "put your thumb in your mouth! Quick!"

"My *thumb?*" asked Brubaker.

"Left!" Vito snapped. "Your left thumb!"

"Yeah, your left!" Louie shouted. "In your mouth! Now!"

"Okay, okay," Brubaker said, raising his left thumb in slow motion to his mouth. "I'm doing it, see?" His thumb disappeared.

"Nobody will be hurt," Louie said, "Slow, now, slow . . . everybody move *away* from the door and *against* the wall. . . . That's it."

"You guys are crazy!" Jesse said, as they started to move. "You can't—"

Louie poked his gun at Jesse. "Quiet, I said!"

Jesse suddenly shot his hands over his head, and the women gasped at the sudden move as they cowered against the wall.

"No, no!" Louie said. "Don't put your hands over your head! I didn't tell you to put your hands up! Put them behind your back—all of you! Not you, with the thumb!"

The two women and the young black man obeyed, clasping their hands behind them.

"Okay, Vito," Louie said, "get his gun."

Vito moved cautiously to Brubaker's left side. There was, somehow, a twinkle in Vito's eye—an old dog doing new tricks, and he was having fun.

"Don't move," Vito cautioned Brubaker. "I'm just gonna help you with your thumb, while I get your gun. Be nice, huh?"

With his left hand, Vito applied a firm upward pressure to Brubaker's left elbow, sinking the man's thumb to the hilt, deep into his mouth. With his

132

right hand he gingerly unsnapped the holster strap and lifted the guard's gun out. Then he looked up at him and smiled disarmingly.

"The safety is *on*, right, pal?"

"*Mm-hmm!*" mumbled the guard, meaning yes. Vito released the man's elbow, looked quickly down at the gun, and snapped the safety off.

"Oh, my God!" Fat Opal whimpered. "I think I'm going to faint!"

"Nobody's gonna faint!" Louie barked, passing the law. "You hear me? *Nobody faints!*"

"Yes sir!" She hiccupped a little whining sound deep in her throat.

"And don't *cry*, for goodness sakes!" Louie complained. "Crying makes me nervous!"

Fat Opal put a hand over her mouth, trying to stifle her spasm.

"Okay, Vito!" Louie said, "take your people to the conference room!"

Vito waved his gun like a herding staff. "After you, ladies . . . and you, fancy dresser. We're gonna have a conference. Walk nice and slow."

Fat Opal wrapped her arms fearfully around Mio Yamaguchi, Jesse fell in behind them, and Vito followed them toward the conference room at the back of the bank.

Nine minutes to nine. Louie had not taken his eyes off the guard against the wall. "Mister Brubaker," he said, "you and me, we will wait here, for the others."

"Howdynumnm?" asked the guard, around his thumb.

"How d'ya expect me to understand you, with your thumb in your mouth? Go ahead, take it out. We got your gun. It's all right."

"How do you know my name?" Brubaker asked, wiping his wet thumb on the side of his trouser leg.

"Does it make a difference how?" Louie asked. "We know everybody in your family. Lock the door!"

"You know—?"

"Please! No more talking—only waiting! Lock up!"

Brubaker knelt to relock the door.

At the rear of the bank, Mio opened the conference room door and looked back at Vito.

"In, in!" Vito ordered, poking Jesse against the women with the gun.

"Easy with that thing, man!" Jesse said, flinching. "We're goin', we're goin'!"

Vito herded the trio into the long narrow conference room, filled almost completely by a massive walnut conference table and fourteen tufted Naugahyde and chrome swivel chairs. A large matching walnut credenza stood against the wall at the far end of the room, and a fancy white call-director telephone rested on the table, facing the head chair.

Vito slammed the door shut behind him and locked it.

"Ladies, I want you should go to that enda the room," he said, pointing, "one of yez at each enda that sideboard, and put you hands up on it, so's I can *see* 'em. . . . That's right. Good. I'll be witchez ina coupla minutes. Jesse, I want you on the side of the table, there—hands on top."

"What are you going to do to us?" Mio asked evenly.

"Do to you? We didn't come in here to *do* anything to you. You're the safe deposit lady, ain't you?"

"Y-yes," Mio stammered, surprised at hearing her job description from a stranger.

"Right!" Vito said. "Well, we're just gonna make a *safe deposit* outa this room, that's all." He snorted a little giggle at his own joke.

"Hey, man!" Jesse blurted. "You just called me Jesse."

"That's your name, ain't it?"

"Yeah, but how'd you know my name? That's what I want to know!"

Vito smiled at the young man. "Jesse, my boy, we don't always get to find out everything we want to know—know what I mean?"

The young man didn't really know what Vito meant. He just stood there, looking at the gun, trying to swallow the dry fear in his mouth.

"Jesse," Vito said, all business again, "you and me gotta lotta work to do in the next five minutes, so keep your mouth closed and your eyes and ears wide open, y'understand?"

Jesse nodded dopily, as if he were in the middle of a bad dream. Vito reached into his raincoat pocket and took out a stick of white chalk. As the three puzzled bank employees watched, Vito carefully marked two bold V-shaped notches, one at the center of each end of the conference table, each notch about four inches deep. Then he put the chalk back in his pocket.

"Jesse," he said, moving back from the table with his back to the door, "I want you to put you *left* hand in your pants pocket and walk slow to this end of the table. Good. Now turn, with your back to the table. Move a little left, so's you can see the V. . . .that's nice."

With his gun hand, Vito had slowly swung open the right side of his raincoat, carefully pointing the gun directly at Jesse throughout the move. Sewn on the inside of his coat were a series of long denim pockets, each pocket bulging with a different tool, and, wrapped many times around Vito's waist—forty feet of steel cable. Jesse's eyes bugged out at the sight of the hardware.

Vito reached across his body with his free hand, extracted a fourteen-inch cut-all saw, and laid it on the end of the table at Jesse's right hand. Jesse looked down at the saw warily, as though it were a snake about to strike.

"Oh, my *God!*" Fat Opal said, from the other end of the room.

"Please, please, ladies," Vito said. "I told you before, ain't nobody gonna be hurt, here. We just gonna see what a good carpenter Jesse is!"

Jesse looked up from the saw as though the snake had struck. "Carpenter?" He whined. "Hey, man, don't do me that way. I ain't even s'posed to *be* here!"

134

"What do ya mean, y'ain't supposed?" asked Vito, intrigued.

"I mean I always come late, man! Onliest reason I'm here first thing *this* morning is, Mr. Slack burned my ass yesterday for bein' late! Tol' me I was gonna be an outawork *nigger* if I didn't get my black butt behind my cage before nine."

"Hey, hey," said Vito sharply, waggling his gun and shaking his head, "I don't like that word!"

"Yeah, well neither do I," Jesse said, "but the Man uses any word he wants, you dig? That's how it is on the chain gang, man! Can't you see my stripes? You color-blind, or somethin'?"

Jesse was laying down the jive with a trowel, and Vito knew it. He tilted his head and looked the young black man straight in the eye. "A lot of us are on the chain gang, kid. The stripes are a little different, that's all. You and me, we'll talk about it sometime, huh? But right now, *I* am the Man, y'understand? And I want you to pick up that saw, and cut me those notches I marked on the table!"

"Say what?" Jesse asked, hearing but not believing the order.

Vito took one slow, menacing step forward. "I—don't—tease—good,—kid," he said, spacing his words out.

Jesse picked up the saw slowly and lowered it toward the chalk mark. "You really gonna ruin this expensive table, man?"

"No," Vito said evenly. "*You* gonna ruin the table, I'm just gonna show you how. Now cut!"

Jesse didn't move. Not a muscle. He just stood there, the saw in his hand, looking down at the chalk mark. Only his mind was spinning.

Vito sensed an impulse of heroism flash through Jesse's mind. "Listen to me good, Jesse! I'm gonna count to *two*, then I'm gonna pull this trigger—*twice!* Get me? Now cut, I'm tellin' ya!"

He jerked the gun downward suddenly, aiming it at Jesse's crotch. All three captives cried out at the same time.

"Oh, my God!" Opal screamed, looking away. "Something terrible's going to happen!"

"Jesse." Mio shouted, "do as he says!"

"One . . ."

"Hey, don't shoot, man," Jesse shrieked. "I'm cuttin'! Look-a-here! Jesse's cuttin'! *See? Mmm!-Mmm!-Mmm!*"

The saw was already an inch deep into the thick edge of the walnut table, heading for the point of the chalk mark. Vito watched the enthusiasm of Jesse's eager strokes, the light mist of expensive sawdust filling the air, while the two frightened women winced with each grating rasp of the saw. The saw hit the point of Vito's mark, and Jesse pulled the toool up out of the cut with a twang. He looked up at Vito, droplets of sweat starting to glisten on his forehead. Vito nodded his approval of Jesse's first cut and gestured him to proceed with an urgent wiggle of his gun.

Jesse quickly put the saw to the table edge again at the remaining chalk line.

"*Mmm! - Mmm! - Mmm!*" Jesse grunted rhythmically with each stroke.

The sharp teeth of the saw reached the point of Jesse's first cut in nothing flat, and the four-inch triangle of richly grained wood fell to the floor. Jesse looked up from the notch with a sick look on his face.

"That'sa nize!" murmured Vito, smiling like Sunny Italy. Then, with a jerk of his chin, he pointed to the other end of the table.


Six minutes to nine. Minnie saw the blue Impala with the Gerry Ford bumper-sticker in the middle of the block, poking its grill around the *putt-putt-putting* gas company rig.

"Aha! The executive car pool!" she said aloud. "You could set a clock!" A man on the bench glanced up at her from his paper for a second, then went back to his reading.

Minnie watched the car pull to the curb at the front of the bank, discharging the same two passengers she had watched arrive in the very same way, every weekday morning since she had begun her bus stop vigil for The Benefit.

"Him, and his shaa-dow . . . Both the same, and dressed in bloo-oo . . . " As she sang, Minnie was looking across Beverly at the portly branch manager, Harley Wilson, and at Burton Slack, the mortgage manager, but she was thinking about Ted Lewis and his sad spotlight.

Barnes started to turn his Chevy right onto Fairfax, heading for the parking lot behind the bank. Minnie knew this morning routine well. Wilson and Slack would stand out front, impatiently swinging their shiny briefcases, waiting for William Barnes, their assistant vice-president driver, to park his car and walk back around the building so Brubaker could open for the three of them at once. Barnes's park-and-walk-around time: twenty-two seconds.

Suddenly Barnes stopped the car in the middle of the crosswalk, cutting off in midcrossing a buxom blonde who was carrying a giant cruller and a plastic cup of coffee. Minnie watched as Angela St. Clair, teller number six, suffered the leering comments of her immediate superior. Oh, the humiliating price of job security.

"Beauty and the beast," Minnie muttered.

Angela shook her head at Barnes emphatically, her big tits bouncing with the force of her irritation, as she angrily waved the cruller at him to keep moving. One more dirty crack before the light changed, producing a crimson blush, then Angela gave Barnes a parting toss of her puffed up hairdo and sashayed around the back of his car.

"I remember exactly how you feel, sweetheart," Minnie said softly. "Go be a nice person in this world, with a build like you got!"

136

Barnes continued his turn, and Minnie started her timing count. "One . . . two . . . "

Angela flounced up onto the sidewalk and walked over to the bank building, where she plumped her ass petulantly down onto the marble ledge, a few feet from Wilson and Slack.

"Five . . . six . . . "

All of a sudden, the *rat-tat-tat-tat* of the jackhammer stopped dead. The muscular jackhammer operator pulled his goggles up to look in the direction of his frantic helper's pointing. Then he saw Angela, her legs unwittingly crossed to the point of near exposure. He pulled the big digging tool up out of its hole, leaning it against his leg as he stared.

"Fan-ta-ass-tic!" he hollered. The whole intersection could hear his macho mating call. Three other gas company guys in yellow hard hats came running around the big truck to see the object of big Joe's affection, and Joe had himself another long lustful look at the blonde with the big tits and bare thighs, sipping her morning coffee and taking the first big bite of her sugary cruller.

"Je-zuss H. Chri-ist," Big Joe screamed. "What a paira super knockers! Oh-h, would I love to split *that* up the middle tonight!"

Then, laughing, he lifted the point of his heavy jackhammer skyward and pressed the trigger-handle, setting the machine *rat-tat-tatting* in vibrating spasms. His buddies broke into loud cheering and applause as Joe balanced the thrusting one-hundred-and-fifty-pound machine, cantilevered in the air like a Herculean hard-on.

Everybody watching got the message, and a lot of people joined in the raucous laughter, as the pointed digging chisel popped out of its collar in an arcing spurt to the pavement and rolled into the gutter.

Angela's face instantly burned red, and she jumped up to turn away from the obscenity, totally humiliated. Poor Angela! Ever since she could remember—ever since she was thirteen or fourteen—the men and the boys had been doing filthy, nasty things like this to her—whistling at her on the street, grabbing a feel of her ass on the bus, elbowing her tits in elevators, exposing themselves to her in darkened movie houses, looking up her dress from under the bleachers at football games, saying all kinds of dirty, disgusting things to her, sometimes all in one steamy breath, and she just couldn't understand it. For the life of her, poor Angela just could never understand why they always picked on *her*. She never *ever* did a single thing in her whole nice life to provoke that kind of smutty disrespect. Sometimes, it made her cry.

*She* couldn't help it if a sweater looked that way just because she put it on—her tits straining the knit, her hard nipples pushing two big dimples into the wool like permanent press—could she? And she couldn't help how she walked, either. Her back was just arched that way, her ass tilted up like her nose, and her firm round buttocks swayed to each side and then up that way when she walked because that's the way the good Lord had attached her legs to her swiveling hips. It wasn't her fault that she drove every man watching into mad fantasies as she walked by in that jizzy-jazzy swaying rhythm of hers. She didn't move her body that way on purpose, for goodness sakes.

And Angela St. Clair never once put her clothes on that body of hers with the idea of driving the guys wild . . . only to be neat and clean and nice, like her sainted mother taught her, so that *nice people* would like her.

"Eighteen . . . nineteen . . . twenty!" Minnie intoned like a metronome. "Come on, Mr. Barnes—make it twenty-two seconds, like usual!"

Four minutes to nine. Minnie stood up and took off her shawl. From across the street, Oscar nodded and poked Stosh with his finger.

"Go, Stosh! She took off the shawl!"

"Okay, I go. Good luck, Oscar."

"*Forget* about good luck! Und *don't* forget the big tool box, here!"

"Oh, yeah!" Stosh lifted the steel tool box off the dolly and lumbered toward the front door of the bank.

Inside, Louie had moved Brubaker cautiously away from the wall a few feet, so he could see out the front door. "That's far enough. Now, Brubaker, look across the street!"

"But Mr. Wilson is out front!" the guard said nervously.

"Never mind Mr. Wilson!" Louie ordered. "Look across the street—the little fat lady on the bus bench!"

"But they're all here!" Brubaker argued, "Mr. Wilson and Mr. Slack, and here comes Mr. Barnes! I have to open up!"

"You'll open up when I tell you! What'sa matter, you don't see this gun anymore or what?"

"Okay, okay," Brubaker said. "The lady on the bench?" He stood up on his toes to see over the crowd at the front door. "What about her?"

"Does she have on a shawl? A dark green shawl?"

"A shawl?" Brubaker asked, peering across the street. "What are you talking about?"

"*You* don't know what I'm talking about," Louie said, "but *I* know what I'm talking! Is she wearing a shawl? Yes, or no?"

"No," Brubaker said, "she's wearing a light green sweater."

"Good!" Louie broke into a good-natured grin. "So, what are you waiting for? Open up the door for the boss!"

Brubaker knelt down to unlock the front door just as Stosh came barging around the corner behind the little knot of people waiting to get into the bank. Minnie saw the large, gold, company logo emplazoned on the back of Stosh's blue coveralls. Guardian Security Systems, it said, enclosed within a large badge-like shield.

"Hmm! That's very fancy," Minnie observed.

"Don't forget what to say!" Louis warned Brubaker as the door-lock clicked open. "And don't forget I'm here with the gun, either!"

Brubaker stood up and pulled the door wide open. Stosh, his arms outstretched to full wingspread, enclosed the small crowd from behind, cramming them all inside like a New York subway guard during the rush hour.

Harley Wilson hated for anyone to even touch him. "Here, here!" he shouted, "The bank's not open yet!"

"You can't come in here!" Slack objected, looking up at Stosh.

"I beg your pardon, gentlemen." Louie moved quickly out from the wall, waving his gun. "But the bank *is* open, and he can come in. He's with me!"

Angela saw the gun, put her hand to her mouth to stifle a little scream, and dropped her coffee all over the floor.

"Okay, everybody," Louie barked, "move over here, away from the door! Quick!"

"Move, move!" said Stosh, his arms still corralling the group as he pushed them all to one side, against the wall.

"Brubaker, lock the door!" Louie ordered.

The guard kneeled to do as he was told.

"What *is* this, Brubaker?" Wilson asked, astounded.

"Tell him!" said Louie.

"Well, sir . . . Mr. Wilson, sir . . . ".

"Tell him what I *told* you to tell him!"

"Mr. Wilson, sir," Brubaker recited, red-faced, "I'm sorry to have to tell you to put your hands behind your back, and walk slowly to the conference room, sir."

"Put my hands where and do what?" Wilson asked, outraged, ignoring Louie's gun.

"Do like he says!" Louie's eyes narrowed. "What'sa matter with you? When a man in a uniform tells you to do something, you do it! All of you!"

The employees looked at Wilson, as though watching to see which fork he would pick up to eat the salad. Wilson returned Louie's stare, then slowly put his hands behind him. The others followed suit.

"Brubaker," Wilson said, "are you involved in this?"

"We are *all* involved, Mr. Wilson, sir," Louie answered, quietly. "Enough talking, already. Walk!"

They all seemed rooted to their spots.

Stosh swung the heavy tool kit gently into Wilson's rear end, nudging him toward the conference room. The rest fell in docilely behind him, and Stosh brought up the rear, like a sheep dog herding his flock.

Inside the conference room, Vito had Jesse on top of the table, straining against the steel cable, which he had already looped around the table, through the notches, under Vito's supervision. Jesse compressed the cable-

139

tightening tool closed with a final grunt and looked to Vito for his approval. "How's that, boss?"

Vito reached over with his free hand and tested the tautness of the steel cable, pulling it up as hard as he could. "You do good work, Jesse. I'm glad I hired you."

Jesse started to get down off the table.

"No, no!" said Vito. "Stay where you are. You're not finished yet."

Vito opened his raincoat hardware store, removed the crimping tool from one of the denim pockets, and tossed it onto the table with a clatter. Both women jumped at the noise.

"Take it easy, ladies," said Vito. "Nobody gets hurt unless somebody tries something dumb. This gun ain't gonna go off by itself!"

Jesse, who had the crimping pliers in his hand, seemed to be enjoying the heft of them too much for Vito, who swung his gun back. "Ya know what I mean, Jesse?"

"Yassuh, Mistah boss!" Jesse answered eagerly. "I don't want no hole in this suit, man! Whatchyou want me to do with this thing?"

Vito fished a bunch of cable grommets out of his coat pocket and spilled them onto the table. "I want you should squeeze these collars around both pieces of cable, where they cross, about every six inches. And squeeze tight—very tight!"

"Tight. Right!" Jesse squeezed the first collar on. "I don't know what you fixin' to do, man, but you sure come ready to get the job done!"

There was a knock on the conference room door.

"What's that?" Jesse asked, as if he had never heard a knock in his life.

"Who's there?" Vito demanded, backing toward the door, his gun trained on Jesse. "Don't move, Jesse—I'm nervous enough!"

"Mr. Wilson!" shouted the testy knocker. "Open the door!"

"Oh, my God!" said Opal.

"Mr. Who?" Vito asked.

"Here is Vlasic, Vito!" Stosh yelled through the door. "I got people for you!"

"Hold them out there!" Vito hollered, "We're not ready for them yet! I need three more minutes!"

"You *slow*, Vito!"

"My assistant—he's slow!" Vito yelled back. "You hear, Jesse? You got only three minutes, so move you ass!"

"I'm movin', man! Jus' as fast as I can. I ain't no mechanic, y'know!"

"Yeah, I know." Vito was wiggling his gun at Jesse, moving it up and down, aiming at every part of him all at once. "And I ain't no real good shooter, either—y'know what I mean?"

Freshly encouraged by the prospect of bullet holes scattered over his entire person, Jesse squeezed faster and squeezed tighter, swearing and grunting and whimpering with the pain in his wrist as he tightened each

140

collar snugly around the cable, while Vito smiled and nodded his approval.

Outside, the tempo of the traffic was increasing. Minnie watched the allegro movement of the nine A.M. intersection symphony from her bus stop box seat. *Accelerando!* Faster and faster, racing toward its daily climax. Minnie's eyes darted over the scene, keeping tempo with the swirl of traffic, seeing and recording everything, totally unnoticed as she played point man at Citizens' Bank for The Benefit.

"Here he comes," said Minnie, "the Empire State Building." Floyd Davis was the easiest approaching employee to spot. He was almost seven feet tall, always got off the bus one stop early to get in his morning walk, bouncing up and down rythmically on the balls of his feet with each step, a towering, long-haired pogo stick, dominating the sidewalk traffic on his way to the bank, the ever-present law books under his arm.

"The books, the books," Minnie mused. "Always with the books. Well, listen, you gotta give him credit. If he wants to be a lawyer, he's gotta study the law, that's all."

Floyd leaned against the bank and flipped open his book of torts, knowing that Brubaker never opened up for a lone employee.

Henry McInnerny walked briskly out of the alley behind the bank and down Fairfax toward the front entrance. "He-e-ere's Henry P.!" Minnie announced, quickly standing up and removing her sweater just as McInnerny passed Oscar.

Oscar gave her a nod and started pushing the dolly slightly downhill to the corner, following McInnerny to the front door. Oscar had one hand on the dolly loaded with the explosives, and the other in his coverall pocket, on his gun.

Minnie looked across the street to her left, at Abe, rocking back and forth from one foot to the other. She knew what that meant—Abe and his nervous pee whenever he was about to go onstage. His cue was coming up, and she could see his moustache twitching in tickly discomfort. "Tough luck, Silver," she said. "You'll just have to wait. It wouldn't kill you."

Only a few more to come. If they came together, she and Abe would cross together. If they straggled, Abe would go first, and she would follow Abe, escorting the last one or two into the bank by herself.

Inside, Brubaker was getting into the spirit of things. "She took it off!" he announced excitedly. "She took off her sweater!"

"How many people?" Louie asked.

"Two," Brubaker answered. "Mr. McInnerny and—" He stopped at the sound of an insistent metallic tapping on the glass door.

Louie jumped at the noise. "What's that, what's that?"

"Aw, that's just Mr. McInnerny," said Brubaker. "He always clicks a coin against the glass—can't wait to get in! He's a pain in the ass, pardon my French."

"So? Let the pain in the ass in." Louie said.

"Yeah, right." Brubaker knelt to unlock the door.

As the door swung open, Oscar started to push the dolly inside, but McInnerny suddenly grabbed the front of the dolly, stopping it on the sidewalk. Oscar's hand tightened around his gun.

"Just a moment, here!" said McInnerny officiously, "Who are *you* with?"

"I?"Oscar asked, as if it were a stupid question. "I am with Guardian Security Systems, of course." And he pointed to the logo on the pocket of his blue coveralls.

McInnerny looked at the logo and back up at Oscar. "You're here kind of early, aren't you, Tommy?"

Oscar resisted the reflex he felt to glance down at the name on the pocket. "You call, we come," he shrugged, "no matter what time. 'Malfunction of timer on the vault'—my partner is already inside."

"Oh! Right. Sorry to hold you up," McInnerny apologized. "You can't be too careful in a bank, you know. Here, let me give you a hand with that."

Minnie couldn't believe it. McInnerny rolled the explosives inside, followed by Floyd Davis, his nose still in his book, followed by Oscar, who turned and winked at her as the door closed. The she saw Brubaker relock the door, the short scuffle of confusion, the people moving away from the door, and she knew that everything was going according to plan.

There was another loud knock on the conference room door.

"Don't get your water hot!" yelled Vito. "We need another minute, goddamn it! *Aspette!*"

"Okay, Vito," Stosh yelled, "I give you *one more* minute, but I got big crowd people here, you know?"

"Yeah, yeah," said Vito. "In a minute!"

Jesse gave a final grunt as he cinched the last collar tight and let the crimping pliers fall out of his sore hand onto the table.

"Good job, Jesse," said Vito. "Now slide the pliers down to me, *easy*."

Jesse slid the tool down to Vito's end of the table. He picked it up, watching Jesse carefully, and replaced it in a denim pocket in his raincoat.

"Now what?" Jesse asked, sitting cross-legged on the table, sweating from every pore.

"Two more quick jobs, and we let the people in!"

"Two?" Jesse moaned, exhausted. "You kiddin' me, man. I ain't used to this manual labor."

"A-ay, Jesse," Vito said, jerking his gun, "I don't wanna hafta fire you, get what I mean?"

"I can dig it, man!" Jesse held up his hands. "I was just jivin', you know? What you want me to do?"

"Lemme see you stand on the table," Vito said, "and pull up on that cable."

"Hey, man! That's an easy one!" Jesse straddled the cable as he pulled up on it, hard. The cable came up off the surface of the table only about four inches, at the center.

142

"Perfect!" said Vito. "Only one more job."

Vito opened his raincoat and removed a pair of wire cutters. He slid the tool onto the table.

"What you want me to do with these?" Jesse asked, taking the cutters.

"Cut the phone."

"You gotta be puttin' me on, man. I mean, this *here's* just a thousand dollar table, but this big white mother is the whole damn telephone company, you dig? They'd fry my black ass if I cut *this* thing, man!"

Vito studied the young man for a moment. "Okay, Jesse, I respect your respect for other people's property, see? So I ain't gonna force you. Just slide the cutters back down here."

"That's cool, man," Jesse said gratefully, sliding the cutters.

Vito picked them up and moved toward the table. "Okay, Jesse, get off the end of the table and stand with the ladies, down there." Jesse did as he was told, the two women looking at him with a new respect.

"*I'm* gonna take the responsibility for the phone," said Vito, moving cautiously to the instrument. "It's only right." He leaned over the table and with one clean snip of the cutters severed the thick wire at the base of the instrument. The white phone cord slithered over the edge of the table and fell to the floor like a dead snake.

"Oh, my God!" said Opal, delivering the eulogy.

"Okay, Jesse." Vito snapped. "Put the phone under the table, quick!"

Jesse hesitated.

"Hey, Vito!" Stosh yelled in, "Louie wants to know what's the holdup?"

"Come on, Jesse," Vito barked, "grab the phone! It's disconnected. Ma Bell will never even know you touched it!" Jesse came forward slowly. He picked up the instrument, flinching as if he expected it to ring in his hand, and set it gingerly on the floor under the end of the table.

"Farther under! The wire too." Vito said.

Jesse kneeled and moved it a little farther under the table, on top of its cord.

"Okay," Vito said quietly. "I think we're ready for company."

Vito was sweating now, too. Cautiously, he backed to the door, his gun still covering his captives. "All right, Stosh," he shouted. "I'm ready for your people! I'm gonna open the door, and I want 'em to come in, one at a time, turn right, and walk to the end of the room." Vito opened the door.

Minnie checked her watch. Two minutes past nine.

"Why are they late?" she said. "Don't they know it's not nice to keep a person waiting on a cold corner?" She pulled part of her shawl back onto her lap, and resumed her scanning of the intersection.

"Well! It's about time!"

There. The last arrivals, off the bus on her corner—the beautiful people, windows one and four, the Washintons, Lowina and Sidney—no relationship except for color and after work, ha-ha. As they alighted, Minnie

143

watched Sidney touch Lowina tenderly on the cheek. He kissed her full mouth gently, their bodies close, in the shadow of the bus. Then, as they turned, he gave her a pat on the fanny, a loving till-tonight smile, and their daily good-bye was completed. Lowina waited for the light to change at the direct-route crosswalk, and Sidney ran to make it the long way across Fairfax, then Beverly, then back across Fairfax again to greet her innocently at the front door of the bank.

Suddenly Minnie saw the dirty white station wagon pull to the curb in front of the bank.

"My God, I don't believe it! She should be home already, with that belly. Oh, boy, have we got a problem!"

A bus, blocked behind the station wagon, was honking at the driver of the wagon stopped at the section of red curb. The honking didn't bother Betty Lundy, Mr. Wilson's very pregnant private secretary. She kissed each of her three little kids in the back, and then rolled to her left to kiss her bespectacled husband at the wheel.

"She shouldn't even be *touching* him, for goodness sakes!" Minnie said. "She's gotta be in her eighth month, at least!"

Betty Lundy managed to roll herself out of the station wagon, miraculously landing her two swollen feet on the sidewalk. She whirled on the rude hissing bus, puffed her cheeks out, and held her big belly between her two hands like a watermelon at the woman bus driver. The passengers at the front of the bus burst out laughing.

The bus driver shrugged a how-was-I-to-know apology, as the station wagon pulled away from the curb. The three little kids were waving good-bye to their mother out the rear window, and the little white plastic statuette of Jesus was swaying on its chain from the rearview mirror.

Sidney and Lowina applauded loudly as Betty joined them at the front door.

"Oh, my God!" Minnie said. "I'm so busy watching the bouncing belly, I forgot the shoe!"

Quickly she leaned over and undid her left shoe, holding it up and waggling it for Abe to see, just as a bus at her bench revved up its engine, spewing the gaseous fumes right in Minnie's face.

Abe saw the shoe and took four giant steps to the corner while Minnie scrambled to get her shoe back on her foot, just as the bus door closed and the bus pulled away.

Minnie looked up, staring in disbelief at her shawl as it disappeared under somebody's arm, boarding the getaway bus.

"Hey, stop, stop!" she hollered after the bus. "Somebody is stealing my shawl! He-ey!" She ran after the bus for a few yards, the people on the sidewalk scattering out of her way. The bus, of course, was deaf.

"Did you see that?" Minnie asked the people standing around. "Some-body got on the bus with my shawl, *in broad daylight!* Did you see?"

144

Each passerby she appealed to quickly turned away. After all, who wants to become a witness to a shawl-snatching?

"Can you imagine?" Minnie continued to wail. "Right in front of my eyes! What kind of a world is this? A person isn't safe on the streets—"

Minnie cut herself off as she saw Abe, already across Beverly, waving at her and hopping from foot to foot as he waited for the light to cross Fairfax to the bank. She scooped up her sweater from the bench, grabbed the shopping basket, and quick-waddled into the crosswalk.

DON'T WALK was flashing, Minnie was running, her untied shoe was gallumping, her purse was flapping, the cars were starting, Abe was crossing, and Brubaker was jumping up and down inside the bank like he was watching O. J. Simpson go off-tackle from the five-yard line on the last play of a game.

"She made it!" Brubaker screamed at Louie. "She scared the shit outa me. A VW almost hit her, making a right. Jesus Christ, you shoulda seen her."

"Never mind the hollering, Brubaker," Louie said. "The VW was lucky, believe me. Open up!"

Brubaker knelt to unlock the door for the last three employees and the last two bank robbers. As the door opened, Minnie and Abe shoved the startled trio stumbling into the bank, Minnie taking care not to push Betty too hard.

"Here, here!" Louie said, waving his gun. "Over here, people, away from the door. Don't make a noise. No, no! Don't put your hands up! I didn't say 'stick-'em-up!' Why does everybody hold up their hands when you point a gun? Move over here. Lock up, Brubaker!"

They all put their hands down and moved away from the door as Brubaker locked it.

Abe broke into a trot toward the back of the bank.

"Hey," Louie yelled at him, "where the hell do you think you're going?"

"I don't think!" Abe shouted over his shoulder, "I know exactly where I'm going! I'll tell you about it when I get back, if you want!" And he skidded into the men's room.

"Is this a holdup, or what?" Sidney asked, looking around the bank. "Where is everybody?"

"Your friend Mr. Brubaker here will tell you all about it," Louie said.

"Good morning, folks," Brubaker said, getting up. "The bank is being held up this morning, but they have assured us that—"

Betty Lundy gasped, grabbing Sidney's arm for support.

"But, you're not going to—" said Sidney.

"Nobody's going to be hurt," Brubaker said quickly. "All we have to do is keep calm and cooperate."

"*Keep calm?*" Betty shrieked. "I didn't even come to work this morning! Yesterday was my last day! I just came in to clear my desk and take some things home! My husband is coming back for me during his lunch hour!"

"Lady, lady," Louie shouted, "take it easy. Nobody's hurting you. Just listen quiet. He'll tell you what to do. Everything will be—"

"Wait a minute!" Sidney said. "You don't mean to say you're going to keep a pregnant woman in here while a holdup's going on!"

"Whata ya lookin' at me like that?" Louie asked. I didn't make her pregnant, did I?"

"That's not very funny, mister," said Lowina, who seemed to be holding her breath all this time. "A lot of very serious things can happen to a woman this close to her time, if she—"

"Yes, I know, little girl," Louie said. "Also a lotta serious things might not happen at all if she *is* here. Go ahead with the instructions, Brubaker."

Brubaker put a gentle hand on Betty's shoulder, talking quietly. "We've got to do as they say, Betty. The bank's funds are insured, and we don't want anybody to get hurt, do we?"

"What about this poor woman?" Sidney pointed at Minnie. "You're not going to keep her in here, too, are you? She's not a bank employee, she's just a customer!"

"Boy-oh-boy!" Minnie laughed. "Have you got the wrong customer! Wait, I'll show you!"

She dug down into her purseful of junk, finally coming out with a huge old revolver, which she held expertly pointed at the ceiling. They all took a flinching step backward.

"I am no customer today," Minnie said. "Today, I am the official housemother, that's what I am!"

Sidney shook his head in disbelief. "Lowina," he said, "do you believe this is happening?"

Lowina shook her head the very same way. "I surely do not."

Brubaker stepped back in to complete his spiel of welcome. "All right, folks, we want you to clasp your hands behind your backs and I'll walk you calmly to the conference room. You'll receive further instructions there."

They all started to move.

"Wait a minute, wait a minute!" Louie wiggled a gimme-gimme hand at Brubaker. "I'll take the keys now, Lefty."

"Oh, yeah." Brubaker started to undo the keyholder attached to his holster belt.'

"No, no!" Louie said. "Just take off the whole thing—the belt, the holster, everything."

"But this belt holds my pants up."

"Never mind." Louie said. "That's not your responsibility anymore. We'll take care of your pants. Don't worry! Just take off the whole belt and slide it to me on the floor."

Brubaker did as he was told, sheepishly holding his loose trousers up with both his hands when the belt was removed. Just then, Abe came

146

waltzing out of the men's room with a relaxed smile on his face, rubbing his hands together in anticipation of the exciting day ahead.

"Reporting for duty, sir," he said to Louie, stiff-arming a salute. "Waiting out in the cold is hard on the plumbing, you know?"

Louie's eyes narrowed at the mock salute. "No horsing around, Abe, I'm warning you."

"Who's horsing? I'm not horsing, honest."

"You better not!" Louie picked up Brubaker's belt. "Here, take this to Stosh, and find out if Vito is ready for these people. And hurry up—it's a quarter after already!"

Abe took the belt and holster. "The keys, too?"

"Yeah, the keys too! And Abe, will you please take off those goddamn dark glasses? I'm lookin' at you, and I'm talking to myself!"

"You don't like my glasses?" Abe asked, hurt. "I thought they made me look . . . you know—"

"Abe," Minnie said, in her deepest do-it-now voice, "take off the glasses!"

"Okay, okay!" Abe walked back to Stosh with the belt, pocketing the dark glasses and muttering as he went.

In the conference room, Vito had all the hostages at the far end in a straggling line against the wall. Most of them were quiet, but Wilson and Slack were whispering to each other in terse conspiracy.

"A-ay, you two!" Vito pointed his gun at them. "Spread apart! I don't want no talkin' till I get yez all sittin' down, get me?" The two men moved apart. "Okay, let's see," Vito said, considering the seating arrangement. "You! You, Wilson!"

"Are you speaking to me?" Wilson asked, looking around.

"You're Wilson, ain't ya?"

"Yes, I am but—"

"Then don't gimme no buts! I hate buts! *Capish?*" Vito poked his gun forward for emphasis. "We're gonna get started with the sittin' down. Wilson, you go to that end. Just put your briefcase on the sideboard, there, and sit in the head chair. Now!"

Wilson slowly placed his case on the credenza and sat in the chair, contemplating the place where the telephone belonged on the table as though it were his navel.

"You look good there," Vito said, nodding. "Your the bossa this here bank, it's only right you sit at the heada the table, right?"

Wilson's answer was a sarcastic tightening of his lips.

"Okay, next. . . .You!" Vito was looking at Mio. "What's you name?"

"Me?" her voice cracked, and she cleared her throat. "My name is Mio Yamaguchi."

"Yeah, right," said Vito. "You just sit down there nexta the boss. You'll be the boss's right hand girl today!"

Mio sat, silently looking at her folded hands as if they held prayer beads and the answer to her quiet fear.

Abe poked his head into the conference room. "Hey, Vito, we got some more customers for you. Louie wants to know are you ready for them?"

"Any girls?" asked Vito, not even turning his head.

"Girls?" Abe asked, bewildered.

"Yeah, *girls*. You forgot what are girls?"

"Yes, there are, uh, two girls . . . "Abe said. "Why?"

"Never mind. I know why," Vito said. "How many men?"

"One."

"Two to one—good," Vito said. "Send 'em in."

Abe handed Stosh the holster belt and walked back toward the front of the bank, shaking his head as if to rattle up some sense out of the conversation he'd just had. "He's ready," he said to Louie, halfway there.

"All right, Minnie," Louie said, "they're all yours. Take 'em back."

Minnie lowered her gun and smiled sweetly at her charges , all three of whom returned her disarming smile with the staring eyes of held-in terror, like kindergarten kids on their first day of school.

"Don't be afraid," Minnie said, motioning for them to start walking. "Nobody will get hurt today, if you are good little boys and girls, understand?" The Washingtons nodded dumbly, and they all started walking back toward the conference room, Minnie and her gun bringing up the rear.

"Tell Stosh to come up here, right away!" Louie shouted after Minnie. His gun still held Brubaker, who was busy holding his pants up.

"Okay, Minnie," Vito said, when they reached the conference room, "send 'em in here. I'll have 'em all ready for you in a coupla minutes." The new trio marched into the room, and Vito saw Betty Lundy. *"Mamma mia!"* he cried, slapping his forehead. "Hey, Minnie, we gonna *keep* this lady with the baby?"

"That's right, Vito. Louie says we keep everybody."

"But Minnie," Vito said, "a lady with a baby!"

"Vito," Minnie snapped, "Louie *says!* she turned and whispered to Stosh, who headed for the front.

"'Louie says,' 'Louie says!'" Vito shook his head. "I hope Louie knows what he's doin'!"

Slack had moved back close to Wilson and was whispering something to him, gesturing furtively toward the floor under the table.

"Hey, you!" Vito hollered. "I told you, no talkin'!"

Slack backed away from Wilson. "May I ask just one question?"

"Yeah, sure. Ask."

"Just what is it you intend doing to us?" Slack's eyes were shifting nervously back and forth.

Vito looked at the man as though he had just been accused of kicking a crippled dog. "Doing to you? We din't come in here to do nothin' to you!"

148

"Then why do you have us all in here, threatening us with your guns?" Wilson wanted to know. "And what is the meaning of this cable cut into this beautiful conference table?"

"Oh-hh, please! I'm sorry I didn't explain everything to yez in advance!" said Vito.

"Vito, Vito," Minnie said, "keep it moving, already!"

"Yeah, right." Vito agreed. "Now I'll tell ya what we're gonna do. You people are gonna sit down at this table, boy-girl-boy-girl, until we run outa girls. I'll tell ya who sits where. You!" He pointed his gun at Slack. "Yeah, you, with the question. You sit next to Safety Deposit there."

Slack looked at Mio as if he was checking the next seat in a movie house, and sat down.

"That's right," Vito continued. "Okay, next. You, the pretty one." He meant Lowina. "You sit next to *him*."

Vito saw the flash of distaste on Slack's face as Lowina sat down next to him, and so did Minnie. Sidney had maneuvered around so that he was standing next to Lowina, and now he was pulling out the chair next to hers.

"You wanna sit there?" Vito asked him. "That's okay—sit. Let's start down the other side, see how we come out here. . . . You —Blondie!"

If looks could kill, Vito would have dropped dead on the spot.

"My name is not Blondie!" she said, the ice crackling. "My name is Angela."

"No kiddin'!" said Vito. "I gotta niece somewheres named Angie!"

"My name is not Angie, either!" she corrected him. "My name is Angela. A-N-G-E-L-A!"

"A-ay, you're a very good speller! You go to the heada the class, right next to Mr. Wilson there. Sit down! And you can bet your sweet ass I'll remember your name, Angie!"

Angela tossed her head and sat down next to Wilson. This was going to be a terrible day for Angela, she just knew it. This morning, there was Barnes. In the crosswalk, he promised again today to give her the thirty-five dollars for her torn bra. Imagine! A grown man, married too, with a good job, trying to tear her sweater off in the photocopy room, forcing her up against the machine, groping at her, actually wrestling with her as she tried to fight him off, until one of her special custom-made brassieres just tore right in two. And for what? Just to get one of his sweaty hands on her tits.

What did they see in that, anyway? What pleasure did they get? Her huge breasts had always been just a burden to *her*. How many times she had wished that she were flat-chested, and skinny, and absolutely unattractive to the male animal, because that's all a man *was* to Angela—a vicious, wild-eyed beast with fourteen pairs of grabbing hands. She felt so dirty when she told the priest about Barnes at confession, even though *she* hadn't done anything sinful—she was only the victim.

At the front of the bank, Brubaker was now swimming in Stosh's blue

149

coveralls, sleeves and pantlegs rolled up, mocked by the large gold letters on his back, Guardian Security Systems, and by the name on his breast pocket, Hector.

Stosh was stuffed into Brubaker's bank guard uniform, looking like a teenager in sprout at the wrists and ankles as he tried to figure out how the belt and holster were supposed to go on.

"That holster won't fit on your right side, you know," Brubaker said.

"Whatta ya talkin' about?" Louie asked. "Why not?"

"Because it's a left handed holster."

"Oh, sure!" Louie scoffed. "And I suppose your gun is a left-handed gun, too!"

"That's right," Brubaker said.

"How about the bullets?" Abe asked. "They're left-handed, too?"

"Listen, Brubaker," Louie said roughly, poking his gun at him. "You're in a rotten position to be playing April Fool jokes with us."

"Honestly, I'm *not* playing—"

"Hey, Louie," said Stosh, puzzled, "he's right. This gun holder goes on right on *left* side, but wrong on *right* side."

"Are you crazy?" Louie said. "Lemme see that thing!"

Stosh handed him the gun belt. Louie held the belt around his waist in both hands, sliding the holster along the belt to his right hip, then to his left hip, then to his right again, while they all watched. Louie was getting dizzy from the turning and the looking down.

Suddenly Brubaker saw his chance. He lunged at Louie and swatted the gun out of his hand. The gun went flying up against the wall at the front, with Brubaker after it. Louie tried to grab Brubaker as he leaped past him, but he was off balance and could only brush Brubaker's sleeve before he stumbled and fell, sliding across the shiny floor, stopping against the teller's counter. Brubaker dove the last nine or ten feet, grabbing for the gun, but it went skittering off along the wall as Abe, galvanized into sudden hysteria, started yelling, "Oh, my God, God, God!" and aiming his gun with both hands at Brubaker, who was scrambling for Louie's gun on his hands and knees. As Abe yelled, Stosh bounded toward the fallen guard, arms spread high, screaming, "Goddaa-aam!" Brubaker got hold of the gun and flipped onto his back to face the onrushing Pole, screaming, "Freeze!" But the sleeves of Stosh's oversized coveralls had come unrolled in the melee and completely covered the gun in Brubaker's hand. Abe hollered, "Stop, stop!" as Brubaker struggled to free the barrel of the gun from the sleeve, but it was too late. The angry Polish giant was airborne, diving at Brubaker right in the line of fire of Abe's gun. And when he landed, it was like a ten-ton human drop hammer, crunching his prone opponent instantly unconscious against the wall with a sickening, floorshaking thud. The gun dribbled out of Brubaker's sleeve and onto the floor.

150

Oscar came loping out of the safety deposit room, his gun in his hand, to peer over the counter at the source of the commotion. He saw an eerie, frightening scene. Abe stood there, frozen, his face ash-white, whimpering incoherently as he held the gun in both his shaking hands, his trigger finger half tightened, still aiming the weapon directly at Stosh, who lay gasping for breath atop the motionless Brubaker.

From his place on the floor, up against the counter, Louie saw Abe's panic. Just then, Minnie came running around the corner to see what all the yelling was about. Louie stopped her in her tracks with a quick hand up and a finger to his lips. As Minnie stared at Abe's shaking back, Louie very slowly lifted himself to a sitting position. Stosh remained stock-still on his back, staring into the barrel of the gun.

"Abe . . . " Louie's tone was calm, soothing.

"Yes, Louie?" Abe whispered hoarsely, locked in his paralyzed position, his eyes popping with fear.

"Abe . . . I want you to listen to me—very carefully."

"Okay, Louie." Abe trembled as if he were holding onto a high voltage wire he couldn't let go of.

"Abe . . . you are *all right*," Louie continued. "I want you to . . . very slow, lift your hands . . . straight up to the ceiling. Can you do that for me?"

"I'll try, Louie. . . . " Abe's jaw tightened, the muscles bulging out in little spasms of effort as he concentrated on Louie's instruction. Then, in a painful slow motion, as if the gun weighed twenty pounds, Abe's hands began to rise, until at last he was pointing it almost straight up at the ceiling. Stosh was still holding his breath as his eyes followed the gun barrel upward. Minnie's lips were praying soundlessly.

"All right, Abe," Louie said softly. "That's high enough. Now I want you . . . very slow, now . . . to *loosen* your finger on the trigger. Loosen very slow."

Abe stood there, teeth clenched, sweat rolling down his neck, as he stared up at his trembling hands.

"Abe? Did you hear me?" Louie asked gently.

"Yes, Louie. I heard." Abe's voice shook like his hands. He closed his eyes tightly, exerting all his will on the muscles in his hand that would release the locked trigger finger.

"I want you to tell me when it's loose," Louie said.

"I think . . . it's loose," Abe whispered, his eyes still closed.

"You think—or you know?"

"Yes," Abe said with a sigh, "it's loose." He opened his eyes.

"Don't move yet, Abe! Now listen . . . I want you to pull your finger *out* of the trigger hole . . . and tell me when it's out."

Minnie clasped her hands together and looked upward. Abe held his

151

breath, watching his finger as though it belonged to somebody else's hand. Slowly, the cramped forefinger uncoiled and came out of the trigger guard, straightening along the barrel of the gun.

"Louie, it's out!" Abe said, breathing again. "My finger is out!"

"Thank God," Minnie said. "Thank God!"

"Stay right there, Abe!" Louie said firmly. "*Don't move!*"

Stosh and Minnie watched as Louie got up and walked quietly to Abe's side. He reached high above Abe's head, gripping the barrel of the gun firmly in his hand. "Okay, Abe. You can leggo the gun."

Louie held the gun in place aloft while Abe gingerly straightened his fingers, releasing the weapon. Like two leaden weights, his hands fell to his side.

Minnie ran to him, taking him into her arms, comforting him as he began to cry in relief. "*Shah, shah,*" she kept saying, "it's all right, Abe. Everything is all right. *Shah, shah.*"

Oscar saw his exit cue and retreated to the safety deposit room. "*Ach, widerlich!*" he muttered. "*Dumm Narren!*" And his agile fingers worked like little precision machines as he spliced the wires from the thermite pans to the dynamite cluster to the blasting box. The soldered joints could have passed muster with any government inspector. There would be no misfiring if Louie decided that they had to use their ultimate weapon.

The brace of wires crisscrossed the floor of the Safety Deposit room, the taped dynamite sticks were capped, and Oscar was almost ready for Vito and his keys.

Stosh and Louie looked down at Brubaker, crumpled on the floor, his legs pretzled under him, and bleeding from his nose and mouth.

"Goddamn fool!" Stosh said, shaking his head.

"Never mind," Louie said. "He was just doing his job. Go get some wet paper towels from the restroom. We'll wake him up and clean up this blood."

Louie took off his overcoat, rolled it into a pillow, and put it under Brubaker's head. He straightened the guard's legs and saw that the man was coming to his senses.

"Did you see?" Abe asked Louie, as he pulled away from Minnie. "I almost pulled the trigger! I almost *killed* that stupid idiot!"

Stosh came running back out of the men's room with the wet towels.

"You hear, you dumb Polack?" Abe screamed at him. "You almost made me kill you!"

"What you talk?" Stosh handed Louie the wet towels. "You couldn't kill mouse! Flea, maybe. But not Stanislaus Vlasic! Only God will kill Vlasic— on a day when He is very, very strong, and I am very, very tired!" Then he put his arm around Abe's shoulder and gave him a medium squeeze, laughing his deep laugh.

152

"It's not funny, Stosh!" Abe said, still shaken. "You jumped right in front of my gun!"

"I know, I know," Stosh said. "But better *without* gun. Then nobody get hurt."

"Nobody get hurt?" Louie mocked him as he dabbed at Brubaker's bloody face. "You almost squashed this man into a pancake."

"Couldn't help, Louie. You saw—he was pointing gun!"

"I know, I know," Louie said. "All right, the emergency is over. Get back to your jobs, all of you. Minnie, go back with Vito. Abe, get the TVs—they go on in a coupla minutes!"

"But that's Vito's job." Abe complained.

"Vito's busy, Abe. Do like I tell ya!" Louie said sternly, and Abe scooted obediently toward the rear of the bank.

Stosh retrieved the gun belt, putting it to his waist again. "Louie, how I gonna use left-handed gun belt and left-handed gun?"

Louie looked up at the giant. "Stosh, who are you today?"

Stosh frowned at the riddle for a moment. "Oh-hh," he said, "I am bank guard today! Right?"

"Ri-ight!" said Louie. "So if you are bank guard today—"

"I am left-handed today! Okay!"

"Okay!" Louie said, anointing him with a squeezing spritz of wet paper towel. Stosh flinched at the sudden cold spray, then smiling broadly at his leader, he buckled on Brubaker's belt, with the holster on his left hip.

Vito had all the hostages seated in the conference room, except Jesse. There were only three chairs empty, and Jesse started to sit in one, leaving a seat between McInnerny and himself.

"No, no, Jesse," Vito said, "I still got work for you!"

Jesse made a sour face. "Aw-ww, man, why'ncha get off my case?"

"Just push the chair into the table, Jesse," Vito said.

"Don't worry," Minnie said. "He's gonna save it for you, I promise."

Alternatives tumbled through Jesse's mind as he looked at the men at the table and then back at Vito's gun. He sighed and pushed the chair against the table.

"That's a good boy!" Vito smiled. "Now, you see this tool kit, here? I wantcha to pick it up and put it on the table."

As Jesse turned to move toward the box, Wilson and Slack exchanged a glance, and Wilson quick-peeked under the table. He saw the telephone, not more than six inches from his feet. Jesse bent down and lifted the heavy metal tool box, setting it gently on the table.

"Okay, Jesse," said Vito. "Now open it, and dump it out ona table."

"*Dump* it?" Jesse asked.

"Yeah, yeah! I'm talkin' English, ain't I? Dump it out!"

Jesse opened the box and dumped the contents out onto the table. The clattering pile of handcuffs and steel locks sent a fearful chill through everyone at the table. They all spoke out at once.

"Oh, my God!" Opal gasped, predictably.

"What the hell—?" Slack started.

"Oh, mercy!" McInnerny said.

"Oh, no!" Angela shrieked.

"Jesus Christ!" Barnes said.

"See here, now!" Wilson shouted, jumping to his feet. "You can't—"

"Quiet! *Quiet!*" Vito yelled above the tumult, sweeping the room with his gun. "Everybody *shut up* and *sit down*, I'm tellin' ya!"

Vito's sudden anger quieted the room abruptly. Even Wilson shut his mouth.

"That's better!" Vito said, simmering down. "What's-a-matter with you people? Don't you know a man with a gun can get nervous with all that noise?"

"Excuse me," Wilson said very quietly, "but I want you to realize I am responsible for the safety of these employees, and I—"

"Excuse me," Minnie cut in, "but today, *we* are responsible for them— and you! Don't worry. We are going to take very good care of everybody, Mr. Wilson."

"This bank holdup is a federal crime," Wilson persisted. "I suppose you know that, don't you?"

"Holdup?" Minnie was astonished. "What makes you think this is a holdup? This is no holdup!"

"It's not a —?" Wilson stared at her incredulously. "Then what is it?"

Minnie stared back at the man, her fat arms akimbo, her chubby little fists planted firmly on her hips. "Mr. Wilson," she said finally, "as far as you are concerned, this is a *sit-in*. And if you know what is good for you, you will sit down and shut up—excuse my language—and you will do as you are told! Understand?"

Wilson sat back down.

"Come on, Vito, get going!" Minnie continued. "The vault is gonna pop open in five minutes."

"You heard the lady, Jesse," Vito said. "*Rapido, rapido!*"

"*Rapido* what, man?"

"Come on, Jesse, you're no dummy. You ain't kiddin' *me!* You are gonna put these on those and lock them to this!" As he spoke, he pointed from the cuffs to the hostages, then he snapped the cable up from the table with a *twang-splat* that made everybody jump, especially Jesse. "Okay, Jesse. Pick up one paira cuffs and one lock. We'll start with Mr. Wilson."

Jesse did as he was told, approaching Wilson with the cuffs like he was walking the last mile. "I'm sorry, Mr. Wilson," he said, snapping the handcuff on Wilson's left wrist.

154

Wilson looked up at him suspiciously. "Are you in on this business, Williams?"

"No, sir!" Jesse said, snapping the cuff closed on Wilson's right wrist. "I'm just doin' like the man says! He got the big gun, and I'm my mama's only son! Know what I mean?"

Slack shot the scat-poet a sharp dirty look. Jesse caught it and returned a big Uncle Tom smile, wide open and dripping with honeyed venom.

"Whatcha want me to do with this, man?" Jesse asked Vito, holding up the small lock in his hand.

"That," said Vito, "goes through the middle link in the handcuffs—around your cable, and then ya lock it. Simple?"

"Yeah, man." Jesse took hold of the connecting chain between Wilson's handcuffs. "Through the middle link, like *this*, ooh! And around the cable, like *that*, ow! Then a snap like *that*, mmm-mm! Yeah, man, that's what that *is*, all right—sho' nuff simple! And bad!"

Jesse was smiling a real smile now. The shackles were on the big white mastah, for a change, and he just couldn't hide the pleasure of it.

Securely fastened to the conference table, Wilson looked up at Jesse with a pink-slip look in his eye. Everybody in the room knew it for what it was.

It was no surprise to Jesse, either. For weeks McInnerny had been on his back for his tardiness. And Slack had taken a fiendish delight in chewing him out for entry errors at least twice a day since he went to work at the window. He would poke Jesse in the chest with a stiff finger and say, "I'se gwine hafta put yo' black ass to the backa the bus, boy—lessen you learn two an' two is *fo'*! You is infectin' our nice new computer system with your own *illiteracy!* Get me, nigger?"

Every time he'd back Jesse up against the wall near the men's room for one of his darky dialect lectures, Jesse had to fight the urge to zip out the knife he always carried in his back pocket.

As for Mr. Wilson, he had paid more attention to Jesse in the last five minutes than he had the whole year he had worked at the bank. Wilson seemed to have that executive knack of looking right through black, as if it wasn't even there. And now, Jesse knew damn well that this was his last day at Citizens' bank.

"You comfortable, Mr. Wilson?" Jesse asked solicitously.

"I'm fine, Williams," Wilson replied. "Just fine."

"Wait a minute," Vito said. "Lemme see ya lift your hands to your chin."

Wilson tried to reach his chin. He made it about halfway, the handcuffs hurting the top of his wrists when the cable abruptly cut short the upward movement of his hands.

"Perfect." Vito smiled proudly at Minnie. "Okay, Jesse, next."

"Who's next, boss?" Jesse asked as he picked up another pair of cuffs and a lock.

"We do all the men first," Vito said, pointing at Slack. "Him. He's next."

Jesse's eyes gleamed as he bent eagerly to his assignment. Slack knew damn well that Jesse hated his guts. And Jesse knew he knew it.

"Take it easy, boy," Slack warned, as Jesse took hold of his wrist.

"I ain't your boy today, Massa Slack," Jesse jived, pointing at Vito. "I is *his* boy! See that big black pistola?"

"This is no time to fool around, Williams!"

"I know it's no time to fool around," Jesse said, putting the cuffs on Slack. "And you know what? I ain't!"

"He's just doing what I tell him to do, Mr. Slack," Vito said. "Tighter, Jesse!"

"Yes, sir!" Jesse squeezed Slack's handcuffs closed tight enough to lift the man's ass right up off his seat, then he snapped the lock around the cable. "You okay, Mister Slack?" Jesse asked.

Slack did not answer. Jesse had not expected an answer.

"Come on, Jesse, let's keep it movin'," Vito said. "Blondie's boyfriend's next."

Vito was pointing at Barnes, and Angela flushed crimson as Jesse moved between them with a pair of handcuffs and a lock. Barnes was an okay guy to Jesse most of the time, but Barnes was into ethnic familiarity. It was his way of convincing all the green and purple people that he had a heart full of brotherhood and not even a scintilla of racism in his lilywhite soul. He was too thick-skinned to know it, but he was a repulsive pain in the ass to Jesse when he came on this way.

"Hey, my main man," he once said to Jesse, in the men's room, "I know you black dudes are sexually superior to us whiteys! And I can handle that, you know? But I'm really curious, man. Make me privy to the dimensions. Just how big a dangle you hangin' man? Ten inches? Twelve? Come on, Jesse, you can trust me with your secret, man!"

"Shi-it, man, whatchyou talkin' about?" Jesse said, trying to be cool.

"Come on, man," Barnes said, "lay it out right here on the sink. I will, too, even though I know I'm going to suffer by comparison."

Jesse looked at Barnes standing there leering, holding the tab of his zipper at the ready. He felt sickened, a dull nausea welling up. Barnes had started these slimy conversations before, and Jesse wasn't too good at handling them. He only knew he had to cut them off, terminate them, before he did something crazy like vomit on the man, or grab him by the throat.

"Come on, Jesse, zip down and haul that meat out!"

"Mister Barnes," Jesse said, trying to control his voice, "I may be your meat out there in the bank, but not in this room, dig? This room is off limits, and right now you are gamblin' with *my* limits, you know what I mean, man?"

Barnes stood there with his jaw hanging slack, as Jesse tossed his used

156

paper towel into the wastebasket and walked out of the men's room, shaking his head in disgust.

Vito snapped his fingers hurry-up, and Jesse attached Barnes to the cable with a snap of a lock. "You are perfectly safe now, girl!" Jesse told Angela as he pointed to the handcuffs on Barnes. "See? No hands!"

It was just too much for Angela. She bent forward onto the table, her head in her arms, her shoulders heaving as she burst into tears. Jesse jumped back, as if he had just stepped on a puppy's paw. "What'd I do?" he asked the room, "I didn't do nothin'!"

"Never mind, you!" Minnie shouted. "You get away from her!"

"Over here, Jesse!" Vito said pointing at Sidney. Jesse moved away gladly.

"Angela, darling," Minnie tried to comfort her, "there is no reason to cry. Nobody is going to hurt you here."

It was no use. Poor Angela was inconsolable and continued to weep her bitter tears of hurt and humiliation.

Wilson secretly welcomed her outburst of tears. It was almost as though it were a preplanned diversionary tactic to cover his own daring rescue action. Without moving his upper torso, his attention seemingly on Angela, Wilson cautiously stretched his foot forward under the table, reaching out for the telephone on the floor.

Mio Yamaguchi, seated across the table from Angela, reached over and put her hand gently on the sobbing woman's head. "It's okay," she said. "You go ahead and cry."

Wilson felt the toe of his shoe touching the phone. Slowly he raised his foot, feeling for the receiver. He could feel his shoe passing over the buttons—and now he was sure that the top of the toe of his shoe was just under the receiver. He could feel it. He started to cough, his throaty hacking even louder than Angela's bawling. At the same moment, he deftly lifted his foot, scooping the receiver astride the top of his shoe and carefully bringing it toward himself. When he felt it was close enough, he tipped his foot, dropping the phone receiver silently onto the carpet. Only then did he stop coughing.

"That's a terrible cough you got there, Mr. Wilson," said Minnie. "Would you like, maybe, a glass of water?"

Wilson glared at her. "No, thank you. A glass of water is *not* what I would like. What I would like is to be told what you people are trying to do!"

"Mr. Wilson," Minnie observed, "we are not trying. We are *doing*."

"Do you think you can possibly get away with this—" Slack demanded, "threatening all these innocent people with guns, endangering lives—?"

Minnie and Vito both zeroed in on Slack with their guns. "No more talking!" Minnie said fiercely. "Only sitting! Do you hear me?" Her features

157

shook with fury, and in that flaring instant everybody in the room realized that this woman would do anything she had to do to accomplish her mission. Anything.

Angela had stopped crying and was looking up at Minnie with two huge, teary, blue eyes.

"That's better, Angela sweetheart," Minnie said kindly. "Crying is only for frightened children. There is nothing to be scared about here. You're just getting a day off, that's all."

Angela did not appreciate the special attention. She put her head back down on her arms, trying to shut out this terrible day.

Minnie shrugged, waving at Vito to continue the lock-up procedure. "C'mon, c'mon, keep it moving. We're not here to hold anybody's hand!"

There were four television cameras in the bank's main room, one in the safety deposit room, and two outside, focused on the drive-in teller's area. Abe was just finishing up with the last one inside, the one trained on the long line of teller's windows that ran almost the full length of the bank. Standing on a high bookkeeper's chair, he shook Louie's can of shaving cream vigorously and pressed the button on the can, spritzing the foaming lather into the camera lens until the lens hood was loaded with a healthy glob of the thick white gook. "Don't worry," he said to the camera, wagging a promising forefinger, "we'll give you plenty for the six o'clock news, believe me!"

At the front of the bank, Louie and Stosh had Brubaker resting in a chair they had rolled out of one of the offices. Louie looked back and saw Abe waving his hands at the TV.

"Hey, Abe!" he hollered. "What the hella you doing? It's a quarter of, goddamn it, get those phones!"

"Okay, okay!" Abe said. "Who's got the cutters?"

"Vito's got them," Louie yelled. "Move, Abe, move!"

Abe moved briskly toward the conference room.

Louie turned his attention back to Brubaker. His left eye swollen almost shut, he sat hunched over holding a badly sprained limp left wrist with his right hand, making little moaning grunts.

"Tsk, tsk, tsk," Louie shook his head.

Brubaker looked up at Louie with his good eye.

"Stosh, go get Minnie's bandana," Louie ordered. "I'll make a sling for his arm."

"I don't know, Louie . . ." Stosh said, hesitantly.

"Whatta ya mean, you don't know?"

"Louie, this man could be hurt bad *inside*. I think we better let him out, so he can go to hospital." Brubaker gave Stosh a look of unbelievable gratitude.

"You crazy?" Louie snapped. "Stosh, don't gimme any trouble! Nobody

158

gets outa here until we all get out! Get the bandana. *I'll* do the thinking, you hear me?"

"I hear you, Louie," Stosh mumbled, and headed for the conference room.

A telephone began to ring. Once. Twice. Louie started to holler, "Abe, where are you? Abe! Abe!"

Abe came running out of the conference room, almost colliding with Stosh, a pair of wire cutters in his hand, his eyes wild as if he had never heard a phone ring in his life. It rang again. Before Louie could stop him, he grabbed a receiver on the nearest desk.

"Hello? Citizens' Bank."

"Hang up, Abe!" Louie screamed.

Abe took the phone from his ear, looked frantically at Louie, then blurted into the phone, "Wrong number! Sorry, I gotta cut you off!" With which he snipped the phone cord between the receiver and the instrument with the wire cutters.

Louie's look of absolute disgust traveled the length of the bank, striking Abe right between the eyes.

"I'm sorry, Louie," Abe said, "but I . . . I couldn't help it. You hear a phone ring, you answer it, you know?"

"Abe, I'm telling you," Louie warned, if you don't cut all the phones in this bank in the next sixty seconds, I'll do some cutting on you, you know what I mean?"

"Don't talk foolish," Abe giggled. "You're too late for that."

"What I got in mind, Abe," Louie said, "I am *not* too late."

"I'm going, I'm going," Abe said, grabbing himself by the crotch.

"And cut them off at the *instrument*—not the receiver," Louie shouted after him.

Abe scurried around from phone to phone with his wire cutters, decapitating Ma Bell's snakes all over the bank—all except one, Louie's command phone for Phase Three.

In the safety deposit room, Oscar worked like a master chef. He squinted as he consulted—for guidance only—the recipe for thermite on page forty-two of *The Anarchist's Cookbook*. All the ingredients for his thermite cake were premeasured and neatly laid out on a Dave's Deli linen napkin spread on top of the dolly:

½ lb. aluminum powder, finely ground
1½ lbs. iron oxide, powdered
4 oz. barium peroxide powder
4 U-loops wire filament, stiffened with airplane glue
2 1-ft. lengths 3" diameter lead pipe, threaded
2 predrilled 3" caps, threaded

4 empty cloth tobacco pouches
1 coil solder, flux core
2 doz. splicing posi-clips
plumber's putty

Oscar took an extra moment to read and savor the technical description aloud:

"'These materials, properly assembled for detonation, equal: thermite' . . . yes. 'Properties und Specifications: On ignition via flammable fuse, thermite attains instant combustion at heat of 2800 degrees Farenheit. Within twenty seconds of combustion in a sealed metal enclosure, the fused material experiences unique exothermic reaction, leaping instantly to white heat of approximately 5000 degrees Farenheit, at the same time releasing subatomic heat und pressure of astonishing magnitude.' Hmm-mm. . . . 'This accelerated "heat leap" causes this incendiary substance to melt or incinerate, in a gravitational path, through any manmade material, irrespective of density or thickness, including molybdenized or case-hardened steel, in a matter of a few fiery seconds.' . . . .Schön, sehr shön."

Precision watchmaker's implements seemed to leap into his agile hands from the fitted pockets of his tool apron as he bent to his work—a twist of the needlenose pincers, a crimp, a drop of solder, a turn of the tiny screwdriver, the spooning of the powders, the deliberately gentle mixing, the cautious tamping into the pipes, the caps turned on just so, as though he were adjusting a living, beating heart valve, and each individual step painstakingly scrutinized under his jeweler's loop, each connection passing the meticulous inspection of the Stein test—perfection or start over.

Oscar Stein was an old-world craftsman. The little gnome from Hamburg was an artist, here perhaps contriving his last and most important work of art. Picasso's very last painting could very well fetch millions at auction, but could it affect social change? Stir the conscience? Put food in the belly of an old man on the last day of a month with thirty-one days?

Bent over low, the coil of duplex wire between his legs, Oscar backed out of the safety deposit room, unrolling the wire toward the counter near which he had placed the blasting box on the floor. This was to be Louie's command post: the Safety Deposit counter at the rear of the bank's main room, directly opposite the front doors—the one live telephone, the binoculars, the blasting box.

Oscar attached the skinned end of one wire run to its brass terminal at the blasting box above the battery, turning the knurl-nut finger-tight. Then he capped the other wire with a splicing nut. "So!" he said to himself.

Standing at the counter on his tiptoes, he held his hand high over his head and snapped his fingers three times. He was ready for Vito and the master key.

*

160

Louie was delivering Brubaker to the conference room, his damaged wrist slung in Minnie's scarf, one eye swollen completely shut, and unable to straighten his back.

"*Psst!* Louie!" Oscar hissed. "Where is Vito? I need Vito!"

"I will send him right out," Louie said.

"I need him immediately!" Oscar insisted. "You people are destroying my schedule, Levine! No key—no cake!" Oscar waved an exasperated palm and disappeared back into his munitions lab.

The decorum in the conference room was incredible. Eleven hostages, locked in place to the steel cable, sitting perfectly still, docile yet attentive, as though they awaited the reading of a will. Only Jesse was still free.

A round of gasps broke out around the table as they all saw the banged-up Brubaker helped into the room.

"Oh, my God!" Opal said, for them all.

"See here!" Wilson demanded, "What have you done to that man? I thought you said no one would be hurt!"

"S'alright, Mr. Wilson," Brubaker mumbled. "I'm okay, just bruised."

"What happened?" Slack asked. "Why did they beat you up?"

"Nobody beat anybody up!" Louie said.

"They didn't beat me up, honest." Brubaker agreed. "I just made a move on them, and they made one on me. *Right* on me!"

"Who is in charge here?" Wilson was pounding his fists on the table, pulling everyone's hands up and down in the process. "I demand to know who's in charge!"

"Who is in charge?" Louie repeated. "We are in charge. Isn't that plain?"

"I mean . . ." Wilson sputtered, "which one of you—?"

A phone rang. Abe came running to the door of the conference room. "Louie, the phone's ringing! What'll I do?"

"Don't do anything. I'll do. You finished cutting?" The phone rang again.

"Yeah, finished," said Abe. "Now what?"

"Follow me," Louie said, moving to the door. "Vito, make it snappy in here! Oscar is ready for the key."

"Tell him I'll be right with him," Vito said, leading Brubaker to a chair. "Okay, Jesse, only *one* hand with this one. Put the other cuff around the cable, get me?"

"Right." Jesse snapped a cuff on Brubaker's good wrist.

Wilson took a quick peek under the table at the phone. Though the phone was still ringing, there were no button lights showing on the instrument. It didn't make sense.

Jesse snapped Brubaker's other cuff to the cable. "You okay, m' man?"

"I'm A-OK, my man," Brubaker said, with a pained but friendly grin.

Louie lifted the receiver off his ringing command-post phone, depressed the lit button and immediately pressed the hold button down. The second line began to ring, another button lighting up. Louie repeated the procedure, rudely consigning the second caller to limbo along with the first.

Now he pressed the third line button and dialed 938-3113, which was line number four. As soon as it started to ring, he depressed the hold button on line number three, and pressed the line four button. "Hello, good-bye," he said, pressing the hold button again.

Methodically, he dialed line number six from line number five, tying *them* together with the hold button, dialed line number eight from line number seven, and so on, through all sixteen lines on the call-director system, disabling each line until the whole instrument was flashing like a Christmas tree in a toy store window.

Wilson thought he was losing his mind as he peeked under the conference table with each cut off ring of the phone. No button light. How could that be? When a phone rings, a light lights. Reaching forward carefully, he depressed a different button on the phone with the point of his shoe, covering the click with a noisy cough. Another short ring. Again, he peeked. Still no light. Impossible!

The new telephone system released the two outside calls on lines one and two, and both button lights went off. Louie quickly dialed from one to the other, marrying them with the hold button till death would them part . . .

Ma Bell had finally stopped ringing, her lines all firmly connected in a conspiracy of silence by a rotary of sixteen consecutive busy signals. Citizens' Bank was completely cut off from the outside world.

Jesse stood behind the chair next to Brubaker's, looking at Vito.

"Take a load off your feet, Jesse," Vito said quietly, pointing his gun at the chair. "You done good work."

"Hey, man," Jesse said with a happy idea, "I could run across to the drugstore if you want—bring everybody a coke!"

Vito smiled. "A coke don't come next. You come next. Sit down."

"But just look at all these poor people," Jesse said. "Can't you see how thirsty they—"

"What's-a-matter, you don't hear good?" Minnie asked. "The man said sit down, so sit down!"

"Yes, ma'am!" Jesse scrambled for the chair. "Looka-here, Jesse is sittin' hisself right down, Yes, Ma'am!"

Vito handed Minnie his gun and picked up a pair of cuffs and a lock.

"Hey, man, lemme see can I do it myself," Jesse said. Vito handed Jesse the lock and handcuffs. Jesse slipped the little lock through the center link of the cuffs and snapped the lock around the cable. Then he deftly snapped himself into the handcuffs. "How 'bout that, man?" Jesse grinned broadly at Vito. "I done incarcerated my own self!"

"Jesse, you are some funny fella," Vito observed cryptically.

"Huh?"

162

"You been a good assistant, kiddo, but now you're holdin' me up, and it ain't so funny," Vito warned. "You wanna tighten 'em—or you want me to?"

Jesse looked at the handcuffs, halfway up his forearms. "Oh-h, yeah, looka-here! I guess I just put 'em on a little too high, huh?"

Jesse quickly shucked the cuffs down to his slim wrists, where he knew damn well they belonged, and cinched the bracelets snugly. Vito backed away and retrieved his gun. As ever undaunted, Jesse beamed an ear-to-ear smile at every grim face at the table.

"We-ell, brethren and sistren—" he intoned, like a Sunday morning preacher. "Here we is—all together!"

Louie and Abe appeared at the conference room door. "Okay, Vito," Louie said, "we're ready for McInnerny. The vault is open."

There was a new tenseness now, and everyone felt it. Vito fished in his pants pocket for the key to the locks. The other pocket. No key. He patted his jacket pockets.

"Come on Vito, come on!" Louie said.

"Twenty locks, twenty keys . . ." Vito muttered, digging from one pocket to the other. "I only brought two, but they're here somewhere."

"Vito!" Louie shouted, "you mean to tell me—"

"Oh, yeah!" Vito said. "Jeez, I almost forgot!"

Quickly, he retrieved the steel toolbox, setting it on the table. He opened it and peeled the tape off of two small keys adhered to the underside of the box lid. "Smart-aa-ass, huh?" he said to Louie, tapping his nose.

"Never mind, already," Louie said. "Unlock him!"

Vito moved to McInnerny's lock. McInnerny was shaking like Don Knotts, rattling the whole length of the cable. Vito held the lock steady, turned the key, and the lock snapped open. He unhooked it and popped it into his pocket, handing Minnie the two small keys.

McInnerny just sat there, shaking and looking at Wilson as though Wilson could invoke a reprieve from whatever was about to happen to him.

"Up, up!" Louie ordered, waving his gun.

McInnerny seemed nailed to his chair, his eyes blinking in panic.

"It's all right, Henry," Wilson said. "Just go along with them."

"But, but . . ."

"Come on, McInnerny!" Louie's patience was wearing thin.

"Go along, Henry," Wilson urged, calmly. "And remember—*people before property*. Just do as they say."

McInnerny rose shakily to his feet, his eyes still pleading with Wilson. "How ab-bout the combina-com-bination?"

"Anything they want, Henry," said Wilson. "People before property." Louie grabbed McInnerny roughly by the arm and led him out. McInnerny was mumbling. "P-people before p-property, p-people before p-property," with every step.

"The key, Vito!" Louie said over his shoulder. "Oscar wants the big key—now!"

"Yeah, yeah, the big key," Vito said. "Comin' up!" He walked deliberately to the head of the table, between Wilson and Mio. Very slowly he raised his gun, aiming it directly between Mio's eyes at point-blank range. Everyone in the room froze.

"We need the key, little girl," Vito said, very quietly. "The big master key for the boxes."

Mio didn't move a hair. Her eyes met Vito's over the barrel of the gun without a trace of fear.

"Did you hear what I said?"

"Yes, I heard."

Vito waited a moment for more. "Well, let's have it!" he said, poking his gun even closer.

"No."

"What'd you say?" Vito shouted.

"I said, No."

"Whatta ya mean, No? Have you got it on you?"

"No."

"Well, you know where it is, don'tcha?"

"Yes," Mio said. "I know where it is, sir."

Vito was beside himself with frustration.

Wilson was shaking his head. "Don't be foolish, Mio," he said. "Get him the key."

"No, sir." She said quietly. "I won't."

"Vito," said Minnie, sensing a Japanese standoff from the other end of the room, "you got no aces up, Vito. You better shuffle the cards."

Vito looked at her for a moment, weighing her unsolicited advice. "What the hell'sa matter wit' you, Japanese girl?" he yelled suddenly. "Can'tcha see this gun in your face?"

He had scared himself more than Mio, who sat perfectly still, looking back at him with an unnerving sloe-eyed serenity. "Yes, sir," she said evenly, "I see your gun, and I am frightened . . . for both of us. But I will not give you the key."

"Mio," Wilson said, "please be sensible—"

"Wait a minute, wait a minute!" said Minnie. "Let *me* ask her. Listen, Mio Yamaguchi. The man is pointing a gun at you. He is prepared to use that gun. Why won't you give him the key, for goodness' sakes?"

Mio slowly turned her head to face Minnie. "Because nothing in the Safety Deposit room is bank property. . . . Because the contents of those boxes are the personal property of our depositors, who expect that property to be *held in trust*."

"Oh-hh, I see . . ." Minnie said.

Mio turned back and looked up at Vito over his gun. "I will do nothing

164

foolish to try to stop you," she explained, "but I will do nothing to help you destroy that trust."

Vito glared at her; and Mio returned her own steady gaze.

From the far end of the table, Floyd Davis, who had deigned to look up from his law book just long enough to watch the confrontation, whispered two words in admiration, *"Hai Samurai!"*

A smile almost flickered across Mio's face, and everyone in the room understood the meaning of what they had witnessed.

"It ain't solitaire in the park, Vito," Minnie said quietly, jerking her head toward the exit. "You just lost one."

Vito was stuck in his own stare, mired in humiliation, his jaw working back and forth from side to side. "You think I need your key, little girl?" he growled at last. "Well, that's what you think!"

He took two angry steps back to the tool box, flung the lid open, tore another piece of tape from the underside, and returned to face his Oriental opponent again. "You see these?" He held two large blank key slugs up in front of her face. "I'll make my own key. How do ya like that?" Then, he shoved his gun back into his belt as though that was what he had planned all along, and strode toward the door.

Mio Yamaguchi and all her ancestors smiled inscrutably at the sight of Vito Morelli trying to save face.

"They're all yours, Minnie," Vito said scornfully. "I'm sicka them."

He reached into his pocket, took out McInnerny's lock, slapped it into Minnie's hand, and stalked out of the room, holding his head as high as he could under the circumstances.

In the world outside the bank, it was just another Thursday, chugging toward ten o'clock.

Astride her three-wheeler, the meter maid rounded the corner onto Fairfax, her eyes sweeping the parking meters for the telltale red flags. The meter at the florist's van still had a few minutes to go before the violation flag would flip up, and the meter maid rode on, not noticing how little time was left on the meter—or the slight rocking of the van. No red flag, no second look.

The heavy traffic in the intersection had subsided, settling down into the medium noisy hum that the urban ear ignores. The buses were fewer now and further between, almost empty as they made their obligatory stops for the few who had not yet reached their Thursday morning destinations.

Outside Dave's Deli, the gas company crew was on a coffee break, sitting on the curb, trying to swallow the sludge that Dave passes off as coffee at a quarter a cup, trading bad dirty jokes poorly told but raucously laughed at anyway.

A few lucky oldsters who were on the early end of the mail delivery were gathering at the front of the bank, waiting to cash their checks, clucking

165

away at each other about their aches and pains and their grown children in other cities.

The sun was much warmer now, shining a bright April Fool's spotlight on the big show about to be performed at the corner of Fairfax and Beverly. God was in His heaven, Louie Levine and his gang were in the counting house, and all was right with the world.

It had taken only a few minutes to distribute the change funds to the teller's windows, and Louie was escorting McInnerny back to the conference room.

"Hey, Louie," Stosh said, from the front. "They start to line up outside."

"Whattayou expect, no business? It's the first of the month! Take it easy, we got a coupla minutes yet."

Louie and McInnerny disappeared into the conference room.

"Myself, I am ready any time," Abe said from window three.

"Welcome back, Mr. McInnerny!" Minnie said brightly. "I was waiting for you, before I start my class! Come in, come in, we saved your chair for you."

McInnerny dumbly headed for his chair, a large piece of white paper rattling in his hand.

"You got his lock?" Louie asked Minnie.

"Don't worry about a thing, Louie. I got his lock, I got my gun, I got my whistle, I got my nice stool, and I know my job. You just go take care of your business."

"Never mind, smart-aleck," Louie said. "I don't go until he's hooked in. Gimme the lock."

Minnie gave the lock to Louie, who quickly secured McInnerny to the cable.

"You sure you don't need anything?" Louie asked Minnie.

"Nothing," she said.

"Okay. In about a minute and a half . . ." Louie checked his watch, "we open for business!" He turned to leave the room.

"You'll *what?*" Wilson cried out. "You'll open for *what?*"

Louie turned back to face the apoplectic bank manager. "*Shhhh!* What's-a-matter with you? You want I should tape your mouth, all of you? There will be no hollering in here! There will be only *whispering* in here, you understand me?"

"But . . . but you said 'open for business'!" Wilson managed to keep his voice to a whisper.

"That's right," Louie said. "So?"

"You . . . you mean the bank? You're going to *open the bank?*"

"Of course, the bank. You know the hours better than I do—ten o'clock to three o'clock, right?"

"But-but . . ."

"Listen, Mr. Wilson," Louie said gently, "I know it's a little confusing for

166

your day to start off like this, but if you just relax and take it easy, everything will turn out all right, trust me."

"Trust you?" Barnes butted in angrily. "You think we're just going to sit in here quietly while you animals rob this bank? You're crazy!"

Louie's easy manner soured immediately. He walked menacingly to Barnes's chair. Bending over slightly, he slid his hand onto the top of the man's head, parting the hair in clumps between his spread fingers. Then all at once, he squeezed a tight fist, pulling the hair painfully as he jerked Barnes's head a sharp quarter-turn to face him.

"Listen, you!" Louie hissed, close enough to bite Barnes's nose. "Lemme straighten you out. We didn't come here to rob this bank. And we didn't come here to hurt anybody, either. But nobody is going to stop us today, you hear? I'm telling you plain. You make just one move, one stupid noise, and that nice little lady there will shoot you in the guts, and blow her whistle *after!*" He tightened his fist even more, pulling the hair harder. "Do you understand me?"

"Yes!" Barnes gasped, his eyes full of tears.

Louie released his hand, pushing Barnes's head away. Everyone breathed again. "That's better," Louie said, satisfied that he had made his point. "Anybody else got anything on your mind that you want to get off your chest?"

"Yes, please." Wilson cleared his throat. "You seem like a reasonable man . . ."

"I *am* a reasonable man."

"Well, then . . . I mean . . . you must know that you *can't* open this bank under these conditions."

"Why can't I? I got the key!"

"I mean, it's outrageous!" Wilson said, trying to speak quietly. "You can't hold all these people hostage like this, in chains! There are women here—a pregnant woman! You're all armed. You can't let people into this bank, endangering the lives of innocent people. Do you realize the possible consequences of this vicious act?"

Louie looked at the man, judging his tension and feeling his own. "My dear Mr. Wilson," he said quietly, "you can see that we didn't make up our minds to do all this just yesterday. Yes, we realize the risks we are taking, and we understand what the consequences could be. But we are ready to take the responsibility and any consequences for our actions today. You call this a vicious act? No. A dangerous act? Yes. But absolutely necessary."

"*Necessary?* A bank robbery necessary?"

"Ah-hh, but we are not *robbing* your bank." Louie smiled, holding a forefinger aloft. "We are *negotiating* with your bank."

"Negotiating?" Wilson asked, bewildered. "What do you mean, you're neg—?"

"Listen, Mr. Wilson," Louie said, checking his watch, "I would like to

167

have a nice conversation with you, but we don't have the time just now. I gotta open up!" And he turned to the door.

Wilson pounded both his fists on the table, completely out of control. "But what are you people *doing* in this bank?" he cried out hysterically. "What the hell is going on here, today, for God's sake?"

Louie turned back. "Mr. Wilson, I told you to stay quiet!"

"I'm sorry, I'm really sorry," Wilson whined, "and we will stay quiet, I promise. But don't you understand? It's my duty to know what's happening here!"

"Yes, I understand," Louie said calmly. "Let me simply tell you this way. . . . We are all here to take part in a special seminar in advanced civics." He turned and left the room. Wilson's mouth was still open as Louie closed the door.

Minnie faced her class of prisoners with a pleasant smile and cleared her throat for attention. "Ladies and gentlemen," she began, "let me assure you once more, there is no reason for any of you to be afraid. We do not plan to hurt anybody."

Brubaker groaned at the news. His swollen wrist was throbbing with every beat of his pulse, shooting sharp pains up his arm. He was beginning to fear that it was broken. He knew for sure that one of his ribs was.

"I am in here with you," Minnie continued, "to watch out you don't get yourself hurt."

Barnes turned in his chair to face the teacher, trying to ease the painful muscle spasm in his neck inflicted by Louie's chiropractic lecture.

"As long as you behave like ladies and gents," Minnie went on, "everything will be hunky-dory. But if any of you try anything funny—like he said—I will have to shoot. I got no choice. I can't give you demerits."

Jesse and Floyd both giggled.

"Gentlemen, gentlemen!" Minnie said, "I am not being funny! When I'm making a funny, I'll let you know! And I'll tell you something else: They took me one day to the mountains, way out on Mulholland, and I learned to shoot this gun. But I found out I'm not such a good shot. I shoot quick, but *not too straight,* if you know what I mean." She looked around the table at the baffled faces. "I'm trying to tell you," she explained, "if one of you makes me shoot, God knows which one—or how many of you—I'll hit with the bullets. You understand me?"

No one volunteered a response. Finally, after a long moment of thoughtful quiet, Floyd Davis lifted his head from his book. "We know what you're saying, lady. You're saying that each of us here had better be responsible for the actions of the entire group. Is that right?"

Minnie looked at him with open admiration. "Oh, boy," she said, "are you gonna make some Philadelphia lawyer! By the way, ladies and gentlemen, my name is Minnie. We're all gonna be in here together most

168

of the day, and I don't see why we shouldn't be friends. So please—call me Minnie!"

"Most of the day?" Wilson said. "You can't keep these people locked up like this most of the day! Without food, without water, it's inhuman!"

"Believe me, Mr. Wilson, it won't be so inhuman. Don't worry! You'll have water to drink, you'll have a nice lunch we got coming in for you. And later, you will even be allowed to go to the toilet, if you need to; you only have to raise your hand. We are not *barbarians*, you know."

"No," said Slack, "you're just simple criminals, that's what you are. And stupid ones, to boot! The police will put an end to this insanity in short order! There's no way you can keep us in here most of the day!"

Minnie lifted her chin. "For your sake, Mr. Slack," she said ominously, "for everybody's sake, it better be until three o'clock at least, I'm telling you."

"Three o'clock?" asked Wilson. "What's three o'clock?"

Minnie considered her answer for a moment. "Three o'clock is your closing time, isn't it?" she asked cryptically.

Wilson tilted his head in confusion, waiting for Minnie to say more. But she had said all she was going to say, and every person in the room felt a chill as they looked at Minnie's expressionless face.

The piece of paper McInnerny was holding began to rattle again.

"What have you got in your hand, Henry?" Wilson asked.

Too deep in a daze to answer, McInnerny passed the sheet to Jesse, who switched it from one manacled hand to the other and passed it to Opal, who passed it to Barnes, who passed it to Angela, who delivered it to Wilson at the head of the table. He read aloud in a flat voice.

"'Receipt. Received of Henry P. McInnerny, Eight Thousand Dollars and no cents, to be used as change fund for windows number two, three, and four, Citizens' Bank. April Fools' Day, 1976. Signed, Abe Rockefeller, head cashier.'"

He looked up from the handwritten receipt as though he had awakened in an asylum.

"You see?" said Minnie brightly. "Everything is strictly on the up and up!"

Wilson closed his eyes in abject surrender to the madness.


Nine fifty-nine. An old lady, one hand shading her brow, was peering into the bank, impatient for the doors to open so she could be the first one in to cash her Social Security check.

Inside, a last-minute scurry was on to accommodate her and the small crowd waiting to get in.

Stosh was just finishing the arrangement of the red velvet traffic control ropes that directed customers to the operative teller's windows.

169

"No, no, Stosh," Louie said from his place at window number four. "You gotta block off the safety deposit counter, remember?"

"Oh, yeah!" Stosh quickly moved a brass stanchion so that the long rope cut off entry to the safety deposit area.

Oscar, bent over ass-up, was scooting backward toward the counter, taping down the wires running across the floor to the explosives in the safety deposit room.

"Oscar, will you hurry up?" Louie said. "It's ten o'clock, for God's sake!"

"You don't have to wait for me." Oscar pointed to the logo on his chest. "I'm the Guardian Security, remember?"

"Oh, yeah. Well, where the hell's Vito?"

Oscar looked disgusted. "Where do you *think* is Vito? Vito is still fiddling around with his fancy key cutter. I told you he would make us late!"

"Vito!" Louie shouted. "Godamn it, everybody's waiting, Vito!"

"I'm coming, I'm coming!" Vito rushed out of the safety deposit room. "Here, Oscar, here is your custom-made master key! Both our boxes are open. Don't say I never done nothin' for you!"

Oscar snatched the key and headed back into the safety deposit room as Vito hurried to his place at window number two.

Louie took a last check down the length of the counter. "Vito, the raincoat! Take off the raincoat!"

"No wonder I was so hot!" Vito peeled his raincoat off, rolled it into a ball, and dropped it under his counter with a loud hardware clunk.

"Okay," Louie said. "Is everybody . . . ready?"

"Ready, Louie," Stosh said, at the front door.

"Places, second act places!" Abe singsonged to himself.

"Abe?"

"I was ready since yesterday!" Abe said, nervously patting the extra two thousand dollars in the cash drawer.

"Vito?"

"Ready, Louie," Vito answered, eyes up reverently as he quickly crossed himself.

"All right," Louie said, watching the second hand on the large wall clock sweep past the eight. "Remember . . . calm, quiet, nice and easy. Everything is gonna go bee-ootiful—like peaches and cream! Dont' forget, Stosh, a nice good morning to everybody!"

"Good morning, Louie!" Stosh said, saluting grandly.

"That's nice, Stosh. Very nice."

The second hand hit the twelve straight up. Louie took a big breath. "Okay, Stosh. Open up the candy store!"

Stosh knelt to his job just as Oscar poked his head out of the safety deposit room. "Gentlemen," he announced in a loud whisper, "the cake is ready for the candles, und the pies are in the oven!"

170

"Curtain going up," Abe sang to himself, "second act curtain!"

Stosh swung the door open, and a small crowd of customers pushed in to do their banking.

"Good morning!"

"Nice morning, isn't it?"

"Good morning, good morning!"

"How are you this morning?"

"Good morning!"

Nobody even looked at Stosh as he greeted them one by one, just as they had never looked at Brubaker on the first of the month. The first of the month was no time for saying good morning to a stranger. Just get in the bank and get to the teller's window with your check. Get the money, then get to the supermarket and home before some kid knocks you down on the street and takes it away from you. That's what the first of the month is for.

The bank had been·open for fifteen minutes, and it was incredible. Business as usual at Citizens' Bank. The lines moved along the velvet ropes without a hitch. The tellers were a trifle slow, but very efficient, verifying the IDs, and checking the endorsement signatures, and counting out the crisp new money.

They rubber-stamped documents with the time-honored little grunts of transaction completion, they initialed intrabank accounting forms, they punched buttons on their individual computer terminals in a perfunctory manner that indicated they knew exactly what they were doing. And every customer seeing the props and hearing the counter sounds felt secure in the knowledge that the records were being meticulously kept.

Under the new management, of course, the on-line computer system had never even been dialed up, nor did it matter at all which stamps were officiously zomped onto which documents. The transactions taking place in Citizens' Bank on April 1, 1976, would never see the light of day, and months afterward, the bank's accountants would still be hopelessly lost trying to follow the audit trail scattered by The Benefit.

"All right, Mrs. Anderson," Abe said to the woman at window three as he counted out her money, "fifty, one hundred, one hundred and twenty, one hundred and forty, one hundred and sixty, and seven fifty, and *here* is your hundred-dollar bonus."

The woman looked at the new hundred-dollar bill Abe had laid on top of her change. "Wha—What's this for?"

"It's like this, Mrs. Anderson," Abe said confidentially. "The governor has declared a hundred dollar bonus for all Social Security recipients this month."

"But . . . but Social Security is federal."

"You see?" Abe said brightly. "Just goes to prove how much our governor *cares* for the old people of his state!"

"Well, uh, do I have to sign something for this?"

"No, that's perfectly all right," Abe assured her. "Your check endorsement is enough."

"Well, Hallelujah in the mornin'!" said the woman, stuffing her purse before her dream could evaporate. "Thank you very much indeed!"

"It's my pleasure!" Abe said.

"Have a nice day," Stosh said, holding the door open. The woman scooted by him and out of the bank as though she were on a skateboard, clutching her purse to her body for all she was worth. Stosh grinned, not the least bit put out that she had not heard his good wishes coming or going.

"Two hundred and ten, two hundred twenty, and fifty cents." Vito counted the cash out at window number two with the nonchalant style of a blackjack dealer. "Don't go away, Mr. Sheinbaum. Here's your bonus—a hundred dollars."

"That's not mine," the man said, pushing the bill back at Vito.

"Oh, yes, it is!" Vito replaced it on the man's pile. "The governor declared it. It's yours!"

"Wait just a minute!" Sheinbaum said, suspiciously fingering the bill. "It doesn't matter what the governor declared. The HEW will just deduct this money from my *next* month, that's all!"

"Oh, no," Vito assured him. "This time they will not give with one hand and take away with the other, believe me!"

"Yeah!" said Sheinbaum, invoking an ancient prayer, "from your mouth to the Social Security's ears!"

"Ri-ight! You got it perfect, Mr. Sheinbaum! That's exactly how it's goin', take it from me!"

"All right," said the man, pocketing his money, "I'll take it. But next month, if they take off a hundred dollars, I'll come looking for you!"

"Right, you do that, Mr. Sheinbaum!" Vito said, as the man left the counter.


Ten forty-eight. Louie made a quick survey of the activities in the bank as he stamped an alleged deposit receipt for a customer. All quiet on the western front. It was too good to be true. Fantastic. A fat little old yenta holding thirteen hostages perfectly controlled and silent, and five old cockers in dark wigs operating a large and busy branch of a major Los Angeles bank—and not one speck of trouble in forty-eight minutes.

About ten-thirty, a woman had come in to use her safety deposit box, but she was planning to put in, not take out, so when she was told Guardian Security Systems was installing a new computer alarm system in the vault and that no one could enter the room until they were finished later in the day, she went happily on her way without a complaint. In fact, she congratulated Louie on the bank's policy of keeping abreast of the latest

172

security technology. He assured her that he would pass her feelings on to the branch manager himself.

Ten fifty-five. A big red-faced man stepped up to Louie's window with a long canvas bank bag containing checks and currency. Louie referred to the deposit slip the man had filled out as he totalled the contents of the bag. "Forty-two hundred dollars exactly, Mr. O'Neil." Louie stamped the man's receipt. "Eighteen hundred and fifty dollars in checks, and the balance in cash."

"Be sure you get this deposit posted to my account before the end of today's business," said the man. "I wrote a large check yesterday, and I'm sure it'll come in for payment first thing tomorrow."

"Oh, yes, sir, Mr. O'Neil. We wouldn't want to have insufficient funds in your account, no, sir! You are our largest cash customer so far today!"

"Is that a fact?" asked O'Neil, not even looking at his receipt. "Well, have a good day!" And he left the window.

"So far, I'm having!" Louie said, crossing his fingers.

Eleven seven. The Benefit was still a big hit inside the bank, gliding along as though Guy Lombardo was playing an easy waltz and everyone was dancing with his or her own partner. Louie and his gang had already handed out over thirty-five hundred dollars in bonuses, and the lines of qualified white-haired recipients were still going strong. Even Oscar had stripped off his coveralls and was now manning window number five to help handle the crowd.

Outside, the intersection traffic stopped and went, stopped and went, as though nothing at all were happening in that part of town, besides the changing of signals.

Big Joe leaned all his weight on his *rat-tat-tatting* jackhammer, making as much noise and raising as much dust as he could before lunchtime, endangering China with the depth of his ditch, but nowhere near the buried gas line he was probing for.

The meter maid was just slipping an overtime parking ticket under the windshield wiper of the florist's van, unable to hear the deep grunts from within over the noise of Joe's jackhammer and the idling motor of her own three-wheeler, double-parked at the side of the van containing a young man who would never again accept help from a stranger on the road as long as he lived.

The big neon Time-to-Eat-a-Knish clock in the front window of Dave's Deli read 11:10. Under the clock, a handpainted sign proclaimed Dave's Deli Delivers! Anytime! Anyplace! Inside the deli, the huge garlicky slabs of corned beef and pastrami responded to the swirling steam heating them to succulence for the mad slicing of Dave's lunch hour. The venerable waitresses, starched and brittle, most of whom had juggled plates at Dave's for more than a dozen years, were barking their prelunch commands at the Mexican busboys.

173

"Two coffees coming up, gentlemen!" Dave said to the two uniformed cops sitting down to his counter. "One black for the white officer, and one white with sugar for the black officer, right?"

The cops no longer even smiled at Dave's daily chatter.

"Hey, man, what'd you do to your coffee this morning?" Bush, the black cop, asked. "It's good for a change!"

"Listen," Dave said, "I didn't hear you complaining yesterday."

"We never complain, Dave," said Cassidy, the cop who wasn't black. "You know that."

"What's to complain?" Dave asked. "Some easy job you guys got—a free uniform, a badge, a fancy car, Chief Davis lets you stop for coffee every morning, you dodge a few lousy bullets, and twenty years later, you get a fat pension!"

Bush laughed. "You really got us figured," he said. "And that'll cost you a piece of cheesecake!"

"That'll cost *you* a piece of cheesecake, if you want cheesecake. I only pay taxes and coffee for protection. Besides, it would spoil your free lunch at McDonald's!"

"*Olé, matador!* That's what I like to hear, *mi patrón!* You telling it like it is, man!"

Cassidy turned to give the speaker a dirty look. It was Gonzalo Díaz, of course, Dave's resident Cantinflas and head bus-boy, sticking his nose in to cheer his boss from the cheap seats on the sunny side as he wheeled a cart laden with a large take-out order past the lunch counter.

"Hey, wait a minute, Gonzalo!" said Dave.

"Yes, *mi patrón?*"

"Is that your birthday lunch order already?"

Gonzalo popped his eyes open wide, bending his body slantwise, his long fingers splayed out in that stylish comic tamale dance of his when he was putting chili sauce on the gringo-bird. "It ain't *my* birthday, man!"

"I know it ain't yours," Dave said, trying to get a straight answer. "I mean, is that the *Wilson* birthday?"

"I don't have no birthdays!" Gonzalo said, ignoring Dave's question and sailing right into his act. "I was hatched in Tehachapi out of a big egg *ranchero* in the middle of a field of refried *frijoles!* You know that, man; I tol' you all about it! I'm not just a poor—"

"Hold it, hold it!" Dave moaned. "Gonzalo, please—"

"I'm not just a poor, disadvantaged Chicano born in the *barrio,* man! I'm an eagle! César Chávez took *my* picture to use for his flag, man!"

"Okay, okay, Señor Eagle!" Dave said. "Where is the cake?"

"Oh, *patrón!*" Gonzalo said in mock hurt. "Do you think Gonzalo would forget the most important thing of the whole birthday?"

He shot his cuffs back and knelt, whipping a large napkin off a box on the lower shelf of the cart as though a bull were charging into the arc of his

174

graceful veronica. *"Mira, patrón!"* he announced. "The famous birthday cheesecake of the famous Dave's Deli! Happy Birthday, Mr. Wilson!"

The two cops had revolved on their counter stools to follow Gonzalo's spiel and to get a look at the cake. Gonzalo peeked up at them from under the cart, his hand pantomiming a gun.

"Good morning, officers. How's the crime in the streets today? Bang, bang! You guys rip off any good grass lately? I might know somebody who's buying!"

"Take it easy on the fuzz, Gonzalo," Cassidy warned. "I may have to check out your papers."

"Hey, officers," Gonzalo apologized elaborately as he rose, "I'm just fooling around! That's how we are sometimes, us Chicanos. We like to sing and dance, and fool around, man . . . forget our troubles in the ghetto, you know?"

"On your way, Pancho Villa," Dave said good-naturedly, "before your Mexican mouth gets you in hot water with the law. And I need you back here in fifteen minutes, no more!"

"I already got that message from the beautiful *Señorita* Bernice," Gonzalo said, with a jerk of his head toward Dave's harridan hostess. "I'm on my horse, *patrón*. I'll be back soon as I empty my wagon. And, oh, excuse me *por favor*, officers, for jazzing you, eh? I was just carried away with my outgoing sense of humor, you know? I'm really crazy about 'Police Story'! *Hasta la vista!*"

Gonzalo rolled his getaway cart out of the deli and onto the busy sidewalk, leaving Officer Cassidy with his mouth open and something uncomplimentary on his mind.

The bank clock clicked to eleven thirty as Louie looked down the length of the counter. Everything was still moving smoothly.

Abe's line at window three was the slowest, and Stosh alertly kept the line shortened by continually redirecting people at the end to one of the other windows. It wasn't that Abe didn't know his job. It was just that he was having such a good time acting out his elaborate show of checking the IDs, double-stamping the dead-end accounting records, and counting out the new money with the flair of a Las Vegas dealer. And when it came to the giving of the hundred dollar bonuses, he was absolutely outrageous. He was Andrew Carnegie, presenting a free clinic to the lower east side. He was Black Jack Pershing, bestowing the medal of honor on the battlefield of the war to end all wars, the king of Sweden, conferring the Nobel prize for all the humanities. Blessed are the givers, and Abe felt so blessed with the giving, he could hardly stand it.

"Yes, Mr. Soloway," Abe was saying to a man finally leaving the window with his bonus, "it's a wonderful thing the governor is doing! Wonderful! He should run for President, at least!"

Two elderly black women stood third and fourth in Abe's line, checks in hand, passing the time of day in the hushed tones reserved for church and banks as they patiently shuffled toward the window. A six-year-old girl, beautiful in her starched yellow dress with matching socks and hair ribbons, was clutching her grandmother's worn hand, slowly walking around her like a Maypole, jealous of the conversation that was not about *her*. Grandmothers being used to the boredom fidgets of little children, the slow spinning did not inhibit the gossip of the two women.

Finally, exasperated with the lack of attention, the little girl tugged insistently on her grandmother's dress. "Granmaw, granmaw!" She pulled down hard on the woman's hand.

"Just a minute, child."

"Granmaw, granmaw! I gotta tell you something!"

"Now, Odessa, you just stop that fidgeting," the woman scolded. "Your grandmother's almost to the window, sakes alive! Only be another minute!"

Grandmothers can wait, but little girls can't.

"Granmaw, granmaw! I can't wait another minute!" Odessa cried, pulling down hard.

"I swear, child," the woman sighed, bending over to her charge, "you're surely going to be the death of your poor old grandmother before the sun sets this day! Now, what is it you have got to tell me this very minute!"

Odessa pressed her mouth to her grandmother's ear, whispering urgently and hopping up and down at the same time.

"Heavens, child!" her grandmother said, "I've been waiting in this line for nearly a half hour and I'm almost to the money window! I can't take you now, I'd have to go to the very end of the line!"

"Don't *want* you to go!" said Odessa, stamping her foot. "Wanna go by my own self! An' I got to go now!" She pulled her grandmother down again for another desperate whispered message. It seemed to be a clinching argument.

"Odessa, you sure you can tend to yourself now?"

"Yes, ma'am!" And she started to skip away.

"Now, Miss Odessa, you come back out directly you're finished, hear? Grandmother is not going to go in after you. We have a lot of nice things to do today, and we still have a long ride on the bus, and we don't want to get there when all the lions and tigers are asleep, do we?"

"No, ma'am."

"And one more thing. Come close, dear." She bent to whisper in the child's ear.

Odessa nodded about ten times in a row as she listened.

"Yes, ma'am, I'll remember." Then she held four fingers up for her grandmother to see.

The old woman smiled, patted her grandchild on the head, and Odessa made a beeline for the ladies' room.

176

"Oooh-h, wheee!" said the woman in front of Odessa's grandmother, "that little girl-child is gonna own this world, if that's what she wants!"

Odessa's grandmother beamed with pride. "She surely owns my world, right now."

Another old gent turned away from Abe's window, furtively pocketing his money in a vest pocket and buttoning his coat over it, and the two women moved one place closer to the wicket.

Stosh saw Gonzalo Diáz and his delicatessen cart through the glass and swung the door open wide. "So early you come with lunch for party?"

"Hey, man," Gonzalo said, turning his head to watch two girls pass the bank, "I just do what my boss tells me, y'know? He tells me deliver now, I deliver now. Where do you want this indigestion?"

"Follow me." Stosh led Gonzalo back through the crowded bank toward the conference room, where the catered luncheon would be served.

Inside the room, Wilson was pleading with Minnie, "It's just common decency, and it's a reasonable request! All I'm asking is that one of your people make *one* phone call for me. Even a jailed criminal gets that much consideration! Six senior executives of a major corporation will be waiting for me at the Jonathan Club fifteen minutes from now, and I just want them to be told that—"

Minnie was tired of nodding patiently. "I'm very sorry, Mr. Wilson, I don't care if you got a dozen VIPs waiting for you at the Whatta-ya-call-it Club, today is not your day. Today is *our* day. Don't worry, they wouldn't go hungry. They'll eat lunch without you."

"That's not the point!"

"The point, Mr. Wilson, is that today you are incommunicado, that's all. Just make believe you are laying around on your boat at Newport Beach today. Take it from me, you'll feel a lot better."

A one, one-two knock at the door got Minnie down off her stool, fanning the group with her gun as a reminder of her vigilance. Carefully, she opened the door a crack and saw half of Stosh.

"The food!" Stosh whispered. "The food is here!"

"So soon?" said Minnie. "It wasn't supposed to be until twelve o'clock. All right, I'm opening up."

Minnie opened the door wide. Suddenly, Stosh sidestepped Gonzalo's cart, grabbed him firmly by the shoulders, shoved man and cart into the conference room, and closed the door behind himself.

"*Ee-eechola!*" Gonzalo yelped at the bizarre sight of the hostages manacled to the table. "What's going down here, man?"

"Don't get excited." Minnie pushed Gonzalo and his cart further into the room. "It's nothing so unusual—a sit-down lunch for thirteen, that's all!"

Gonzalo's hands flew off the bar of his cart as though it had suddenly

177

become red hot. "A sit-down—? Hey, let me outa here!" He whirled toward the door and found himself belly to belly with Stosh.

"No, no!" Stosh said, belly-bumping him backward. "No out today—only in!"

Gonzalo turned to Minnie, suddenly aware of the gun poking at him from her sweater pocket. "Look, man, please . . . I gotta get back to Dave's for the lunch rush!"

"Don't be silly. I wouldn't cheat you out of that pleasure," Minnie said, kindly. "You'll serve lunch here!"

Gonzalo looked at Minnie as though she had just dropped down from another planet. Then, as he stared at her, a glint of recognition seemed to grow in his eyes. "Hey . . . hey!" he said, pointing at her excitedly. "I know you. Don't I know you?"

Minnie shrugged. "Do you?"

"Sure, man. I know I seen you before!"

Wilson's ears almost snapped to attention. An identification, even of only *one* of the criminals, would be vital information for the police, if he could only get to that phone at his feet.

Gonzalo was snap-snapping his fingers at Minnie, jogging his memory for her identification. "*Ay, ching-gow!* I know I know you! You . . . you're . . ."

"I'm . . .? I'm . . .?" Minnie was waving a come-on hand, as though encouraging her partner playing Password.

"I know who you are!" he shouted at last, clapping his hands together victoriously. "You always come in and buy the day-old bread at Dave's! Right?"

"You know me, all right," Minnie nodded. "I'll tell you the truth, I'm glad you don't have the job to carve my tombstone, the way you know me!"

Gonzalo looked at her, chagrined; and Wilson groaned inwardly with disappointment.

"Anyhow," Minnie continued, "you got a job here that fits you to a T. You'll stay, you'll serve lunch, you'll eat with the nice people. It wouldn't be so bad."

"But, but . . . it's not my job to serve on the outside, man! I just deliver, y'know? And I get into plenty of big trouble when I take too long on a delivery, so—so let me cut outa here, eh? Please?"

"I promise you," Minnie said, "you won't get into trouble with Dave today. You got a perfect excuse: You are a hostage." She was smiling at him warmly, almost lovingly.

Gonzalo felt suddenly disconnected from all reality, like an actor playing a part in somebody else's dream.

"A hostage?"

"But also a lunch guest," Minnie said graciously.

"You're putting me on!" Gonzalo cried, waving his hands wildly.

"She ain't puttin' you on, man!" Jesse piped up from his place at the table. "They got the whole bank taken over. There's five or six of 'em, and they all got guns."

"You better believe it!" Stosh said, slapping Brubaker's left-handed holster awkwardly with his right hand.

Gonzalo looked up at Stosh, who didn't even need a gun to detain him, and decided quickly to turn his persuasive talents to Minnie. "Aw, come on, man," he pleaded, "you got plenty of nice-looking people for your party. You don't need Gonzalo!"

"Gon-za-lo!" Minnie said, repeating his name as though it were an aria encore. "Oh-hh, what a bee-ootiful name! Gonzalo, I would like you to meet our other lunch guests. These are the nice people who usually operate the Citizens' Bank. And this, ladies and gentlemen, is Gonzalo!"

"Aw, don't do that, man," Gonzalo said irritably, "I don't wanna meet nobody! I don't wanna even be here, man."

"Gonzalo, you didn't notice I'm a woman?" Minnie asked.

"Huh?"

"I'm a woman," she repeated.

"Yeah, I can see that, man."

"So how come you call me 'man'?"

"We call *everybody* 'man'" he said as though everybody knew that.

"Why?"

"Don't ask *me*, man. That's the way it is!"

A few of the younger people at the table gigled at Gonzalo's sweeping statement of fact. Minnie cooled the gigglers with an icy look.

"Well, my dear Gonzalo, let me tell you how it is in here," she said, all business again. "You came in too late for the house rules, so I'll tell you special: Everybody in this room is going to spend most of the day here. We are all going to be peaceful and very nice to each other. This way nobody will be hurt, and maybe something good will come from this day. But if anybody here tries to throw a monkey wrench into the proceedings with any monkey business, I will have to shoot this gun. . . . You understand me, Gonzalo?"

Minnie took her gun out of her pocket so Gonzalo could get a good look. The effect was instantaneous.

"Oh, yes, yes," Gonzalo said in a hurry, keeping his eyes on the gun. "I understand English very good, man! . . . uh, I mean *Señora!*"

"Oh-h, Gon-zalo," Minnie said, "that's nice. Very nice! All right. So-o, let's eat lunch, *Señor!*" She whipped the tablecloth off the top of the cart, revealing the heartburning display of one of Dave's extra-special super king-size assorted party delicatessen lazy Susan trays.

"Would you just look at this layout, everybody!" Minnie said, slapping her cheek in admiration. "I don't even believe my own eyes! Look at the sandwiches—hot corned beef, pastrami, lox with cream cheese, chopped chicken liver, sliced turkey with Russian. And look at the side dishes—bee-ootiful sour tomatoes, and new kosher pickles, and sliced sweet Bermudas, and pickled herring in sour cream, yet! It's a regular feast, a banquet fit for royalty! And wait, wait!" She pocketed her gun and wiggled a finger at Gonzalo, motioning him to bend an ear for a secret question. Then, shielding her mouth with a pudgy hand like a little kid, she whispered eagerly in his ear. Gonzalo nodded Yes in response.

"And afterwards," Minnie announced with delight,—"we have a special *surprise dessert!*"

No one cheered. No one spoke. No one even looked the least bit interested in the huge mounds of assorted delicacies before them. Despite Minnie's appetizing overture to the luncheon, this crowd was clearly going to be tough to play deli to.

Wilson's stomach had turned at the very instant the heady garlic perfume had reached his pinched nose, Slack's mouth had twisted at the sight of the sour tomatoes, Barnes couldn't stand the sight or the very idea of chicken innards, chopped or not, and McInnerny, who was sitting closest to the sliced Bermudas, started to cry and cough at the same time.

Minnie Gold had an unerring sense of audience response, and she knew at that moment that her lunch intro needed a certain gimmick to get this crowd into the spirit of the show. A captive audience is not necessarily an enthusiastic audience, and a full-house benefit crowd is the absolute worst of all.

A quick glance at Stosh, his eyes glued on the huge tray, and Minnie had her gimmick.

"Mr. Guard," she said, "you would like maybe a little taste of something here?"

Stosh was momentarily disconnected, riveted by the sight and smell of the food.

"Mr. Guard!"

Stosh jerked himself out of his gastronomic reverie with a foolish start. "You talk to me?"

"Yes, you!" Minnie said. "You see maybe *another* guard someplace? I said, would you like a sandwich, a pickle, a *nosh?*"

"You think I should?"

"I'm inviting you, ain't I?" Minnie said, as if to a son-in-law. "G'wan! Take, take, eat, enjoy!"

Shyly nodding in apology to the people at the table for being first in the chow line, Stosh ambled over to the cart, his eyes devouring even more than his giant stomach could hold. Decisions did not come easy to Stosh. There he stood, as they all watched, the tip of a huge forefinger in his freely salivating mouth, his hungry eyes darting from sandwich to sandwich, from the pickles to the tomatoes and back again to the meat-laden sandwiches.

180

But Minnie didn't rush him. She had her eye on her audience at the table, and by the time Stosh finally popped a thick kosher pickle slice into his mouth, the juice squirting down on his chin from the force of his first eager bite, she knew—like Ethel Merman knows—that she'd have them eating out of her hand.

At last, Stosh chose a heaping corned beef on rye from the very top of the pile. Backing to the door, he daintily amputated a full quarter of the sandwich in a single bite.

"How is that? Good?" Minnie asked him.

"*Mmm-mm-gmm!*" Stosh was chewing happily.

Minnie looked back at the table. Her timing had been perfect. One clearing throat, two mouths swallowing saliva, a pair of flaring nostrils, and two shamelessly licking lips. The reluctant diners were now all at once slavering, ravenous, absolutely dying for kosher delicatessen.

"Okay, Gonzalo," Minnie said. "Just put the whole lazy Susan on the middle of the table. Everybody will help themselves—very informal."

Gonzalo lifted the huge tray from the cart as Jesse and Opal parted wide to let him in with it.

"Watch out for the wire in the middle," Minnie cautioned. "That's it, good. Now, Gonzalo, you will come here and sit down in your reserved seat next to Mr. Brubaker."

Gonzalo moved toward the chair Minnie had pulled out, his eyes shifting warily from Minnie's gun to Stosh at the door to the empty chair next to Brubaker, then to the open pair of handcuffs locked to the cable, waiting for him.

Brubaker lifted his head from the table at the mention of his name, and Gonzalo suddenly noticed the man's battered face and his arm in a sling.

"Hey, man, *¿qué pasó?* What happened to you?"

"Simple," said Brubaker. "I tried to do what *you're* thinking right now. If I were you, I would sit down."

The wisdom of Brubaker's advice struck home immediately, and Gonzalo sat. "I don't believe this, man," he said, shaking his head miserably.

"*Señor* Gonzalo," said Minnie quietly, "do yourself a big favor. *Believe* it." She reached over and snapped the handcuffs around his wrists, then turned to her dining-roomful of guests.

"Come on, everybody, what are you waiting for? Eat, eat! There is plenty for everybody. I wasn't sure how many, so I ordered for thirty!"

The steel cable swayed back and forth, handcuffs clicking against one another, locks sliding to and fro along the cable, the lazy Susan spinning clockwise and back as the newly hungry crowd attacked Dave's deli tray as if they hadn't eaten all week.

Opal passed a turkey sandwich down for Mr. Wilson. Angela removed the thin slices of lox from atop her cream cheese and had one of her favorite

181

sandwiches. Barnes opted for corned beef, and Jesse winced as he passed him a little paper cup of mayonnaise for it. Lowina offered Slack a corned beef sandwich.

"No, no!" he said, pulling back. "I don't want it."

"It's good corned beef," Lowina said.

"No. I don't think I want any."

"I'll have a corned beef," Mio said, reaching over to take it.

"Turkey, Mr. Slack?" Lowina asked, reaching back to the tray again.

"No, no! Don't touch it!" Slack jumped in his seat. "I'll get mine later. Take it away, dammit!"

Lowina was stunned, blinking at the man as he glared at her, the turkey sandwich still held in her hands.

"Mr. Slack," Minnie said, "It's perfectly all right to accept kosher food from black hands, you know."

"What the hell are you talking about?" Slack snapped.

"I know what she's talking about," Lowina said quietly, putting the sandwich carefully down in front of Slack. "You didn't want me to sit next to you, either."

"I . . . I didn't what? What do you mean?"

Lowina didn't answer. She just looked at him. Sidney gently put his hand on her forearm.

Jesse broke the heavy silence in the room. "They all on to you, Massa Slack," he said quietly.

"Shut your mouth, Jesse," said Barnes, pointing a warning finger.

"Yassuh, Mister Barnes," said Jesse, smiling easily. "You right. I don't hafta open it no more. I done said everything that's on my mind."

"Mr. Slack," Minnie said, "if I knew you felt like that, I'da put you between Lowina and Sidney like an Oreo cookie."

Jesse giggled.

"I don't feel like that!" Slack exploded.

"Like what, Mr. Slack?" Minnie asked innocently.

"Like . . . like you're implying!" the man sputtered. "I've never shown disrespect for another color . . . for another person because of his skin color in all my life!"

"*Tsk-tsk-tsk!* You felt it all your life, but you never *showed* it? Is that what you mean?"

"No, no! That's not what I mean!" he blurted, squirming in his seat. "I'll have you know that I follow, to the letter, the guidelines of the Equal Employment Opportunities Act, and . . . every other piece of civil rights legislation laid down by the federal government."

"Really!" Minnie said, drawing him fully out.

"Yes, really!" Slack shouted. "And so does Citizens' Bank. For your information, the work force of Los Angeles County is made up of twenty-four point five percent ethnic minorities, and Citizens' Bank is currently

182

employing more than twenty-*eight* percent of its entire staff from these minorities. I'm very *proud* of that!"

The man was pale and shaking with righteousness.

"Izzat so-o?" Minnie said. "I see, said the blind man."

"We all see," said Sidney, who usually didn't say much.

"Gonzalo," Minnie said after a moment, tapping him on the shoulder, "pass the paper napkins down the table please . . . *por favor.*"

"*Si, si, Señora,*" Gonzalo passed the stack of napkins along. "You know what, *Señora?*" he said, looking at Minnie with new respect. "This whole crazy thing . . . whatever is going on here . . . I *believe* it, man!"

"Please. Just one moment, please," Oscar said, stopping the man about to step up to his window. "Stay behind the rope for a moment, und I will be right with you." Oscar leaned over the low partition to Louie in the next cubicle, fidgeting while Louie finished with a customer.

"This is insanity, Levine!" Oscar whispered tensely. "It's after twelve o-clcock. You *must* call for Phase Three! It's already a miracle that we haven't been discovered!"

Louie smiled at his next customer, calmly holding up his palm, motioning the old man to wait in place. "Oscar, you are going to drive me crazy," Louie hissed through his plastic smile. "I am in charge here. I will decide when is Phase Three. You get back to business!"

"But we can't go on like this!" Oscar insisted. "You are forgetting why we are here. We didn't come here to operate a bank, for God's sake!"

"You are telling *me* why we're here?"

"I am telling you that we are not keeping to our schedule. I am telling you that you arc cndangering the whole project—everything!"

A pencil in Louie's hand snapped in two as he felt the sudden hot flush at the back of his neck. "Oscar, if you don't move back to your window right now, I will reach over and choke you! That's what *you* are in danger of, you hear?"

"I hear, Levine, I hear," Oscar said. "So remember: It is on your head."

Oscar moved back to his window and motioned his next customer forward.

Stosh came out of the conference room, furtively dabbing the corners of his mouth with a paper napkin, and headed for the drinking fountain.

Odessa's grandmother was now next in line at Abe's window, looking anxiously toward the rest rooms for her granddaughter as Abe counted out the money for the woman in front of her. She had never seen anyone count out paper currency with such panache. The bills seemed almost to tap-dance as he snapped them one by one onto the counter, forming a symmetrical green fan for the customer to pick up.

"One hundred twenty, one forty, one sixty, and seven fifty, all American money, Mrs. Jordan," Abe said, smiling broadly.

"One forty, one sixty, five and two are seven, and fifty cents. . . . Thank you, sir," Mrs. Jordan said, snatching up her monthly income and stuffing it into her purse.

"Wait just a minute," Abe stopped her. "Here is your hundred-dollar bonus!"

"My what?" the woman asked.

"Your hundred-dollar state bonus, Mrs. Jordan. Haven't you heard? All Social Security recipients are getting it this month. The governor declared it the minute he found out so many old people were running short. Isn't that nice?"

Mrs. Jordan tucked her chin way in, pulling her head back on her long neck, like a suspicious ostrich, as she looked down at the hundred-dollar bill. "You doin' a April fool joke on me?"

"Does this *look* like a joke to you, Mrs. Jordan?" asked Abe, holding the bill out. "If this is a joke, you can laugh all the way home from the bank!"

She looked at him, unsmiling. Then she tilted her head quizzically, as though to inspect the bill's authenticity.

"It's real! See?" Abe turned the bill horizontally. "Benjamin Franklin, the same as your other one. Here, take it. Just don't spend it all on a *young man*, you know what I mean?"

She was slowly shaking her head. "No. No, thank you just the same," she said nervously. "I can't take what's not mine."

"It's yours, really!" Abe insisted as he grabbed her hand and forced the bill into it. "If you don't take it, it'll screw up our books, you know?"

"Shoot, what do *I* care 'bout your books?" the woman said, trying to reopen her fist, which Abe was holding tightly closed around the bill. "They said my brother-in-law cheated once on the unemployment, and they put him on the inside for six months. I take that money—they'd just throw a old black woman like me on the trash heap!"

Abe shot his hand up, waving for Stosh, holding onto her hand and talking a mile a minute all at the same time. "Mrs. Jordan, I assure you, it's not cheating! The hundred-dollar bonus is yours, it's strictly legal!"

Stosh had walked quickly to Abe's window and was standing next to the woman as she continued to struggle with Abe.

"Come on now, mister, you get that money away from me! I got all mine here—a hundred and sixty-seven fifty, and that's all I want!"

"Shh-hh! Just calm down, Mrs. Jordan," Abe said, handing her fist into one of Stosh's huge mitts. "The guard will explain it to you. Mr. Guard, would you please assure Mrs. Jordan that the hundred-dollar bonus is on the level—and help her to the front door?"

"Oh, sure!" Stosh put an arm around the woman's shoulder and started hustling her toward the door. "Come, Mrs. Jordan, right this way!"

"Don't want no explanation," she objected, "and I don't need no help to no door, neither!"

184

But the woman was buried under Stosh's arm like a walking football and could hardly be seen or heard as he escorted her gently but firmly to the front door, breathing hot corned beef on her all the way. "Believe me, Mrs. Jordan," he said as he took her out the door and onto the sidewalk, "every old person that cashed Social Security check here today gets extra hundred dollars. It's the law!"

"The *law?*" the woman asked spinning around dizzily as Stosh let her go without warning, "I don't wanna have nothin' to do with no law!"

"Very smart!" Stosh said, nodding soberly. "Have good day, now!" He gave her a smiling salute and disappeared back into the bank.

The befuddled old woman continued to turn like a wobbly top, revolving in slow motion and utter confusion in the middle of the busy sidewalk as people walked by her.

Down the block, Bush and Cassidy, the black and white cops, came out of Dave's Deli and got into their black and white squad car, forcing Big Joe to get off the fender of the police car and find someplace else to sit while the other men dug the asphalt chunks out of his trench.

"Hey, man! You see how long you guys've been in there?" he shouted to the cops, pointing at the trench he had dug right past the length of the police car.

"Yeah," Bush said, laughing. "Keep pumpin', man!"

The old black woman stopped turning. Slowly, she unclamped her stiff fingers and straightened out the hundred-dollar bill, staring at it fearfully, as though it were a one-way ticket to San Quentin.

Shakily, she walked back to the front door of the bank, waving the offending bill at Stosh through the glass. Stosh smiled and nodded, thumbing her on her way. She turned back to the street, now in a panic, out of control. Frantically, she grabbed at the arm of a man passing. "Here, mister!" she screamed. "Take this hundred-dollar bill. I don't want it!"

The man flinched, jerking his hands up as though she had pointed a gun at him, and fled from her, muttering about a crazy world filled with crazy people.

"Please, please! Oh, God!" the old woman started to rave, flailing her arms in the air. "Oh, Lordy, please! Somebody take it! Take it, it don't belong to me! Save me, save me!"

Startled passersby quickly gave her a wide berth, dodging around her as though she were a madwoman.

"Help! He-elp me, somebodee-ee!" she shrieked at the top of her lungs, as she ran off the sidewalk and right out into the middle of the street, wildly waving the hundred-dollar bill like a flag.

The black-and-white was accelerating to make it through the changing traffic signal at Fairfax.

"Holy shi-it!" Cassidy yelled as he saw the woman, right in front of them. Bush slammed on the brakes and twisted the wheel hard to the right,

185

sending the squad car into a squealing sideways skid, the tires burning rubber until the rear end of the car finally came to a lurching stop at the old woman's feet.

In that last sickening millisecond, Bush saw the wild-eyed woman go down in a heap like a clubbed calf, just as the car behind them banged into the side of their police car with a crunch.

A driver in a Volvo, jackrabbiting out at the change of the light on Fairfax, jammed on his brakes at the sound of the crash to his right, and was instantly rear-ended by the red Mustang behind him. The Mustang's front wheels jumped right over the Volvo's rear bumpers, landing high up on the Volvo's trunk, where it continued crazily chug-chugging forward.

People came running into the streets from everywhere, several rushing out of the bank, some from other buildings, some from a tour bus in the CBS parking lot—all intent on seeing how fast they could get in the way.

Stosh ran to the front door of the bank to look out at the tangled scene. He saw the crowd gather around the fallen old woman lying in the street. Then he saw the two cops scramble out of their vehicle. That was all he needed to see. He raced back to tell Louie that The Benefit was about to be discovered.

"Is she dead?" yelled a guy at the back of the crowd.

"How do I know?" asked the man bending over her with her wrist in his hand. "I'm not a doctor!"

Cassidy and Bush were pushing through the crowd, horns were starting to honk behind both accidents, and a fist fight had broken out between the drivers of the Volvo and the Mustang, their vehicles still locked together on Fairfax.

"Back up, back up. Police officers!" Cassidy shouted as he elbowed people out of the way and knelt to examine Mrs. Jordan. The frail little woman was lying flat on her back, rigid as an ebony branch, her eyes tightly closed, her fists folded over her bosom, the hundred-dollar bill sticking up out of one of them like a newly minted lily.

Cassidy felt the woman's wrist for a pulse.

"Feel anything?" asked Bush.

"Nothing," said Cassidy. He slipped his hand through the woman's flowered blouse to feel her heart.

The stiff little victim suddenly snapped her knees to her chest like a spring-steel bear trap, her eyes blazing open.

"What you think you're doin' with your hand in there, boy?" she screamed at Cassidy, who was having a difficult time pulling his hand out with her bony knees pressed hard up against his arm.

"Take it easy, lady," he said, finally extricating his hand. "What were you trying to do? You almost got yourself killed!"

"What you think I was tryin' to do, boy?" She was struggling to get to her feet. "I was tryin' to get somebody to pay attention to me, that's what!"

186

"Hey, wait a minute, momma!" Bush said. "Don't try to get up, now."

"I ain't your momma, boy," she snapped, pulling herself up by his belt. "And I sure ain't gonna lay in the middle of the street all day!"

"You sure you're all right, now?"

"My poor ol' body's all right, boy," she said. "It's my troubled soul that needs tendin' to!" And she started to shake uncontrollably, holding the hundred-dollar bill out to him.

"Here, let's get you out of the street, momma," Bush said, putting his arm around the woman's shoulder and walking her stiffly to the sidewalk.

"Okay, folks," Cassidy shouted to the crowd, "show's over! Move along, now."

The crowd dispersed, grumbling and swapping eyewitness accounts of the accident, while the two cops negotiated their frail charge across the sidewalk.

The old woman was punching the hundred-dollar bill into Bush's stomach. "Take it, take it!" she howled. "I don't want it!"

"Just put your money away, ma'am," Bush said, pushing the bill away. "We're going to get you an ambulance to make sure you're not hurt."

"Don't want no amb'lance! I jes' want you to take this damn hundred-dollar bill away from me! It don't belong to me, I don't want it, and I won't have it!"

"What do you mean, you don't want it?" asked Cassidy.

"I mean it's not mine. And I don't wanna get in no trouble! What in the world do I have to do to give away a hundred-dollar bill anyways? Is the whole world crazy?"

"Take it easy, lady. Just calm down a minute and tell us what happened," Cassidy said. "Now, where did you get that bill?"

"Oh, my Lord," she cried in frustration, "they give it to me right in that bank! They're crazy people in there, givin' money away, whether you want it or not!"

"Giving money away?" Bush asked. "What do you mean, *giving?*"

"Why you axin' me all these silly questions, boy? Why don't you jes' help me? Help me! Here, take this outa my hand! Please, please, take it!"

The woman moaned a pitiful glissing moan as she slumped slowly, her back sliding down the marble wall of the building, until she sat bump on the sidewalk. She tried to throw the hundred-dollar bill at the cops standing over her, but it only fluttered back in her lap, where she swatted at it, howling in terror as if it were an attacking bumblebee.

Both cops quickly bent over her again, and a new crowd immediately formed around them on the sidewalk at the sound of the fearful screaming.

"Easy, easy, momma!" Bush put his hands under her arms to pull her up. "We're here to help you."

"Well, then, help me, help me!" she shrieked, slapping at Bush and sweeping away the hundred-dollar bill, which Cassidy quickly retrieved.

187

"Hey, what are you doing to this poor woman?" yelled a big woman, elbowing her way through the crowd and swinging her purse at Cassidy. "Let her up! What's the matter with you? You oughta be ashamed!"

"Hold it, hold it!" Cassidy cried, trying to dodge the rain of blows. "We're helping her! She was just—"

"That's how you *help*?" the woman shouted. "You knock her down and take her money?"

"Take it easy, lady," Cassidy said, holding his baton in both hands, shoulder high to the crowd. "Nobody's being hurt here, folks. We're assisting this woman. Just move along. That's it, people, just clear the area. . . . That's right; thank you very much."

The crowd dispersed, as if they had business of their own to mind.

"See if you can get her calmed down," Cassidy said to Bush, "while I go call in for the paramedics."


Inside, Louie was on the phone at the safety deposit counter, where he had just finished making his media calls. As soon as he got through to the Los Angeles Police Department, he could call for Phase Three.

"Hello, LAPD? I wanta report a bank holdup, please. . . . Hello! Hello! . . ."

Louie shook the receiver in his left hand, as if to wake somebody.

"I don't know whether they hung up on me," he said to Stosh, "or whether they're switching me."

"Louie, please," Stosh said, "no more phoning! They come in any minute!"

"Hello? Oh, yes, hello! Am I connected with the party where I can report a bank holdup? Good. How-do-you-do? . . . Yes, Sergeant Bailey, I am calling to report a holdup and occupation of the Citizens' Bank on the corner of Fairfax and Beverly. . . . Of course Los Angeles!"

"Louie, please, Louie!" Stosh pleaded.

"What?" Louie asked on the phone. "My name? You crazy? You don't recognize an anonymous phone tip when you get one?"

Oscar suddenly came limping back to the safety deposit counter in a big hurry. "Levine, this is crazy! There is a police car outside! Und a big crowd of people! Phase Three should begin right this instant, I'm telling you!"

"Okay, okay!" Louie said, covering the phone with his hand. "I got the right guy!" He uncovered the mouthpiece. "Hello? Excuse me, can you hold the phone a minute? . . . No, no, I'll be right back. Just a minute!" He covered the phone again. "Okay, Stosh, go! Check out the rest rooms, then lock the front door. Hold your hand up high when you get it locked, and we go into Phase Three!"

Stosh headed for the men's room—nobody at the urinals, no shoes showing under the booth doors. He left the room quickly, turning left. The sign on the ladies' rest room door flashed a red light in Stosh's brain, and he stopped dead in his tracks. He had never been in a ladies' rest room in his life, but Louie said "Go" and Stosh was going to go, no matter what.

Cautiously, he turned his back to the door—Nobody looking directly at him. Green light. He backed into the room.

"Any woman in here?" Stosh asked, still facing the door.

As she had promised her grandmother, Odessa had counted aloud to four and had just torn the toilet tissue at the proper perforation. Startled by the scary deep voice, she stuffed the paper into her mouth and held her breath so no sound could escape.

No answer. Stosh swiveled around for one quick peek—no one at the sinks, no shoes under the booth doors. He shot out of the door and into the hall in an embarrassed sweat.

Stosh had done his best. It really was not his fault. From a height of six feet six inches, it is impossible to see the dangling shoes of a six-year-old child under a toilet booth door. Men in high places often overlook the little people.

Stosh reported to Louie at the command phone. "Nobody in toilets."

"Okay," Louie said. "Go to the front door—now!"

"How about sign?"

"I'll tell you when to hang the sign! Go, go!"

Stosh walked briskly toward the front, begging their pardon as he bumped into several people on the way.

"Yes, yes," said Louie into the phone, "I'm still here, Sergeant. I'll be with you in just a minute. I am putting you on the hold button." Click. Louie smiled wryly at the memory of all the times people had put *him* on "hold."

Stosh turned the key and stood up quickly, holding his hand high above his head. Louie saw the signal and suddenly started whacking the telephone onto the counter as hard as he could. Everybody in the bank whirled around to face him and the awful racket.

"Okay, everybody, *stand still!*" he shouted. "*Nobody move!* Now, Abe, your speech! Vito, go to Minnie!"

Vito ran to the conference room as Abe vaulted up onto the counter at window three in a flash, waving his hands above his head. "Ladies and gentemen! May I have your attention, please? We got a little emergency, and I want—"

A woman screamed and started running for the front door.

"Let's get outa here!" a man yelled to his wife.

"No, no! Listen to me!" Abe hollered. "Don't try to get out! *Stand still and listen!*"

Stosh jerked his gun out with his left hand as several people ran toward the door. The screaming woman screamed again, but she stopped with the rest as they all saw the gun and backed away.

189

"Ladies and gentlemen, please!" Abe cried out. "I want you to listen to me very carefully! There is *no danger;* nobody will be hurt!"

The crowd of customers suddenly started a babble of frightened questions.

"Quiet! Be quiet!" Stosh yelled, waving his gun. "Stand still!"

"You will be silent!" Oscar called out in his high-pitched voice from behind the counter, his Luger pistol now shaking in his hand. There were new gasps from the crowd, and several women put their hands over their mouths to keep from screaming.

"Please, ladies and gentlemen," Abe said, slowly drawing his gun from his belt and pointing it carefully up at the ceiling, "I want you all to be calm. . . . This way, *we* will be calm, and nobody will have to be hurt. Do you understand me?"

They were quiet now, and pretty much standing still, instinctively huddled together like a flock of sheep surrounded by marauding wolves.

"That's better," Abe said, no longer shouting. "Now listen to me. We are going to let you all out of the bank—" A sudden chatter of relief broke the short silence. "Quiet, now, quiet. We are going to let you all out, but we have to do it in an orderly way, so nobody gets hurt. There are police outside, with guns, and we do not want an accident. Now, I want you all to raise your hands over your heads—"

A black woman suddenly broke from the crowd, running toward the back of the bank, waving her arms wildly and screeching, "Odessa! Odessa! Ode-es-ss-a!"

Louie saw her move and stepped out to cut her off, grabbing her in his open arms, where she struggled for a moment, screaming incoherently. All at once she collapsed, slumping totally limp in his arms like a doll of rags. Louie gently laid her out on the floor. Odessa's grandmother had fainted dead away.

The crowd started to surge toward the fallen woman.

"Nobody move!" Louie commanded, as he quickly felt her pulse. "It's all right. She's okay. She only fainted, that's all. Go ahead with the instructions, Abe." He grabbed a seat cushion from a secretary's chair and put it under the unconscious woman's head.

"All right," Abe continued, "everybody put your hands up high. . . . Ladies, just raise your purses with your hands."

"Oh, my God, my purse!" one woman cried.

"Don't worry," said Abe, wiggling an assuring palm, "nobody will take anything from you. This is not a stickup!"

A short burst of surprised jabbering came from the crowd.

"People, please!" Abe complained. "How can I tell you how you are going to get out of here, if you are not going to listen to me?" They quieted, immediately attentive again.

"All right. Everybody got hands up? Good. Now, I want you all to face

190

the front door . . . slow, slow. . . . Keep your hands up. . . . That's nice. . . . You are doing fine."

They were like automatons now, obeying Abe's commands willingly, hoping that quick obedience would get them quickly out of the bank.

"Now listen carefully, everybody. . . . Next, we are going to make a big bunch, right in the middle of the bank, between those two big tables—wait, wait—don't move till I tell you. I want the ladies to be in the front, closest to the door, and the men in the back, understand? All right, start to walk to the middle of the room. . . . That's it, take it easy . . . ladies first . . . nice and slow . . . "

Louie and Oscar were kneeling over the unconscious black woman.

"Is she really only fainted?" Oscar whispered.

"Yeah, she'll be all right," Louie said, "but she's not gonna wake up in time to walk outa here."

They both looked down at the woman, out cold, but still clutching her purse and a little yellow sweater.

"I got an idea." Louie pointed to a swivel chair behind a desk. "Get me that chair—she'll ride out!"

"Wait a minute!" Abe was yelling at a little man. "You, *you!* . . . Are you a lady? Move back, back with the rest of the men!"

The man clutched his wife's arm even tighter. "She's my wife, for God's sake!"

"I asked you for your marital status?" Abe asked. "Move back, I said!"

"Move back, for goodness sake!" a woman pleaded. "Let us get outa here!"

"Don't worry," Abe said to the man as he moved to the back, "you'll see her again outside. She'll nag you plenty before it's all over! All right, let me see a nice round group, a *little* closer together."

Louie and Oscar had the black woman seated in the chair. Louie tried to put the yellow sweater around her shoulders, but it was too small, and kept falling off, and she kept falling forward. Oscar grabbed the sweater and quickly tied it snugly around woman and chair, solving the problem.

But something was still troubling Louie as he peered curiously at the woman's face. "That's funny . . . " he said.

"What's funny?" Oscar asked.

"She was hollering 'Odessa, Odessa!' . . . Does she look Russian to you?"

Oscar looked more closely at the woman. "Black Russian?" he said.

"Go-wan!" Louie wheeled the swivel chair around to the front of the crowd. "Grab this!" he ordered the two women in front. "Push her out when you go."

The two women put their hands on the back of the chair.

"Oh, my God!" Louie suddenly remembered, running back to the phone. "I forgot all about Sergeant Bailey!"

"No, no! Don't turn around!" Abe barked at the crowd. "You should look only in front of you—straight ahead! That's better. . . . Okay, we're almost ready now, folks."

All at once, the blob of humanity started to move toward the door.

"Hold it!" Abe yelled, "Nobody moves until I tell you to move! Okay, Oscar, Stosh, ready for the red velvet!"

Stosh and Oscar hove to in a hurry, gathering the red velvet ropes off the brass standards. The stunned crowd watched wide-eyed, as the ropes started to form a circle around them on the floor.

"That's right," Louie was saying on the phone. "The Citizens' Bank has been taken over, that's what I said. . . . The group? Never mind. An unidentified group. . . . Of course I know who we are! You think we came in here without knowing who we are? Let me tell you something, before we get outa here today, *everybody* will know who we are! . . . No, no, I'm not getting angry. I understand, you're just doing your job. And I am just doing my job, too! . . . How many in our group? Don't worry: We are enough of us to do what we came here to do! . . . No, I can't tell you that. I'll talk about that only to the Chief of Police. That's right! Now listen, we are all heavily armed, and we—Wait a minute, you'll have to hold on again. . . . I'm telling you: If you want more information, you'll just have to hold the phone, that's all!"

Louie pressed the hold button agan and turned his attention to Oscar and Stosh as they bent to their job, connecting the snap-locks from rope to rope around the tightly bunched flock of customers.

Outside, Officer Bush was also bending to his job on the sidewalk.

"No-siree! Not on your life, boy!" Mrs. Jordan was saying. "Ain't no way I'm gonna give you my name, not 'lessen you tell me I'm under arrest! No suh! Minute I give you my name, I know I'm in trouble!"

Bush shook his head in frustration. "But I tell you, ma'am, you're not in any trouble, and you're not under arrest! I just need to get some information from you, and I got to start with your name."

"Don't hafta give my name 'lessen I'm under arrest" she said, shaking her head. "I know my rights, boy! I got so *few* of 'em, I know 'em by heart!"

"Then would you just tell me where you got that hundred-dollar bill, and why you don't want it?"

"I done told you! They give it to me in that bank. What's-a matter with you, boy? You got the money, I ain't done nothin', so just lemme up and lemme go!"

"Exactly who gave it to you in the bank?"

"The man in the cage, who d'you think? I give him my gov'ment check, a hundred and sixty-seven fifty, and he give me a hundred an sixty-seven fifty cash money, and then . . . he give me that extra hundred-dollar bill to boot!"

"Did you tell him he made a mistake?"

"'Course I told him!" she replied. "He says, 'This bank don't make no

192

mistakes.' He says, 'Our governor is passin' out a hundred-dollar bonus to all the old people this month.'"

"Did you try to make him take it back?" Bush asked.

"That's what I'm tellin' you, boy! He wouldn't take it back—just kept tellin' me it was mine, 'cause I'm old and I deserve it. Told me not to spend it on no young man. . . . Shoot! He even had the guard man to take me out the door, so's I couldn't give it back!"

Bush shook his head slowly, trying to make sense of it. "That sounds crazy," he said.

"Ain't *me* that's crazy," Mrs. Jordan said. "It's them people in that bank!"

Stosh and Oscar had their covey of customers neatly packaged, securely surrounded by red velvet rope, and ready for self-shipment out of the bank on Abe's command.

"Please, you people on the outside," Abe directed. "You hafta hold the rope tight at your waist; otherwise you won't be able to fit outa the door!"

"Hurry up, will you!" cried a woman in the middle of the pack, "I'm suffocating here!"

"Okay, okay! We're almost ready to go.Now remember: I will tell the guard to open the doors, then I will count to three, slow . . . *then* you will start walking—slow and easy—starting with your left foot. When the whole bunch gets through the door, you all turn left—*left,* you got it? Be sure you hold onto the rope until you get to the corner. Then, the people on the outside will drop the rope to the ground—and you're all on your own. Anybody got any questions?"

Nobody had questions.

"Okay . . . " Abe said, taking a last look at the crowd, which looked like a giant bundle of asparagus. "Mr. Guard, you can open the doors."

Stosh knelt to unlock the doors.

"Oscar," Louie said quickly, "get on the other side of the door from Stosh. They'll need a push to get through!"

Oscar ran limping to one side of the entrance as Stosh pulled both doors wide open.

Outside, both wrecks were being cleared out of the middle of the street. Officer Cassidy had exchanged license and insurance information with the driver who had rammed into the squad car, then had released him. Officer Bush had parked the black-and-white against the curb, its mangled passenger-side doors hanging sprung open in testimony to the collision.

"Feeling better now, ma'am?" Cassidy asked the black woman. "Let's get you up off the sidewalk, all right?"

"Yessuh, thank you, suh," she said, as each cop took an armpit, hoisting her to her feet.

"Now, then," Cassidy said, "we want you to take us back into the bank and show us just who gave you this hundred-dollar bill—"

The woman struggled to pull her arms out of their grasp. "Oh, no! I ain't goin' back in that crazy bank, no, suh!"

"But all we want to do is return the money," Bush said. "Then you can go home."

"Oh, my Lord!" she wailed hysterically, pulling her arms loose and starting to whirl around and around. "Whatcha tryin' to do to this old woman? Help! He-elp, Po-leece!"

And all of a sudden, she lurched forward and collapsed in a heap again, sitting on the sidewalk with the two cops bending over her and another crowd gathering.

"Ladies and gentlemen, before you go, I would like to congratulate you," Abe was saying, "for your cooperation, for keeping your heads cool, and following—"

"Abe, I'm warning you!" Louie growled.

"I'm sorry," Abe said. "All right, I'm going to start counting. I will count to *three*, then I will say 'Go.' . . . Do *not* start until I say 'Go.' . . . One . . . two . . . three. Left foot first . . . Go!"

The red-velvet-tied bunch lurched forward on its left foot, pushing Odessa's grandmother toward the door.

"That's good. . . . You are doing good," Abe said. "Slow . . . slow. Keep your hands up high. . . . That's nice . . . "

A man carrying a canvas bank bag full of currency started into the bank just as Odessa's grandmother reached the front door, the casters of her chair blumping over the threshold.

The two women in front screamed at him. "Get outa the way! Coming out, coming out!"

The man took one look at the bizarre herd of humanity coming at him, spun around and started running like hell, the heavy bag thwunking against his leg as he raced down the block toward the two cops. "The bank, the bank!" he sputtered, pointing back as he ran. "They're all. . . . they're all tied up! They're coming out of the—*Jee-sus Chri-i-st!*"

Stosh pushed the crowd in on one side, and Oscar on the other, squeezing it out of round as though it were a balloon full of air, until, all at once, the pushed-in mass grunted and popped through the doorway and out onto the sidewalk.

"You're out!" Abe screamed after them, jumping down off the counter. "Turn left! *Le-eft!*"

The crowd veered to the left as Stosh and Oscar banged the doors shut.

"Now, Stosh, the chain!" Louie yelled. "And the sign, the sign!"

"Holy Shit!" Cassidy said, as he saw the crowd lumbering toward him.

"Get up! Quick, momma!" Bush pulled Mrs. Jordan to her feet and shoved her headlong into the open squad car. "Get in there, and stay down!"

194

"Oh, my Lord, have mercy!" Mrs. Jordan buried her face in the driver's seat, covering her head with her purse and whimpering pitifully.

Both cops scrambled around to the street side of their squad car, diving to the pavement as they drew their guns.

"Judas Priest, will you tell me what the hell that is!" Bush said, as the bundled crowd marched past them toward the corner like a gigantic centipede.

"Jesus, I don't know," Cassidy said. "That's the weirdest thing I ever saw in my life! Hey, that big guy had a bank bag!" He raised up, trying to aim his revolver at the man hurrying away with the canvas bag, but the moving crowd cut off his view. "I can't get a shot off, dammit!" Cassidy yelled. "Those people are in my way. . . . .I'm going after him! Get on the radio! We need back-up!" He galloped after the man with the canvas bank bag.

Bush crawled to the driver's door and pulled it open. Mrs. Jordan lifted her head and screamed as loudly as a terrified old lady can scream, right into the cop's startled face. Bush ducked as though he'd been shot at, banging his nose hard against the car's door-sill.

"Here, take *all* my money!" the woman shrieked, shoving her purse at him. "Just let me go home! Please, please!"

"You're all right," Bush said, holding his nose, "I'm just gonna use the radio. You gotta stay right there, you hear?"

"Oh Lord, save me!" the woman cried out, covering her head again with her purse. "Save me, God, *save Leona!*"

Bush reached across and grabbed the radio mike, flipping the speak switch as his nose began to bleed.

"Yes, thank you for waiting," Louie was saying into the phone. "I can talk now. . . . That's right, Citizens' Bank, at Fairfax and Beverly. . . . Never mind what we want, Sergeant. I will tell the Chief what we want! Now listen, we are all heavily armed, and we are holding hostages . . . all the bank employees, and one busboy—What? . . . A joke? Listen, Mister, this is exactly the opposite of a joke, you hear me? We also have a bomb in the safety deposit vault. . . . No, not a timer. We have a whatta-ya-call-it, a plunger. . . . Never mind. That's all. No more free information. . . . You what? . . . Wait a minute! You calling me a *liar?*"

Louie was shaking with anger as he listened to the cool official voice of the Los Angeles Police Department.

"Oh-h, I see. . . . April Fool, hah?" Suddenly he pulled his gun out of his belt and pointed it at the ceiling. "Well, listen to *this,* Sergeant Bailey. You'll *hear*—maybe you'll believe!"

Louie pulled the trigger twice fast. The recoil of the first shot cocked the gun in his hand so that the second shot slammed into a fluorescent light fixture, showering pieces of glass and plastic all over him.

Vito came tearing out of the conference room. "What the hell hap-

195

pened?" he yelled, seeing Louie bent over with the phone in one hand and brushing the debris off his shoulders with the other.

"I shot off my gun, that's what happened!" Louie shouted, covering the mouthpiece.

"At who? Where?" Vito whirled around in all directions, looking for an enemy.

"At the dumb cop on this phone, who do ya think?" Louie said.

"You shot at a *cop* on the *phone?*"

"Shut up!" Louie barked. "Can't you see I'm still talking?" He took his hand off the mouthpiece as Vito looked from Oscar to Stosh to Oscar in confusion. Oscar put a shushing finger to his lips.

"Hello? You still there?" Louie shouted into the phone. "Good. So now you see . . . this is no joke, and I am no April Fool! No, I will talk *only* to the Chiefa Police. . . . No, no, don't waste time with me with his assistant. If the chief is too busy right now, just tell him to call me. We have almost three hours yet. . . . Never mind what happens in three hours. I'll tell the Chief what'll happen! The phone number here is—Oh, you got the number? All right. . . . What? . . . Oh, you're welcome. Thank *you!*"

Louie placed the phone gently back in its cradle, slowly grinning an ear-to-ear smile.

"My friends," he announced quietly, "The Benefit is in touch with the outside world."

The scene outside was bedlam. People were running back and forth and every which way, bent over at the waist with their heads tucked in as they ran, as though rehearsing for a war film. They were skinnied up behind telephone poles, crouching low behind parked cars, peeking around corners of buildings and shouting at each other and waving wildly and pointing at Citizens' Bank.

A whole line of people waiting to get into Studio Forty-three to see a TV game show deserted the outer balcony at CBS and were scurrying across the parking lot to get a closer view of the bank, squealing delightedly as they ran toward the danger.

As the crowd of people released from the bank reached the corner, the red velvet rope dropped to the ground. The freed captives exploded in all directions, tripping over the rope and falling all over each other in their panicky flight, leaving Odessa's poor grandmother to roll eerily backward down the sidewalk toward the bank, her swivel chair finally bumping smack into a street light standard, spilling her out of the chair and waking her out of her faint with a rude sprawl on the concrete.

At the sound of the gunfire, Big Joe and the gas company crew had scrambled for their lives into the back of the big yellow truck. In his panic to reach safety, Big Joe had detached himself from his bucking machine but

196

hadn't unhooked the locking link from his trigger handle, which left his jackhammer *rat-tat-tat*ting a solo Saint Vitus's dance out in the middle of the street. Nobody in the yellow truck was about to risk trying to make it to the generator truck to cut off the pumping air.

Officer Cassidy, his back flattened against the insurance company window, a few doors from the bank, was waving his gun high over his head, frantically yelling to people who couldn't hear him to clear the street.

Dashing back across the sidewalk to the squad car, Cassidy ducked up and down behind the vehicle, surveying the chaos.

"SWAT, dammit!" he screamed to Bush, still on the radio, "Tell her we need SWAT! Tell her they got the bank chained shut, and a red highway explosive sign at the door. Tell her somebody's fired two rounds in there, and a crowd of people tied up in a red velvet rope just walked out of the bank, heading east on Beverly. No, no! Wait a minute! Don't tell her that *last* thing: She'll think it's April Fool!"

Odessa's grandmother pulled herself groggily to her feet, clinging to the light pole for a moment. Seeing the little yellow sweater on the sidewalk, she snapped suddenly awake as though someone had slapped her. She scooped the sweater up and started to run stumbling toward the bank, holding the sweater low by the shoulders as though she were about to put it on a child, and screaming at the top of her lungs, "Odessa! Odessa!"

Cassidy saw the woman coming. "Hey, lady, get back! Get back, dammit, there are people with guns in that bank!"

"My little girl's in there!" she screamed, unheeding.

"No, no!" Cassidy ran out from behind the police car and intercepted the hysterical woman at the door to the insurance office, locking her in a bear hug and pushing her struggling and screaming through the door and inside. "What's the matter with you, lady? You crazy? Didn't you hear me instructing you to halt?"

The woman kept pushing against him, trying to get back to the door. "Let me out!" she screamed. "My baby's in there!"

"Whoa, whoa!" Cassidy said, pushing her into a chair, as the office workers gathered around. "Now, just try to calm down, ma'am."

"Calm down?" she howled. "Don't you understand, officer? My little girl's in that bank!"

"Okay, okay, take it easy," said Cassidy. "She work in there?"

"No, she doesn't *work* in there! She's my granddaughter!" The woman held the little sweater up for him to see. "She's only six years old!"

Cassidy shook his head as though someone had just belted him. "Jee-sus Christ! Are you sure?"

The woman broke down and started to cry, rocking back and forth, the yellow sweater pressed tightly between her hands. One of the women in the office knelt down beside her, taking her into her arms.

"Take care of her. Keep her in here!" Cassidy ordered, jerking the door open. "Nobody out this door, understand?"

He slammed the door and ran ducking and dodging back to the squad car.

Though everyone in the conference room had eaten, Dave's super king-size deli tray seemed hardly to have been dented. Most neglected were the pastrami and the pickled herring, but Minnie knew that would be corrected the moment the food was taken into the main room, within Abe's arm length. Abe Silver had a passion for two things in life—Minnie Gold and hot pastrami, most of the time in that order.

On taking his first bite out of a hot pastrami sandwich, Abe would always say, "Ah-hh, sweet Rumania! Dee-licious! No doubt about it—pastrami is the *second best* taste I ever had in my whole mouth!"

And Minnie would always ask, "Oh-h, yeah? And what is the *best* taste?"

And Abe would answer, with a wicked wink, "Aha! If I told you—then you'd know everything that I know!"

"Don't worry," she would say, winking back, "I know you . . . and I know!"

"Izzat so? You think you're such a woman of the world," he would say. "So tell me, if you know."

"Never mind," Minnie would say, with the last word. "I know . . . and that's enough!"

Of course she knew. And Abe knew she knew. Can two children live together for fifty years and not know everything about each other? Of course not.

Knowing is one thing, but if they were ever to *tell* each other, then they could never ever have that conversation again. And hot pastrami would never ever again be the second best taste in the world.

Louie came into the conference room wiping his hands with a paper towel. He hated it when his hands sweated.

"Ladies and gentlemen," he said, "I'm sorry if we had to be a little rough with you to . . . to get you situated so we could do our work. Also, I'm sorry we had to keep you in the dark about what was going on, but I'm sure you understand that we have to—"

"Look here!" Wilson exploded, his face beet-red. "We understand nothing! We only know we're being held hostage, chained up like animals by a bunch of vicious maniacs! What do you think you're doing, terrorizing innocent people—a badly injured man, young girls, a pregnant woman—people who never did anything to hurt you. Do you understand what a terrible thing you're doing?"

"Oh, yes, Mr. Wilson, we understand very well what we are doing. And we also understand that it must be done."

"Well, I know what you're doing, too: You're robbing a bank, that's what you're doing! You're committing a federal crime!"

198

Louie studied the angry man at the end of the table for a moment. Then he nodded slowly. "Yes, Mr. Wilson, we are committing a crime . . . it's true. But if that's all we were doing here, we coulda taken the money, and we coulda been gone a coupla hours ago. No, we are not robbing a bank, Mr. Wilson. We are communicating."

"Communicating?" Wilson repeated the word as if he'd never heard it before. "What are you talking about?"

"Oh, we know what we are talking about, believe me," Louie said. "But we got this terrible problem. Nobody *listens*. Nobody pays attention. You're right, my friend. There *is* a federal crime being committed. So how do we get them to open their eyes? Maybe we hafta spit in their eyes . . . they'll wipe out the spit *then* maybe they'll see us."

His audience sat spellbound, though his rhetoric was incomprehensible to them. They were held by his quiet power, and by his eyes, in which they could sense a frightening life-or-death commitment to his cause.

"But I almost forgot," Louie said, breaking the silence. "I came in to let you know we are not operating the bank anymore. I tell you, you people gotta go through a lot to do your job. I got a new respect for banking, yes sir! Anyway, the bank is clear of customers, and don't worry: Everybody who came to the windows before the police car came was well taken care of! By the way, the two shots you heard? I wanna assure you that nobody was hurt, nobody. I had to shoot the ceiling a coupla times, that's all. I was communicating with the Chief of Police.

"So, now . . . the front doors are locked and chained, and everything is going according to schedule. Now, it's just us . . . and you . . .and them."

A fire engine siren whined down as it passed the bank, turning a corner to stop. Then they all heard another siren and skidding tires. Then another, and another. But in the conference room, no head turned, no hand moved, no eye blinked.

"I gotta tell you one more thing," Louie said. "I pray to God it won't happen, but I gotta mention it. You are in no danger from us, as long as you behave yourself. But in a coupla minutes, the bank will be surrounded by the police. A lotta policemen will be running around outside. I don't think they will be shooting into the bank as long as we are holding you here. But later, if they get nervous, they might try a little tear gas to get us out—"

"Oh, my God!" Opal couldn't help it, it popped right out.

"Jesus Christ!" said Barnes. "You think they'd do that?"

"I don't know," Louie said. "I only said they might. Maybe they won't. But we're gonna bring in some wet paper towels for you, and if it should happen . . . the best thing to do is to put the wet towel up to your face and put your head on the table. Understand?"

Everybody understood. Nobody answered.

"So . . . " Louie said quietly, "everybody get enough to eat?"

The answers were grunts and nods.

"Okay, then, I guess it's our turn." He turned, and opened the door. "Vito!" he yelled into the main room. "Come on in here!" He lifted the lazy Susan tray off the table, returning it to Gonzalo's rolling cart as Vito came in. "Here, Vito," he said, "take your pick and stay in here for a while. I'm gonna feed the troops."

"A-ay," said Vito, spinning the tray. "I don't see no rigatoni."

"C'mon, willya, Vito!"

Vito grabbed a sandwich and a pickle in a hurry, as Louie wheeled the cart past him and out of the room.

"Dinner time, gang!" Louie announced as Minnie followed him into the main room. Abe, Oscar, and Stosh started toward the food cart.

Suddenly, they all stopped dead in their tracks.

Staring up at them from the back end of the room was a little black girl with huge searching eyes. She stood there in a very wet yellow dress, twisting a little ring on her finger and turning back and forth uncertainly as she tried to sort out the strange new scene before her.

What had happened to the crowd? The lines of people at the windows? The pretty red ropes that hung from the shiny brass poles? What had happened to her grandmother? And why hadn't she come to get her from the rest room, as she usually did?

She stopped twisting her ring as she finally found her tongue. "Where's my granmaw?"

The five adults stood in a stunned semicircle, staring down at the child blankly as her simple question echoed in the large room.

The little girl made a sour face and placed her fists on her hips.

"My name is Odessa Hoskins," she announced. "I live at three-four-o-two East Eighty-second Place, and I'm six years old. Now, *where's my granmaw?*"

And still the quintet standing around the food cart showed no sign of the power of speech. At last, Minnie spoke.

"*Nu?* Guess who's coming to dinner?" she said.

She was not trying to be funny, and the four men knew it. "Tell me," she asked, squatting down as if to play jacks with the child, "where did you come from?"

"No!" said Odessa, stamping her foot. "You *first!* Where's my granmaw?"

"Well, uh . . . we don't know," Minnie said. "Was your grandmother in the bank?"

Odessa looked up at Minnie. "Course she was! I can't go anywhere all by myself! I'm just a little girl. . . . Can't you see?"

"Yes, darling, I can see that now. . . . I'm sorry," Minnie said. "What does your grandmother look like?"

"She's black," Odessa said, still talking to a dummy, "just like I am. And she's old, just like you are."

200

"I see," said Minnie. "And what did you say your name was?"

"My name is Odessa Hoskins, and I'm in the high first grade."

"Odessa," Minnie said. "That's a beautiful name for a little girl!"

"I know," the child said proudly. "And it's gonna be beautiful when I grow up, too!"

"Odessa!" Louie said, pointing at Oscar.

"Odessa!" said Oscar, nodding back at Louie.

"I told you that woman didn't look Russian!" Louie said.

"Hey, Louie," Stosh said, "what we do with little girl?"

Louie looked at the giant Pole, his arms spread wide as though embracing all their confusion. Then he looked down at the little girl, frowning and clicking his tongue as he struggled with his terrible decision. Odessa crossed her arms and stood her ground.

"I take her out of bank!" Stosh announced in a booming voice.

"Oh, no!" Louie snapped, whirling on him.

"Levine, it is insane to keep her in here," Oscar said.

"He's right, Louie," Abe agreed.

"No, No!" Louie shouted. "She stays right here!"

"Louie, please . . . for God's sake!" Minnie said.

"I take her out now!" Stosh moved toward Odessa. "Come little girl, I take you to your grandmother."

Stosh took hold of Odessa's hand and started for the door.

Louie stepped out to block his way. "That's enough, Stosh!" he barked, putting his hand on his gun. "Stop right there!"

Stosh kept moving forward. "Get outa my way, Louie."

"I said stop, goddamn you!" Louie yelled, jerking his gun out of his belt and pointing it at Stosh's stomach. Stosh stopped as Odessa let out a bloodcurdling scream. Minnie gasped, shrinking into Abe's arms as Vito came tearing out of the conference room, gun in hand.

"Holy Jesus! . . . What the hell!" he said, skidding to a stop.

"Stay out of it, Vito!" Louie's eyes were riveted on Stosh, who carefully pushed the child behind his legs to shield her.

Vito slowly lowered his gun, pointing it at the floor as the two men stood facing each other, Louie's gun inches from Stosh's belt.

"Leggo of her, Stosh," Louie said quietly, raising his gun to aim at Stosh's chest.

Stosh looked at the gun. "You would use gun, Louie?" he asked. "On me?"

Odessa wrapped her arms around Stosh's leg and buried her face in his trousers, whimpering as they all waited for Louie's answer.

"You leggo of the little girl, Stosh," he said, "and I'll put away the gun. Listen to me. . . . Do it now, Stosh."

Stosh looked down at him in that direct, gentle way of his. "You don't

201

answer question, Louie," he insisted. "You shoot me if I don't?"

Louie's eyes were narrowed almost shut, and they could all hear the grinding of his teeth as he stared hard at the big man.

"I . . . don't know, Stosh," he said at last. "Please . . .don't make me find out. I only know one thing. . . .This little girl is a gift from God! We have to keep her here with us."

"What are you—crazy, Louie?" Abe asked. "Whatta ya mean, *gift?*"

"No, no. I'm not crazy," said Louie, shaking his head. "Don't you people understand what you got here? This little girl might save all our lives today. This little girl, my friends—is our *gas mask!*"

Louie was right. As much as they hated the idea of keeping a six-year-old girl hostage in a place where people were running around with guns in their hands, they all knew that Louie was right.

"Goddamn, I don't like," Stosh said slowly, "but goddamn, maybe little girl *is* come from God. Maybe now nobody be hurt, hah?"

"I hope not, Stosh." Louie stuck his gun back in his belt.

"Okay." Stosh reached behind his leg. "It's okay, little girl. . . . Don't cry, Everything be okay!" And he scooped her up into his arms. "You and me, we play games, hah?" he laughed, holding her high over his head.

Odessa looked down from her lofty perch at the laughing potato-face and somehow felt better immediately. She hicupped one postcrying hiccup, then she began to giggle infectiously as Stosh turned her over and over in midair tossing her and catching her and tickling her and rocking her from side to side until she was laughing hysterically.

And they all watched the children at play, and they smiled, completely forgetting for the moment where they were.

Minnie came to her senses first. "Come on, Stosh, that's enough! You'll make the poor child you-know-what in her pants! Besides, I gotta try to get her dress dry. Give her to me."

Stosh caught her one last time and lowered her gently to the floor, like a forklift handling a crate of eggs.

"You like that, hah?" he asked her. She gave him a rapid succession of nods, still gurgling with laughter. "Okay! We do more later, maybe, okay?"

Minnie took Odessa's hand. "Tell me something, Odessa," she asked, leading her back to the rest room. "How did you get your pretty dress so wet?"

"It's not *so* wet," said Odessa, as the two of them disappeared from view.

Oscar shook his head grimly. "I don't like it, Levine. I don't like it at all."

"Listen, Oscar," Louie said, "I don't like it either. That's the way it is, that's all! But if we're lucky—"

An ear-splitting racket suddenly exploded from the conference room—banging, knocking, whacking, shouting. Vito raced back into the room just in time to see Wilson succeed in blumping his lock through the notch and

202

disappear under the table, knocking his chair over backward as Angela screamed in anguish.

"Mr. Wilson!" she shrieked, "you get up from there *this minute!* Mr. Wilson!"

Another first for Angela St. Clair—an executive vice-president and bank manager on his knees, staring point-blank at her crotch, and she couldn't do a thing about it except to squirm frantically from side to side, hiking her short skirt higher and higher up her struggling hips. "Mr. Wilson, Mr. Wilson, Mr. Wi-ill-son!"

"Where is Wilson?" Louie shouted to Vito as he and the others burst through the door, guns drawn.

"Down here," said Vito, beckoning from the end of the table as he squatted.

The four men knelt to peer under the table at Wilson, on his knees, suspended by the handcuffs still locked to the cable, his hands held in a frozen grasp, a frustrating foot and one-half above the telephone.

"What are you tryin' to do, Mr. Wilson?" Vito asked, trying desperately not to laugh. "See how the other half lives?"

"Reminds me of somebody I know," Abe observed archly.

"Shut up, you!" Vito said, grinning.

The scene under the table was like a surreal football huddle, the hostages were all straining against their bonds, craning their necks as far as they could to peer under the table, watching Wilson, red-faced and perspiring, dangling over the instrument he had hoped to use to arrange their rescue.

"I was trying to get . . . to the phone," Wilson croaked.

"Aw-ww, that's too bad! Why dincha *ask* me? I coulda saved you a lotta trouble." Vito lifted the phone up off the floor and held the severed wires under Wilson's nose. "Y'see, this telephone is outa order at the present time."

"That," said Sidney Washington, deadpan from the edge of the table, "is a communication gap!" Almost everybody laughed.

"A-ay, that's very good!" Vito said.

Wilson's head hung in humiliation, like the rest of him.

"Get him up outa there, Vito," Louie ordered.

"Yes, please, please!" Angela whimpered.

"My pleasure," Vito said, digging for his key. "Mr. Wilson, you really think we'd be dumb enough to leave a live phone around this close to a smart man like you?"

The lock snapped open and Wilson ducked out from under, bumping his head smartly on the table in his rush to get back in his chair.

"Hey, take it easy," Vito said, snapping him back onto the cable. "We don't want nobody to get hurt, y'know?"

The phone began to ring in the other room. All heads turned at the sound. Quickly, Vito scooped the phone off the floor and set it on the table in front of Wilson.

"Prob'ly for you, Mr. Wilson," he said.

Jesse and Gonzalo laughed as Wilson stared at the useless instrument.

"Come, Levine!" Oscar said. "Enough fooling. Answer the telephone."

"Don't get your water hot. I'll answer, I'll answer." Louie strolled out of the conference room as the others followed. "If it's who I think it is, they'll wait for me, don't worry."

Louie reached the phone and let it ring one more time.

"Get back to the door, Stosh," he said, and picked up the phone. "Hello? . . . Yes, this is the gentleman—Who? . . . Wait a minute! Hold the phone!"

Stosh and Oscar were jumping up and down at one side of the front door. Louie looked outside just as a police ambulance, its siren running down, slowed to make the turn onto Fairfax, pulling up behind the fire truck parked kitty-corner from the bank. A SWAT personnel carrier careened around the corner onto Beverly, disgorging a dozen running, black-uniformed men carrying automatic weapons, dodging and ducking to their assigned positions across from the bank.

"Hey, Louie, Jesus!" Stosh hollered. "Must be hundred men outside running around. Everybody got guns!"

"Whatta ya expect?" said Louie. "It's about *time* they got here. I called them fifteen, twenty minutes ago." He picked up his binoculars to get a better look.

"Looks like Polish Army," Stosh said. "No head. All feet."

"You are dreaming, Vlasic," said Oscar. "The Polish Army would not find their way here until tomorrow!"

"Listen, Oscar," Stosh warned with a dirty look, "I can make fun. You don't can make fun."

Peering through the binoculars like General Patton surveying a battle scene, the mouthpiece of the phone clamped under his armpit, Louie could see dozens of uniformed cops, their guns drawn, bent over and running every which way outside. Cops with bullhorns were shouting at crowds of pedestrians, ordering them away from the intersection. All civilian traffic was being rerouted, and men in blue coveralls were running long wooden barricades out into the street. Sirens screamed in from every direction as Louie watched the black-and-whites skidding in to converge on Citizens' Bank and The Benefit.

Louie put the binoculars down, took in a big breath and blew it out. "So this, my friends is Phase Four."

"Ja," Stosh said.

"Ja," Oscar said.

"Pray to God," Abe said, from behind the counter, "nobody should be hurt."

204

"Okay, everybody . . . quiet!" Louie took the phone out from under his arm. "Hello? I'm sorry, there was a lotta noise in here. Who did you say you were?"

"Clear this goddamn sidewalk, Lopez!" a police captain hollered out of the public phone booth. "Everybody down!"

"Hello? Who's calling?" Louie asked again, trying to hear over the noise in the background.

MacAdoo kicked the booth door closed. "Hello! This is Captain Michael MacAdoo, Los Angeles Police Department. I am in a public telephone booth diagonally across the street from your location. I am in command of a special task force of personnel and equip—"

Louie interrupted him as soon as he could. "Oh, how-do-you-do, Captain Michael MacAdoo, across the street in command! Did Sergeant Bailey give you my message that I want—"

"Just a minute, please," MacAdoo cut in politely, "we'll get to Sergeant Bailey in a minute. First, I am required to verify that I am in contact with the individual who is the leader of the group holding the bank."

"Listen, if it's required, it's required," Louie said. "I'll verify this for you. You are talking to the leader. I'm him."

"Can you identify yourself, please?" MacAdoo asked.

"Identify? To you? Listen, Captain, *who* I am is not important right now. I'll tell you what is important right now—and the time is running out—I wanta talk only to the Chiefa Police. *Person-to-person*, do you hear me?"

"Yes, I hear you just fine," MacAdoo said.

"No, no—not hear me just fine,'" Louie said. "Do you understand me?"

"Yes, sir, I understand you," MacAdoo said, carefully choosing his words. "Sergeant Bailey has reported your request to speak with the Chief. However, I must tell you that the Chief is in San Francisco today, attending a law enforcement conference. We are attempting to contact him there on your situation."

There was an awkward pause in the conversation. MacAdoo opened the door of the hot phone booth to get a little air. Louie ground his teeth in frustration. He was not prepared for the possibility of the Chief's being out of town. He had counted on a face-to-face confrontation. That was the plan.

"San Francisco, hah?" Louie said, his mind spinning with alternatives.

"Yes, sir," MacAdoo pushed the booth door closed. "Captain Robeson is Commanding Officer at Parker Center in the Chief's absence." MacAdoo felt a little stab as he made the statement. It was the first time he had ever referred to Robeson as his superior, and he didn't like it one bit.

"Lemme get this straight," Louie said. "They are holding a law enforcement conference on April Fools' Day?"

"Correct," MacAdoo said. "It's a three-day meeting—the first through the third. But I can assure you that Assistant Chief Robeson has complete authority to act while the Chief is out of the city. I am in radio contact with him on this emergency, and he has asked me to inform you that—"

"Hold it, hold it! Do me a favor—don't inform me anything from an assistant! I did not come here to communicate with assistants!"

"Yes, sir, I understand that, but until we get you into direct communication with the Chief, I suggest you listen to some information I have for you. It's for your own safety."

Louie paused a moment, thinking. "Okay, make it quick. I'll listen."

"I'll be as brief as I can," MacAdoo said. "This is the situation—"

Two men in civilian clothes suddenly ran ducking zigzag from the barricade to the phone booth, one of them rapping sharply on the window, waving an ID folder. MacAdoo turned in annoyance, squinting through the glass.

"Who the—goddamn it, get the hell out of here!" MacAdoo hollered, his hand over the phone. "Lopez! Lopez! Get these people away from me! Are you asleep out there, for Christ sake?"

Corporal Lopez ducked out from behind the ambulance and grabbed the two men roughly by the arms, dragging them away from the booth.

"Captain MacAdoo!" one of them yelled, "it's Doctor Harmon and Doctor Kell—"

Lopez had pulled them down behind the fire truck. MacAdoo kicked the door shut.

"Hello? I'm sorry, I was distracted for a minute," he said. "There's a lot going on out here."

"I can see that," Louie said. "In here, it's nice and quiet."

"That's good," MacAdoo said. "I hope it stays that way."

"That, my dear Captain," Louie said, "is all up to you."

"Yes, sir," MacAdoo said mechanically. "All right. Now, this is what we've got. We know that you are holding hostages—twelve or thirteen hostages. I want you to know that our primary concern in this situation is for the safety of those people."

"That's nice. I am very glad to hear you say this," Louie said. "Looking outside at the artillery, I am worried about their safety, too, believe you me."

"Right," MacAdoo said. "Now, we *also* know that you are armed, and I want you to be aware that we are taking your Dangerous Explosives sign seriously."

"That's a good idea," Louie said. "They are serious explosives."

"All right, now," MacAdoo said, warming to his message. "This is the situation. We have a major task force out here. Our units are deployed, completely surrounding the bank on all sides—the SWAT team, automatic weapons, the works!"

"Yes, Captain, I see them! What are you trying to tell me? That your army is bigger than my army? That you can kill more people, or what?"

206

"No, sir, I didn't say that!" MacAdoo said quickly, "I just want you to be fully aware of your position. I want you to know that you and your accomplices are contained. An escape would be impossible."

MacAdoo paused dramatically to let his words sink in. Louie waited patiently through the pause for what he knew was coming.

"It is my duty now to order you and your associates," MacAdoo directed, "to disarm your explosive device, if you have one, put your weapons on safety, slide them carefully out the front door, and walk out of the bank with you hands clasped behind your heads. Is that clear?"

Now Louie made MacAdoo wait.

"Hello, hello? . . . Are you there?" MacAdoo shouted.

"Ye-es, Captain, I'm still here," Louie said finally. "And you make yourself perfectly clear. Now let me make myself also perfectly clear, so we will both know where we stand. We are inside—contained, as you say. But this is exactly what we planned, Mister Captain MacAdoo. We are on the inside, for a change, and you are only on the outside, looking in."

MacAdoo frowned as he ran his fingers through his graying blond hair. "I . . . don't think I understand you," he said. "You planned to get caught *inside* the bank?"

"Oh, no!" said Louie. "We planned to catch *you* on the *outside*." He smiled to himself at his apt turn of phrase. "Now listen, Captain," he continued, "you are running out of time, already. It's after one o'clock. You got less than two hours altogether."

"Why?" MacAdoo kept his tone casual. "What happens in two hours?"

"How many times I hafta say it? . . . I'll only tell the *Chief* what happens! Now you listen to me. If the Chiefa Police is in San Francisco, I'm sure they got telephones there. So my advice to you is, you get a-hold of him quick, and you tell him he better call me long distance in a hurry. Is that clear?"

"Yes, sir, perfectly clear. But can I tell him what it is you want?"

"No, thank you, Captain. I want him to hear what we want straight from the horse's mouth, y'know what I mean? Oh, by the way, he can call me here *collect*. I'll okay the charges!"

"But—" MacAdoo began.

Louie slammed the phone into its cradle.

MacAdoo ducked out of the phone booth and ran low to the protection of the fire truck, where Lopez crouched with SWAT Lieutenant Stryker and the two men he had pulled away from the booth. Stryker's walkie-talkie chattered a metallic message at his ear.

"Check. Hold your positions," Stryker said into the speaker-phone. "Everybody loose and easy. Out. We're set, Whitey," he said to MacAdoo.

"Right," MacAdoo acknowledged. "Lopez, dammit, I told you to get these people out of here—"

"Captain, Captain," one of the civilians spluttered, wiggling his card under MacAdoo's nose, "Doctor Harmon and Doctor Keller, don't you remember?"

MacAdoo showed no sign of recognition. "Huh?"

"The Political Insurrection seminar," Harmon said.

"Oh, yeah. The shrinks, right?" MacAdoo recalled vaguely. "Well, what the hell are you guys doing here, at a time like this?"

"This," Harmon replied, "is our first assignment."

"This is your what?" MacAdoo blurted. "On whose orders?"

"Assistant Chief Robeson."

"Assis—? When?"

"Fifteen, sixteen minutes ago," Harmon said, checking his watch. "He caught us at Cedars-Sinai Hospital. We were only a couple of minutes from here."

"Jesus," MacAdoo muttered, checking his own watch. "He called you before he called me!"

Harmon was confused. "I don't understand what you're—"

"Okay, okay!" MacAdoo cut him off. "You can stick around, but stay out of the way, right?"

"Wait a minute, Captain," Harmon said. "I don't think you're tuned *in* to why we're here."

MacAdoo looked at him blankly.

"Our assignment is *first* contact."

"Are you crazy?" MacAdoo bellowed. "There are people in there with guns, holding hostages, demanding to talk with the Chief, threatening to blow up the place. . . . You people can't be involved in a dangerous emergency like this!"

"An emergency like this," Harmon said, "is exactly why our unit was formed. Remember the name of our team—Political Insurrection Emergency Squad, right? Well—this is it!"

"Bullshit!" MacAdoo shouted. "This is a bank robbery, not a *demonstration*, for Christ's sake!"

"Oh, no, Captain! And you know it as well as I do. Whoever they are, those people want something other than money. They didn't come to rob the bank. They came to *capture* the bank, and it looks like they've done a damn good job of it. Now, do you want to get back on the phone with them—or do you want me to?"

MacAdoo stared balefully at Harmon, the chip of official directive perched firmly on the Ph.D.'s shoulder.

"Son of a bitch! Lopez, get on that radio! I want to talk to Captain Robeson, and I want him right now—red alert!"

"Yes, sir!" Lopez ran low to the police car parked just behind the ambulance, MacAdoo and the two doctors scooting behind him.

While all this was going on outside, Minnie Gold was in the middle of an astonishing cultural exchange in the ladies' rest room. She had discovered

208

the first known toilet portrait sculptress prodigy in America, perhaps in the world.

Upon entering the rest room with Odessa, Minnie had been greeted by an exhibition of six fist-sized sculptured heads fashioned out of a mixture of soaked and squeezed paper towels and toilet tissue *a la maché*, stuck up on the mirror all in a row. The Museum of Modern Art was never graced by a more startling one-woman show.

Michaelangelo's fingers were blistered and cracked by his years of marble chipping, Picasso's loose trousers were stained with urine from pissing the patina on his outdoor bronzes, and so it follows—Odessa's yellow dress was simply wet with *her* art.

Now Minnie was pointing at the faces, one by one. "So . . . this one is your mother, and this is your grandmother, and this is your Aunt Exine— that's a pretty name, too!"

"*Awnt* Exine," Odessa corrected her.

"I'm sorry, Awnt Exine. And who is this?"

"That's my sister Lena! Isn't she the most beautifullest girl in the whole world?"

"Could be," said Minnie, taking a second look. "And who is this one?"

"That's mean Mrs. Miller, that's who that is." Odessa made a face. "I had her in kindergarten."

"You really got her frowning, haven't you?" Minnie observed.

"That's just how she looks all the time, too—like a mean old witch! I just wish God would make her die!" Odessa said, holding her hands up at Mrs. Miller, like threatening claws.

Mrs. Miller's face reacted immediately, as if rehearsed, coming away from her adhesion to the mirror and committing suicide, as she plummeted between the sinks to the tile floor with a loud smacking splat.

"Look, look!" Odessa giggled, pointing to the glob that had been Mrs. Miller. "God heard me! I wished she was dead, and she died!"

Minnie was horrified. "Odessa! That's not nice, to wish somebody would die!"

"Why not?" the child asked righteously. "She's all the time wishing us kids would die!"

"No! I can't believe that—a teacher?"

"It's true, it's *really true*, cross my heart! She says there's too many children in the world—'specially poor children, that's what she says!"

"But Odessa, darling," Minnie reasoned, "that's not the same thing."

"Is so!" Odessa said certainly. "Besides—how's God gonna make it so only *rich* kids get borned?"

Minnie shook her head with no answer in it, and quickly changed the subject. "Listen, sweetheart," she said, "I notice all these faces are ladies. How come you didn't do one of your daddy?"

"Don't have a daddy," the little girl said simply.

"G'wan!—Everybody's got a daddy," Minnie said without thinking.

"Not *me*," Odessa said, looking directly up at Minnie. "My momma and my granmaw, both of 'em, told me I don't *have* a daddy—and they never, never tell a lie!"

Minnie bit her tongue—for what she had already said, and for what she knew she must not say.

"Come, darling," she said, taking the child's hand. "We'll go out and find you a place to wait for your grandmother. Maybe I can find you some paper to draw on. . . . You like to draw?"

"Uh-huh," Odessa nodded. "I'm a good drawer."

"I'll bet you are!" Minnie opened the rest room door. "By the way, are you also a good cheesecake eater?"

"Oh, yes, ma'am!" Odessa said, and the two girlfriends left the powder room.


Assistant Chief of Police Jack Robeson sat at his new desk on the twelfth floor at Parker Center, looking over the city toward the trouble at Citizens' Bank while he listened on the radiophone to MacAdoo's frustration.

"Wait a minute, Mac!" Robeson said, pushing a half-eaten sandwich out of his way. "Just back up a minute, dammit. I know it must be rough out there, but I don't think I'm getting through to you. I just told you I talked to the Chief in his sickbed at his hotel in Frisco—the poor man could hardly talk—and I gave him a status report on this thing—"

MacAdoo tried to interrupt.

"Just let me finish, Whitey!" Robeson said. "I gave him—"

"If you want to finish anything with *me*," MacAdoo said, "you'd better not call me 'Whitey,' Jack."

"Aw, come on, man," Robeson said. 'That's your nickname, isn't it?"

"To everybody but you, Jack," MacAdoo said evenly. "Everybody but you."

Robeson shook his head wearily. "Okay, Mac, if that's the way you want it, you got it." He looked back down at his notes. "Now, I gave the Chief your report verbatim, dammit, and I'm telling you that *his* instructions—verbatim—are as follows: *No* LAPD or Sheriff's personnel are to attempt forced or covert entry into the bank while hostages are being held. . . . Two: *No* police gunfire or tear gas unless there is gunfire or explosive action from inside the bank *first*—f-i-r-s-t—and then, only *after* a three-minute telephonic or bullhorn warning, heard-and-understood verified. . . . And Three: You are to recontact the people inside, try to get them to let an unarmed member of the PIES into the bank for a parley. Maybe one of the doctors can find out who these people are and what this damn thing's all about. Got it?"

MacAdoo did not answer. He just sat there, hefting the speaker-phone in his hand as if it were a rock he wanted to throw at somebody.

"Mac? Do you read me?"

210

Still no answer.

"Are your instructions clear, *Captain?*" he repeated.

"Yes, sir!" MacAdoo snapped back, like a cadet. "They must be very clear up in the tower where you're sitting, but it's a helluva way to run a stick-up, if you ask me. Ten-four, over and—"

"Hold it, Mac!" Robeson barked, disallowing the sign-off. "Mac . . . I'm going to have to ask you to repeat those orders."

Lopez looked away in embarrassment at the indignity forced on his superior officer. MacAdoo gritted his teeth and repeated his instructions, in a martinet shorthand.

"Yes, sir. No entry while hostages are held, no fire except in answer to fire, following a three-minute verified warning, and I'm to try to arrange a parley inside for one of the PIES."

"And I mean really try, Captain."

'Yes, sir. Is that it, sir?"

"Yes-sir-that's-it-sir." Robeson parroted. "But I'm telling you, MacAdoo, this personal crap is going to have to stop between us. . . . It's getting in the way of our work, man."

"I don't know what you mean, sir."

"Oh, yes, you do," Robeson said. "I mean—we've gone through the little official contest, and I won by a couple of percentage points. Okay, that puts me here and you there. That should've ended it, but the beat goes *on* with you, doesn't it?"

"I'm only talking about my street scene out here, Captain," MacAdoo said. "I don't know what you're talking about."

"You know what I'm talking about, all right," Robeson said, not letting up. "I'm talking about maybe you and me working it out in the Academy ring, like they used to make us do when we were plebes. Maybe three or four rounds of black and white sweat, and we could get it out and over with, hear?"

"I hear you loud and clear," MacAdoo said. "But I've got a more pressing problem on my hands right now. Ten-four, Cap'n Jack. Over and out."

MacAdoo nudged Lopez with his elbow. "Get out a minute, Lopez. Tell Harmon I'll be right with him."

Lopez got out and slammed the door. MacAdoo sat there, clenching one fist, then the other. So this was how it was going to be—sucking official hind tit to a black man, from now to retirement.

MacAdoo wiped the angry sweat off his upper lip with the back of his hand and got out of the squad car, slamming the door hard.

"Okay, Doctor Fix-it," he said to Harmon. "You're first in the zoo, *if* I can get them to give you a pass."

With that, he ran low to the phone booth to call Louie again.

Just after one o'clock, news of the bank break-in hit the airwaves. Almost every local radio station broadcast the story, and, of course, they all had the

211

story all wrong. According to them, a gang of four bank robbers was trapped inside the bank before they could escape with bags full of cash, so the gang had taken twenty-two customers and employees hostage in order to bargain their lives in exchange for a getaway. They had so far sent the body of a black woman they had murdered out to the police, strapped in a chair, to show that they meant business, and they had a plastic bomb taped to three hostages inside, set to go off at three o'clock, Pacific Standard Time. The identity of the gang was unknown, but "authoritative news sources" were quick to broadcast guesses ranging from a newly organized SLA to the nortorious Scotty Derringer gang out of Oklahoma City.

Though it had been her own radio station that first broke the story, Joy Newsome, intrepid KFWB newsperson, just didn't feel right about the report. Somehow, the details didn't seem to add up to a simple bank robbery to her. It was more than that. She could smell it.

She wheeled her white KFWB Mercury with the huge black NEWS 98 painted on its sides out of the circle drive of the Century Plaza Hotel, where she had just covered a crowded news conference luncheon sponsored by Save-a-Tree and attended by the Mayor and three Councilmen running for reelection.

Car 98, Newsome's mobile news unit, looked like a porcupine of radio antennae as she turned east onto Olympic Boulevard, the Tac 2 chattering its stacatto dispatches in her ear. It sounded like war, like the Watts riots, like the day of the SLA shoot-out. All available units, Fire Department assistance, SWAT, code personnel, bomb squad, the works.

Joy Newsome reported her position to her station, rounded the corner onto Fairfax, and stepped on the gas toward Citizens' Bank.

Odessa Hoskins sat on two telephone books in Mr. Wilson's big leather chair in his private office. Minnie was busily taping the artist's output onto Wilson's walls. Odessa's medium was his multicolored felt-tip pens, her canvases were his big desk pad scratch sheets, and his office by now looked like the end-of-term art contest at an inner-city grade school.

She had already completed drawings of his plump family, his sailboat heeled into the Newport wind, his two beautiful collies, and his teenage son proudly holding a string of dead fish, all freely copied from the handsomely framed photographs in his office, and she had polished off two pieces of Dave's cheesecake to boot. She was faster on the draw than Dali, and she was having a marvelous time.

"I'm all out of pictures," Odessa said abruptly. "I'm gonna draw you."

"Me?" Minnie asked coyly. "You wanna draw me?"

"Sure," Odessa said, "I can draw you real good. Sit down right here, and smile."

"Could I have it when you're finished?" Minnie asked.

"If you want it, you can have it. If you say please."

212

"Oh, of course I'll say please!" Minnie sat down, holding her chins up for all she was worth, as though she were posing for the senior Wyeth.

"Even cold," Abe announced with a leer as he chewed his sandwich, "even cold, hot pastrami is the second best taste in the whole world!"

Oscar and Louie cackled while Stosh looked at him blankly.

"Maybe," Stosh said grudgingly. Then suddenly, he lit up. "But *bigos* is *first!*"

Abe looked at him quizzically. "Bigos? What the hell is bigos?"

"Poor Abe, what *you* know about eating?" Stosh scoffed. "Bigos is beautiful Polish stew! Got sauerkraut and fat pork and garlic sausage and fried duck and—"

"Stop, stop!" Abe held both hands up. "You're making me sick! I wasn't talking eating—I was talking *eating!*"

"Hah?" Stosh asked.

The telephone rang.

Louie finished his last bite of pickle, let the phone ring a third time, and then answered. "Hello?"

MacAdoo recognized Louie's voice immediately. "Hello, this is Captain MacAdoo, across the street—"

"Listen, Captain MacAdoo across the street," Louie interrupted rudely, "I told you before, I don't wanna talk to captains! I only wanna talk with the Chief, can'tcha understand English?"

"Yes, sir, I can," MacAdoo said, "but I'm sure you understand that I'm just out here, taking orders from my superiors."

"So? What do your superiors order?"

"We haven't been able to contact the Chief in San Francisco, yet," MacAdoo lied, "but we're still on it. He may just be between locations."

"We are *all* between locations, my friend," Louie said. "Why do you waste my time? Just call me when you get a-hold of the Chief—"

"Wait, wait, don't hang up! I'm calling you now on orders of Assistant Chief Robeson, downtown—"

"What'sa matter, he can't call me himself?"

"No, he . . . he's going to try to get over here personally," MacAdoo said, stalling, "but he's asked me to—"

"I see," Louie said. "He is also between locations, hah?"

"Yes, sir, but until he gets here," MacAdoo was talking fast, trying to keep Louie on the phone, "or until we can reach the Chief for you—you must realize that this is a very dangerous situation. I've got fifty or sixty armed men out here, the intersection is cordoned off, and—"

"Hold it, hold it! Why are you telling me things I already know? You like to talk on the phone?"

"No, sir, I don't." MacAdoo tugged at his sweaty shirt. "Believe me, this is one kind of phone conversation I do not enjoy. And I can tell you I don't

213

like this predicament, either. You've put a lot of innocent people in terrible jeopardy, you know."

"Listen, Captain, don't talk to me about innocent people in jeopardy today, I'm warning you!"

"Wait a minute, now. Just calm down. The last thing in the world we want to do is get overemotional here. First thing you know, somebody does something foolish and we've got a *shoot-out* on our hands. We don't want that, do we?"

MacAdoo let his deadly question hang there. And Louie listened to the heavy silence, his eyes slowly narrowing.

"It sounds to me, Captain," Louie said finally, "like you are getting a little *itchy* out there. . . ."

"No sir, absolutely not. My orders are to maintain a safe standoff condition, and that's exactly what I'm going to do unless you give me a reason to do otherwise."

"So it's all up to me, hah?"

"That's about the size of it, mister."

"Easy, take it easy!" Harmon cautioned, standing next to MacAdoo at the open phone booth.

MacAdoo gave Harmon a harsh look and continued. "Now Assistant Chief Robeson has suggested that I arrange a parley between you and our Doctor Harmon."

"A what with who?"

"A parley, a nice, calm, face-to-face conversation," MacAdoo explained carefully. "We'd like you to allow Doctor Harmon to come into the bank with you—*unarmed*, of course—to discuss this situation with you . . . see if we can't defuse a very dangerous condition until Chief Robeson gets here."

"Listen," said Louie, "we *don't* need a doctor, we *don't* need a plumber. I told you, what we *need* is the Chiefa Police—somebody who can make a decision, give the orders to get us what we want, you understand?"

"I hear you," MacAdoo said, "but it could be a half-hour or more before Chief Robeson gets here. This is your show, but I'm telling you—the longer we're out here with guns and gas, and the longer you're inside with hostages, the hotter this thing is going to get."

"Captain, that's the second time you've threatened him," Harmon pointed out, unable to contain himself any longer. "Don't *do* that. That's *very* inciteful."

"You say it's my show, hah?" Louie said. "*You* are not involved in the danger here, is that what you are telling me?"

"I'm only telling you like it is," MacAdoo said. "You people started this thing. . . . I'm just here to end it—that's my job. And I hope that we can accomplish that without people getting hurt."

Vito stuck his head out of the conference room. "Hey, Levine! I got people in here gotta go to the toilet!"

214

"How about talking to the doctor?" MacAdoo asked again.

"How 'bout letting these people go to the john, Louie?" Vito repeated.

"Wait a minute!" Louie said. "Everybody's talking to me at the same time! Listen, Captain, you'll hafta call me back in about ten minutes. I gotta let my people go to the toilet." He hung up.

"Okay, Vito," he decreed, "ladies first, two at a time, Minnie goes with them. Abe, get Minnie out here, tell her to lock the little girl inside. Come on, move!"

"What did he say?" Harmon asked MacAdoo, who was looking at the dead phone receiver in his hand.

"He said to call him back in ten minutes. Something about letting his people go to the toilet."

"Well, that shows a little consideration on his part, at least," Harmon said.

"Doctor, these people are not considerate. Hell, these people are armed criminals committing a federal crime. You act as if you'd like to invite them home to dinner!"

Harmon felt the back of his neck tighten. "And you're acting as though the quicker you can anger somebody inside into an overt act of violence, the better you're going to like it!"

"What the hell are you talking about?"

"I'm talking about what our job is here today," Harmon said. "These people know they are caught, they know they're surrounded, and they know they're going to have to bargain their way out of there if they're going to avoid bloodshed. The most important thing to them right now is their ego."

"Ego?" MacAdoo scoffed. "Who the hell gives a good goddamn about their *ego*? We're sitting on a keg of dynamite out here!"

"For your information, Captain," Harmon said with an edge, "we care a good deal about their egos. These people are experiencing a very dangerous trauma in this circumstance—dangerous to them, and to us. We have to assume that they are at what we call their 'paranoid peak.' Unless we want all hell to break loose, it's our job to listen to their demands calmly and negotiate a way for them to save face."

"It's not my job to save faces, Doctor. It's my job to get those hostages out of there alive!"

"That's right," Harmon agreed. "That's our job. But you can't accomplish one without the other. The least little threat on our part will be interpreted by *them* as an open act of hostility, and their response will most certainly be violence!"

The veteran cop looked at the doctor oddly for a moment, then a faint smile played across his face.

"Well, Doctor," he shrugged, "it's a violent world."

215

"Right," Harmon said. "The animals among us make it that way."

The two men crouched behind the fire engine, eyes locked, each knowing the other very well.

"You sure you're all right?" Minnie asked Betty Lundy as they left the ladies' room to return to the conference room.

"I'm fine," said Betty, "except the baby is starting to really press down on my bladder, you know? I feel like I have to pee all the time."

"I know, I know," Minnie said sympathetically.

"Oh, you have children?" Betty asked.

"No," Minnie said, "but I almost did, many years ago. I miscarried in my sixth month."

"Oh, I'm sorry. You never tried again?"

"Oh, boy, did we try!" Minnie said archly. "My husband Abe especially—like he was trying for the Olympics! But sometimes, no matter how hard you try, trying isn't *doing*, you know what I mean?"

Betty had been listening attentively, but she had no clue as to Minnie's meaning. Minnie ushered her back to her place at the conference table. "Listen," she whispered in Betty's ear, "any time you wanna go, just raise your hand. I'll take you to relieve yourself."

Betty nodded thanks.

"Okay, Vito," Minnie said, "it's your turn with the boys. I'll take over here."

"Far out!" Jesse said.

"Good news!" Floyd seconded, coming out of his book.

"Okay, men," Vito said. "I ain't takin' no chances. We go one at a time, clockwise around the table—"

"Clockwise?" Jesse moaned.

"Sorry, Jesse, you'll just hafta hold on a little longer, *Capish?*"

Jesse's pained expression made it clear he understood.

"Okay, Minnie," Vito said, "I'll take the lawyer here first."

Minnie moved to unlock Floyd.

"He's got an accent of some kind, I'm telling you," MacAdoo was saying to Harmon and Keller. "I know damn well they're foreigners."

"What kind of an accent, Captain?" Keller asked.

"I don't know. Just a foreign accent."

"Latin? European?" Keller persisted.

"How the hell do *I* know?" MacAdoo said irritably. "I'm no accent expert."

"Have you found out who they are and what they want, Captain?"

The three crouching men were suddenly staring into a microphone thrust into their midst by a graceful feminine hand, displaying at least one ring on each manicured finger.

216

MacAdoo whirled angrily around at the young woman squatting next to them. "What the hell—?"

"Joy Newsome, KFWB," the pretty young woman said, smiling. "How many hostages are they holding? What are their demands? Any shots fired yet?"

"What the goddamn—?"

The woman moved the microphone closer to MacAdoo's lips.

He cut off the curse in his mouth, clapping his hand over the head of the open mike. "What the hell do you think you're doing in here, lady? Lopez? Lopez!"

"Was the black woman in the ambulance *shot*, Captain?" she asked, unperturbed, as though MacAdoo were running a press conference.

"What black—? Listen, girl, you turn this damn thing off, and you get your little butt out of here, now! Lopez!"

"I can't go until you let go of my mike, Captain," said the intrepid reporter.

MacAdoo released the microphone as Lopez came running up. "I'm going to get your ass, Lopez! Where the hell were you?"

"I was in the ambulance with the paramedics, Captain, and—"

"I want you to get this stupid reporter and her tape recorder the hell out of here! Way behind that barricade!"

"Yes, sir," Lopez panted. "But they've got a—"

"Now, right now, Lopez!" MacAdoo hollered. "Do you read me?"

"Yes, sir!" Lopez grabbed Joy Newsome by the elbow.

She poked the still-open microphone up to MacAdoo's mouth again as Lopez started pulling her arm. "How many people are holding the bank, Captain?"

"Lo-pez-zz!" he screamed in anguish, waving both hands frantically.

Lopez pulled her roughly to her feet and started hustling her to the barricade.

"Down!" MacAdoo yelled. "Keep her down!" He watched them disappear behind the crowded barricade, Newsome's microphone poked close to Lopez's moving mouth.

"Je-sus Christ, can you *believe* that?" MacAdoo moaned.


"Keep 'em movin', willya Vito," Louie ordered. "I'm expecting an important telephone call."

"We're goin' as fast as we can," Vito said as he led Barnes back toward the conference room. "A coupla them had important business to do in there."

"That's Dave's pickles," Abe said.

"That's Dave's everything!" Oscar said.

"I only got a few more," Vito said, taking Barnes inside.

Jesse was already on his feet in the starting blocks. "You got no heart, man!" he groaned. "I'm dyin'!" And with that, he was through the door, scooting toward the men's room, with Vito in close pursuit.

"One order of Dave's knishes to go!" Abe hollered, and they all laughed.

Barnes moved quickly to his place next to Angela.

"No, no, Mr. Barnes," Minnie said, beckoning him back. "I'm gonna switch you places with Jesse. Come, sit here." She pulled Jesse's chair out for him.

"Why *there?*" Barnes asked, looking at the chair as though it were contaminated.

"Never mind why. Because I say so, that's why."

Barnes flushed. "But damnit, I don't see why I—"

"Please, Mr. Barnes," Minnie warned, slipping her hand into her pocket with the gun, "don't make trouble for me!"

"I'm not the one who's making trouble, lady," Barnes said. "I'm perfectly happy where I've been sitting, and I don't see why you pick on me to move into his chair, that's all."

"Why? Because I had a special request in the ladies' room, that's why!" Minnie let it slip out without thinking. "Now you satisfied? Come."

Barnes turned an accusing glare at Angela, who returned his gaze with a steady flight of daggers of her own.

"Come on, Mr. Barnes," Minnie said, "be a good fellow. What difference does it make where you sit, after all?"

They all watched as he slowly turned away from Angela and approached Jesse's chair, hating every step.

"That's better." Minnie leaned in to relock him to the cable. "You'll see, you'll be just as comfortable sitting here, as—"

Suddenly Barnes grabbed for Minnie's gun with both hands, leaping out of his chair and jerking the gun barrel and Minnie's hand with it, high up over her head. Everyone in the room was all at once yelling and screaming as Barnes struggled to break Minnie's frantic grip on the gun.

"Abe! Abe! Abe!" Minnie screamed even louder than the others as she held onto the gun for dear life.

Barnes, much taller and stronger, was yanking her off her feet, pulling her arm painfully out of its socket as he thrashed her back and forth, slamming them both up against the wall. Minnie was flailing at him, trying to hit him with the steel lock she still had in her left hand, but he had her sweater stretched up in front of her face—she couldn't even see him. She could only feel the terrible pain in her shoulder as he jerked and twisted her arm viciously upward.

Desperately, she pulled hard away from him for a split second, stepped quickly to her left, then grunted as she lifted her right knee sharply, with all her terrified might, delivering a crushing blow *right to the balls*.

Barnes let out a shattering primal scream that could have been heard a

218

jungle away. His fingers sprang loose from the gun, and he flopped to the floor in a painful writhing heap.

Tearing through the door with their guns drawn, Louie and Abe reached Minnie's side to see Barnes rolling back and forth on the floor, clutching his groin.

"My God!" Minnie looked down at him, glassy-eyed. "I did it! I can't believe it—*I really did it!*"

Every man in the room could feel Barnes' excruciating pain as he lay groaning on the floor, drawn up in a tight ball, trying to catch his breath.

And every woman put her hands over her eyes, or looked away—all except Angela St. Clair, who just couldn't help herself as she watched Barnes squirm and moan. At that moment, she didn't care if he never paid her back for her torn bra. The fates and Minnie Gold had at last gotten her even with the number-one male chauvinist pig of Citizens' Bank, and it was a pleasure to see him keeping his hands to himself.

"Abe, oh, Abe!" Minnie cried, seeing him there for the first time. "I'm sorry! I'm so sorry!" She fell into his arms sobbing.

"Whatta ya sorry?" Abe asked as he led her from the room. "He deserved it, didn't he? Did he hurt you, the son of a bitch?"

"My arm, he hurt my arm a little," she whimpered. "But *him,* the poor man— I must've almost *killed* him, I kicked him so hard!"

"Don't worry," said Abe. "You don't kill a man so easy."

"And all I could think of was that it was *you* I was kicking, Abe. *You!*"

"Me? Why *me?*"

"I don't *know* why," she wailed. "I couldn't *help* it. The second I kicked him there, I could only feel your pain, Abe—*yours!* Oh, God, Abe, I'm so *sorry.*"

Abe held her tightly as she wept in his arms. "Minnie, Minnie," he murmured, patting her head. "Minny the ninny . . . shah, shah. It's okay, he'll be all right, I promise you."

Little by little, she quieted down. Then she lifted her tearful face to look up at him with a crooked smile.

"Thatta girl," Abe said, gently scooping a tear from her cheek. "That's my shining Gold."

Minnie sniffed loudly, the way women do after a foolish cry.

"And listen," Abe said, chucking her under the chin, "I guarantee, you didn't hurt me. *Mine* are as good as new. I'll show you anytime you want! They are sterling silver—"

She knew his punch-line, of course, and joined him in nodding unison: "All they need is a little polishing up every once in a while!"

"Ri-ight!" Abe said, turning her out of his arms and slapping her on the rump. "You better get back in to the little girl. I'll help out in the meeting room."

"Oh, all the excitement," Minnie said. "I almost forgot about her. I mustn't let her see I been crying." And she shuffled toward Wilson's office, dabbing at her eyes with her sweater.

Barnes was still on the floor with Louie standing over him when Vito brought Jesse back into the conference room.

"A-ay, I can't leave you people alone for a minute," Vito said. "What the hell happened here?"

"This dummy tried to take Minnie's gun away from her," Louie explained, "so she gave him the big knee."

"*Maron!* 'This dummy' is right!" Vito said, looking down at the injured man.

"Aw, man!" Jesse said. "I'm always missing out on the good stuff!"

"That's enough outa you, Jesse," Vito said. "Sit down in your chair."

"Okay, man, I'm sittin'."

"No, no!" Barnes grunted with difficulty, "don't sit there! You're supposed to change places with me!"

"I'm supposed to what?" Jesse asked.

"Please! Please, Jesse." Barnes struggled painfully to his feet. "Don't ask questions, just change places with me. That's the way she wants it, I'm telling you!"

Jesse took one fearful look at Barnes, doubled over, his hands clutching his crotch.

"Gotcha, man!" he said, "I'm movin'!" He was in Barnes's chair in a flash, his hands folded on the table like a kid on the first day of school.

Barnes limped to Jesse's chair, and Louie helped him sit down.

The phone rang in the main room. "Telephone, Levine!" Oscar shouted.

"I hear, I hear." Louie walked out to the phone, put his hand on it, waited through a second ring, then picked it up. "Hello, is this the Chiefa Police, or only a cop?"

"Hello, this is Captain MacAdoo, across the street. It's been exactly ten minutes—"

"I know, I know."

"What's your answer on the doctor?" MacAdoo asked.

"What's your answer on the Chiefa Police?"

MacAdoo paused for a moment. Maybe he'd better tell him about the Chief. Maybe his unavailability would help get the doctor inside. God, how he hated to talk to these people. Who the hell did they think they were, demanding to negotiate with whatever government official they wanted while they terrorized innocent people and endangered the lives of his men? The Chief of Police, for Christ's sake—why not the Governor? Or the President of the United States? The death penalty, that's the answer. Get the fucking death penalty back, and all this terrorist shit would end in a hell of a hurry, by God.

"Hello? Did you hear my question?" Louie asked.

220

"Yes, yes." MacAdoo came out of his law-and-order reverie. "About the Chief of Police . . . well, I'm sorry to have to tell you . . . Assistant Chief Robeson finally reached him in San Francisco, but he's sick in his hotel room with the swine flu. He's got a dangerously high temperature, and the doctor up there wouldn't even let him talk on the phone."

"Your Chiefa Police has got the *swine flu?*" Louie grinned in spite of himself. "I wouldn't even make a comment."

"Yes, sir," MacAdoo said, not getting it. "So you see, due to circumstances beyond our control, the Chief is simply not available. Now, we want to cooperate with you on this thing, get everyone out of danger as soon as we can, but you have to meet us half way. Right now, we have no idea what it is you people want, so how about letting the doctor in a for a little talk? We'll both know better where we stand. . . . How about it?"

"Yes . . . not available . . . where we stand . . ."

An old man's mind sometimes falters when faced with a change in plan, a new set of hurdles. He clucked his tongue nervously against his upper palate, setting a dull tempo, trying to get his mind back in gear.

"Whatta you clucking, Louie?" Abe asked, putting his hand over the phone. "What does he say?"

"He says the Chiefa Police is sick in bed in San Francisco," Louie said dully. "He says the Assistant Chief has all the same authority, and he says he is on his way here. But in the meantime, he says, he wants us to let in a doctor, to talk to me."

"A *doctor?*"

"Not a regular doctor," Louie explained, "a talking doctor."

"Und so?" Oscar asked. "What is your decision, Levine?"

Louie shook his head stubbornly. "We didn't come all this way just to talk to a doctor," he said. "We will wait for the Assistant Chief of Police."

"Und what if the Assistant Chief doesn't come?" Oscar asked. "*What then?*"

"If he comes, he will be here," said Louie, steadily answering Oscar's searching gaze. "If he doesn't come, he will be someplace else—and we will find out if you know your business, watchmaker." He put his hand on the blasting box.

Abe shuddered. The threat was real for the first time, and he knew it.

"Levine," Oscar said, "we are all in this thing together, from the beginning, to the ending—und one thing that I know for sure—we also did not come here to find out if I know my business. I say we talk to the doctor."

Louie looked at Oscar, right into him in that steely way of his. Oscar didn't even blink.

"That's what you say, hah?" Louie asked. "What about you, Abe? What do you say?"

"Louie, I gotta say Oscar is right," Abe said. "The more time that goes by not talking, the more things can go wrong for us. I say we talk to the doctor. Minnie would say so, too."

Vito escorted McInnerny out of the restroom and across to the conference room. And still, Louie studied the two men.

"Hello, hello!" MacAdoo said irritably, over the phone.

Louie removed Abe's hand from the mouthpiece. "Yes, Captain, I'm here, I'm here. Don't get your water hot. Okay, we will take the first step *your* way. We will see the doctor. Here is what he will do . . ."

Through the booth window, MacAdoo nodded emphatically at Harmon and Keller.

"Ollie, I'm not going inside," Harmon informed Keller. "*You* are."

The younger man was caught completely off guard. "But why me?" he asked, pushing his glasses back up his nose. "I thought you had decided that you—"

"I know," Harmon said, "but I've changed my mind, for two reasons. First, you're really more experienced at this sort of thing, and second, I seem to have at least some influence over MacAdoo. He can't be trusted out here alone. I don't know what's eating on him, but he could destroy our very first assignment, and get some people killed in the process."

Keller watched MacAdoo, gesturing wildly in the phone booth at something Louie said.

"You're right, Mark," Keller said. "He's a grenade. If he blows. . . . No problem—I'll go in."

"Sir, I think you're really taking advantage of your position to put us through this kind of nonsense," MacAdoo was saying, "but we'll do it just like you say. Are you in a position to see directly across the street?"

"Don't worry about where my position is," Louie snapped, "I'll see what I *need* to see. You just get the doctor in his place."

"Yes, sir," said MacAdoo. "That's exactly what I'm going to do. Now, I'm going to leave the phone booth, so don't hang up. It'll take me a minute to get the doctor squared away and get a bullhorn, okay?"

"Yes, yes, okay already. So *do* it."

MacAdoo stood with the phone in his hand, hefting it like a billy-club. Then he dropped it, letting the wire slide through his fingers until the receiver hung swinging back and forth against the glass. He barged out of the booth, glaring across the street at the bank, and rejoined the two doctors. "Lopez! A bullhorn, on the double!" he yelled.

A uniformed cop came running low from behind one of the squad cars in the street, carrying a bullhorn, which he handed to MacAdoo.

"Where the hell's Lopez?" MacAdoo shouted after the cop as he continued to run past crouching low.

"I don't know, Captain," the cop shouted back. "Haven't seen him in a while!"

"Son of a bitch!" MacAdoo muttered. "I'm going to shit in that taco's

222

packet this time! Okay, Doctor Harmon, this is what he wants you to do. He wants you to get over there on the sidewalk, directly across the street from the front door of the bank, and then he wants you—"

"Wait a minute, Captain," Harmon said, "*I'm* not going in. Doctor Keller's going to go. Tell *him*."

"I thought you said you were going to go?"

"I know," Harmon said, "but it's better this way."

"Hell, it makes no difference to me which one of you goes," MacAdoo said. "The whole damn thing's a waste of time anyway, just another stupid Police Commission idea to get in the way of law enforcement, that's all."

"We'll soon see, won't we?" Harmon said.

"Okay, Captain," Keller said, "I'm across the street from the front door of the bank. Then what?"

"Then he wants you to take your clothes off," said MacAdoo.

"My clothes?"

"Yeah, right. That's how he's going to make sure you're not armed. Maybe he doesn't trust doctors, huh?"

"All my clothes?"

"I don't know," MacAdoo said. "He tells *me* on the phone. I tell *you* on the bullhorn. That's how he wants it."

"Well, I'm not much of a specimen," Keller said, starting to pull his jacket off, "but if that's what he wants, that's what he gets."

"No, no," MacAdoo said, "don't take them off here—he wants to see your whole strip act in front of the bank."

"Okay," Keller said, getting up, "here goes!"

"Names, Doctor," MacAdoo reminded him, "get me names. Of the hostages, too."

"I'll get all the information I can," Keller said. "Keep it nice and quiet out here, men. I'll see you in a few minutes."

MacAdoo headed for the phone booth with his bullhorn, and Keller started across the street toward the point directly opposite the bank, loosening his tie. For some reason he looked down at his shadow, cast directly in front of him as he walked. A curious thought struck him. As long as he could keep his shadow moving, he knew that he would be all right, that he would be alive. Stupid thought.

Keller reached the appointed spot and faced the bank. No traffic moved in this major intersection. To his right, firemen watched him from their truck. To his left, armed police personnel, in and out of uniform, hovered behind the open doors of squad cars and emergency vehicles, their guns trained on the bank. Behind the barricades, he could make out the crowd of two or three hundred people watching him. Over his right shoulder, he saw the TV camera trucks moving forward. He looked up to see sharpshooters standing at the open windows of nearby buildings and on the roofs, including the roof of the bank.

Keller tried to see into the bank across the street, but the sun's rays made a perfect mirror of the bank's massive front doors, and all he could see in them was his own reflection.

Suddenly, MacAdoo's bullhorn blasted everything else to absolute silence. "Keller! Your coat and tie!"

Keller removed his jacket and tugged at the knot of his tie. He tried to pull it free of his shirt, but the sweaty collar held it fast. He reached up behind his neck, unfolded his collar and extricated the tie.

The crowd watched attentively as he waited for his next instruction.

"Drop them!" MacAdoo barked, poking the bullhorn out of the booth.

Keller dropped his jacket and tie on the sidewalk.

"Okay—your shirt!" MacAdoo boomed.

Keller tugged his shirt up out of his pants, unbuttoned it, and pulled his arms out of the soaking wet sleeves, revealing a flabby, freckled, pear-shaped body that suddenly started to blush crimson from the top of his forehead downward to his navel. He dropped his shirt on top of his jacket.

"Your shoes—one at a time!"

MacAdoo had relayed Louie's order without editing, and many in the crowd laughed as Keller took off his shoes "one at a time," setting them neatly together next to his jacket.

"Now your socks!"

"Oh, shit, not my socks!" Keller said. He bent to do as he was told. At that moment, his glasses slid off his nose and fell to the sidewalk. He snatched them up and saw that one of the lenses had cracked into a perfect star-burst, right in the center of the glass. His head dropped forward disgustedly, and a compassionate groan went up from the crowd. He cleaned his glasses with the top of one of his socks and put them back on.

MacAdoo poked his bullhorn out again. "Pick up your shoes, and shake them!"

Keller heard, but didn't understand for a moment, shaking his head and frowning at MacAdoo.

"Of course, stupid," Keller said to himself as the light went on. "He wants you to shake your shoes so he knows you're not concealing a weapon." He shook his shoes out upside down.

"Okay, you can put them on," MacAdoo blared out. "But don't tie the laces!"

Keller put his bare feet into his shoes. He hated that worse than anything. He could feel his clammy feet, with the grit from the sidewalk sticking to them, glued to his inner soles, and it sent a shiver up his back.

"Now, roll up your pants!"

Keller gratefully started rolling his trouser legs up. Thank God, he was going to be allowed to keep his pants on. He couldn't remember which pair of boxer shorts he had put on this morning, but that didn't bother him. What bothered him was why he was trying to remember.

"Higher, higher!" MacAdoo blasted. "Above the knees!"

224

Keller quickly complied, revealing a pair of spindly hairless calves.

"Turn your pockets inside out!"

Keller emptied his pockets onto the pile of clothing, taking a moment to slip his wallet into his jacket pocket and to remove a small flat object. Then he pulled his trouser pockets inside out.

"Turn around! Show him your back pockets!"

Keller about-faced, exhibiting the two limp pockets flopping out in back. Then he faced the bank once more.

"Raise your hands over your head!" MacAdoo commanded.

Just then, Lopez, sweating and red in the face, came running up to MacAdoo at the booth. "Captain, Captain, they want you to come to the ambulance, they've got a—"

Louie saw Keller's hands go up. "What is he holding in his hand?" he screamed into the phone. "I don't want anything in his hands!"

"Get the hell out of the way, Lopez!" MacAdoo yelled, swinging the bullhorn at him. "Can't you see I'm on the phone, goddamn it?"

"But, Captain—"

"Lopez! Come here!" Doctor Harmon shouted. "Get away from him!"

"What the hell are you trying to do to us?" Louie shouted into the phone. "You think I can't see what's going *on* out there, or what? You wanna get people *killed*, for God's sake?"

"Easy," MacAdoo said. "Take it easy. We're not trying to *do* anything. Just let me see what he's got in his hand, okay?"

"I don't care *what* it is!" Louie hollered. "I don't want anything in his hands, you hear?"

"It's a notebook," MacAdoo said.

"A what—?"

"A notebook—you know—to take *notes* in." MacAdoo poked his bullhorn out of the booth toward Keller again. "Show him your notebook! Riffle the pages, so he can see it's a book!"

Louie saw Keller open the harmless little book and riffle its pages. "All right, I see it's a notebook. He can bring it in."

Brubaker came limping out of the rest room, leaning heavily on Vito's shoulder. "You gave me a great job here, Levine," Vito griped. "I hadda operate this guy's zipper for him!"

"Never mind," Louie said, covering the phone, "You're perfect for that job. How many more you got?"

"Only one," Vito said, "the busboy is the lasta the Mohicans."

"Well, hurry it up, willya? We got a visitor waiting."

Vito helped Brubaker toward the conference room.

"That man needs doctor, Louie," Stosh said from the front.

Louie frowned. "Listen, Mr. Guard, you pay attention to your own business! What the hell's going on here? Everybody thinks everybody needs a *doctor* all of a sudden!"

Stosh turned back to the front door as Vito brought Gonzalo out.

"*Eechola!*" Gonzalo said, looking out the front door. "Hey, man, you guys are on the TV! *¡Mira, mira!* Look at those cameras over there! You guys are gonna be on the news, man!"

"Hey, *Señor.*" Vito grabbed Gonzalo by the ear and turned him around. "I thought you said you hadda take a leak! You wanna skip it?"

"No, no, man," said Gonzalo quickly. "I'm goin' right now, pronto!" And he hurried toward the men's room with Vito right behind him.

"Hello, in there," MacAdoo said on the phone. "The doctor's all set. Shall I send him across?"

"The doctor will have to wait a minute," Louie said, once more scanning the scene outside through his binoculars. "I got one more hasta finish in the bathroom."

Across the street, Keller stood stiffly in place, his hands high above his head, trying not to move a muscle. His glasses had slipped down to the tip of his nose, but he was afraid of reaching down to push them back in place. The slightest gesture at this point could be interpreted with suspicion by the people inside, and there would be no telling what irrational thing they might do. He had seen it happen before.

In the glass of the bank's front door, Keller could see the milky pink whiteness of his body in the bright April sun, and he knew that five more minutes of exposure to the elements, and he would surely fall victim to an itchy sunburn or a croupy spring cold or both.

Vito brought Gonzalo back out of the men's room. "Hey, man," the young man said to his captor, "how 'bout just let me go to the front door and check out all the action, eh?"

"Get outa here!" Vito jerked his gun toward the conference room.

"Okay, okay!" Gonzalo said, holding his hands up and resuming his bouncing stride. "Don't get excited, man. I was just foolin' around, okay?"

Louie watched the two men disappear into the other room. "Hello? Captain MacAdoo?"

"Yes, I'm here."

"All right, MacAdoo. You can send your doctor across the street. But be a smart fella. We got people watching you. Don't do anything foolish. Don't *lose yourself* a doctor, you know what I mean?"

"There will be no police action of any kind while the doctor is in the bank," MacAdoo said. "I give you my word."

"I don't need your word, Captain," said Louie. "I got your doctor!" With that, he cut MacAdoo off with the hold button.

MacAdoo let the phone drop and stepped all the way out of the booth. "All units hold your positions!" he shouted into the bullhorn as he swiveled left and right, repeating each instruction. "Hold your positions! I want absolutely no movement out here! No movement! Holster all handguns! Holster all handguns! Stand by!" He pointed the bullhorn at Keller. "Okay, Keller! You can cross the street!"

Keller felt himself gulp as he started forward to the curb. His shoe

226

slipped half off when he stepped down in the street, but he managed to keep it on with a quick forward movement of his foot. Then he shuffled awkwardly ahead to cross the boulevard.

It seemed to Keller as though the street was a soggy mile wide, and as he finally reached the other side and stepped successfully up onto the curb, both shoes still on his feet, a few people in the crowd burst into jeering applause.

MacAdoo blasted a stream of stacatto orders through his bullhorn at the crowd. "Quiet! Quiet, you people! I want quiet out here! Move those people back! Quiet! That's a man's *life* out there!"

Keller stood right in front of the doors to the bank, his nose almost touching the glass, his mind racing, his temples pounding, his mouth dry, his glasses slipping, aching to scratch an itch at his left shoulder blade—and longing to be anyplace on earth except on the spot where he was standing at that moment.

"I should open door now, Louie?" Stosh asked.

"No. Let him stand," Louie said. "I will tell you when."

Again, Louie peered through the binoculars, looking past Keller to the street and to the CBS parking lot beyond. He took a last swing to his right to see MacAdoo, standing at the booth, with the phone at his ear. Then he took a long close-up look at Keller, trembling at the door.

"This is a *doctor* . . . ?" Louie asked nobody in particular. He lowered the binoculars and set them on the counter. "Nobody calls anybody by their *names*, everybody understand? All right, Stosh, listen to me. I want you to let him in, then lock the doors—with the chain—then I want you to search him, understand?"

"But, Louie, his pockets are all out—empty."

"Stosh . . . can you tell me if he has a gun strapped to his leg?"

Stosh nodded foolishly, then removed the chain and unlocked the doors, swinging one door open wide for Keller's entrance.

Keller stepped inside.

"Stop right there," Louie commanded, and Keller stopped.

Stosh quickly secured the front doors and knelt to search Keller's trousers, patting the man's legs gingerly from knee to waist.

"I'm not armed," Keller said hoarsely.

"Nothing," Stosh confirmed, returning to his post at the side of the door.

"All right, Doctor." Louie crooked a finger. "Come to me."

Keller shuffled slowly through the long room to the safety deposit counter, where Louie stood with Oscar at his side.

"You can put your hands down, on the counter," Louie said.

Keller lowered his cramped arms and placed his sweaty palms down on the counter, his notebook between them.

"Now, Doctor—*if* you are a doctor—" said Louie, "what can we do for you?"

"My name—" Keller cleared his throat. "My name is Doctor Oliver E.

Keller. Until early January of this year, I was a member of the faculty at UCLA, in the department of psychiatry."

"Oh-h, a brain doctor," Louie said.

"Yes, uh, sort of."

"So now you are a *policeman*, hah?"

"No, sir, I'm a . . . I'm just a professional consultant to the, uh, Los Angeles Police Department," Keller stammered, reaching for an absent breast pocket. "My . . . my identification is across the street . . . in my jacket pocket."

"I don't need no identification," Louie said. "You're a *cop*, that's all—plain and simple."

"No, not really, sir," Keller differed carefully, trying to get both eyes in focus despite the one shattered lens of his glasses. "I'm a member of a new professional group formed by the Commission which oversees the police department, to *advise* them on civil, uh, disturbances of this kind. It's our function to discover the causes of these, uh, events, and, uh, to negotiate with the people involved, in an effort to avoid violence. We are in *no way* a law enforcement department. I'm here to try to help you, do you understand?"

Louie had listened respectfully while the young man earnestly described his function.

"Oh, yes, I think I understand," Louie said with a caustic little grin. "So what can I do for you, Officer?"

Keller felt the needle of Louie's sarcasm and backed off. "Okay, okay," he said, using the repeated word as his restart switch. "Let's see if we can start with a few essential facts. . . ." He opened his notebook and slipped out a slim ballpoint pen.

Louie exchanged amused glances with his men as they watched Keller assume the studied casual air of his profession, pen poised to record the momentous interview. "Now, what is your name, sir?"

"My name?" Louie asked. "I have no name."

Keller looked up from his notebook with a puzzled expression. "No name?" he repeated idiotically.

"That's right—no name." Louie said.

Then, slowly, with a certain show of ceremony, Louie reached up and carefully peeled off his curly dark wig, dropping it to the floor and aging thirty years or so, as Keller's mouth dropped open and the pen fell out of his hand.

"I have only a number," Louie explain. "I am just one of the nineteen million old people in this country who are despised, who have been deserted, who go hungry the last week of every month, or steal cat food to eat from the supermarket, or dig for food in the garbage cans. I am only one of millions who are left alone and unprotected to be robbed and beaten up by the hoodlums in the streets. Why should I have a name?"

228

Keller stared in shocked disbelief as Oscar, too, pulled his wig off and threw it on the floor. The young doctor turned to see Abe and Stosh also shedding their mops of false hair.

"But . . . good God!" Keller was staring aghast at the white hair and the balding heads. "You're all old people!"

"What'sa matter?" Louie asked, "You're surprised that a bunch of old people could get angry enough at their condition to *do something?*"

"No, I . . . I'm just . . . God! Old people!" Keller felt weak-kneed, almost faint, as he looked from one aged face to the other.

"Okay, okay," he said, trying to regain his composure. "I . . . I have to admit that this is the, uh, last thing in the world I could have expected to find in here. But, okay . . . this is the situation, and we have to *deal* with it."

"That's right, my boy," Louie said quietly. "This is the day we will deal with it. It's about time."

"Yes, sir." Keller's gears were starting to mesh. "Now, I'd like us to be fair with each other, okay? I've told you my name—it's Doctor Oliver E. Keller. You can call me Doctor, or Doctor Keller, or even Oliver, if you like. It's, you know, hard to communicate with someone unless you can call them by name, so what can I call you? Just give me a first name, it doesn't even have to be your real name—"

"What difference does my name make?" Louie asked irritably. "Just call me 'old man,' like they do on the street—He-ey, wait a minute!" He interrupted himself, pointing at Keller. "I know you from someplace, don't I?"

"I don't know, sir," said Keller. "Have we ever met?"

"Oh-h, yeah, in the newpaper," said Louie. "You're 'Oliver Keller, the Remarkable Feller,' right?"

Keller blushed.

"Yeah," Louie continued, "you're the man who went up on top of the Arco Tower Building downtown and talked that GI without legs—You're the man who talked him into coming down off the roof, right?"

"Yes, sir, I am," Keller admitted modestly. "I'm surprised you should remember that. That was almost three years ago. I was consulting psychiatrist for the Veterans' Administration at the time."

"How could I forget such a thing?" Louie said, waving to his group to gather around. "You know what this man did? Listen to *this*. . . . A coupla years ago, just after the POWs came home from Vietnam, a young soldier who had his legs blown off—He was an officer, right?"

"Yes, very sad," Keller said. "First Lieutenant John Sheridan—he was a patient of mine at the VA hospital."

"Yeah, a First Louie, like me." Louie smiled at his pun. "Anyhow, one night this young soldier escapes from the hospital—in his wheelchair, mind you! He just wheels himself out in the middle of the night. They look all

229

over for him for a couple of days, but they can't find him anyplace. All of a sudden, the next thing you know, he shows up on the roof of the Arco Tower *in his wheelchair*. Only God knows how he got himself up there—and he's shooting his machine gun in the air and hollering down at the top of his lungs, right in the middle of downtown Los Angeles during the lunch hour!"

"How do ya like that!" Abe said.

"And what is he hollering about?" Louie continued. "He is crazy with anger because he came home from Vietnam without his legs to find Nixon still selling guns and fighter planes to the Arabs on one side, and to Israel on the other!"

"My God," Stosh said.

"And what does he want? He wants to talk on the TV. He wants to tell the people that *we* are helping to make a war—that's all he wants. He wants to show Nixon the stumps of his legs, and to tell him to stop selling the weapons of death and mutilation."

"He was a very sick man," Keller said, shaking his head. "He had very serious mental problems."

"Ah-hh, mentally sick is one thing," Louis reasoned, "but right and wrong is another. Was he wrong? No, he was not wrong!"

"But he was endangering the lives of hundreds of people in the streets below," Keller argued. "He had four live grenades strapped to his body, and he was threatening to jump off—fifty-two stories to the street—if his demands weren't met! It would have been a major disaster!"

"More of a disaster than another Mideast war?" Louie asked, as though Keller could answer such a question.

Keller shrugged his inability to respond.

"So, anyway," Louie continued, "they call for Doctor Keller here, and he goes up on the roof—very brave, I gotta admit. I mean, the soldier was only a cripple in a wheelchair, but he had a loaded automatic rifle in his hands, after all! And like today, a thousand cops and a thousand guns, a big crowd stood around watching and waiting and kibitzing. A lotta nice people were yelling up to the soldier not to listen to the doctor and to jump, already. A helicopter was flying around—it was a madhouse! But the doctor talks and he talks, and after a while he calms the soldier down with some mumbo jumbo, and he *promises* him that he will get his story out. Sure enough—finally the kid gives up his gun and comes down crying with the doctor."

"A very fortunate outcome to a terrifying event," Keller said. "That was a frightening day for everyone concerned."

"For everyone *concerned*, hah?" Louie pondered another meaning of those words for a moment. "So listen, listen to the finish," he said finally. "When they get down to the street, the reporters ask the soldier what made him change his mind, what made him come down on the elevator? And he says, like a nursery rhyme, he says: 'Oliver Keller is a remarkable feller.

230

Oliver Keller, he's O.K.'—Do ya get it? O.K.—stands for Oliver Keller! And *this* was the little headline on the story in the newspaper! Can you imagine? Never mind *why* he was up there in the first place. He was just another long-haired hippie war protester back from the war who went a little nuts, that's all! And he didn't get to tell his story on TV in his own words, so the headline was just a joke poem! They made a *dirty little joke* out of this young man's anger and his pain! How do ya like that for concern?"

Keller stood silently looking down at his own hands on the counter.

"Und what happened to this soldier?" Oscar asked quietly.

"I don't know," Louie said. "Doctor?"

"I was sent up there to save lives," Keller protested, "and to protect property, and I was lucky enough to succeed at my assignment!"

"What happened to the soldier?" Louie repeated.

"The last I heard," Keller answered, "he's at Camarillo State Mental Hospital."

"Camarillo, hah?" Louie nodded grimly. "So . . . he is still a prisoner of war, right?"

No one spoke. There was nothing to say.

Vito stuck his head out of the conference room. "Hey, can somebody come in here and—oh, excuse me," he said as he saw Keller.

"What'sa matter?" Louie asked him. "Whatta ya want?"

"Can somebody come in here and take over for me for a coupla minutes? I gotta go to the toilet."

"You been in and outa there a dozen times with your people, for goodness' sakes," Louie said. "why didn'cha go?"

"You ever try to take a leak with a gun in your hand?"

"You," said Louie, turning to Abe. "Take over for him in there."

Vito hurried toward the men's room as Abe walked to the conference room.

Keller craned his neck, trying to get a glimpse into the conference room as Abe quickly shut the door behind him.

"So, Doctor Keller," Louie said, all business again, "you came in here also to save lives and protect property, hah?"

"That's correct," Keller said carefully. "But more than that, we believe that confrontations of this kind can only be concluded safely—without bloodshed—if both sides are willing to establish between them a spirit of mutual respect and, uh, trust. Now, I want to assure you that I have come in here in that spirit."

"Izzat so?" Louie said. "I can see right away, you got a golden tongue, Oliver Keller."

"No, seriously," Keller said, loosening up a little, "I'm here to help, but I need your help, too . . . so I can get a feel for what's going on here . . . so I can understand why you're doing this, and just what it is you want."

231

"That's simple enough," Louie said. "Why? Because we are old people, at the end of the line, and we would like to be allowed to live—until we die. What we want? We want somebody to *stop, look,* and *listen!*"

"I see," Keller said, studying Louie's face, wondering how much he might bend the dangerous commitment the old man had made to this fateful day.

"Do you really see, Doctor?" Louie asked.

No word games, Keller thought. This man will not stand for them. No ploying around with this old man. Just try to draw him out for information. Don't test his anger . . . because his anger is old, and deep, and deadly. "No, of course I don't see," Keller said with a frank smile. "How can I see what *you* see?"

Louie looked at Keller, noting the coincidence of the young doctor's half blindness in the cracked lens of his glasses. "You're right, Doctor," he said. "But maybe some day, you will be able to see with *both* eyes."

"If you help me," Keller said, feeling a new license to dig in, "maybe that day can be today."

"Maybe," Louie said. "We'll see."

"All right," Keller said, referring quickly to his notebook. "Since you won't tell me your name—and I can understand that, I really can—will you at least identify your organization for me?"

"Organization?"

"Yes. I mean, is this a political group, or a religious action of some kind, or—my God, you're not the *Gray Panthers*, are you?"

"Whatta you talking about?" Louie sneered. "Listen, we are not the Gray Panthers, we are not the Black Panthers, and we are not the Spotted Panthers! Yes, we are a bunch of old cats, that's right—a bunch of helpless old cats who have been left out in the cold to go hungry, and we finally got tired of crying meeow-meeow!"

Keller was sorry he'd asked the question.

"You see this?" Louie lifted the whistle that hung around his neck. "This is a rape whistle, a gift from Chief Davis. So today, these old cats are whistling rape!"

Without warning, Louie blew a shrill blast on the whistle that went right through Keller to his bare feet, making him wince so hard that his eyes squeezed shut. He opened them just in time to see Vito come tearing out of the men's room with his gun in his hand and ready for action.

Keller shot his hands up in the air.

"Hold it, hold it!" Louie shouted at Vito. "Everything is okay—I'm just communicating with the doctor."

"Jeez, you scared the hell outa me again!" Vito said, shoving his gun back into his belt.

Keller dropped his hands, with a moaning sigh.

232

"Do ya think you're gettin' through to him?" Vito asked, wiggling a little finger in his ringing ear.

"I think that he is hearing me now," said Louie, nodding at Keller. "The next step, is listening."

"Look here," Keller said, testily, "I told you that I came in here prepared to listen, but frightening me certainly won't accomplish anything. We have a very dangerous situation here. I'm sure you realize that."

"Oh, yes, Doctor," Louie agreed. "We realize."

"Well, then, tell me," Keller dared to ask, "do you really believe that you had to commit a federal crime—to put all these people in jeopardy of their lives—in order to be heard?"

Louie studied the younger man's face, sensing that the professional shell was cracking—that he was, indeed, starting to get through to the person underneath.

"Well, tell me the truth, Doctor," he said evenly. "Would you listen to me—yesterday?"

"But . . . but *I'm* not really the right person for you to discuss your grievances with," Keller said. "There are, as you undoubtedly know, agencies that are in place for that specific purpose, if you have valid complaints."

"*If?*"

"I didn't mean that," Keller said quickly. "I'm sure they *are* valid, but don't you think that you could get more satisfaction by going through legal channels, rather than by committing this criminal act of violence?"

"No, no, young man," Louie said, wagging a finger. "What we have created here—is a fact!"

"A fact?"

"Yes," Louie explained, "a fact that cannot be ignored, that cannot be overlooked or postponed or amended by somebody telling us to fill out an official application in triplicate just for the right to live like a human being. This fact we have created must be dealt with—today!"

"But don't you understand?" Keller was losing his poise again. "You are threatening the lives of people who have nothing at all to do with your problems. How can you hope to gain sympathy for your cause—no matter how just it is—by behaving like a gang of terrorists?"

Louie squinted at Keller, both hands knotting into tight fists. Oscar quickly laid a restraining hand on Louie's forearm.

"Listen, young man," Louie said, controlling his temper, "you're on the *wrong side* of this counter to talk like that to me!"

"I meant no disrespect, sir," Keller said quickly.

"Terrorists, hah? You call us a gang of terrorists? Well, maybe you're right. But don't you read the newspapers? Don't you notice, that people listen only to *gangsters* lately?"

233

"Come on, now," Keller challenged. "Do you really think that this kind of criminal act can be an answer to your problems?"

"The answer?" Louie said. "Oh, no, my young Doctor Freud, you will not catch me in that trap. I am too old to have answers. Young people like you will have to come up with the answers. I only know that we are doing something today that is necessary. We have perpetrated a shocking event so somebody will listen, so somebody maybe will *do* something to save this endangered species, this bunch of abandoned old cats."

"But surely, sir, you realize that ours is a society of law? The police must terminate this kind of outlaw behavior, they have no choice."

"Terminate?" Louie chuckled. "Look at us—you think we have something to lose? Don't you understand—the sooner we die, the better we'll feel. We just can't pick a time and terminate, that's all. We rust, we spoil—but we don't die so easy. Yet every day the old animal must eat, and try to stay dry and warm. Never mind happy, never mind respected or loved—just dry and not hungry, not humiliated. Would your 'society of law' be more comfortable if we just went away quiet and laid down happy on our dump heap?"

"I can't seem to make my point with you," Keller complained, rubbing his forehead for a moment. "Look, you're obviously an intelligent man, a well-read man. Surely you understand that civilization would soon be converted into a jungle if this kind of behavior was permitted every time—"

"Doctor, you dare to talk to me of civilization?" Louie demanded. "In what context? Watts? Attica? Kent State? The eighty-year-old man in Minnesota, sick in bed alone in his house, he didn't pay the gas bill for two months, they turned off his gas without even knocking at his door and let him freeze to death in his bed in thirty-below? *This* is the civilization you wanna defend?"

"No, sir, and I think you know that," Keller said, not giving up. "Be fair, now, those are all excesses you've cited—aberrations of a society put under pressure. But we've learned valuable lessons from those terrible events, and it seems to me that society is reaching back for a worthwhile moral ethic again! We've just got to give our legal institutions the chance to reestablish moral order."

"I can't believe it," Louie said, shaking his head. "Now you're talking *law and order*, for God's sake! You are a psychiatrist? A social scientist? How can you look at the present without regretting the past? Without fearing the future?"

Keller had no answer.

"You wanna know the truth, Doctor?" Louie continued. "You are *not* 'O.K.' You know what you are? You are a pimp, in here trying to sell soiled merchandise, that's what you are."

Oliver Keller, M.D., Ph.D., fiddled with the pages of his notebook, humiliated by an old man who had not even gone to high school.

"Go on, my friend." Louie said quietly. "Go take a hike. Peddle your fish

234

someplace else. Go find a halfa man somewhere, and talk *him* out of his reason for living. . . . The people in here are still in one piece, thank God, and we will not surrender so easy our last chance to tell our story to the world. Your society will deal with us today on our terms, not on yours."

Keller's mind raced. What the hell happened here? Had he argued too much? Preached too much? Pressed the old man too hard? Not listened enough? Had he made the fatal mistake of acting the role of adversary, rather than understanding friend?

What the hell had happened to the months of intensive training for the PIES? Had he not even learned the basic charter of the new department? "To neutralize organized acts of terrorism against society with reasonable powers of persuasion, rather than the use of traditional police fire power." Had he learned nothing during the long weeks of seminars with experts in the fields of criminal psychiatry, forensic tactics, political psychology, and revolutionary rhetoric? And what about the long days he spent at the UCLA Drama Department, being tested by the realistic improvisations with armed actor-terrorists who threatened the lives of their hostages if their demands were not met? How could he have bungled his job with this old man? How could he have allowed himself to commit the one unforgiveable sin of his profession—to become emotionally involved?

"Doctor Keller!"

It was Louie's voice again, jerking him back to reality.

"Did you understand what I said? Our interview is over. Mr. Bank Guard, you can take the doctor out now."

"No, no, please! Look, let me just try to explain—"

"No, no, it's *useless*," Louie said bluntly. "You and me, we don't communicate. We don't even talk the same language. I think I know what I'm talking about—and you think that you are listening."

"But . . . but wait just a minute. You said that what you have created here was a fact, isn't that right?"

"Yes. So?"

"Well, then," Keller reasoned, "in order that we can both cope with that fact intelligently, would you mind answering just a few factual questions?"

"Listen, Doctor—"

"I promise I won't argue," Keller said. "Just factual questions and answers. You are holding hostages, is that a fact?"

"Yes, that's a fact."

"How many hostages?" Keller asked, marking his book.

"I don't know. A dozen, thirteen, fourteen—What'sa difference how many?"

Don't argue. Just keep the old man talking. It's vital to stay inside the bank to get every bit of useful information possible.

"Okay," Keller said, making a note. "Has anyone been hurt?"

Louie hesitated a moment. "Not really."

Stosh cleared his throat, and Keller turned at the sound.

"Well . . ." Louie reconsidered. "One man, the guard—he tried to be a hero, you know? So before you could say Jackie Robinson, he got himself banged up a little bit. Nothing serious, he'll be all right."

Keller turned again to see Stosh's reaction. The big man was looking down at his shoes, and Louie was moistening his lips as Keller turned back. Body language. The old man was off balance for the first time.

"I would like to see the hostages now, please."

Keller's brazen request caught Louie completely off guard, and the young doctor's unyielding gaze made him even more uneasy. "You gotta lotta balls, you know that, Doctor?" he said.

Oscar tapped Louie on the shoulder, turning him around for a private conference as Vito joined them in a short walk away from the counter.

"Don't go away," said Louie over his shoulder. "I'll be right back."

Keller listened intently, but he could make nothing out of the whispered caucus.

After a moment, they returned to the counter.

"Tell me, Doctor," Louie said, "how long do you think it'll take for the Assistant Chief of Police to get here?"

"I don't know," said Keller. "I didn't know he was coming."

"You didn't hear MacAdoo ask him to come?" Louie asked.

"No, sir. I did not."

"Und what did I tell you?" Oscar said, nodding sagely.

Louie looked past Keller and out to the street. "Son of a bitch liar!" he muttered. "So he waits for his target practice, hah?"

Keller's expression had not changed, but he understood Louie perfectly.

"All right. Come, Doctor," Louie said, "follow me. I will take you in to see the hostages, and then I will give you a special message for Captain MacAdoo, who came here to shoot his gun."

Louie opened the door for Keller to go into the conference room.

Doctor Keller had been inside the bank for exactly fourteen minutes, but so many things had happened outside that it felt like fourteen hours to Captain MacAdoo.

Keller had just entered the bank when Betty Lundy's husband Francis, returning to pick up his pregnant wife, was stopped by Officer Cassidy, now manning the police barrier one block east of the bank.

"Turn right, turn right!" the cop shouted, as Francis nosed his station wagon across the intersection, unmindful of the barrier.

"What's the matter with you, Mister?" Cassidy yelled, running around the wagon to Francis as he finally braked to a stop, sending the little plastic Jesus clicking against the windshield. "Don't you see this emergency barrier? I said turn right here. This street is closed!"

"What do you mean closed? I'm coming to pick up my wife—she works in Citizens' Bank!"

236

"You sure she's in there?" the cop asked.

"I brought her to work this morning myself!" Francis said. "What's going on here?"

"Just turn your motor off, take your keys, and get out of your car."

"You mean just leave the car right here?" Francis asked, getting out.

"Hey, Doug!" Cassidy yelled to his partner. "I'm taking this guy over to Captain MacAdoo. He says his wife is in the bank!"

"What *is* all this?" Francis asked fearfully. "What's happened?"

"Captain MacAdoo will tell you all about it," the cop said. "Now, this is what we're going to do: You and I are going to cross the street right here, we're going to run into the CBS parking lot over there, then we're going to turn and run west across Fairfax to that telephone booth over there, see it?"

"Yes, I see it," said Francis. "But tell me what's—"

"No time for that. Just follow me—stay close and run low!" Cassidy ran crouching across the street to the parking lot, with Francis close behind.


"She can't be in there, ma'am," MacAdoo was telling Odessa's grandmother in the ambulance. "Nobody would hold a little six-year-old kid hostage. She must be lost in the crowd around here someplace."

"Officer, don't be telling me she can't be in there." Odessa'a grandmother said, "and don't be treating me like an ignorant old black woman, either! I'm a retired school teacher, and when I say my granddaughter is in that bank, I know exactly what I'm talking about. Those people weren't even aware she was in there when they cleared us out because she was in the rest room at the time!"

"All right, ma'am," MacAdoo said. "I believe you. Now, you just stay quiet in here with the paramedics. We'll check for your little girl."

MacAdoo backed quickly out of the ambulance, jerking his head at the paramedic standing outside. "Sedate her," he said out of the side of his mouth.

"Yes, sir!" the paramedic said, stepping into the ambulance.

Just then, Stryker ran over to MacAdoo. "We got a break, Mac! Two of my men on the roof of the bank just located an exterior return air supply duct for the air-conditioning system, and they skinned off the service plate. We've got an unrestricted straight shot down to the main unit for our gas. Two or three of these new G-pellets down the duct, and they'll be begging to come out of there in about three minutes—special delivery!"

"That's great," MacAdoo said. "Can't use it, Lieutenant. Thanks just the same."

"I don't mean right now," Stryker said. "I mean as soon as the doctor comes out."

"What makes you think he's coming out?" MacAdoo asked.

"You don't think they're going to hold him in there?" Stryker said incredulously.

"I don't know, and I don't really give a damn!" MacAdoo said. "That's Robeson's responsibility, from now on. He's running this show from his chair in the tower, and we do nothing without clearance from him!"

"But you're the Field Commander, Whitey," Stryker said. "He can't do that to you in a situation like this!"

"I know he can't—but he has! I'm just an executive observer here, that's what I am. And you're a SWAT team with no swat, get it?"

Stryker's walkie-talkie came to life. "Lieutenant? Harrison here—on the roof."

Stryker flipped his talk-switch. "I read you, Bud. What have you got?"

"Tobin and I just heard some pounding," the voice said. "At first we thought it was coming from inside the bank, maybe from the crawl space, but now we think it's coming from a van parked at the curb next to the bank on Fairfax. Can you make out that florist's van on the east side of the street from your location?"

Stryker peered across the street at the back of Vincent's van. "Check! I can see it, Bud. Seems to be rocking back and forth!"

"Yes, sir. We're looking right down on top of it. Somebody's in there, wants to get out real bad!"

"Right, over and out!" Stryker snapped. "Agnello! Agnello, come in, do you read?"

"Yes, sir! Agnello here!" a voice answered. "We see the van from the alley, Lieutenant. Nobody behind the wheel."

"Okay, I want two men with a bar to spring open the rear door of that van," Stryker ordered. "On the alert—it may be one of *them*, locked himself in. Move!"

Two SWAT team cops came flying out from behind the bank, guns drawn, one with a crowbar in his hand, running low to the rear of the van. The man with the bar didn't even try the door, which he would have found open. He just planted the bar chisel between the doors, springing them open with one heave.

"Freeze!" the two cops yelled, squatting low as they shoved their guns through the rear of the van.

"Holy shit!" one of the cops said.

"What—is that?" said the other.

"That" was Vincent's driver, still taped and bound, his clothes sopping with sweat, his forehead battered and bloody, his long hair a tangled mop, kneeling among the crushed funeral sprays, facing the sidewalk side of the van, where he had been beating against the wall with his head.

The two cops scrambled into the van and pulled the tape off his bloodied face.

The young man spat out his snapdragon salad. "Jee-zus, thank God you're the cops! I've never been so glad to see cops breaking in on me in my whole fucking life!"

238

The two cops didn't understand what he meant at that moment, but it became clear to them later, when they sat with him in a squad car while he recounted the terrifying story of his early morning abduction.

"Anything, Lopez?" MacAdoo shouted to his aide, standing in the booth with the phone at his ear.

"Nothing," Lopez answered. "Still on hold. It's boring."

"Yeah? Well, stay awake, dammit."

An officer, bent low in battle-trot, came running in toward MacAdoo from the west Beverly barrier. "Excuse me, sir, there's a man raising hell at the barrier—a Mr. Olson—says he's regional vice-president of Citizens' Bank, insists on seeing the officer in charge. You want him let in?"

MacAdoo looked painfully toward the heavens. "God, what else is going to happen to me today? Yeah, what the hell—let him in. Let *everybody* in. We'll have a goddamn block party here!"

The cop turned to run back to his post, just as MacAdoo looked up to see Cassidy and Francis approaching. "Captain, this man says his wife works in the bank!" Cassidy said breathlessly.

Huffing and puffing, Francis nodded vigorously, trying to see MacAdoo through his steamed-up glasses. "That's right . . . my wife. . . . She's in the bank. . . . What's going on . . . in there?"

"What is your name, sir?"

"Lundy . . . Francis X. Lundy. . . . My wife's name's Elizabeth."

"Okay, Mr. Lundy, just take it easy—and get your breath. Nobody's been hurt in there yet, that we know of."

"Hurt?" Francis yelled. "What do you mean, hurt?"

"Well, just calm down now," MacAdoo said, "and I'll tell you about it."

"I'm all right, I'm all right!" Francis gulped, grabbing MacAdoo's arm. "Tell me what's happening, please!"

"Well, there are some people in there holding the employees hostage. But, as you can see, we have the bank completely surrounded, and everything's under contr—"

"*Hostage?* My God!" Francis screamed, jumping to his feet. "My wife's eight months pregnant! This was her last day. I just brought her in to clear out her desk!"

"Easy, easy!" MacAdoo yelled, and he and Cassidy pulled the distraught man back down behind the fire truck.

"Oh, my God!" Without warning, Francis broke out of the grasp of the two cops, leaped to his feet again, and ran screaming into the street, racing across the intersection toward the bank, his arms windmilling furiously, his voice cutting through the air like a siren. "Eee-liz-a-beth! I'm com-ing, Eee-liz-z-beth!"

MacAdoo grabbed the bullhorn. "Get him! *Stop that man!!*"

A SWAT cop crouching on the street side of the florist's van came tearing out after his man, intercepting Francis with a crushing flying tackle that sent them both sprawling into a tangle with the air hose of Big Joe's jackhammer, just as Stosh showed up at the front door, gun in hand.

The cop was up first. He yanked Francis away from the front of the bank by the back of his belt and shoved him down behind the gas company truck. Stosh stepped back, out of sight.

"Way to go!" Stryker shouted across to his man. "Bring him back around! How 'bout that flying tackle, Mac? Classic SWAT if I every saw it!"

MacAdoo turned away from the smug SWAT leader as Doctor Harmon came running up.

"I want to talk to that man, Captain," the Doctor said. "If he has a pregnant wife in there, he could very well be our psycho-guilt key for release of the hostages."

MacAdoo looked at him blankly.

Just then, the cop from the south barrier came running in low, escorting a distressed and rumpled, bulky bank vice-president.

"Peter Olson, Captain," the banker said, handing MacAdoo his business card and reciting the rest of it as the captain read along. "Executive Vice-President, Citizens' Bank, Central Office, Western Region, Downtown."

"Mr. Olson, meet Doctor Harmon, special duty LAPD."

The men quickly shook hands.

"Where have they got the dynamite, Captain?" Olson asked, trying to maintain executive calm.

"We don't know that they have dynamite," MacAdoo replied. "We don't know that they have any explosives *at all,* for that matter."

"But what about the sign on the door?" Olson asked.

MacAdoo sighed. "We do know they have a sign on the door claiming that they have explosives, but we don't know if these people are aware of the truth-in-advertising laws."

"I see." Olson was not amused. "Well, how do you plan to get them out of there?"

"Right now," MacAdoo said, not bothering to hide his chagrin, "we're trying to talk them out."

"Talk them out? Aren't you equipped with tear gas out here?"

"The Captain's got gas out here, Mr. Olson," Harmon cut in, "but there are a lot of people in there, and—"

"I know there are people in there," Olson said matter-of-factly. "That's who tear gas is made for, isn't it, Doctor?—people who break the law, people who threaten life and property?"

"There are also a dozen or so of *your* people in there," Harmon noted, "innocent people, including a pregnant woman . . . people who did nothing but come to work for you this morning."

"Don't you think I know that, Doctor? By the way, Captain," Olson continued, opening his briefcase, "I brought a complete personnel list with

240

me for this branch." He took a sheaf of papers from his case and started shuffling through them. "That stupid little bitch!" he muttered. "I asked my girl to give me our western section branch personnel rosters, and she's given me the damn *eastern* section. I ran out of the office so fast I didn't even check. But I can give you the top two or three names by memory, there's—"

"That's okay," MacAdoo said, "you don't have to remember them—Doctor Harmon's associate will come out with a list of the hostages. Won't he, Doctor?"

"If he gains their confidence," Harmon said pointedly. "And if there's no more threatening action out here. I also expect him to come out with a next-of-kin list, and phone numbers. I'll see you get a copy, Mr. Olson."

"Easy, Doctor," MacAdoo said, interrupting the flow of hostility between the two men. "I'm sure Mr. Olson's main concern is for the safety of his people. Let's see what the psychiatrist comes out with, Mr. Olson. There's plenty of time to take aggressive measures, if they're necessary."

"A psychiatrist?" Olson asked, astonished. "You've got a psychiatrist in there talking to those people?"

"That's right."

"That's crazy! What the hell can a psychiatrist do about a bank holdup, for God's sake?"

"We're not at all sure it is a bank holdup," Harmon said. "Our best information so far is that they've been in there, holding the premises since a little before nine o'clock this morning."

"Nine this morning?" Olson was aghast. "Why weren't we informed? The first I heard about it was simply when our computer system got no response from this branch's transaction terminals during the dial-up polling procedure."

"You weren't informed," MacAdoo told him, "because we didn't learn about it until after eleven."

"They've been operating the bank since it opened at ten," Harmon said, as if that explained everything.

"Operating?" Olson blurted. "What do you mean operating? Our bank?"

"That's right. They've been manning the teller's windows, cashing checks, taking deposits, and giving money away."

"*Giving money*—Oh, my God!"

"So you see," Harmon continued, "they are probably not robbing the bank at all. If they wanted to do that, they'd have been in and out a long time ago. They're after something other than money."

"What the hell else is there in a bank, besides money?"

"Leverage, my friend," Harmon said. "All you have to do is read the papers. People with a beef against society these days don't believe in assembling peaceably to get their grievances redressed through the system. They don't believe in the system anymore. They're resorting to hijacking, kidnapping, terrorizing, perpetrating all kinds of antisocial crimes just to get their story told in an environment that is so threatening that it can't be ignored. And in order to save lives, we've got to learn to handle these outbreaks on those terms—not with police fire power."

Olson stared at him as though he were a raving lunatic. "Antisocial? Environment? What in the world has that got to do with a bank holdup? Have you people gone crazy? The thugs in there are threatening lives and a hell of a lot of our depositors' money! They've got to be stopped, and now— with any kind of weapons you've got."

MacAdoo was silent, enjoying the argument.

"Let met get this straight," Harmon said. "Are you ready to trade lives, Mr. Olson, just to protect money that's insured?"

"That's not the point. Negotiating with criminals is not law enforcement—it's absolute stupidity. You sit out here and massage these terrorists with conversation, holding their hands while they got you by the balls, and you'll have these gangs knocking over banks all over the country!"

Stryker's walkie-talkie started to chatter, and they all turned their attention to the urgent communiqué from the SWAT team across the street.

"How many men—say again?" Stryker asked.

"Two men," the voice cracked. "One big, one small. The victim says he's pretty sure both suspects were wearing wigs."

"Where did this happen, Agnello?" Stryker asked. "And what time?"

"Right on Beverly Boulevard, sir, about eight blocks east of this location. The victim's time estimate is seven forty-five A.M., shortly before the terrorists took over the bank. He says they came at him out of an old camper pickup truck parked at the curb, which he thinks is still there."

"Here, give me that," MacAdoo said, taking the field radio. "Agnello, Captain MacAdoo here. I want you to take the victim and two of my officers in a squad car to the location he's described and shake down the suspect vehicle. I want license, registration, a run-down on any articles inside—the works. And get back here A.S.A.P., got that?"

"Yes sir!"

"On your horse," MacAdoo snapped. "Over and out."

MacAdoo handed the radio back to Stryker. Both men were faintly smiling.

"There's our break, Stryker," said MacAdoo, massaging his palms in anticipation. "Maybe now we'll find out who these animals are. Then we'll know exactly how to snap the trap shut."

Harmon saw the look they exchanged between them, and he felt a chill as he looked back across the street at the bank.


Louie and Keller came out of the conference room.

"Wait, please!" Keller said. "Before you close the door, let me take the

242

guard and Mrs. Lundy out with me. They both need medical attention. Please."

"What you talking about?" Louie shut the door and walked back to the counter. "The guard's got only a sprained wrist, and maybe a cracked rib, for goodness' sakes. He could wait a week to see a doctor. And the pregnant girl—she's blooming like a big sunflower! What does she need a doctor? She needs to turn her back on her husband for a while, that's all she needs!"

"Whatta ya think they *been* doin' for the last coupla months?" Vito cracked.

Oscar and Louie guffawed, while Stosh shook his head somberly at the front door.

"Do you really think that's funny?" Keller demanded. "How can you people joke at a time like this? You're surrounded by dozens of armed police, the SWAT team is out there with tear gas, the fire department have their high pressure hoses connected . . . you're putting everyone inside and outside this bank within a hair of death. Please don't joke with me. It's obscene!"

"We are not really joking, my good doctor," Louie said quietly. "Don't you understand? Old people no longer laugh at life. Only at the coming of death—to throw her off balance a little, see? The Angel of Death is no angel . . . so you gotta laugh in her face when she tries to take you out dancing—you know what I mean?"

Keller looked at the three men behind the counter, studied their faces returning his gaze with steady, knowing eyes, and suddenly he felt as though he were the one under the microscope, as though he were the societal germ threatening an infection of anarchy.

And in that moment, held fast by the piercing eyes of these three old men, Keller had a fleeting glimpse of perception into the true meaning of this confrontation. He was peering into the sad eyes of men, each of whom had experienced three-quarters of a century ending in hardship and humiliation—and he was only *thirty-seven*.

The fact was simple—a conflict of interest.

And the fact was plainly written on their plain faces. Each of these men had committed himself to the probability of his own death on that day.

"Okay," Keller said, reopening his notebook. "If your demands are reasonable, I'm prepared to go back out and try to negotiate them for you. Can you list your grievances for me?"

"No, no, Doctor," Louie said. "Not over a counter, not this time."

"Well, do you have them in writing?"

"No, we are finished writing," Louie said, shaking his head. "No more letters or petitions or applications—no, no. Writing from an old person has a certain way of getting into file cabinets, stored away someplace, away from the light. No, this time we will tell our story face-to-face, looking them straight in the eye, so the whole world will hear."

"But I don't understand what you're asking for!"

"We are not asking—we are telling," said Louie. "You tell Captain MacAdoo to telephone the Chief of Police, wherever he is, or whoever he has to call who can give the word. We want a press conference with the TV, the radio, and the newspapers, all of them *before* three o'clock. They will come to the drive-in window on the side of the bank—before three o'clock, you understand?"

"But that's impossible," said Keller, looking up at the big wall clock. "That's less than an hour and a half from now!"

"Never mind impossible," Louie said. "They are all here already—see? Across the street in the parking lot? The eyes and ears of the world. I called them all myself! All they gotta do is cross the street!"

Keller looked out across the street at the crowd of newspeople with their equipment assembled on the lot. "I . . . I don't know. I can only try." He turned toward the door. "I can't promise anything—"

"Wait a minute, not so fast!" Louie said.

Keller stopped, bewildered. "Is there something else?"

"My dear doctor, the something else is the most improtant thing of all! This news conference will *not* begin until Mr. Ernest P. Whitehead is at the window. *He* is the man we will interview for the people of the press!"

"Whitehead? Who is Mr. Whitehead?" Keller asked, jotting the name in his notebook.

"You don't know who is Mr. Ernest P. Whitehead? I can't believe it! You? A social peacemaker, a student of current events, a fancy consultant to the police department—and you don't know who is Ernest P. Whitehead?"

"No, sir. I'm sorry, but I don't."

"You ever hear of such a thing?" Louie turned to ask Oscar and Vito.

"Tsk-tsk-tsk!" Vito clucked.

"Why, Mr. Ernest P. Whitehead is only the Director of Social Security for the whole western region of the United States," Louie intoned. "That's who he is!"

"I see," said Keller, writing down the title.

"I see, said the blind man!" Louie mocked him. "No, no—seeing is not knowing. And even knowing, is not understanding! Lemme try to make you understand, really understand!"

Louie reached into both his coat pockets, pulling out several small items which he slapped angrily down onto the counter. "See this, Doctor?" he said, pointing. "What is it?"

"Uh, three envelopes of sugar."

"That's right," said Louie. "I steal them from Dave's delicatessen, so I will have sugar for my tea at home. And what's this?"

"Two small bars of hotel soap, I think," Keller said, suffering. "And, this looks like, like, uh . . ."

"*Toilet paper*," Louie prompted, "folded-up toilet paper. Don't be

244

ashamed to say it, we all have to *use* it. The Ambassador Hotel, the last civilized hotel in Los Angeles, still has individual bars of soap in the lobby men's room. I go there about once a week, on my four-dollar bus pass, before lunch time, and when the men's room attendant goes out to eat, I go in and help myself to the soap and toilet paper."

Keller shifted uncomfortably from one foot to the other.

"Wait, wait," said Louie. "I didn't get off the subject, don't worry. I'll come back to Mr. Whitehead. Anyway, after I got these valuables in my pocket, I take a walk to the end of the lobby. I always find a newspaper somebody threw away, *The Times*—sometimes the real *Times* from New York—and I sit on a sofa, and I read the paper. I relax, I lounge, I look around, I rest myself for the bus ride home. Imagine! Me, sitting like royalty in a place with marble floors and velvet drapes and crystal chandeliers and God knows what! It musta cost a coupla million dollars just to build that lobby—today, nobody could even afford to build it—and this old pauper, this piece of garbage that has been thrown away, sits in the lap of luxury, reading the news of the day! You see, we really do live in a free country! And free is very good, but free is not necessarily *living*. Tell me the truth—is it living, when old people in this country have to go sneaking around stealing little pieces of soap and toilet paper? Tell me, is that nice? Is it?"

"No, sir. It's not nice," Keller said. And he meant it. His eyes were watery, and in his throat he felt a salty lump of understanding which he could not swallow away.

"But Mr. Ernest P. Whitehead—" Louie continued, "I don't think *he* knows about these things. Or if he knows, maybe he thinks it's okay, hah?"

"Well . . . I can't believe, that if these things were brought to his attention—"

"You can't believe, hah? But you don't know Mr. Whitehead, so I'll tell you about him—how hard it is to get his attention. Then maybe you'll see. Then maybe you'll know why we are doing this thing today. It was a year ago, just before Christmas. A delegation of old people, people like me, who steal from the markets and what not like I do, living from month to month and from hand to mouth on the Social Security dole, we went up to Mr. Whitehead's office in the Federal Building, with a petition. We had over a thousand names on it. I signed it, every old cocker for miles around signed it. It musta been a roll of paper a block and a half long. Anyway, about a dozen of us carried it up to his office that day—men, women, black, white, some born here, some immigrants, even one a crippled old woman who walked with a little aluminum cage she pushed ahead of her with every step. And what did the petition say? What was our complaint? We got a raise in the benefit that summer—five percent, a miserable few dollars! But you think the landlords didn't hear about it? And how, they heard! So they put their heads together, and just in time for Thanksgiving, the lousy landlords raised all the rents twenty, twenty-five dollars a month—twice as much as the raise from Uncle Sam!"

"No," Keller said.

"Sure! *Why not?*" Louie went on. "It's a free country, isn't it? The old farts are getting more money from the government, so let's get ours! What can they *do* about it? Where they gonna *go?* Let's relieve them of the extra benefit now, while the getting is good—before they croak, and the stinking room hasta be fumigated and repainted maybe for the next victim!"

"Come, get to the point," said Oscar quietly. "It's already one thirty. Our man will be coming back from lunch."

"I'm getting, I'm getting," said Louie. "So we went up to see Mr. Whitehead, could he maybe do something to stop the rents going up for no good reason, you know? But you see, Mr. Whitehead didn't make the appointment with us personally—a lowly assistant made the appointment. So you know what he did to solve the problem, when he found out what we came to see him about? I'll tellya what he did! He quick sneaked outa the building by a back elevator and got on an airplane to Washington, D.C., the home of the brave! And when they told us that he flew the coop so he wouldn't hafta listen to us, we got so angry, so furious, we refused to leave the office. Later that night, when a local radio station heard about it, they broadcast the story on the news, and dozens of other old people came to join us from all over the city, with food and bedclothes and protest signs, and we all jammed the waiting room of his office until he would come back to listen to us. We stayed *two nights* and *three days* in his office and in the halls, sleeping on the floor, begging to be heard. This man was there, he'll tell you!"

Oscar nodded his head in silent witness to the facts.

"We occupied his office and held our sit-in until somebody ordered the Federal cops downstairs not to let any more food into the building—can you imagine? These were old people, people in their seventies and eighties, not gangsters, not criminals! But because we were disturbing the peace, which really means the status quo—because we were such a big threat to society, Doctor—they were gonna starve us out! On federal property, mind you, property that belongs to all the people!"

Louie stopped speaking for a moment, breathing heavily with the emotion of his story. He glanced up at the clock.

"So, to make a long story a little shorter, we had to come out. We couldn't hold out anymore, with no food. So that was the end of our demonstration, the end of our petition to our government!"

"But what about the petition?" Keller asked, "Did you leave it?"

"Leave it? Leave it for what? To be buried in a dark filing cabinet someplace? Oh, no! We took it out with us. And then, when the Federal cops were leading us outa the building, the little old lady, the cripple with the metal walker, she fell over and passed out. She had diabetes, the old

246

lady, but she didn't tell anybody. With all the excitement of the petition and so forth, she forgot to give herself the insulin shot that morning, and she didn't bring any with her. Who knew we would be up there three days? But she was stubborn—she wanted to stay there until the end, with the rest of us—so she stayed until the end. The cops quick rushed her to the nearest hospital, which happens to be the Veterans' Hospital right across Wilshire Boulevard, and two days later she died in a diabetic coma. So they didn't let her sit-in on Federal property, but they did let her die on it."

Keller shuddered. He felt empty and dry, like a wrung out floor mop. "And what happened to the petition?" he asked quietly.

Louie smiled a sour smile. "I hafta tell you? We had over two hundred people standing in the rain for her funeral—more people than she ever knew in her whole life! The petition? We buried it with the old lady. It's in her coffin. It's rotting in the county cemetery, with her body."

Keller winced. What could he say? What could anyone say to these angry old people to convince them that there was a better way?—a less dangerous way, a legal way, through the system. No Ph.D. pitch in the world could sell the system to these people now, and Keller knew it.

"So, my friend," Louie said, "now you know Mr. Ernest P. Whitehead. You think we have a right to interview him?"

Keller nodded slowly. "Yes, I think you have the right. I only wish you had chosen another way."

"*This* was the only way left for us," Louie said.

"And if we can arrange this interview with Mr. Whitehead," Keller said, "and this press conference—what will you do afterward?"

"Afterwards?" Louie shrugged. "Afterwards we will come out and go our way. We will let the hostages go, and nobody will be hurt. But it must be before three o'clock!"

"And if not?" Keller asked. "If this conference *can't* be arranged the way you want it?"

"If not," Louie said, "then Citizens' Bank will close at three o'clock. For good!"

"When you say—the bank will close," Keller inquired carefully, "How do you mean . . . ?"

"Do you play pinochle, Doctor?"

"Play what?" Keller asked.

"Pinochle. A game of cards."

"No, sir, I, uh, don't play cards."

"Well, in pinochle," Louie explained patiently, "if you are a good player, you hold back your trump until just the right time—you never play it until you need it, see? And when you play out a trump card, you play only a card high enough to win the trick. but the highest trump cards, you save until the end—for the kill! To win the game. You understand?"

Clearly, Keller did not understand.

247

Louie reached to his right, behind the opaque glass counter divider. Slowly, he slid the blasting box into view, to the center of the wicket, as Keller stared wide-eyed.

"This—is trump," Louie whispered, raising his eyebrows. "This is our *pièce de résistance*. You get it?"

Keller got it.

Louie turned to Oscar. "Watchmaker, tell the doctor what this is, so he can write it down in his book. I want Captain MacAdoo across the street to know what is our ten of trump."

Oscar moved into position at the window, and Keller saw his gun for the first time, tucked into his belt. The mere sight of it sent a sharp chill through him. The LAPD had instructed him in a nominal course on firearms, but he had never before seen a weapon such as Oscar's, only pictures. It was a German SS officer's Luger, its white pearl handle gleaming, its swastika medallion burning Keller's eyes.

"This is a blasting box, manufactured by the Atlas Dynamite Company," Oscar explained proudly. "It is old, but also in perfect working condition. Beautiful wood, isn't it? It is powered by a brand new twelve-volt automobile battery—a Sears Die-Hard—und it is connected individually to two types of explosive devices, which we have placed in the safety deposit vault—see the wires running under those tapes?"

Keller looked up from his notebook to peer over the counter at the neat tapes running along the floor.

"One of the devices," Oscar continued, "is a simple black powder charge, direct detonation—similar to dynamite—weighing approximately twelve pounds."

Keller took in a sharp breath as he noted the weight of the charge in his book. "And the other device?"

"The other apparatus was much easier to come by," Oscar said with an elfin grin, "but it is much more exotic, und much more powerful—*much* more. It is a mixture, called in America by the name thermite. It was used by the French resistance forces to destroy railroad bridges controlled by the Nazis, und when a loaded troop train was on *top*—it was something to see, believe me! It is composed from the most common elements—a little aluminum powder, some powdered oxide of iron, a few tablespoons barium peroxide powder, simple combustion filaments—but when you put them all together . . ."

"Get outa town!" Vito said, supplying the punch line.

"We don't have too much, of course—only about two pounds," Oscar went on. "But if it is detonated, it is easily capable of the total destruction of the vault, all the contents—und also probably more."

"My God!" Keller gasped. "How can you even consider setting off a terrible blast like that? You could kill everyone in this bank! You can't *do*

248

it!" He reached across the counter and grabbed Louie's lapels, shaking him. "You can't! You mustn't! *I won't let you!*"

"Get away from me!" Louie screamed, pushing Keller back from the counter. "We mean business! What the hell do you think this is—just a song at twilight? If they will not listen to us before three o'clock—they will listen to *this!*"

Suddenly, Louie put both his hands on the blasting box plunger, pushing it down hard to the hilt—SWACK!

Keller hit the deck face down, tiny shards of glass from his shattered lens showering the floor.

There was no blast.

Slowly, Keller raised his head from the floor to see Louie and the other men grinning down at him, amused at his fright, like fraternity brothers hazing a hapless freshman.

"It's all right, Doctor," Louie said gently. "You are not hurt. You're still alive. You can get up."

Keller just sat there, blinking.

Louie carefully turned the blasting box around on the counter so that Keller could see the open back of it from his place on the floor.

"You see," Louie said, taking hold of the unattached wire lead and bending the end of it out from the box, "you are dealing with responsible people. This hot wire does not get connected up until five minutes to three, if our demands are not met. Sooner, if the police try to interfere."

Keller sat staring at the broken glasses in his hand and shaking his head hopelessly. "I can't understand it," he muttered.

"What can't you understand?" Louie asked.

"I just can't understand how a man of your intellect can be involved in an act of violence like this."

"Nonsense!" Louie sneered. "Intellect is no answer to human crisis. It's only a joke—a burden. A man's intellect becomes his greatest curse at the same moment he realizes that wisdom—*wisdom*—is the only goal he cannot reach!"

Louie's forefinger pointed sagely aloft with his pronouncement as he scowled down at Keller, a man beaten into submission with rhetoric, with ideas, with words—the very tools of his own profession.

"Come on, get up from the floor," Louie said. "You gotta go now—we're running out of time. You did your job in here, now you got messages to deliver."

"I failed my job in here," Keller confessed, replacing a shoe he had lost in his fall. "I failed to probe under. I didn't get *close* enough to you, didn't let you get close enough to me—so that I could make you see that you are doing something terribly wrong here."

"Baloney," Louie said. "The closer we get to each other, the less we see.

249

Didja ever watch people on a crowded elevator? They're standing so close they could pick each other's teeth—but all they see is the ceiling of the elevator, nothing else."

Wearily, Keller got to his feet and stood awkwardly in the middle of the room, the bits of glass crunching under his shoes. "Is there nothing else I can say to get you to stop this madness, to get you to listen to common sense, before people get hurt or killed?"

"Nothing," Louie said. "Besides, sense that is only common, is capable of accomplishing nothing. You just do the rest of your job—deliver my messages. Good-bye, Doctor Keller. Be careful crossing the street."

Keller stood still for a long moment, looking at Louie. "Thank you. . . . I'm sorry," he said incongruously, then he turned toward the front door.

"You don't hafta be sorry," Louie said. "Just get me Whitehead."

"I should open up now?" Stosh asked.

"So how will he get out if you don't open up?" Louie asked.

Stosh snapped the big lock open and started to undo the chain.

"And remember, Doctor," Louie said as Keller turned back to listen, "you saw only our *ten* of trump. . . . I didn't show you the ace!"


"Hello? Hello?" Louie shouted into the telephone.

"Hello!" Lopez said.

"Captain MacAdoo?"

"No, sir, this is Officer Lopez."

"Another assistant, hah?"

"Say again, sir?"

"Never mind," Louie said, "just tell Captain MacAdoo that his doctor is coming out."

Stosh opened the door, and Keller was out on the sidewalk, squinting into the bright sun as some people in the crowd across the street applauded his reappearance.

MacAdoo hardly even noticed. "Now let's get this straight, Huntsinger," he said, trying to make sense of the cop's report. "You are telling me that there's a dead body in that old pickup truck, with a funeral spray saying Rest in Peace on it?"

"Captain," Lopez interrupted, "Doctor Keller's out of the bank! He's standing there waiting for instructions, I think."

"Dammit, Lopez, can't you see I'm busy here?" MacAdoo snapped. "Wave him to get his ass over here! Chrissake, doesn't he know where he's supposed to go?"

Lopez ran out into the open and started waving as MacAdoo turned back to the group just returned from their investigation of Stosh's pickup. "How

250

about it, Carney," he said to another cop, "did you see what Huntsinger saw?"

"We *all* saw it, Captain," Carney replied.

"With the flowers and everything?" MacAdoo asked.

"I told you, Captain," the young blond driver spoke up impatiently, "the Rest in Peace farewell spray fell out of my van. That's why I fucking stopped in the first place! Now, can't I just take my van and split out of this insanity? My boss is going to be pissed!"

"Take it easy, Sonny," MacAdoo said. "You're not going anywhere, and your van isn't going anywhere. We've got to get a full statement from you, and your van is evidence—probably got fingerprints all over it."

"Shit!" the young man said with feeling. "First, I'm ripped off and tied up by a couple of bank robbers, and now I'm being held captive by the whole frigging police department! Can I at least make a phone call? Would that be asking too much?"

"In a few minutes. Just settle down. Now when these two men abducted you, did you see a body in their truck?"

"I was nowhere near their stupid truck!" the driver wailed in exasperation. "I was out in the middle of the street trying to pick up my goddamn flowers, when these two guys jumped me, shoved me into the van, and taped me up. Mine was the only body *I* was interested in! I thought I was going to be raped—and that's not my thing, you know?"

MacAdoo, exasperated, turned his attention back to the cops. "Were you able to determine the cause of death?" he asked.

"No, sir," Huntsinger said. "The body showed no evidence of gunshot wounds or stab wounds, only bad bruises about the face."

"How bad?"

"Pretty bad," said the cop. "The left eye of the deceased was swollen shut, his forehead had a lump the size of a golf ball, and he had very marked edema over a large area of the left side of his neck."

"Any sign of a weapon?"

"No, sir," Huntsinger said, looking at his partner.

"Well," Carney said, "there was an empty wine bottle in the cab—could have been a weapon."

MacAdoo turned half away in thought, a faint and private, vengeful smile touching his lips. "Homicide," he announced bluntly. "These people—these bastards—have committed a murder!"

He and his men slowly turned to look across at the bank, each seeming to crouch a little lower, sensing a new and greater danger from the enemy.

"What'd you get on the vehicle check?" MacAdoo asked.

"Registered owner, Stanislaus Vlasic," Carney answered, referring to his notes. "Last address, eight thirty-one and a half Gardener Avenue, Los Angeles, nine-o-o-three-six. I don't even know how the computer came up

251

with it—the vehicle has nineteen seventy-four plates. Should've been cited every time it hit the streets."

"Good job," MacAdoo said, grabbing Carney's notes. "Get back to your posts."

Doctor Harmon came running over from out of the fire department ambulance. "It's useless, Captain," he panted. "The pregnant woman's husband can't be any help to us—the poor man's hyperventilating, The paramedic's got a bag over his face in there."

"I don't think we're going to require his help, Doctor," MacAdoo said cryptically. "Hey, Stryker!" he shouted. "Front and center!"

"How about it, Mac?" Stryker asked. "Do we SWAT or don't we?"

"I'll know in a minute. Follow me!" Crouching low, MacAdoo ran to his command car, followed closely by Stryker and Harmon.

"What are you doing?" Harmon asked him. "What's happened?"

"Your people in the bank have *killed* a man, *that's* what's happened." MacAdoo snapped his speaker switch on.

"In the bank?" Harmon asked, bewildered.

"Captain MacAdoo here," he barked into the mike. "I need Captain Robeson—Code Three!"

"Where's Doctor Keller?" Harmon asked.

"Where you been? He came out of the bank a couple of minutes ago," MacAdoo said, swiveling around. "Lopez signaled him to cross the street over there—oh, shit! That stupid taco delivered him right to the goddamn press!"

There was Keller, in the CBS parking lot, he and Lopez surrounded by cameras, microphones poking in his face, cables tangled around his legs, a crowd of reporters pressed around him high and low, craning, pushing, bombarding him with their barrage of questions.

"How do you spell your name, Doctor?" a reporter shouted.

"I'm sorry, I can't make any comment. You'll have to talk to the captain."

"Anybody hurt in there?" Joy Newsome poked in.

"No, I'm sorry, I can't—wait a minute, I better answer that. *No,* no one's really hurt at this time."

"Who are they? Who are the terrorists?"

"I'm sorry, please let me through—"

"What are their demands?"

"Are they black or white?" a black reporter asked.

"Please, please—what difference does it make if they are black or white?"

"Does that mean they're black?" the reporter asked.

"Of course not!" Keller shouted. "They happen to be white. Several of the hostages are black, but—"

"Are they threatening to kill the hostages?" Newsome asked.

"Clear the way!" Lopez yelled, pushing forward. "Let the doctor through! Outa the way!"

252

"No, no!" Keller said, pulling back from Lopez's grasp to answer the query. "They haven't threatened to kill anyone. They're simple holding the hostages as leverage to negotiate, and that's what we're trying to do right now, if you'll let me through—please!"

"Negotiate for what?" asked a huge reporter in a blue ABC-TV news jacket, who was blocking Keller's way.

"I can't answer that—please! I've got to get to the captain and back to the people in the bank. They're very disturbed!"

"What are they disturbed about?" the big newsman asked, accidentally knocking Keller in the front teeth with his microphone.

Keller clutched his mouth.

"Sorry," the newsman said.

"I mean disturbed in the clinical sense!" Keller shouted. "And so am I! Now, dammit—get out of my way!"

Keller lowered his shoulder, charged right into the big reporter, knocking him aside, and grabbed Lopez's outstretched hand. Together, pushing and shoving, they took their leave of the ladies and gentlemen of the press.


"Dammit, Jack, I'm telling you what we got here!" MacAdoo was shouting into the radio microphone. "We got armed terrorists inside holding all the bank employees hostage. One of them's a pregnant woman— the paramedics are out here treating her husband, who's hyperventilating. There may be a six-year-old female inside the bank—I've got her hysterical grandmother out here. I've got SWAT, and the fire department, and the bomb squad, and a bank vice-president pushing me. I've got a nasty gay driver of a florist's van these people knocked over on their way to the bank. I've got a clobbered-up intersection out here that looks like World War II . . . and now I've got a dead body on my hands that was found in a vehicle identified as belonging to the people inside! Now if *that* doesn't qualify for terminal response, I don't know what will!"

"You haven't answered my question, Whitey," Robeson's voice came through crisp and calm. "You said Doctor Keller has come out of the bank. Do you have his report?"

MacAdoo winced at the use of his nickname. "He's out of the bank," MacAdoo said, "but he's lost in the crowd someplace across the street. Hell, Jack, it's liable to be fifteen minutes before he can get to the command car, and the guy I talked to in there keeps harping about a three o'clock deadline. We've got less than an hour to make a move!"

"What does he say will happen at three o'clock?"

"He doesn't say, dammit, but with one dead man on our hands already, do we have to guess?"

"No, Mac, we don't have to guess," said Robeson. "We have to find out. We're not going to risk lives again on a situation like this with terminal police action just because we can't keep our cool. That's why the PIES have been assigned to this one. What we don't want is another long hot summer in L.A., you know what I mean, Captain?"

"No, sir, I don't know what you mean," MacAdoo said. "Nobody out here is getting hot. We are keeping our cool. We are in control. But you know as well as I do—we let time slip by at this point, and the advantage all goes one way. Theirs. We'll just be giving them time to get organized, so they can set the ground rules. Terrain that we should control is going to become their territory, sure as hell, and—"

"Hold it, Mac—"

"Just let me finish!" MacAdoo said, his anger rising. "You're there and I'm here. I've got fifty or sixty men exposed out here, and I don't like military funerals—do you?"

There was no response.

"Now," MacAdoo continued, "we've got adequate fire-power, and we've got gas. SWAT has located a perfect insertion point on the roof. Five or six cannisters, and we can clear that bank in ten minutes—no fuss, no muss— and that's my recommendation. *Now, for the record,* from your field commander, sir! Do you read?"

There was another tense pause. "Are you alone in your car, Mac?" Robeson asked finally.

"No, I'm not. I've got Doctor Harmon and SWAT Lieutenant Stryker here with me."

"Clear your car, please," Robeson commanded crisply.

The two men stood clear of the command car, and MacAdoo slammed the door.

"Captain," Robeson said, choosing his words carefully, "I appreciate your recommendation, and I hear you loud and clear. You think you have a homicide connected with the bank takeover. But until we have verification of that, or until there is gunfire from the bank, or until Doctor Keller agrees with your recommendation—we are *not* going to use gas on these people, is that clear?"

"Yes, sir, Captain, that's clear," said MacAdoo, steaming. "But let me remind you that as field commander, I have the uncontestable right to a judgment call *on the scene*—that's department policy. So I'm informing you, sir, that I'm clearing SWAT to set up and stand by."

"Okay, that's what you're supposed to do," said Robeson. "But I've got my orders from the chief, and now you've got *yours*. So you're on notice, Captain—any reckless disregard of those orders, and the monkey's on your back."

"You're the only monkey on *my* back, sir," MacAdoo snapped.

Robeson held his breath for a moment. "Okay, Mac," he said, "now we both know who you're really gunning for out there, don't we?"

"I don't know what you mean, sir," MacAdoo said innocently. "I'm just

254

out here fighting for law and order and my pension—just doing a cop's dirty job the best I know how."

Robeson didn't respond.

"Is that all, sir?" MacAdoo inquired.

"When you find Doctor Keller, MacAdoo," Robeson said, "I want to talk to him. We'll take his report together, got that?"

"Yes, sir," MacAdoo said, grinning. "Over and out." He jumped out of his squad car like a boxer ahead on points, and coming out of his corner for the last round. "Get your cannisters up on the roof, Stryker, and stand by," he ordered.

Olson and the young van driver came running over to the car to converge on MacAdoo as Stryker barked orders to his men across the street. "Stryker here, Stryker here. Come in Agnello."

"Yes, sir. Agnello here."

"Six cannisters up to the roof and stand by. Repeat—stand by."

"Yes, sir!" the voice crackled.

"What do you mean, stand by?" Olson parroted. "This is ridiculous, what are you waiting for?"

"Listen, Captain," the long-haired driver whined, "can't I just get my buns out of here? I gave all my information to that big officer over there— he knows more about me than my mother does!"

"I'll bet he does!" MacAdoo said. "Okay, Sonny, you can take off—please! But your van stays!"

"Thanks loads!" the young man said bitchily. "Cops and robbers—it's been a real thrill!" And he bounded away toward the barrier.

"How about it, Captain," Olson said, "when are you going to get your men in there and put a stop to this thing?"

"Look, Mr. Olson," MacAdoo said, "I didn't need that fag hippie bitching at me, and I don't need you getting on me, either. Why don't you just go over there and sit in that squad car around the corner, while we do what we have to do? I'll call on you if I need you, okay?"

It was not a request, it was an order, and Olson didn't like it one bit. "Now, see here, Captain," he said, waving his arms, "you've got no right to—"

"Captain, Captain!" Lopez yelled from the middle of the street, as he and Keller came scooting across.

"It's about time, Doctor," MacAdoo griped, turning away from Olson.

"What's the story, Ollie?" Harmon asked, crowding in.

"You'll never believe it!" Keller gasped, trying to catch his breath. "They're a bunch of old men!"

"*Old men?*"

"What do you mean, old men?" MacAdoo asked.

"I mean old men!" said Keller. "Senior citizens—all over sixty-five. One of them told me he was seventy-eight!"

"You sure they weren't wearing wigs?" MacAdoo asked.

"No. They took their wigs *off* when I was in there—I saw them! Five old men! And what they want is a—"

"Hold it, Doctor," MacAdoo said. "Get in the car. Captain Robeson wants your report the same time I get it."

"Old people . . . I can't believe it," Olson said, shaking his head. "What are they doing in our bank? We never did anything to hurt old people."

Keller slid across the seat behind the wheel, and MacAdoo got in beside him, rolling the window down as the rest of the men all gathered around to hear the report to Robeson.


"I tell you, Louie, that was boy from flower truck!" Stosh insisted.

"I believe you, I believe you." Louie was peering through his binoculars at the command car. "So what?"

"So they know we stole truck, that's what!" Stosh hollered.

"Big deal," Vito said. "The parking meter's on red, too! Take it easy, Stosh."

"Take easy, take easy. I don't know how to take easy! I think we in big trouble, that's what I think!"

"Do me a favor, Stosh," Louie said. "Don't think—just watch!"

"Okay, I watch, I watch," Stosh grumbled.

"So, Levine? What do you think?" Oscar asked.

Louie saw the men crowded around MacAdoo's command car. Olson was waving his arms in argument with Harmon; Stryker was hunched over, barking into his speaker-phone. He could see the two heads in the squad car, MacAdoo's and Keller's, moving agitatedly as they passed the radio speaker back and forth between them.

"I think," Louie said slowly, as he studied the scene, "they don't know what to do yet."

Then, Louie saw a SWAT cop on the run, a gas mask flopping at his belt and two more in his hand, racing to Stryker with one and dropping the other into the command car onto MacAdoo's lap.

"So?" Oscar asked. "You look, you look—but what do you see?"

"I see trouble," Louie whispered hoarsely, "I see insanity, that's what I see. . . . Hook up the hot wire on the box, Oscar."

"*The wire?* But it is only ten minutes past two."

"I know what time it is, Stein," Louie said. "Do like I tell you . . . slow, easy, no excitement."

Oscar moved to the blasting box, put a tender hand on each side of it, and stared into the open back of the device.

"Stosh," Louie said, "I got a job for you. Come back here—I don't wanna holler."

As Stosh reached the counter to get his assignment, Oscar wedged in the

256

wooden safety block he'd made to hold the blasting handle at its high position, then he fastened the hot wire lead to the copper lug, and tightened the thumb-screw.

The inside of the command car was like a daylit cave, each voice crystal clear and crackling as the terse information passed back and forth by radio, the faces peering in from the outside of the car, turning more and more ashen as Keller reported the facts on the notched table and the steel cable and the handcuffs and the guns and the grenade and the Molotov cocktails—and the terrorists' demands, and the terrible threat of three o'clock.

"Five men, armed," Robeson repeated, "all with handguns—is that right, Doctor Keller?"

"Yes, sir."

"Five old men, no *young* men, is that right?"

"Right. I didn't see any others, Captain."

"Any sign of a little girl inside the bank?"

"A little girl? No, sir, no little girl."

"And the only injuries were to the bank guard—sprained left wrist, and a possible rib fracture, correct?"

"Correct," said Keller. "And they wouldn't let me take him out for medical treatment, either."

"Were you able to get a description of their explosive device?" Robeson asked.

"Yes, sir," Keller referred to his notebook. "They have two separate devices, both connected to an old-fashioned highway blasting box as a manual detonator, and both located in the safety deposit room, which they—"

"Holy Jesus!" Olson screamed, jumping up and down. "The worst place possible, goddamn it!"

"What do you mean, the worst place?" Keller asked him. "That's the safest place, farthest away from the people in the conference room."

"That's not what I mean! It's the only place in a bank that's impossible to insure! We could be sued for millions if they blow it up!"

"Impossible to insure?" Harmon asked.

"Of course!" Olson yipped, as if everyone in the world knew it. "Nobody knows the value of what's in those boxes, except the depositors!"

"That's right," said Stryker. "I never thought of that."

"A bank can only insure that space at minimum coverage, and you can bet your bottom dollar every damn box-holder in the bank will file a maximum claim! My God!"

"Keller, Keller! What's happening?" Robeson asked. "You're cutting in and out—"

"It's okay, Captain," Keller said. "Just a little noise outside."

"Continue your description of the explosives, Doctor," Robeson said. "And have Lieutenant Stryker listen, too."

"They have a dynamite charge," said Keller, "approximately twelve pounds . . ."

Stryker frowned.

"The second device they described, is something called thermanite—sorry, *thermite*. A little old guy—a German, I think—ticked off the elements of this explosive for me. Aluminum powder, powdered oxide of iron, barium peroxide powder, combustion filaments—"

"Jesus H. Christ!" Stryker bellowed.

"Repeat that, Doctor Keller," said Robeson. "The last few words were garbled."

Stryker reached over and took the radio mike from Keller. "Lieutenant Stryker here, Captain. That was me before, and what I said was 'Jesus H. Christ.' These people know what they're doing! You know what thermite is? A couple of ounces of that stuff will melt right through an engine block in nothing flat—I've seen it! They say how much of it they have in there, Doctor?"

Keller looked at his notes. "Two pounds," he said.

"Two *pounds?* Good-bye Citizens' Bank, Captain! If that stuff's in properly enclosed containers, and I'm *sure* these people know enough to pipe it, it could blow this corner right off the map of L.A.!"

"Oh, God!" Olson moaned, looking up to where his God was supposed to be.

"Doctor Keller?"

"Yes, sir?" Keller took the mike back.

"You were inside," Robeson said, "you've talked to these people. If we don't get this Mr. Whitehead over there, or if we refuse to let them have their press conference—what do you think they'll do?"

Keller fussed nervously with his notebook for a moment. "Captain, if these people do not get their demands," he said carefully, "if they are not permitted to present their grievances . . . it's my considered opinion that they will blow up the bank at three o'clock sharp."

"You can't wait until three o'clock!" Olson cried out, pushing his face into the car. "You've got to stop them, now! I can't believe you people, sitting out here with all these men and all this equipment, talking about what *they're* going to do. They're only a few decrepit old men, for God's sake!"

"Olson, if you don't stay quiet and let us get our job done," MacAdoo said, poking him in the chest with a stiff finger, "I'm going to have you removed physically, do you understand?"

Olson backed off.

"Doctor Keller? On a scale of one to ten," Robeson asked, "how sure do you feel that they would detonate their explosives?"

"Ten," Keller said.

258

"Why are you so positive?"

"I just know they will," Keller said. "These old men are emotionally committed beyond retreat. They have *no* psychic alternative. "Let me put it this way, Captain. Have you ever seen your father really angry? So angry, he could kill?"

Suddenly two shots rang out from inside the bank. People screamed, running back from the barriers and around buildings. Cops dived for cover behind their vehicles. MacAdoo and Keller flattened themselves out on the seat of the squad car. A fireman, playing out hose, fell off the fire truck onto the street and crawled under the big machine for cover.

Atop the bank, four SWAT cops scattered to the edges of the roof. The startled cop who was hoisting the tear gas cannister basket up from the alley below let his rope slip out of his hands, dropping his cargo to the cement twenty feet below, barely missing SWAT Sergeant Agnello. Two of the pellets were activated on impact, hissing their burning vapor out into the alley, sending five or six SWAT cops scrambling out from behind the bank and racing across the street. The gas fumes spewed up out of the basket, the ghastly cloud spreading along ground level, filling the alley and spilling out onto Fairfax Avenue.

In the alley, the poisonous fog was being pulled upward in a ghostly flume as it was sucked up into the kosher poultry store by a fresh-air intake fan, routing people out onto the street with their hands to their faces and setting the choking chickens to squawking out a horrendous torrent of noise.

"MacAdoo? MacAdoo! Don't forget me, man," Robeson shouted on the radio. "What's happening? Do you read? Come in, come in!"

MacAdoo scrambled for the fallen speaker mike on the floor and flipped the switch. "MacAdoo here! Sorry, Jack—they just fired two shots off in the bank! We're all taking cover! Over!"

"Get your warning in, Mac!" Robeson barked. "A three-minute warning, before any action! Do you read? Over!"

"I read you, Jack," MacAdoo said, "but my command car is exposed, so I can't get out with my bullhorn, and the phone booth we've been using is within direct line of fire! You're going to have to phone into the bank from down there. Let me know when my three minutes start. You're open. Over."

"Roger. Dialing right now. Stand by, Mac!"

Stryker's walkie-talkie began to chatter excitedly. "Lieutenant Stryker! Harrison here! Lieutenant, do you read?" The voice sounded tinnier through his gas mask.

"I read you, Bud," Stryker snapped. "Over."

"Lieutenant, we're up here on the roof of the bank. You know those shots that were fired just now?"

"Yes, yes, Harrison. What about them?"

259

"Well, one of them came right through the roofing up here—hit Magruder right in the heel of his boot!"

"Is he hurt bad?"

"No, sir, just a bloody nose, sir."

"Say again—bloody toes?"

"No sir, N for Nellie—*nose*. He kneed himself in the nose when the bullet hit!"

"Oh." Stryker was having trouble putting the picture together. "How about the other round?"

"I don't know, sir. That was the only one we saw," said Harrison. "But we got another problem. Grodner dropped the cannister basket when the shots were fired, and a couple of them went off—chased our men right out of the alley!"

"You're kidding!" Stryker blurted angrily.

"No, sir, I'm not."

"Agnello, Agnello!" Stryker shouted into his walkie-talkie. "This is Lieutenant Stryker, Channel Two. Do you read me?"

"Yes, sir, Lieutenant. Agnello here!"

"Why the hell didn't you report to me *immediately* on that cannister accident, Agnello? I can't direct traffic on this operation, unless you men keep me informed! Over."

"I was just going to, sir," Agnello said, "when Harrison took the channel. I thought you could see it all from your position. I'm just issuing masks to my men from the truck."

"That's terrific, Agnello, because you're going to need them, mister! Tell you what I want you to do, Agnello. I want you to get six more cannisters up on top of the roof—do you read me?"

"Yes, sir, but—but the basket's burning gas in the alley, sir!"

"I don't care what the basket's doing in the alley, Agnello!" Stryker shouted, "I only care about what *you're* going to be doing! And I don't care how you get it done. *Lob* them up there if you have to. Grodner will be happy to catch them! Got it?"

"Yes, sir!"

"Okay—move! Now! Over and out!"

Stryker watched Agnello and two other SWAT cops lope across the avenue and into the gas cloud, masked heads down, each gingerly nestling two gas cannisters in his arms.

Louie picked up the phone on the third ring. "Hello?"

"Hello? Is this Citizens' Bank?" Robeson asked, "the Fairfax branch?"

"Ye-es," Louie replied courteously.

"Who am I speaking to, please?"

"You are speaking to the man you called," Louie said. "You got the right number, don't worry."

260

"This is Captain John Robeson, Assistant to the Chief of Police, Los Angeles Police Department. I'm calling from Parker Center. Are you the leader of the group holding the bank?"

"How do ya like that?" Louie said. "All you gotta do is shoot off a gun, and right away—the whole world shows up to listen to you!" He nodded smugly to his cohorts, who nodded back at him in sage agreement. "So what took you so *long*, Captain John Robeson, Assistant to the Chief of Police? You know what time it is?"

"Yes, sir, I know what time it is," Robeson said, "but it was necessary to evaluate Doctor Keller's report before contacting you."

"So? Contact," Louie said. "Now what do we do?"

"Who were the two shots fired at?"

"Who? I fired two shots at the ceiling, that's who!"

"Why did you shoot at the ceiling?"

"Why? Because your Captain MacAdoo across the street is taking too much time," Louie explained. "Too much running around out there, nobody is telling me what's going on, and I'm getting nervous, you understand?"

"Yes, sir, I understand." Robeson said. "It's a dangerous situation, isn't it? A lot of lives being threatened. How do we solve the problem without people getting hurt?"

"Simple," Louie said. "You get us what we want before three o'clock, and the whole thing is solved—one-two-three!"

"I'm sorry," Robeson said evenly, "but we just can't solve your problem that way, sir."

"Whatta ya mean, can't? You mean you *won't*, don'tcha?"

"I mean," Robeson said, quoting the book, "that it is my duty now to order you and your associates to assemble at the front of the bank, open the door, slide all your weapons out onto the sidewalk, and walk out of the bank with your hands on top of your heads. You have exactly *three minutes* to comply with my order, prior to police action. Is that clear?"

Louie's eyes narrowed, and his friends knew at once he had just heard something that infuriated him.

"So you are Captain MacAdoo's boss, hah?" he asked.

"Yes, that's correct."

"And you give him his orders, hah?"

"Yes," Robeson agreed, trying to follow.

"So, in three minutes, you will give him an order that will blow up this bank! Is that what you want?"

"No, sir," Robeson said. "That seems to be what you want, man. The decision is *yours*."

"You listen to me!" Louie shouted, his rage splitting wide open. "You know damn well what we want! Doctor what's-his-name told you what we want! We do not want to *kill* people! We want only to *talk* to people!"

Robeson remained silent for a moment, letting the steam escape, allowing Louie time to sense his authority.

"Did you understand my order?" he asked Louie again. "Or would you like me to repeat it?"

"Listen, Mr. Captain—Mr. Assistant Chief of Police—you can repeat your order until you are blue in the face, instead of black. We are staying exactly where we are, until you bring us who we asked for, or until three o'clock. It's up to you!"

"How did you know I was black?" Robeson's question popped out before he could even think about it.

"How did I know? Because I'm *listening*," Louie said, "and I'm hearing the voice of a black man, that's how! What'sa matter, you're ashamed I can tell from the way you talk?"

"No, but I—"

"Can't you tell from the way I talk, that I am an immigrant, for goodness' sakes?"

"Yes, as a matter of fact, I can," Robeson said, amused in spite of himself.

"Of course!" Louie said. "Listen, you worked yourself up to a very important job in this world. You shouldn't be ashamed of your accent! I'm not ashamed of mine! Remember—you and me, we didn't *have* accents until we came to this country!"

The tension was broken momentarily, and in that moment Robeson sensed that he was talking to a man of reason, a man of good humor. "You're sure right about that!" he said good-naturedly.

"You bet your sweet life I am!" Louie observed immodestly. "I'm right about a lotta things."

"I'll bet you are," Robeson said, lapsing into an easy conversational tone. "Tell me, how old are you, sir?"

"Me? I'm seventy-eight on August fifteenth. Old enough to be your father, hah?"

"You certainly are," Robeson said, and he saw the flash of his angry father's face once more.

"We are *all* old in here," Louie said, "but I'm warning you—we are not old enough to be children! We are not afraid of the dark, or of loud noises, and we will not walk out of this place until we accomplish what we came to do. Make up your mind, my friend, we're not gonna sneak outa here with our tails between our legs just because you got a gun and you holler 'Hands up!'"

"You will not release the hostages and surrender the bank, unless we concede to your demands—is that what you're saying!"

"Surrender? No, sir!" Louie said. "Not on your life—or on mine, either. It's too late. It took too much anger to get us here. We won't back out now."

"You don't leave me much choice, do you, old man?" Robeson asked.

262

"Don't worry, my dear Captain," Louie promised cryptically. "You will have a choice! Good-bye—"

"Wait, wait! Don't hang up! I want you to hear my order to the Field Commander at the site." Robeson flipped the switch on his radio make. "Captain MacAdoo, do you read? Robeson here. Come in."

Louie covered his mouthpiece with his hand. "Hey, Stosh!" he shouted, "are you ready?"

"Ready, Louie!" Stosh hollered back from inside Wilson's office. "You tell me when!"

"I'll tell you—don't worry!" Louie shouted, as he heard MacAdoo answer Robeson's radio call.

"MacAdoo here. I read, over."

"Captain, I have just had a conversation with the leader of the group holding the bank. He is on the phone with me now, and can hear this communication. I have issued them the order to surrender their weapons and to vacate the bank. The have refused that order. I'm going to authorize you to proceed with your three-minute drill. Any questions?"

"No, sir!" MacAdoo replied, waiting for the positive command.

"One thing more. The two rounds that were fired—were they directed at personnel outside the bank?"

"No, sir, not to my knowledge," MacAdoo said. "No glass was broken. As far as we know, they were firing at something or someone *inside* the bank."

"At the ceiling, Captain!" Louie shouted into his phone. "I told you—at the ceiling!"

"Any gunshot injuries to anyone inside or outside, that you know of?" Robeson asked, ignoring Louie.

"No information on that at this time," MacAdoo lied.

"I gave you the information!" Louie shouted desperately.

Doctor Keller shook his head and gave MacAdoo a dirty look, but he said nothing. He had done all he could.

Robeson's grip tightened on the plastic case of his radio mike as he confronted the most important decision of his police career. The big blue swivel chair at Parker Center was an uncomfortable seat—a seat that Jack Robeson would have to get used to. "Captain MacAdoo?" he said, checking his watch.

"Yes, sir!"

"Maintain contact, Mac. I want a running play-by-play!"

"Yes, sir! Lopez will be at this end."

"O-kay . . ." Robeson watched the sweep hand of his watch hit twelve. "Your three minutes start *now!*"

"Yes, sir! Over and out." MacAdoo laid his mike on the seat and ducked out of the squad car, with Keller after him.

"Did you hear my order, sir?" Robeson asked Louie.

"I heard, I heard." Louie watched MacAdoo waving his arms, pointing this way and that, dispatching the blue uniforms criss-crossing to their battle stations for the attack.

"There's still time to prevent people from getting hurt," Robeson offered. "Maybe from getting killed . . ."

Louie saw the cameras across the way, moving closer—newspeople ducking down behind the short hedge that edged the parking lot. "You're probably too young to understand, Captain," he said. "Death is not really so important. It's only a fact of life. But the *reason* for a death—Ah-h! *Now* you got something important! *Who* got killed, and who permitted it, and *why!* Those are the questions that have a meaning!"

"I've got a question that has some meaning for you, sir," Robeson said. "Are you going to let innocent people get hurt or killed even though you have the chance of stopping it right now?"

"You got a way with words, you know that, Captain?" Louie drew his gun out of his belt and laid it on the counter. "Just tell the doctor that we're hooking up the wire."

"That you're what?"

"Never mind. He'll tell you!" Louie said, and he slammed the phone down in Robeson's ear.

"So? What, what?" Oscar asked, as Louie stared straight ahead.

"Abe," Louie said calmly, "go bring some wet paper towels to the people in the conference room."

"Louie, remember," Abe said, not moving, "we didn't want to hurt anybody, we only—"

"Don't talk, Abe. Just move, you hear?"

Abe ran toward the men's room as Louie scanned the scene outside with his binoculars.

"What do you see, Levine?" Oscar asked.

"Never mind what I see." Louie saw Stryker signaling thumbs up to his men on the roof of the bank. "Is your cake ready? That's the question."

"It is not a cake, Levine," Oscar corrected him. "It is a bomb. Und it is ready to destroy—the bank, und maybe all of us. What will this accomplish, Levine?"

Louie was glued to his binoculars. He seemed not even to have heard Oscar's challenge as he saw Stryker running low across Beverly Boulevard, pulling on his gas mask, and MacAdoo, his gun drawn, racing out to the middle of the street to duck down behind the open door of a police car pointed directly at the front door of the bank.

Louie's command phone started to ring. He made no move to answer it. It rang a second time . . . and a third as Louie continued to stare outside.

"I will answer it," Oscar said, reaching for the phone.

"Don't even touch it!" Louie barked, lowering his binoculars and grabbing Oscar's wrist.

264

"But maybe it's—"

"I know who it is!" Louie tightened his grip on Oscar's wrist, making him wince. "I already listened to everything he's got to say, don't you understand? They are up on the roof with the gas! We got less than two minutes!"

Abe came running out of the men's room and toward the conference room, carrying an armload of dripping wet paper towels.

"Stay in there, Abe, you hear?" Louie yelled. "You too, Oscar—into the conference room!"

Oscar did not move. He just stood there, staring hard at Louie. The phone continued to ring.

"I said go, Oscar!"

"Don't holler, Levine. I am *not* going. I am staying here with you. This is too much to have on your head alone." And he laid his hand gently on top of the blasting box.

"Okay, okay, I won't argue with you," Louie muttered. "Stay if you want."

The telephone stopped in the middle of a ring.

"You see?" Louie pointed at the phone. "His message wasn't so important, after all."

Outside, the sun's angle finally permitted a clear, unreflected view through the glass front doors into the interior of the bank.

Crouching behind the open door of the squad car, a scant thirty feet from the doors, MacAdoo could just make out the two motionless figures behind the counter at the back of the bank. He checked the second hand of his watch as it swept around to the two-minute mark. Then he looked left and right behind him, to see his men on both flanks at the ready.

Across the street, low behind the parking lot hedge, the CBS minicam crew zoomed in for its first closeup of the inside of the bank, sending out the live video coverage, preempting their regular daytime programming to cover the event, just as they had for their prizewinning broadcasts of the SLA shootout during the early hot summer of 1974.

A slow zooming closeup shot of Louie, peering out through his binoculars . . . an unsteady panning shot of Oscar, at his side . . . a slow pan down to Oscar's hand, resting lightly on the plunger of the blasting box . . . a reverse zoom, widening the shot to show the big Citizens' Bank sign, flashing its 5.25% . . . a long panning shot of the tensely posed cops aiming their guns, the police vehicles scattered in the intersection, the gawking crowds behind the barriers, hoping for something terrible to happen . . . a zoom up to the building roofs, bristling with police marksmen, their highpowered M-16s trained on the front doors of the bank . . . and, as the camera moved, the staccato voice-over description of the scene by Bill Martinez, top local crime reporter for CBS News, on his stomach behind the hedge with his microphone, laying his life on the line for the loyal daytime viewers of Channel 2.

The fact of the matter was, the CBS switchboard had already logged over a hundred telephone complaints from irate soap opera viewers demanding an explanation for the unscheduled blackout of "As The World Turns"—just as poor pretty Peggy O'Neal was being wheeled into the operating room to go under the shaky scapel of a hung-over Doctor Dennis Dozier for her long-debated abortion.

Louie saw MacAdoo check his watch again, then raise his officer's hat high over his head for the stand-by signal to Stryker across the street. Then he saw Doctor Keller, still shirtless, with a bullhorn under his arm, as he came galloping out to the middle of the street, standing straight up and obviously adjusting his gas mask, to join MacAdoo at the squad car.

"How do ya like that?" Louie said, "The remarkable Doctor Keller is giving us a signal! He is okay!"

"Ja, I see," said Oscar.

Louie glanced up at the big wall clock to see the second hand sweeping past the two minute mark. "All right, Stosh!" he yelled. "Come out, now!— right to the door!"

Wilson's office door opened and Stosh strode resolutely out to stand in plain view at the front door, just to one side of the DANGER—HIGH EXPLOSIVES sign, with his little passenger giggling astride his shoulders.

There stood Stosh, bigger than most life, a confident grin on his face, holding the tiny ankles of six-year-old Odessa Hoskins as she bounced and giggled on her mount, gaily waving a big yellow balloon with red lettering on it: My Daddy Banks at Citizens'.

CBS was broadcasting the scene—live, and in living color—to an estimated one-half million viewers. The reaction from outside the bank was immediate.

The crowd sent up a loud and scary "Whoo-OOO!" MacAdoo stared at the front door in frozen shock. Behind him, Keller stood slowly upright, peeling off his gas mask.

"Holy Jesus, Joseph, and Mary!" Keller said in a daze, "it's the Ace of Trump!"

MacAdoo looked up at him, bewildered. "What'd you say?"

Keller couldn't even answer him.

"Dirty sons of bitches!" MacAdoo snarled, turning back to the bank.

"Don't lower your hat!" Keller suddenly screamed at MacAdoo.

"What?" MacAdoo popped up like a jumping jack, his hat still held stiffly over his head.

"Keep your hat up in the air for God's sake! Stryker can't see what we see!"

MacAdoo was suspended in a moment of disconnection, his mind poised to snap his hat down at the three-minute deadline to signal Stryker for the gas drop, as ordered, but now—

266

"Oh-de-ssaaah!"

The whining scream cut across the intersection, spinning MacAdoo around to face the ambulance. Odessa's grandmother was struggling desperately with the paramedics.

"That's my little gi-irl!" she wailed. "That's my grandchi-ild! Let go of me-ee!"

MacAdoo turned again to look across the street at Stryker, then automatically checked his watch to see the second hand sweeping to the three minute mark, straight up to twelve.

"No, MacAdoo!" Keller shouted right in his ear, snapping him to attention. "You can't give the order for the gas! Not in this situation! Not without informing Chief Robeson! You're on TV, man!"

MacAdoo stared first at Keller, then up at his hat, then again at the front door of the bank, then at his command car, where he could see Lopez chattering excitedly on the radio-phone.

Stryker stood up, confused, looking to MacAdoo for the overdue signal.

Trembling with frustration, MacAdoo holstered his gun and grabbed the bullhorn from Keller. "At ease, Stryker! Suspend!" he barked. "Come to my command car!"

Stryker acknowledged the order with a nod and flipped his talk switch.

"Bud, this is Lieutenant Stryker, do you read?"

"Yes, sir!" crackled the voice from the roof. "*Now*, sir?"

"No! Negative! We've got a delay of some kind. Hold your positions and stand by!"

"Yes, sir!" the voice responded. "Standing by."

"Roger. Over and out." Stryker ran to the command car, and MacAdoo lowered his hat.

MacAdoo saw the paramedics pulling Odessa's grandmother back into their ambulance as he and Keller reached the command car on the run.

"I told him all about it, Captain!" Lopez cried out as he opened the door. "Chief Robeson is up to date, sir!"

"Yeah, I *knew* I could count on you, Lopez." MacAdoo slid into the seat, taking the mike in hand. "MacAdoo here. Well, *Chief* Robeson, you know what the situation is here, and it's all yours. We've given these people enough time to really put it to us, and they've come up with a beaut! They're calling the shots now, and your field commander is powerless to act—unless of course, you want me to gas a six-year-old kid with a yellow balloon, right on TV!"

Robeson was silent.

"I'm standing by for orders, Chief," MacAdoo said, rubbing it in.

"Well, let's examine our options, Mac," Robeson said after a moment.

"Only one option I can see, sir."

"Shoot," Robeson requested.

"That's right," MacAdoo said quickly. "We can see clearly now through the glass, and the guy who's the leader is in plain sight, and stationary.

Stryker's got two class-A marksmen here with their scopes. *One clean hit* would abort this thing in a hurry."

"Negative!" Robeson snapped back. "That move is *not* within the parameters set down by the Chief, got it?"

"Yes, sir." He smiled smugly at the men looking into the squad car. "I'd like to hear another option, sir."

Robeson paused, as he thought about the Chief of Police in San Francisco, and what he would do if he were here, and about his own recent promotion to the blue swivel chair at Parker Center—and, most of all, about what a sitting target he was in that big chair for the Whitey MacAdoos of the world.

"We'll have to give them what they want," he said at last. "Try to negotiate some people out of the bank in exchange. Is Doctor Keller still there with you?"

MacAdoo handed Keller the radio mike.

"Yes, sir, This is Doctor Keller."

"Doctor Keller, about six minutes ago," Robeson said, "I dispatched a car on a Code-Three from West L.A. Division over to the Federal Building to pick up this Mr. Whitehead and transport him to your location. Total travel time should be twenty to twenty-five minutes, provided he's in the building and provided they can locate him immediately—but we're going to need more time as a cushion. Do you think you can negotiate an hour's extension of their deadline?"

"I'll try, sir. If I can make them believe that we're really going to deliver Whitehead—"

"We'll deliver him all right. If he's in the area, they'll get him there. I've instructed Lieutenant Bowman of West L.A. to place him under arrest, if necessary, but he'll be in your show."

"Very good, sir," Keller said.

"Do you think you can negotiate the release of the female hostages in exchange for our promise to grant them their news conference and interview?" Robeson asked.

"I don't know, sir," Keller said doubtfully. "I don't think they'll stretch that far, but I'll try to insist on at least the child, the pregnant woman, and the injured bank guard."

"Right. Let's get moving on it!"

"But Captain, wait a minute, sir—"

"Yes, what is it?"

"These people are not going to bargain away any part of their leverage just on conversation—just on our stated pledge to comply. They've been given the runaround too many times for that. I can tell you for sure that we're going to have to exhibit some positive action before they'll even discuss negotiating."

"What do you suggest?" Robeson asked.

268

"I don't know, sir. Maybe a partial withdrawal of police personnel?"

"Bullshit!" said MacAdoo.

"No, we can't do that, said Robeson.

"I have an idea!" Doctor Harmon said.. Keller passed him the microphone. "Doctor Harmon here, Captain. How about setting up the news conference while we're waiting for your people to deliver Mr. Whitehead? Maybe that would be a strong enough good-faith action to support Doctor Keller's negotiation."

"Sounds good," Robeson said. "let's do it, Mac."

MacAdoo grabbed the mike. "Set up a news conference now? Before Whitehead gets here?"

"You see something wrong with that?" Robeson asked.

"Number one, I don't think they'll go for it," MacAdoo said. "Whitehead's the guy they want. Number two, you let those press people cross the street, and sure as hell you're going to have that whole mob of civilians over there too! No way to stop it."

Robeson swiveled in his chair, trying to guess how far MacAdoo would go to sabotage his new authority. "Let's do it, Mac!" he said, in a tone that was unmistakably an order. "I think they *will* go for it, and I have every confidence that you will handle the crowd control with maximum efficiency, Captain. As a matter of fact, I think the crowd attendance at the news conference will be an additional safety factor."

MacAdoo listened to the plan for police capitulation with a squinty scowl, exchanging a sour glance with Olson, who was standing outside. Olson walked away in disgust.


Louie watched the men move back from the command car, as MacAdoo got out with his bullhorn. He saw Keller throw his gas mask into the back seat of the car and walk to the phone booth, followed by Harmon. Then, swinging his binolculars, Louie followed MacAdoo, crossing the street toward the press people in the parking lot, broadcasting through his bullhorn for attention.

Louie smiled a self-satisfied smile. "Stosh," he said pleasantly, "you and your little playmate can go back into Wilson's office. You done a good job. Oscar, you can unhook the wire to the box for a while."

"Why, what did you see?" Oscar asked.

"Never mind," Louie said. "Just do like I tell you—and please be quiet. I am getting a nice phone call."

The phone rang, and Oscar blinked in surprise at Louie's ability to foretell the present.

"Hello, Doctor Keller," Louie purred into the phone. "What can I do for you?"

"Hel—Hello?" Keller stammered in the confusion of hearing his name before he identified himself. "This is, uh, Doctor Oliver Keller calling, and I have good news for you."

"So what is the good news?"

"Assistant Chief Robeson has reconsidered," Keller explained, "and he has agreed to permit a press conference provided you agree, in turn, to cooperate in several ways so that it can be held under maximum safety conditions."

"Never mind cooperate, Doctor," Louie said bluntly, "and never mind the mumbo jumbo. What about Ernest P. Whitehead?"

"A police car was dispatched to the Federal Building from West Los Angeles about ten minutes ago, to pick him up and bring him here—if they can locate him."

"Whatta ya mean, if? You locate him in his office!"

"No, I mean, we're not sure we can get him here before your three o'clock deadline," Keller reasoned. "So we're asking for a one-hour extension, to *four* o'clock."

Keller waited for a response, looking nervously at Harmon.

Louie let him wait, his suspicion growing. "You wouldn't shit me, would you Doctor?" he asked, finally.

"What do you mean?"

"I mean it don't sound kosher to me. They really sent a car over to get Whitehead?"

"I am telling you the *truth*, sir," Keller said.

"Okay. I believe you. So . . . I'll give you an extension of *fifteen* minutes. You got until a quarter after three."

"I hope we can make it," Keller said, shaking his head at Harmon and flashing five fingers at him three times.

"I hope you can, too, Doctor."

"There's something else . . ."

"Yeah? What else?"

"We want you to release all the female hostages and the injured bank guard immediately," Keller said, all in one breath.

"You want me to hang up on you, or what?"

"No, no! Please don't hang up!" Keller said quickly.

"Then don't talk such foolishness!" Louie snapped. "You think I would give up the only thing that is keeping us from being tear gassed outa here?"

"There will be *no tear gas*, I promise!"

Louie squinted, tilting his head to one side. "*You* promise? What about Captain MacAdoo with his hat up in the air? Does *he* promise, too?"

Keller knew immediately that he had gone too far, but he took a big breath and plowed ahead. "Now, look, sir, I have been assigned the responsibility of negotiating with you by the chief law enforcement officer of the City of Los Angeles, and when I tell you that there will be no tear gas

270

used, providing you cooperate, I have a right to expect you to believe that I'm negotiating in good faith."

"He assigned you the responsibility, hah? But did he also give you the authority to back up such a promise?"

"It's up to you, sir," Keller said calmly. "You and I can play word games here on the phone while critical minutes tick away—or we can set about making the moves that will get you what you've asked for, and put an end to this dangerous situation. Which will it be?"

Louie saw MacAdoo loping back across the street toward the phone booth, leaving the press people standing in an expectant little knot at the edge of the parking lot. Then he noticed the CBS remote news truck inching forward as men played out the heavy cables.

"We are prepared," Keller continued, "to send the press across the street to the drive-in teller's booth *now*, to set up for your press conference. Are you prepared to release the female hostages and the injured bank guard?"

"Yes and no," Louie said. "The bank guard, yes. The female hostages, no. Impossible."

"You claim to be a reasonable man," Keller said. "Do you call *that* negotiating in good faith?"

"My dear doctor, I am fresh outa good faith." Louie answered. "All of us in here had our good faith pissed on a long time ago. That's why we're here, doing what we're doing."

"What's he giving?" MacAdoo asked Keller in the booth.

"Damn little," Keller replied, covering the mouthpiece. "So far, only the bank guard."

"It figures," MacAdoo said sourly. "Like I said, you can't bargain with terrorists. They take a few hostages, and they think they've got the whole world on its knees. And we're out here helping them get away with it!"

"Okay, Captain," Harmon spoke up, gently brushing MacAdoo back with his arm, "let's let Doctor Keller do his job here. He's just gotten started. We'll let you know when we've made an acceptable deal."

"Let's make a deal!" MacAdoo sneered. "Bullshit! You're over a barrel, and they know it. I'll be in my command car, watching them laugh at you." He turned away in disgust.

Louie saw MacAdoo move away, and he read the body language.

"Hello?" Keller said into the phone.

"Hello, Doctor," Louie said wearily. "I am still here, and you are still there. So?"

"I'm sorry, sir," Keller said brusquely, "but your bargaining attitude is unacceptable. We cannot let you have your press conference unless you release hostages. The bank guard is not enough—and I think you know that, don't you?"

"So sue me!" Louie said. "I'm only trying to make the best deal I can

271

make, just like you are. Give a little, take a lot. That's the American way, right?"

"All right," said Keller, not reacting to Louie's humor. "Let's start making some sense. This news conference is not going to take place without a release of some of the people you're holding. How about the little girl and *three* women?"

"No, that's too much. Remember, Doctor, I didn't make you take off your pants when you came in here."

"Okay, okay," Keller said. "How about the little girl and the pregnant woman?"

Louie's jaw worked back and forth as he thought it over.

"My God, man!" Keller cried out in frustration. "We're wasting valuable time. You're eating up your own deadline!"

"All right," Louie muttered after a moment. "You send the reporters across the street, and we'll *see* about the little girl and the pregnant woman."

"Oh, no! The hostages must be released first."

"Listen, Doctor, I'm getting sick and tired of being told what *must* be! We are here to *change* what must be, don't you understand even yet?"

"All right, all right. Let's try to stay calm, now. I didn't mean to upset you—"

"And don't give me that bunk about staying calm!" Louie erupted. "I'm too *old* to stay calm! I stay calm—I'm *finished*. Now, you listen to me. I'll tell you what *must* be. You must send the press people over here *now*, you understand? If they are not by the drive-in window—twenty feet back from the window—in five minutes, I must bring the little girl out in front again, and Captain MacAdoo must drop the gas, and I must push the plunger, and afterwards, *you* must pick up the pieces! Ya got that? Five minutes—exactly two thirty-five—that's the deal!"

Keller gulped down the ultimatum, and it almost choked him. He had pushed the old man over the brink to an unyielding stance, and he had done it by using the simple forbidden four-letter word *must*. How did he know that nobody says "must" to Louie Levine?

Louie watched Keller come out of the booth and run with Harmon to the command car, where he saw them arguing with MacAdoo inside. Then he saw MacAdoo shaking his head violently as he talked with headquarters on the radio.

"Hey, Louie!" Abe shouted, sticking his head out of the conference room. "The pregnant lady is feeling sick in here. She wants to go to the bathroom! What'll we do?"

"Get Minnie, quick," Louie said, pointing toward Wilson's office. "She'll take care of it."

Abe scooted across to Wilson's office. Louie saw MacAdoo get out of his

272

command car and run toward the parking lot where the press waited, while the two doctors headed back to the phone booth.

"Hello?"

"Yes, Doctor," Louie said. "So what did you decide?"

"I have assured Chief Robeson that you are a fair man," Keller said, "that you are a man of your word, and he has approved our immediate relocation of the press to the drive-in teller's window."

"Twenty feet back from the window," Louie reminded him, as Minnie and Abe hurried back to the conference room.

"Yes, twenty feet back," Keller repeated. "Now, will you be able to hear the people that far away?"

"Oh, yes," Louie said. "The drive-in booth is a very fancy place, all the latest equipment—a speaker in and a speaker out—and I am not hard of hearing, so don't worry."

Keller looked across to the parking lot to see MacAdoo, arms outstretched, awaiting his signal.

"All right, then," he said. "I will give the signal for the crossing, while you gather the hostages you're going to release. I will pick them up personally at the front door and escort them out, okay?"

"I don't have to remind you, no funny business, do I, Doctor?"

"No, sir, you don't."

"That's good, so I won't," Louie said.

Minnie and Abe brought Betty Lundy out of the conference room and headed for the restroom, the ashen mother-to-be leaning heavily on Abe's shoulder.

Louie saw Keller step out of the booth and wave his arm high for MacAdoo. He heard the chatter of MacAdoo's bullhorn, then he saw four men dressed in blue coveralls running two long yellow parade barriers across the street toward the bank driveway. MacAdoo turned his horn back to the crowd of reporters, and suddenly they broke ranks, running across the street pell-mell, cameras and tape recorders flapping, as they elbowed one another out of the way to get prime locations for the press conference.


Minnie ducked out from under Betty's arm as the trio reached the restroom door. "Hold her right there, Abe!" She ran to one of the desks, searching through the drawers frantically.

"What are you looking for?" Louie asked her.

"Never mind, I know what I'm looking for. You pay attention outside! Aha!" She held aloft a pair of long, pointed scissors and ran back to the restroom, hustling Betty inside.

"Hey, hey!" Louie shouted. "What's the matter with her?"

"Mind your own business!" Minnie yelled back, half in and half out of the

273

ladies room door. "This is strictly female! Nothing is the matter. It's perfectly natural!"

Abe walked back to Louie with an anxious look on his face. "I'm telling you, Louie, that woman needs a doctor."

"How do you know?" Louie asked. "You a nurse?"

Abe was suddenly staring out the front door, pointing. "Hey, Louie, Doctor What's-his-name is waving."

Louie turned to see Keller, across the street, waving his arms over his head for attention.

"Go to the front and wave him to come over," Louie ordered, "then tell Stosh to come out here, quick!"

Keller saw a figure approaching the front door, beckoning him to cross the street. As he stepped off the curb, he noticed his shadow moving ahead of him again, and the sight comforted him. When he reached the front door, all he could make out through the glass was Louie's shadowy figure, standing behind the rear counter where their interview had taken place, looking at him through his binoculars.

Keller waited. He knew that Louie would make him wait. He was beginning—just beginning—to know his man.

As he waited, he saw a figure move to the rear counter to confer hastily with Louie, then limp briskly off toward the door to the drive-in teller's booth, carrying a thick stack of paper.

It was Oscar, carrying the special April issue of *The Voice of the Aged* to its special distribution point.

For a moment, Keller's vision was almost completely blocked as Stosh stepped sideways into the front door opening, the ring of keys dangling at his waist. The giant smiled gently down at Keller through the glass, and Keller returned an uncertain smile. Then, from the rear of the bank, he made out two men walking slowly toward him at the front door, one bent over, his arm in a makeshift sling, leaning heavily on the other. Keller recognized them as Vito limped Brubaker to the glass door.

He heard a muffled command shouted from the rear counter, then Stosh knelt to open the door.

"The little girl!" Keller yelled. "Where is the little girl? And the pregnant woman?"

Stosh held up a palm as he clicked the floor lock open. Then, still kneeling, he turned to his left and wiggled a beckoning finger.

Odessa Hoskins pranced out into view, poised and smiling, as though she had been called back on stage to take another bow after stopping the show with her act. She still carried the yellow bank balloon, and in her other hand she held a rolled-up sheet from Wilson's desk pad—the artist-in-residence, exercising her right to retain one souvenir work from her exhibition, her very first life portrait sketch.

Stosh patted her on the head and pulled the door open. "You go with

274

man, now. Good-bye, little kid. Remember big Stosh—and be good girl, ja?"

Odessa giggled up at him, putting her balloon hand over her mouth as she hunched her shoulders up in tickly glee. Then she skipped through the door and out onto the sidewalk to take Keller's hand.

Vito moved Brubaker through the door, shifting his good arm onto Keller's shoulder. "Wait a minute, just a minute!" Keller protested. "Where's the pregnant woman? Where's Mrs. Lundy?" He kicked his foot up against the door as Stosh started to push it shut.

"Mrs. Lundy!" Keller screamed in at Louie. "You promised to release Mrs. Lundy!"

Stosh was struggling to close the door, but Keller's foot was now stuck through, as he continued to holler, while Vito, on his knees, was trying to push the frantic foot out.

"Wait, wait!" Louie shouted from the back. "Open up the door! Let him talk!"

"You are reneging on our deal!" Keller yelled at Louie as Stosh pulled the door open. "You agreed to release these two and the pregnant woman!"

"No, no," Louie said, shaking his head. "You agreed with *yourself* that I should release her. She stays with us!"

"But that's inhuman!" Keller cried, "She's over seven months along! Prolonged excitement like this in her condition can cause—"

"Take it easy. She's all right." Louie said, glancing back toward the ladies' room. "Don't worry about her. She will have a fat healthy baby!"

"But I can't let you, uh, stay pregnant with a—I mean . . . I mean, uh—" He couldn't even finish his protest. His parts were not working. His tongue wagged meaninglessly in his mouth, his brain stumbling hopelessly behind, as he stood there with Odessa tugging on one hand and Brubaker groaning on his other shoulder.

"Give it up, Doc," Brubaker said. "I can tell you—he won't let her go."

"Take those two and be satisfied, Doctor," Louie shouted. "I gotta go now! You bring me Ernest P. Whitehead, you hear? Mr. Guard, you can close the door."

Stosh locked and rechained the door, then Louie tucked his gun into his belt and walked toward the drive-in teller's booth.

Outside, MacAdoo watched the Keller trio hobble across the street toward the ambulance, to scattered applause from the crowd. Keller was sweating freely and lobster-red, Brubaker was bent over in pain, and Odessa still held her scrolled sketch in one hand and the balloon string in the other.

"Granmaw, granmaw!" Odessa squealed, "I got a present for you!"

"Odessa! Oh, thank the Lord!"

Keller let go of Odessa's hand and she ran to her grandmother, who knelt to smother the child in her frail arms. The paramedics helped Brubaker into the ambulance, and Keller turned to face MacAdoo.

"I see you settled for the shitty end of the stick," MacAdoo said.

Keller was about to reply, but thought better of it as Doctor Harmon came running over from the command car. "They've got Whitehead! They estimate they'll be here with him in ten to fifteen minutes!"

"Anything can happen in ten to fifteen minutes," MacAdoo said to Stryker. "Let's get over there and see what's going on."

The four men trotted across the street toward the drive-in window, while Odessa tried to comfort her tearful grandmother.

"Please don't cry, granmaw," she said. "I had a real good time! Much more fun than the old zoo! And my awnt Minnie gave me a present for you, too! Here." And she handed her grandmother a crisp new hundred-dollar bill.

"You're sure you're feeling all right, now?" Minnie asked Betty Lundy as they emerged from the restroom.

"I think so," Betty gasped, between deep breaths. "I think I'll be okay now. . . . I had it once before . . . on my last one."

"What happened?" Abe wanted to know. "A false alarm?"

"None of your business, a false alarm!" Minnie said. "What are you—writing a book?"

"No, but—but we thought that she was, uh, you know, having her labor pains already, and you were—"

"Get outa here, you crazy? You think I would deliver a baby with *these?*" Minnie waved the long scissors in the air.

"Well, how was I to know?" Abe shrugged.

"That's right! So don't even try!" Minnie said. "The waistband on her skirt was too tight for her, that's all. It was cutting off the circulation, so naturally it made her feel like fainting."

"Oh," Abe said foolishly.

"It was a job for Super-Seamstress," Minnie said, snipping the scissors in midair, "not for Doctor Spock."

"Thank God!" Betty said, crossing herself a little one.

"Come, we'll go back inside," Minnie said gently. "You'll sit down, you'll put your head down on the table, you'll feel a lot better, you'll see." And she herded Betty back into the conference room.

"Woman okay?" Stosh asked Abe, from the front door.

"Yeah, Minnie says she's gonna be all right—Oh, my God, *Looka this!*" Abe pointed to a small red spot on the floor. Then another, and another, in a line of dots leading back to the restroom.

"What? Look at what?" asked Stosh as he watched Abe, head bent toward the floor, intently following the path of telltale spots.

"The woman is bleeding!" Abe said. "We got trouble—big trouble!" He

276

jerked the conference room door open. "Minnie, Minnie, come out here!"

Stosh left his post and ran back to look down at the frightening red spots for himself.

"Goddamn!" he muttered. "Goddamn . . . Goddamn . . ." punctuating each spot as he came to it.

Louie and Oscar entered the drive-in teller's booth just as MacAdoo, Stryker, and the two PIES doctors arrived on the scene of the forthcoming news conference. Louie closed the door behind him as Oscar attached his hearing-aid to his lapel.

The crowd of reporters and cameramen had assembled behind barriers that were set up twenty feet back from the window, just as Louie had demanded.

At the sight of the two men at the teller's window, the crowd surged forward, knocking a barrier over right on a cop's foot. The cop howled, and several other cops scrambled in to right the barrier and push the noisy crowd back again as MacAdoo, Harmon, and Keller pushed their way forward and in front of the barriers.

"Move back, you people!" MacAdoo yelled into his bullhorn. "We've got to have order here, or somebody's going to get hurt! Just hold your places, and stand still!"

A loud falsetto voice from somewhere at the back of the crowd piped, "Oink! Oink!" A cop quickly closed in on the source of the insult, and a kid ducked out of the crowd and ran like hell down Beverly Boulevard. Some people at the back of the crowd laughed and applauded.

"Quiet! Quiet, everybody!" MacAdoo blasted on his bullhorn. "If you don't quiet down, I'll have to clear the whole area! Now, it's my duty to inform you people that you're here at your own risk. And I want to make one thing very clear—there is *no such thing* as bullet-proof glass!"

MacAdoo now had the undivided attention of the crowd. "They know that in there," he continued, "and now *you* know it, so for your own safety—no sudden moves out here? *Is that clear?*"

The crowd simmered down to a respectful hush, and MacAdoo handed the bullhorn to Keller, who turned it toward the teller's window.

"How do you want to handle this?" he asked Louie.

Louie bent the microphone up close to his mouth, but he was not yet ready to talk. His eyes were scanning the crowd in a squinting search among the faces, looking for trouble, looking for signs of a possible police trick, while Keller waited nervously for instructions.

"Where is Ernest P. Whitehead?" he finally asked Keller.

"He's on his way," Keller replied through the horn. "He should be here in a few minutes. Do you want these news people to ask you questions, or do you have a statement to make first?"

"I don't wanna see *no guns,* you hear me?" Louie shouted into the mike.

The booth speakers squealed out a feedback, and Oscar adjusted the volume. "No guns! No guns!" Louie repeated.

MacAdoo took the bullhorn again, and turned around to broadcast his orders in duplicate. "Holster all handguns! All handguns on safety and in holsters! You SWAT personnel at the back—move off with your automatic weapons! Move off to the extreme sides!"

MacAdoo returned the horn to Keller. "All right," Keller said, "are we all set now?"

"I don't want *him* in the front!" said Louie.

"Who?"

"Him!" Louie pointed. "Captain MacAdoo, from across the street. I don't wanna look at him in the front!"

Keller turned to MacAdoo, who nodded red-faced and backed away, skirting the crowd to stand in the back with Stryker.

"Anything else?" Keller asked when MacAdoo was clear.

"Yeah—get ridda that horn, for God sakes! I don't wanna be yelled at by no damn bullhorn!"

Keller stepped aside to hand the horn to a cop.

Newsome saw her chance to get in the first question. "Joy Newsome, KFWB!" she shouted across the driveway from her place in front, pointing her microphone toward Louie. "What is your name?"

Louie did not respond.

"Why did you people take over the bank?" another reporter hollered. "And what do you call your group?"

"Is it true that you have a woman hostage in there giving birth to a baby?" yelled the big guy in the blue ABC-News blazer.

Louie turned to say something to Oscar, and Oscar quickly put his hand over the microphone.

Keller stepped back in to front and center. "Did you hear the questions, sir?" he asked loudly.

Louie was shaking his head harshly at something Oscar said, and Keller waited.

Then Louie removed Oscar's hand from the mike. "Ladies and gentlemen of the press," he announced finally, "I wanna thank you all for coming here today, but you are going to have to be patient a little longer. Nothing is going to happen here until Mr. Ernest P. Whitehead shows up—if he shows up—no questions, no answers, nothing. That's all I have to say." He nodded to Oscar, who clicked the microphone switch off.

The restive crowd reacted immediately with groans and cries of frustration, shouting at Louie like an angry, churning mob.

Keller whirled to face them, waving his hands up in the air. "Quiet, please!" he shouted. "Please, ladies and gentlemen! Quiet, quiet!"

"Who is Ernest P. Whitehead?" Newsome screamed above the noise as

278

she jumped up and down, trying to point her microphone at Keller around one of the cops.

"What do these people want?" "Who are they?" "We were called to a news conference!" "Yeah, what the hell's going on here?"

The reporters' shouts grew louder and louder as Keller pleaded in vain for order, waving his arms more and more wildly. Suddenly, a bearded newsman broke out from behind the barrier and ran up to the teller's window, sticking his tape recorder microphone right up to the glass. "What are your demands?" he yelled. "What do you want?"

Louie wiggled a finger at his ear, indicating that he could not hear the man through the thick glass. Oscar slowly drew out his Luger, laying it on the counter as two cops came forward to drag the reporter away from the window.

MacAdoo was in front of the barrier again, blasting the crowd with his bullhorn at top volume. "Attention! You people quiet down, right now! I am giving you final warning—order will be maintained! Just one more outburst like that, and my men will disperse you and clear this area immediately! Is that clear?"

The chastened crowd settled down quickly, and MacAdoo returned to rejoin Stryker at the back of the crowd.

"Doctor, Doctor!" Newsome said after MacAdoo had retired. "Can't you just tell us who Mr. Whitehead is?"

Keller turned toward the booth as though to ask Louie's permission to answer the question. Louie smiled, offering an open be-my-guest palm, and everyone knew at once that the two old men in the booth were not hard of hearing.

"All right, all right, I'll answer that question," said Keller. "Mr. Ernest Whitehead is the western region director of Social Security. The people who are holding the bank have demanded an interview with Mr. White-head in the presence of the press. A police car has already picked him up at the Federal building, and he should be here any minute."

A babble of follow-up questions erupted from the crowd, then cut off abruptly as the newspeople became aware of new arrivals inside the booth.

It was Vito at the door, with Stosh looming behind, both men gesturing wildly, and both jabbering at Louie at the same time.

"I'm tellin' ya, no matter *what* Minnie says," Vito yelled. "Jesus, the woman's bleeding all over the floor! She needs a doctor plenty bad, I'm tellin' ya!"

"And I'm telling *you*," Louie snarled as he poked Vito's chest, "to get the hell outa here and back to that blasting box, you hear? Stosh! Get out front—right now!"

Stosh turned and ran.

A howling scream came suddenly from somewhere in the middle of the

279

crowd, and a hawk-faced woman, beating her breast with her hands and spinning herself around like a dervish, toppled over backward into the arms of the startled people around her. All other activity was suspended as the crowd, the police, and the men in the booth tried to pinpoint the source of the hysteria.

The woman suddenly leaped stiff-legged to her feet. "Jee-zuss, Mother Mar-y-yy!" she screeched, staring to pull at her hair. "It's him! Oh, God, it's him!"

MacAdoo and Harmon pushed through the crowd and reached her at the same time, each grabbing hold of an arm as the woman started jumping up and down to get a better look at the window.

"Tell me it's not him!" she squealed. "Oh, God, please!"

"Who?" MacAdoo yelled at her.

"The man in the window!"

"Do you *know* a man in that booth?" asked Harmon.

"Yes, yes! Oh, God, I wish I didn't! It's my father-in-law!"

"Which one?" MacAdoo asked.

"The little one. The one on the left!"

"What's his name?"

"Morelli," she gasped. Then, as if to exorcise the shame to the entire family on both sides of the Atlantic, she screamed his full name out to the heavens and beyond: "Vito Morelli! God help me, his name is Vito Anthony Morelleee-eee!"

Even half-inch bullet-retardant glass could not shield Vito's ears from that screeching broadcast of his name. "Who the hell is *that?*" he asked, peering out through the tinted booth window as he tried to identify the stool pigeon who had fingered him.

"Gotta be somebody who knows you," Louie said flatly.

"What'll I do?" Vito asked, turning as if to leave.

"Stay where you are, that's what you do," Louie ordered as MacAdoo and Harmon brought the woman forward to the front of the barrier.

She took a sure look and crossed herself. "Pop . . . Pop, how could you *do* this?" She was half moaning, half sobbing. "How could you do this thing to us, how?"

"You know her?" Louie asked.

"Yeah, I know her," Vito said. "Lemme talk to her. I been waitin' for this a long time."

Oscar snapped the microphone switch on.

"Hey, look who's here!" Vito said, greeting a dear long-lost friend. "As I live and breathe, if it ain't my ex-landlady! Ya still change the sheets once every two weeks, if they need it or not, Missus?"

"Look at him in there!" the woman wailed. "Are you crazy? What are you doing in there? An old man with a gun—aren't you ashamed? God will punish you for this terrible thing!"

280

"Yeah? Well, I'll take my chances with Him, lady," Vito said. "We all get punished for different things, ya know what I mean? So how's your big shot husband doin', huh? Still promotin' his big deals?"

The woman looked at him with surprise. "I don't hear from your son no more," she said bluntly. "Didn't you know that? He went to New York, I think."

"Don't you call that chicken punk my son! I don't have no son! So you kicked *him* out too, huh?"

"No, I didn't!" she admitted, without thinking.

"So now ya got no smell of cigars, and no smell of shaving lotion, neither," Vito observed. "How do ya *like* a house with no smells—only your own, huh, girlie? Stinks, don't it?"

The woman shook her head sharply. "What are you talking about, Pop? Don't you realize what you're doing? They'll put you into jail, for God's sake! Come out of there, before it's too late. Please, Pop, I'm begging you!"

"Don't beg me nothin', girlie, and don't call me Pop!" Vito snarled. "Whatta ya think you're tryin' to do, get a cat down out of a tree? You don't kick Vito Morelli outa noplace today—no, sir! I tell ya whatcha do, girlie. You go home and smell your nice clean house, and forget ya ever saw me! You was never a member of my family—never. Ya get me? Capish?"

The woman stood there glassy-eyed, with nothing to say. Then, she turned stiffly and started walking slowly away, with Harmon and MacAdoo supporting her.

"Hey, Josie!" Vito called to her sharply on the mike. "You still unnerstand Italian?"

"What do you mean?" the woman asked, turning back. "Of course I understand Italian!"

"Sure ya do!" Vito said, with a big warm grin. Then, leaning down close to the microphone, he shouted, *"Buon giorno,* Josefina! *Fongool!"* and he slapped his palm loudly to the inside of his right elbow, jerking his right fist rudely up in the air in one of the biggest, most joyous up-yours gestures ever pantomimed in any Italian neighborhood. Laughing uproariously, he turned heel and left the booth.

Oscar flipped the mike switch off as Louie turned and locked the door after Vito. The two men turned to face the crowd like two detached and silent Buddhas.

"How do you like this shit?" said one newsman to the other. "We could waste all afternoon here! Don't these stupid people realize there's news breaking all over town we should be covering?"

MacAdoo loaded Vito's shaken ex-daughter-in-law into a black-and-white. "Take this lady home," he ordered the cop at the wheel.

Just then, Officer Lopez came running across the street like a sprinter on a relay team, carrying Odessa's rolled up sketch as his baton. "Captain,

Captain!" he cried. "I got a picture here the little kid drew of one of the terrorists inside!"

"Let me see that!" MacAdoo said, unrolling the large sheet. The police department sketch artist could not have done better. Odessa's drawing was a remarkable likeness of Minnie, complete to the heart-shaped birthmark on her cheek, and smiling her warm chicken soup smile. MacAdoo looked at the bottom of the page and read the inscription aloud: "'Aunt Minnie, April Fools' Day, 1976, by Odessa H., six and-a-half years old.'"

"That's positive ID, right, Captain?"

"What the hell are you talking about, Lopez? Minnie who?" MacAdoo said sourly. "Besides, this has got to be a picture of one of the hostages. The criminals are all men. Doctor Keller reported five *men*."

"But the little girl said she saw this woman with a gun!"

"Who are you going to believe, Taco? Doctor Keller, or a six-year-old kid with a Crayola? Here—take this back to the kid's grandmother and have them taken home in a squad car. Then get your ass back over here on the double. I may need you—I don't know what for, but just in case."

Lopez rolled up the drawing and went dashing back across the boulevard, just as a black-and-white with siren screaming came speeding up Fairfax and careened around the corner on the wrong side of the street to the front of the bank.

"In here!" MacAdoo yelled from the sidewalk, motioning to the bank driveway. "Pull right in!" He ran alongside the police car as it pulled up to the drive-in window.

The crowd came alive immediately, the newspeople elbowing forward to better their positions.

Louie tapped angrily on the glass with his gun, yelling into the mike. "Back up! Back up that car! Nobody near the window!"

"Too far!" MacAdoo shouted at the cop behind the wheel. "Back it up, and kill your motor!"

Louie and Oscar watched the squad car move back out of their sight. Louie looked up at the convex mirror attached outside the window and trained on the driveway entrance. In it he saw the car stop well back from the window. Then he saw Harmon and Keller running in to converge on the car.

MacAdoo got in the front seat and Harmon got into the back, while Keller stood outside leaning on the rear door. Louie counted the silhouettes of six heads in the car. "They sent us some *delegation*," he observed. "You see, Stein? The system works. The people petition—and Uncle Sam shows up!"

Inside the car, introductions were just being completed.

"How do you do, gentlemen," said Ernest P. Whitehead, pulling at his tight shirt collar. "And this is my assistant, Calvin Overmyer." They actually shook hands all around.

282

"Is that M-c, Captain?" Whitehead asked, "or M-a-c?"

"M-a-c—Scottish," MacAdoo said. "The M-c McAdoos are all potato eaters—micks."

"I'll have to remember that," Whitehead said. Then, turning to his assistant, he asked, "Do you have all the names recorded properly, Calvin?"

"Yes, sir," said the pinch-nosed man at his side, not looking up from his clipboard.

"We're running out of time, men," Doctor Harmon said. "Have you been brought up to date on this situation, Mr. Whitehead?"

The stout man turned his head sharply to face Harmon, his sweaty double chin depositing a droplet on his lapel as it blumped to the right. He hesitated for a moment, trying to identify the chain of authority. Was the police captain in command here, or was it the doctor? Very important.

"I've only been told," he said carefully, "what Captain, uh . . ."

"Robeson," Overmyer prompted.

"Right, Robeson . . . what Captain Robeson could tell me in a very brief phone conversation before I was hustled over here. Something about this bank being taken over by a group of senior citizen terrorists? I mean—that's ridiculous! Just saying it out loud, it sounds incredible! Impossible to believe!"

"*Believe* it, Mr. Whitehead," Keller said. "I spent over forty-five minutes in there with them. They are five old men—all over sixty-five, senior citizens—and all of them are very angry."

Whitehead blinked his civil servant's blink, trying to sort it out. "Well, are they Social Security recipients? I mean—why have they demanded to see *me?*"

"Yes, they are," Keller said, "and you're their target. They are extremely disturbed—stretched to their psychological limits, I'd say—and *you* are the psycho-symbol of their desperation."

"I can't believe it!" Whitehead's blinking was increasing. "Our benefit recipients just don't behave like this. I mean—there are forms and procedures for handling any complaints they may have from time to time—built right into our system for them."

"Evidently," Harmon said, "the group of old men who are holding hostages in there don't feel they can get satisfaction from the system. They've been frustrated at the lower levels, and they're taking these violent means to bypass the counter help, to get to talk to you—in public, don't you see? Sure, we're all shocked out here, because we're used to urban terrorists being young radicals who use violence as a revolutionary tactic. Moral issues aside, it might be perfectly appropriate for a structured society to react to that kind of lawlessness with guns and gas—fight fire with fire, but—"

"Damn right it's appropriate!" MacAdoo muttered.

"But these are old people," Harmon continued, "people who could be our own parents, whose frustration has pushed them over the edge to this terrible act. Whether we like it or not, we're going to have to respond to this one in a special way—their way."

As Harmon spoke, Whitehead sat squirming and sweating and blinking and inserting, "Uh-huh, uh-huh, uh-huh," every time Harmon took a breath.

"But—but this is a local police matter!" Whitehead sputtered between blinks. "I shouldn't be involved in this! The federal government shouldn't be involved!"

"Mr. Whitehead," Harmon said, "you're already involved—right up to your title. These people didn't pick your name out of a hat, you know. Right or wrong, they consider you responsible in some way for their problems."

"I resent that, sir!" Whitehead said. "Now look here, I came here to put in an appearance, to cooperate with local law enforcement in this—this emergency! I broke away from an important departmental budget meeting to come here. But no one informed me that this was going to be a fullblown media event. There are television cameras out there! I mean—I don't have the authority to interview a bunch of criminals in front of the press—I don't care if they *are* recipients! I can't be a party to this. This is just terrorist blackmail! I would just be handing them the United States government as another hostage!"

"Join the club, Mr. Whitehead," MacAdoo said. "That's exactly the spot they've got the LAPD in."

"We're wasting time, men," Harmon reminded them as he checked his watch. "First of all, Mr. Whitehead, it's too late for you not to appear on television. See that camera over there, pointing this way? You're already on. You've been on—and identified—ever since you arrived!"

"Oh, my God!" Whitehead blurted, looking out past Keller at the hand-held minicam with the red light on.

"And in about six minutes," Harmon pressed on, "these old men are going to blow up this bank, if you're not out there talking to them!"

"*Talking* to them?" Whitehead asked, bug-eyed. "Talking about what? I mean—I'm not even prepared for the subject matter. Do you have a list of their grievances?"

"They wouldn't give them to me," Keller said pointedly. "They're saving them especially for you, Mr. Whitehead."

"He-ey! What the hell are we waiting for now?" yelled a reporter in the impatient crowd.

"Let's get this show on the road!" another hollered.

"I'd better tell the people in the bank you're coming out," said Keller, abruptly walking away from the car toward the barricade.

"Wait a minute!" Whitehead shouted after him.

"We don't have any more minutes," Harmon said, pinning Whitehead with his eyes. "Now I want you to listen to me very carefully. You are going to go out there, where Doctor Keller is standing right now, and talk to these men. There is no alternative, do you understand?"

"Uh-huh, uh-huh," Whitehead nodded.

"These men are desperate," Harmon continued, "but they are not afraid. At this moment, they are on a psychic 'high'—they are feeling that the success of their dangerous mission is just within their grasp, so the manner in which you talk to them is psychologically critical. You must speak to them calmly and reasonably, totally ignoring the fact of their threat to explode a bomb. And you must listen to their complaints patiently, making them feel that you see, and have sympathy for, the validity of their grievances. Remember, just *one* inciteful comment from you—and they could instantly be thrown into psycho-panic. Do you understand?"

"I don't know," Whitehead mumbled. "What can I say to them? I mean— I can't solve their problems standing out on a driveway in Los Angeles. These things are handled in Washington!"

"They don't have to know that," Harmon pointed out. "You just make them believe that you're going to do everything in your power to take care of every complaint they bring up, is that clear? Maybe we can get everybody out of this thing alive."

Keller came running back to the squad car. "He told me to tell you," he said to MacAdoo, "that he's giving you back your three-minute warning."

"The son of a bitch," MacAdoo muttered.

"This is it, Mr. Whitehead," Harmon said evenly. "Time to talk to these senior citizens or take the consequences."

Whitehead stared at every face in the car, his eyes shifting nervously from one to the other and finally to Overmyer, who returned his gaze as though he were looking at his squirming superior through a microscope.

"I have no choice, Calvin," Whitehead said. "I'm being forced into this confrontation. You can see that, can't you?"

His assistant didn't bat an eye, didn't speak.

"Open the door, Calvin," Whitehead said. "Bring your brief, and stand by."

The two men got out of the police car and walked hesitantly to the front of the barrier, turning to face the teller's window as the crowd murmured noisily in anticipation.

Louie watched Whitehead, standing uneasily, shifting his considerable weight from foot to foot, with Overmyer standing stiffly at his side. Louie noticed MacAdoo circling the crowd to join Stryker again.

Photographers snapped their fingers to get Whitehead to face them. Flashbulbs popped, camera motors whirred, and tense intimate voices reported into closely held microphones the eyewitness coverage of the big scene.

Whitehead turned front, peering at the teller's window, the flashbulb bursts still etched in his vision as he tried to make out the faces of the enemy behind the tinted glass.

Louie waited, making Whitehead wait, and making sure that the press corps had plenty of time to get their establishing shots setting up his news conference. The voice of the aged was about to be heard throughout the land of the free and the home of the brave, and maybe—at the end of this day—there would be new meaning to the twilight's last gleaming.

Louie tapped his gun on the window, hushing the crowd. Whitehead interpreted the signal as a cue for him to speak. He cleared his throat and started walking forward, "My name is Ernest P. Whitehead, and I am Western—"

"Back up, back up!" Louie suddenly barked into the microphone.

"Oh, I'm sorry," Whitehead said, backing up awkwardly. "I started to say, my name is Ernest P. —"

"Never mind," Louie said. "I know who you are. Who is the man with you?"

"I beg your pardon?" Whitehead asked, with a puzzled frown.

"The man standing there with you," Louie repeated. "Who is he?"

Whitehead snapped his head around to look at Overmyer. "I'm sorry, I didn't understand you there for a moment. That's my executive assistant, C. R. Overmyer."

"Tell him to go away."

"Beg pardon?"

"I am talking in plain English," Louie said. "I said, tell him to go away. I met, already, enough assistants in my life. I am not talking to assistants today!"

Whitehead turned to see Overmyer backing stiffly away. "But he has all my papers," Whitehead complained, "surveys and statistics—"

"We will not be talking about surveys and statistics today, sir. We will be talking about *people* today. People who've got, and people who've got nothing—that's what we'll be talking about."

The crowd stirred slightly as Whitehead gestured a scribbling motion to Overmyer, standing off to the side. He immediately assumed his clipboard stance.

"Before we start, sir," Whitehead said, "can you tell me your name?"

Louie put on a baffled look, his hand to his ear. "I didn't hear you. You will have to talk a little louder, we got this radio set turned up as loud as it'll go. . . ." How many times the people behind the Social Security counters had made Louie repeat his name . . . spell it over . . . repeat his age, his birthplace . . . spell it again . . . his marital status . . . swear again that he didn't know the whereabouts of his grown children . . . repeat, again and again . . . a thousand interrogations in triplicate, a thousand humiliations, times three. "What did you say, Mr. Whitehead? Can you speak a little more clearly, please?"

286

"I say," Whitehead repeated, louder and more distinctly, "I would like to know your name, for the record."

"Why certainly, of course!" Louie said obligingly, "I know your name—you oughta know my name, that's only fair. My name is . . . Number Five-Six-Two, dash One-Eight, dash Four-Nine-Two-Zero." Louie smiled his sardonic smile.

"No, no, please," Whitehead said, "I mean, seriously!"

"Oh, I mean seriously, too!" Louie said seriously. "Don't you remember? You took my name away from me on the day I became sixty-five, and left me only with a number. Go and look me up on your computer. I been a member of your miserable club for a long time. The computer will know me. Come to think of it, the computer is the only one in the government who knows me by my name. Now, I ask you—is that nice? To take a person's name away?"

One of the reporters whistled softly. Whitehead said nothing. He just stood there blinking, bewildered, trying to get a handle on his adversary's rhetoric, and wishing he were somewhere protected from this sort of harassment and abuse, somewhere safely camouflaged and covered up by his own kind—somewhere like Washington, D.C.

"Did you hear me, Mr. Whitehead?" Louie said. "I asked you a question. Do you think that's nice, to take a man's name and throw it away like garbage into a computer someplace? To take away his dignity, to humiliate him? Not because he failed you, or because he became useless—but only because he got to be sixty-five years old! Does that make sense to you?"

Whitehead was swaying under Louie's assault, his bureaucratic bulk swiveling left and right, his eyes shifting back and forth as though he were looking for an escape route. "Well, I don't, uh, I don't know exactly what you're trying to *prove*—I mean, what you're trying to say . . ."

Louie shook his head slowly, smiling a patronizing smile. "I'm not trying to *say*, Mr. Whitehead, Western Director of the Social Security—I'm trying to *ask!* We invited you here in front of these people, only to ask you questions—because we need to understand from your answers, why we hafta kill ourselves every day just to stay alive. You know what I mean?"

Whitehead felt dizzy. The man in the glass booth was orchestrating a terrible nightmare in which he, Ernest P. Whitehead, was the unwilling leading player, being publicly reviled for having committed unspeakable crimes against humanity.

"I asked you a question, Mr. Whitehead," Louie barked. "Do you know what I mean?"

"No . . . no, I'm sorry, I don't." Whitehead mumbled. "I mean—we all have Social Security numbers. We are all part of the Social Security system."

"Ah-hh!" said Louie, his eyebrows arching. "But do you know what it

287

means to be a number in the system when you are poor and over sixty-five—that's the question!"

"Yes, I . . . I think I do," Whitehead said, coming out of his daze to defend himself. "It's my job to know."

"And you know how to do your job, hah?"

"I certainly think I do! And evidently, so do my superiors. I am currently serving at my post for a second administration."

Louie stopped for a moment, judging the man's ego. "From Nixon to Ford, right? *You* think there's a *difference?*"

Several people laughed aloud; Whitehead remained silent. He was beginning to understand that most of Louie's questions would require no answer.

"Well, let us see, Mr. Western Director," Louie said. "Let us see how good you know your job." He turned to Oscar, who handed him a rectangular check-sized document covered with computer print. Louie slapped it up, face against the glass.

"Do you know what this is, sir?"

"Of course I do. But look here, I can't be expected to answer a lot of questions like this—not even knowing who is interrogating me. Who are you people? What political action group do you represent?"

"Political group?" Louie scowled. "Don't talk nonsense! What are you, blind? Can't you see we are just angry old people who are screaming in the darkness of the night for somebody to listen? My goodness, don't you recognize us? We are your tired, your poor, your huddled masses. And now we are your *old*, your *deserted*, your *betrayed* masses. You have forsaken us, sir. Isn't it a crime?"

Whitehead swallowed hard, trying to restart the flow of saliva, while the crowd stood stock-still and deathly quiet, like a graveyard full of tombstones.

"Isn't it, sir?" Louie repeated harshly.

"No, I . . . I don't know, I . . ."

"Well, if you don't know," Louie jumped in, "I'll tell you. We are not a political group and we are not crazy terrorists trying to destroy the world. We are just a bunch of old paupers at the end of the line, and at the end of our ropes. Just a few of the nineteen million old victims who are trying to exist on the dole in this great country. You call it Social Security, and Old Age Assistance, and the Great Society Welfare. These are all made-up words to make it sound like some kind of fancy retirement picnic. But the life we hafta live in order to survive, mister—is no picnic, believe me!"

Whitehead looked down at his shoes and gritted his teeth, realizing that the old man would not be finished talking until his bitter message was delivered in full.

"I'll tell you who we are. Some of us came across the ocean," Louie continued, picking up steam. "We came to see the streets paved with gold, to make a new life in a free country, a better life to pass on to our children.

288

We came by invitation, remember—Emma Lazarus and the lady with the lamp *invited* us—to come over to the great melting pot, to help cook up the American dream. We learned the language, and the laws, and the Constitution, and most of us became citizens. Some, their parents came over from the old country, and they were *born* into citizenship of this wonderful country. Imagine, they were lucky enough to be given the two greatest gifts on the very same day—life and liberty! Noplace else in the world—only in America—are such birthday gifts handed out!"

His passionate words spilled out in a torrent, pounding their primitive power home to the mesmerized crowd. He was JFK and Billy Graham. He was Dylan and Ghandi. He was Moses on the Mount. He was Louie Levine, the voice of the aged, and the people were really listening.

"When we were young, it was a new century, bright and promising in the new country that welcomed every man and every woman who came to dream the dream. And boy-oh-boy, what a dream—such a dream! Such excitement! Every day, a new invention! Think of it—just in my lifetime, and I'm only seventy-eight—the radio, the electric light bulb, the frigidaire, the automobile, the airplane, the polio shots and penicillin, the television box, and God knows what else! And all you had to do to own a piece of this wonderful dream, was to work hard with your shoulder to the wheel, mind your own business, and obey the law. So we worked hard for a lifetime, and we tried to raise decent families. We didn't become rich or famous. We were tickled to death to make a *living* for ourselves, each in our own way, trying not to hurt somebody next to you, because he was also one of the dreamers. So what is the bottom line? Now the century is not so new anymore . . . and we? We are old. You call us 'senior citizens' and 'geriatrics'—not with respect, but with the wish maybe we would just go away and die, and not bother you anymore. For some reason, you don't need us in your American dream anymore. Is that nice? Is that right?"

There were people in the crowd with tears in their eyes, clearing their throats. And Whitehead stood there, blinking and thinking about what awful publicity would result from this day.

"This is terrible, terrible," he said, shaking his head miserably.

"You are absolutely right, Mr. Whitehead," Louie agreed. "Isn't it terrible? So whatta ya gonna *do* about it?"

"No, no . . . I mean it's terrible trying to hear a recipient's complaints under these circumstances—"

"Don't you dare call me a recipient!" Louie shouted at him. "I am a *person*, not a recipient! We are all *people* in here—old people who spent a lifetime giving, not taking! And when we got old, you betrayed us, you left us to the wolves. And when we cry out, you don't listen to us—you humiliate us in triplicate at your counters, and then you bury our cries for help in your dark filing cabinets. That is the reason for these circumstances, that is the reason we broke the law! And today—*you will listen!*"

A sudden burst of applause came from the very rear of the crowd, and everyone turned to see a claque of a dozen or so old people, clapping and chattering and egging Louie on. MacAdoo pointed them out, a cop walked over to stand in their vicinity, and they quieted down.

"You said you knew what *this* was, hah?" Louie asked, displaying the oblong computer document once more.

"Yes, I do," said Whitehead. "It is a monthly Medicare Identification card, issued to the Social Security beneficiary to provide medical services."

"Exactly. Very good. So now, I'm a beneficiary!" Louie turned the card over. "Let me read it to you: 'Present this card to your doctor or other person giving Medicare service each time you see him. He will copy certain information from it, remove a label from it, and return it to you. Unless he obtains a label for each service, he cannot bill Medicare. Please help him by having your card readily available. Thank you.' It also says the same thing here in Spanish for the Latino pauper. You know what *happens* to these, Mr. Whitehead?"

Whitehead had been punctuating Louie's reading with an unconscious series of audible "uh-huh, uh-huh's," and he was still doing it, after Louie's query.

"Mr. Whitehead?"

"What? Certainly I know what happens to them," the big man said. "Each month, millions of elderly citizens on Social Security all over our country use the labels on that card to obtain free medical services. Doctors, pharmacists, and hospitals simply attach these labels to the proper report forms, sending them in to be reimbursed by the government for the services they have rendered. It's a very efficient system."

"So you think you know your job, hah? Well, for your information, Mr. Western Director, this little card is also a very efficient license to steal! You know what most of my friends and I hafta do with this little card every month?"

Louie paused for effect, while Whitehead and the crowd waited for him to answer his own teasing question.

"A few years ago," he continued after a moment, "somebody asked a famous bank robber in the penitentiary why it was that he robbed banks. The holdup man looked at the somebody like he was crazy. 'Simple,' said the bank robber. 'Because *that's* where the money's at!'"

Louie paused again for a second, while everyone waited for the connection.

"Well, *this*," said Louie, waving the card seductively, "is where the money's at! You know what I mean?"

Whitehead's puzzled expression was just what Louie had expected.

"You don't know what I mean, do you?" Louie needled. "So I'll tell you. These labels are good for just one month—you send us a new card every month, right?"

"Ye-es?" Whitehead said, trying to follow.

"So, in the month of April, if I get a liver attack from the macaroni and cheese in the cafeteria, or if a coupla young hoodlums beat me up on the street at night for the few measly pennies in my pocket—these labels are my medical insurance for the month, right?"

"That's correct."

"No, Mr. Whitehead—not correct! You know why?"

"No, sir, I don't!"

"Because on the day we get this card, if we are feeling okay—only the same old aches and pains—we *sell* this card to a certain man on the street for ten dollars."

"Why, for goodness sakes?" Whitehead asked, shocked.

"Why? Because ten dollars is the going price, that's why."

"No, I mean—how in the world could you give up your medical protection for the month, that way? Why would you take that sort of chance with your health for ten dollars?"

"Simple," Louie said. "Because we know at the beginning of the month, when we get the measly check you call our Social Security, that we will not have enough to eat at the *end* of the month. And with this extra ten dollars, maybe we wouldn't hafta go in to steal the small cans off the shelf in the supermarkets—the sardines, and the anchovies, and the cat food. And maybe we wouldn't hafta sneak behind the markets to dig in the big trash cans to find a piece of moldy cheese they throw away, that might still be okay in the middle, or a heada lettuce—"

"Oh, my God, my God!" a woman cried out, putting her hands up to her mouth to stifle her emotions. The TV cameras zoomed in to get their shot as her companion quickly put his arm around her shoulder and led her away.

"Listen, I myself am very lucky," Louie said brightly, breaking the tension. "I haven't been sick or needed a doctor, knock wood, in almost two years."

"But—but this man on the street—he can't do anything with your medical card. It's issued in *your name!* It's non-interchangeable!"

Louie stared out at Whitehead as though he had just announced that a pig was a vegetable. "You know what you are, mister?" Louie nodded sadly. "You are a bigger fool than I thought you would be—and I can only hope that *you* are interchangeable!"

Whitehead flinched at the insult, as several people laughed out loud.

"Whatta ya talking, noninterchangeable?" Louie mocked him. "You think the man cares *who* the card was issued to? He only cares how much money he will get from the doctor for my card, that's all! You go ask your computer under my number, and you will find a coupla fancy doctors, and a few pharmacists—maybe even a hospital—who got paid by Uncle Sam in the last two years for treating number Five-Six-Two, One-Eight, Four-Nine-Two-Zero! They prob'ly collected plenty for taking out my gall bladder maybe, which is still right here and has plenty of gall! Or my appendix nobody's ever even seen! Or for selling me a dozen bottles of insulin for my diabetes I ain't got!"

The people in the crowd were buzzing. Even policemen were shaking their heads.

"And do you really think," Louie continued, "that these labels go only for medical services? Did you ever watch the dope addicts line up early in the morning to buy the doctors' prescriptions for the uppers and the downers, the pills that the pharmacist is just waiting to count out? The addict doesn't hafta have a disease—all he hasta have is the right price in cash, and one of *these labels,* Mister! You think he cares whose name the label is made out to?"

Whitehead felt his lunch starting to repeat on him, and he popped a big white tablet into his mouth.

"So, Mr. Whitehead?" Louie asked solicitously, "Do you think you are learning anything new about your job here today, it shouldn't be a total loss?"

"Just a moment, now," Whitehead said, somehow swallowing the antacid pill and holding a hand up for his turn. "We are perfectly aware that Social Security and its satellite systems are not absolutely foolproof. They are extremely complex systems designed to cope with extremely complex social problems. And we know all too well that every time a government-administered plan is developed and put into place to benefit our ever-changing society, there will be unscrupulous individuals who will invariably invent clever schemes to perpetrate frauds against such worthy social progress. But let me assure you that there are safeguards built into these systems to protect the taxpayer against such criminal frauds."

"Izzat so?" Louie said.

"Yes, sir!" Whitehead said. "These systems are being monitored and investigated for fraudulent billing practices on a continuing basis by a highly experienced staff whose only responsibility is to track down these criminal activities. And when evidence of such wrongdoing is uncovered, it is immediately turned over to the Justice Department for prosecution."

"Just like the evidence on the Watergate bunch, hah?" Louie asked, as even the newspeople laughed and Whitehead shook his head helplessly.

"So let's take a look at what you investigate—and what you don't." Louie said, holding up a small white plastic object which he waved at Whitehead by its short wire stem. "You see this? You know what this is?"

Whitehead peered at the object for a moment. "No, I can't say that I do."

"This, my good man, is a call button," Louie explained. "It is stolen property from the Happytime Retirement Home on Olympic Boulevard, about a mile from where you are standing. You wanna know how I got it? About three years ago, I was a member of one of your citizens' committees to look into some of the problems of the aged. You know the groups I'm talking about: 'We are getting too many complaints from these old people, so let them form a committee, we'll take them around, we'll show them

292

what we are doing to look out for their interests, we'll let them write up reports, they'll keep themselves busy, then they'll feel like their complaints are being investigated.' You know the routine, don'tcha? But when you take a tourist around town, you don't take him to see the *slums,* you take him to Park Avenue, to Beverly Hills, you know what I mean? So we were taken to only the right places, at the right times, and everybody who was to be investigated was ready for us, like a rehearsed show. But not me—no, sir! As soon as I caught wise to the put-up job, I took my committee credentials and I forced my way in alone—a committee of one—into places where nobody expected anybody to come! You wanna know what I saw? You wanna hear *my* report?"

Whitehead clearly did not wish to hear Louie's report, but he knew damned well that his painful trial was not over here and that he was about to hear Louie's report whether he liked it or not.

And so did the media know, as cameras zoomed in and microphones were poked forward as far as arms could extend them.

"My report was simple, and sickening, my friends," Louie said. "I saw old people—sick, helpless old people—in these places they call nursing homes, these stinking morgues where the government and their own grown children go partners to put them in there to die in misery. I saw the old animals rotting from terminal diseases lying in their own filth in beds that had not been changed for days and days . . . crying, like little babies in dirty diapers. I saw the pussy bedsores of neglect, festering on the bodies of people who *used to be* people. With my own eyes, I saw the slop some of these government-licensed rest home operators feed the poor victims who come there to die. And to each one of them, Mr. Whitehead, you mail such a medical card every month. And each one of them, holds such a call button in his or her hand."

He was clicking the call button against the window in a deadly tempo.

"You thought maybe I forgot about this, hah, Mr. Whitehead? Don't worry, I didn't forget. For three years I have carried it with me in my pocket wherever I go—and when I go for the last time it will go with me. Maybe I'll buzz it where I'm going, somebody will *hear* me. I pulled this button loose from the fingers of Mrs. Alice Nickerson, just before the county undertaker came to pick up her body. Look her up on your computer—I'll betcha a nickel some doctor got paid for a coupla blood tests or an X-ray, after she died, even. She was a nice old lady, Mrs. Nickerson. I knew her. She could play checkers as good as any man, and she choked to death on her own blood in the middle of the night at the Happytime Nursing Home. The man in the bed across the hall told me she was ringing this bell for more than four hours during that night, and nobody came to her bed."

Whitehead was looking down at the ground, unable to face Louie anymore.

"My question is, Mr. Whitehead, did you investigate the pitiful death of

293

Mrs. Alice Nickerson, and does your Justice Department know about the Happytime Nursing Home?"

"I can't be sure . . . I . . . the Health, Education, and Welfare Department has thousands of investigations in progress at all times—"

"You are missing the point, sir! I am not talking about *one* old lady, *one* rotten nursing home! And don't give me the business about some other department of the government who is responsible! You will not send me to another office today to stand on another line to fill out another form. The HEW is not here today—you are here today! And you will answer our questions today so everybody can hear! So answer me, Mr. Whitehead. Why must this buzzer be a cry in the wilderness? Why? What are we—a primitive tribe, who take our old people out to the middle of a lonely frozen lake to freeze to death on a certain day, because somebody thinks they are useless? What is happening to us? And whatever happened to 'Honor thy Father and thy Mother'?"

Louie looked out at the man standing there shaken, drained, and speechless, his eyes empty.

Oscar saw the sad faces of the crowd, their shadowy eyes now glazed with a shameful pain. "It is enough," he said to Louie. "Give him the letter."

Louie put his hand quickly over the microphone. "I am not finished!"

"You are finished, I say," Oscar said, and with that, he pressed a large green button activating the exchange drawer, which slid outward with a startling *whoosh-click*.

Two cops in front reached for their holsters. "Hold your places!" MacAdoo barked through his bullhorn.

Louie grabbed Oscar's forearm roughly, twisting the little man's arm. "Take your hand off, Oscar! I'm warning you . . ."

"The letter," Oscar whispered. "It is time for the letter!"

The two old men, locked in a desperate struggle for control of the button, straining with all their strength, stared at each other without a change of expression lest the enemy should become aware of their dangerous disagreement. Then Oscar's wrist started to give, to turn under Louie's twisting. Louie looked down quickly to see the green button clear, then he saw the tattooed number on the inside of Oscar's wrist. D for Dachau—One-Zero-Three-One.

Louie's fingers sprung open, releasing Oscar's wrist. "Oscar," he said, "you are a pain in the ass, the way you are always right—you know that?"

Oscar smiled and pulled his shirt sleeve down with a modest shrug. It was the first time he had ever seen Louie squinting and grinning at the same time. He had not thought it was possible.

"All right, ladies and gentlemen," Louie called, "can I have your attention again, please? It's only a drawer, nothing bad will happen. I'm sorry if it scared you—it scared me, too."

There was a titter of nervous laughter from the crowd.

294

"We would like to ask you some questions, sir!" Joy Newsome cried out, jumping up and down on tiptoe as other reporters also started to shout at the booth.

"No, no!" Louie rapped his gun against the glass. "No questions. You'll wait a moment, you'll be able to ask Mr. Whitehead all the questions you want."

Whitehead shot a terrified glance at the crowd behind him.

"Mr. Whitehead," Louie said, "I know you are a very busy man—you got places to go and important things to do—so I wanna finish with you, okay?"

"Yes, sir," Whitehead said.

Louie wiggled a forefinger. "I want you to come to the window, slow, and—no, no! No policemen!" The two cops in front who had started to step forward with Whitehead stopped moving.

The stout man was now standing at the window, the open drawer slightly higher than his bulging waist, looking in at the two old men smiling out at him.

"You will see in the drawer," Louie pointed out, "a stack of papers. They are copies of a monthly newspaper we publish for ourselves. We call it *The Voice of the Aged,* and this is our expanded April issue, published especially for today, in your honor. You will notice the headline says ERNEST P. WHITEHEAD GRANTS INTERVIEW, and underneath, it says Pledges Personal Report to President." Whitehead stared dumbly down into the drawer.

"Holy Jee-zus H. Christ!" a voice boomed out from the rear of the crowd. "If it ain't Louie Levine! You're doin' great, Levine! Give 'em hell!"

"Shut up, you big dummy!" It was Ida Katz, banging her purse on Henry Hoover's head. "Get outa here, stupid, before the police make you a witness!"

Hoover pulled his head in like a turtle, and quickly turned away to take Ida's advice. But it was too late. Two cops caught up with him as soon as he reached the sidewalk and started giving him the third degree.

Louie saw it all, recognizing Hoover at once. *"Nu?"* he said to Oscar. "Once a schmuck, always a schmuck!"

Louie knocked on the microphone again with his gun. "Now I'll tell you what I want you to do," he said to Whitehead. "First, I want you to pick up the top copy off the pile. The rest are for the members of the press, when I'm finished with you. . . . Go ahead, take one, it won't bite you."

Whitehead carefully did as he was told, making sure not to take two.

"You got there in your hand," Louie noted, "a very interesting social document. The mimeograph is not so hot, but the content of these twelve pages, my good man, is unique in all the world!"

Whitehead couldn't take his eyes off the headline.

"The front page story, as you see, is mostly about you," Louie pointed out, "and how you were nice enough to take time out from your busy schedule to come and talk to us today. Later, when you get a chance to read it, you will really be amazed how accurate a story can be, written two weeks before the event took place! Maybe you would call that 'managing the news'—but it's a helluva lot better than a *lie* that is published *after* the event, I can tell you!"

Whitehead made a sour face at the front page.

"Oh, yes," Louie said, noting his expression, "we tell them who you are, Mr. Western Director, and what you have and haven't done in your job. By the way, if you find a lie there about yourself and can prove it, we will be only too glad to print a retraction for you."

Whitehead looked quickly away from the front page.

"The next ten pages," Louie said, "contain a list of one hundred questions—ten to the page, triple-spaced—contributed to *The Voice of the Aged* by the real experts, the Phi Beta Kappas, the graduate students in the field of gerontology. You know who I mean?"

Whitehead knew who he meant. Everyone knew.

"That's right. The questions come from the sick and the lame and the deaf and the blind—from the humiliated and deserted old people of this country who are saying, 'Listen to us—look at us.' My God, don't you see? You will be looking at yourself."

A murmur stirred the crowd as Whitehead shuffled his feet restlessly.

"And when you can answer *these* questions," Louie said, "these questions from the trash heap, from the exiled elders of your tribe, my friend—then you will know your job."

Oscar clapped his hand impatiently over the microphone. "Come on, already, with the letter, Levine!"

"Okay, okay," Louie snapped, "take your hand away. No, no, Mr. Whitehead, don't roll the paper up. I am going to ask you to read something out loud to the ladies and gentlemen, from the last page!"

"Read. . . ?" Whitehead asked.

"Yes, read," Louie repeated. "You will have the honor of reciting the most important page of *The Voice of the Aged*—our letter to the President of the United States!"

Whitehead took an astonished step backward.

"*After* you take the oath, of course," Louie shouted into the microphone, topping the noise of the crowd.

"Oath?"

"Of course, isn't it required?" Louie asked. "Don't you call *me* into the Social Security office every year on my birthday with my citizenship papers, and make me swear on the Bible that I have made arrangements for my own burial? And that I haven't inherited a halfa million dollars from my grandmother, and that I haven't collected on a sweepstakes ticket, and that I am still living in poverty at the same stinking address, and not being kept by a beautiful young heiress? Don't you make me swear to the 'pauper's

296

oath,' so the computer will send me money on which to go hungry for another year? So turn around, and raise your right hand, and repeat after me!"

"See here," Whitehead objected, "you have no right to force me—"

"You will turn around!" Oscar shouted, waving his Lugar in a circle. "Und you will raise your hand up high! Und you will repeat after him, whatever he says—now!"

Whitehead was turning left and right, longing for a way out.

Then, he saw Harmon and Keller, both nodding at him pointedly.

With a resigned sigh, Whitehead raised his right hand and forced himself to revolve in a slow motion about-face as the cameras zoomed in.

"I swear to my God," Louie intoned.

"I swear to my God," Whitehead parroted.

"That I will personally deliver . . ."

"That I will personally deliver . . ."

"Into the hand of the President of the United States . . ."

Whitehead's eyes widened with a queer pleading look at Louie, who repeated sternly, "*Into the hand* of the President of the United States . . ."

Whitehead turned back to the crowd in final defeat. "Into the hand of the President of the United States . . ."

"The following letter, which I am about to read . . ."

"The following letter, which I am about to read . . ."

"Addressed to him respectfully, by *The Voice of the Aged* . . ."

"Addressed to him—" Whitehead stopped.

"*Respectfully!*" Louie said again.

"Respectfully . . ." Whitehead almost choked on the word, "by *The Voice of the Aged* . . ."

"Who, until now, have had *no voice*," Louie finished.

"Who, until now, have had no voice." Whitehead gratefully dropped his hand to his side and turned back to face Louie once more.

"Good," Louie said, "you done good. Now turn around again and read the letter. It's on the back, inside the black border."

"I think it's only fair to warn you," Whitehead said, "that my pledge to deliver this letter is subject to my being granted an audience with the President."

"That's good enough for me," Louie said graciously. "Now, turn around and read."

Whitehead turned again to the crowd and started to read in a flat, exhausted voice: "Our Dear Mr. President, You don't know who we are, of course, and we don't know you either, only from seeing you on the news on television. But Mr. President, we got a problem—which means you got a problem. And the time is running out for us. We are almost twenty million old—"

All of a sudden, there was a terrible commotion at the inside door of the booth. Angry shouting voices and a loud pounding against the other side of the door cut Whitehead off in midsentence as Louie and Oscar jumped to their feet.

"You crazy? Stay outa there!" they heard Vito holler.

"He'll kill you, Stosh!" Abe screamed.

"*Nobody* kill Vlasic!" Stosh roared as he fought them off. "Goddamn! Get outa my way!"

Louie lunged for the doorknob, and there was a thundering crash and a tearing of wood, as Stosh and the battered-off door came smashing into the booth on top of Louie, knocking him to the floor and tossing Oscar to one side like a twig. At the same instant, a gunshot exploded inside the booth.

People scattered in all directions as a shot was fired from the driveway, and another, followed by the sound of shattering glass. Cops with guns drawn were running and ducking for cover; two members of the SWAT team with their M-16s were flat against the wall of the bank, flanking the teller's booth, which now appeared to be vacant. Reporters and cameramen flattened themselves face down on the pavement as Whitehead hit the ground, rolling himself like a huge beachball toward the booth and under the still-extended teller's exchange drawer, *The Voice of the Aged* still hanging over his head, while everywhere people were running and screaming hysterically as several more shots rang out.

Suddenly Stosh stood straight up in the booth, the front of his guard's uniform covered with blood. "I take woman now!" he hollered down at Louie, on the floor. "You hear me?"

"No! No, Stosh!" Louie cried out. "Please . . ."

MacAdoo, crouching behind a post, drew a perfect bead through a sizeable hole that had been shot out of the booth window, aiming at the wet red bullseye on Stosh's shirt.

"Hey, you!" Stosh yelled into the microphone, pointing right out at MacAdoo. "I bring woman out now! You come around front, bring doctor!"

MacAdoo, astonished by the command, released his trigger finger and pointed his weapon to the ground, gaping at the bloody giant in the booth.

"Move, goddamn!" Stosh jerked his thumb toward the front of the bank, then barged out of the booth. MacAdoo, Keller, and Harmon raced toward the front of the bank, followed by cops, members of SWAT, and press people, all elbowing each other around the corner of the building to the new action site.

Joy Newsome came running low from behind a post toward the teller's booth, just as Whitehead, hugging the wall, started crawling toward the front sidewalk on his hands and knees. Ducking under the teller's window, Newsome reached quickly into the drawer, snatched a fistful of Louie's newsletters, slammed the drawer back into the booth, and ran toward the front of the bank with her big scoop.

Whitehead and Newsome reached the corner of the building at the same instant, she running at breakneck speed, he crawling into a right turn, his feet sticking out perfectly for disaster. KFWB's star female newscaster tripped over Social Security long before her time, scattering her copies of *The Voice* all over the sidewalk, dropping her tape recorder into the gutter, the cassette flipping out into the dirty water, and herself sprawling in a heap at the curb.

Oscar staggered to his feet in the teller's booth, shaking his head and examining himself for blood and the bullet hole he was certain he would find. He cackled his dry little laugh as he noticed the small perforated brass speaker-case of his hearing aid, smashed in, and more useless than ever, dangling out of his shirt. The glass of the booth and the little brass box had absorbed the impact of a police bullet, and Oscar Stein's life had been miraculously saved by the appliance for an infirmity he would never have.

"Levine," he called, looking around, "where are you?"

"Here, Oscar," Louie moaned. "Under the door."

"You are all right?"

"No, Oscar. I am shot . . ."

"*Ach, mein Gott, mein Gott!*" Oscar grunted, as he struggled with the heavy door.

Out front, SWAT had already smashed in both glass front doors and crow-barred the door lock apart. Only the heavy chain remained to be cut through, and a SWAT cop was running to the personnel carrier to get a pair of giant bolt cutters for the job.

"Everybody back!" MacAdoo shouted into his bullhorn. "No news people on the sidewalk! Back off into the street, and *keep down!* Get behind those cars!"

Everywhere, cameras and cops pointing guns were hanging over the fenders and hoods of automobiles. One reporter was even underneath a car parked at the curb, poking his microphone out as far as he could.

The view they were all covering at the moment, into the interior of the bank, was a strange one indeed. Nothing—no sound, no sign of a person—just empty, as though the bank had simply been closed for the night, and ready for the janitors. Only the blasting box, a lone sentinel standing in the center of the safety deposit window at the rear counter, its wooden safety block removed, gave any evidence of an unusual situation at Citizens' Bank, as the big wall clock clicked to four o'clock, straight up.

"Hold, and stand ready," Stryker radioed his squad leaders on the rooftops and in the alley behind the bank. He looked straight up above his head to see four of his sharpshooters, leaning over the bank roof, their M-16s aimed in convergence directly over the front door.

Agnello came tearing around the corner, carrying the big bolt cutters for the chain. He ducked quickly through the broken glass door, and pulled the long handles apart for the cut—then he slammed the handles together and ducked back out through the opening, flattening himself against the wall with Stryker.

"Did you get it, Agnello?" Stryker asked.

"No, sir! Somebody's waving a white sweater out of a door in there."

"I don't care what somebody's doing with a sweater, damn it! Get back in there and cut that chain!"

Everyone saw the white sweater then, sticking out of the door of the conference room at the end of a chart pointer, waving slowly in surrender as Agnello ducked back inside. He snapped Stosh's chain with one easy cut, pulling it off the door handles and onto the floor, like a clanking dead snake.

"Pull the doors open, and out of the way, Agnello!" Stryker commanded.

Agnello slid the cutters out onto the sidewalk, yanked the doors open, kicked the chain away, and scooted out of the bank.

MacAdoo, crouched behind an open squad car door, watched the white sweater waving, through the sights of his revolver, which he now held extended tightly in both hands. For the first time since mid-morning, when he had first arrived on the scene, he was perspiring again. It was always that way with him. It was never fear or embarrassment—it was always anticipation that made MacAdoo sweat.

The sweater continued to wave, and still MacAdoo waited and watched, tightening the muscles of his jaw in tempo with the hypnotic waving of the sweater.

"Nobody is going to walk out to surrender," said an insinuating voice behind him, "until they're sure you've seen their flag and responded, Captain."

MacAdoo turned back to see Keller and Harmon, both standing behind the open rear door of the squad car.

"Your bullhorn is on the front seat, Captain," Harmon said.

"I know where my bullhorn is, Doctors," MacAdoo said. He turned his attention back to the sweater.

"Be a good idea now for you to use it," Keller said.

"Is that an order, Doctor?" MacAdoo asked over his shoulder.

"Not *my* order, Captain," Keller said. "I'm not your superior officer."

The sweater blurred in MacAdoo's vision as he remembered that Keller had been in the squad car at the time Robeson had radioed his orders from the Chief.

"Son of a black bitch!" MacAdoo muttered under his breath. Then, he holstered his revolver and grabbed the bullhorn. "Attention! You people, inside the bank! Attention! This is Captain MacAdoo, of the Los Angeles Police Department! I want you to slide your weapons out on the floor, and walk out slowly with your hands clasped behind your heads!"

The white sweater stopped waving. The pointer tilted downward, dropping the sweater onto the floor. Then the pointer fell to the floor with a clatter.

300

Again, the big room was empty and silent.

"Attention, inside!" MacAdoo barked into his bullhorn. "I'm going to repeat that order! Slide your weapons out, and walk out *now*, with your hands behind your heads! Police personnel, stand by! Fire only on command! Repeat! Fire only on command!"

Stryker radioed the order to his SWAT team as everyone waited for something to happen.

Something did. A gun came spinning out across the polished floor, sliding the entire width of the big room and striking the base of the long teller's counter, firing itself off on impact, blasting a hole in the counter wall, the recoil propelling it in a skidding tangent all the way to the center of the front door, where it finally blumped to a stop against the aluminum threshold.

Then, everything seemed to happen at the same time.

"Wait, wait, Stosh!" a voice hollered from inside, as people outside looked up from their various hiding positions.

"No, goddamn! We go out now!" Stosh roared.

MacAdoo looked up to see Vito, walking tentatively into the main room, where he stopped and peered out the front door, trying to get the lay of the land outside. Vito was unarmed, his gun lying at the front door.

MacAdoo put the bullhorn down on the front seat of the squad car and slowly drew his gun again.

Just then, Abe was pushed backward half out of the conference room as he struggled against Stosh with all his might. "No, Stosh! Wait one minute more! Vito has to fix the box! Quick, Vito!"

"No wait no more!" Stosh bellowed, as if in pain. "Woman is die, goddamn!" And with that, he barged past Abe and out into the main room, carrying Betty Lundy in his massive arms.

Betty was moaning and praying to God and bleeding through her yellow polka-dot dress, all over Stosh's shoes and the floor.

"Stop, Stosh, stop!" Minnie screamed as she barreled into the main room, waving a gun in each hand, high above her head, just as Vito made his move to the blasting box.

MacAdoo jerked his gun up, poking it through the car window at the same instant that Stosh stopped in his tracks at Minnie's command.

"MacAdoo, don't shoot!" Keller cried out from behind him. "He's just going to disarm the box!"

Stosh staggered forward a few steps with the bleeding woman and stopped again, wavering as though he were dizzy and struggling for balance.

Then, as Vito pushed the wooden safety block snugly under the plunger handle, Stosh raised his head painfully toward the ceiling. "Doctor, Docto-rr!" he hollered at the top of his lungs, "get Doc-to-rr, for God's sake! Woman is die!"

301

Keller reached over the front seat of the squad car and grabbed the bullhorn. "Paramedic! Paramedic!" he screamed into the horn at the ambulance across the street. "Stretcher and oxygen! On the double!"

MacAdoo was frozen at his position, his gun still aimed into the bank, as Harmon stepped around his door, slowly reached over MacAdoo's shoulder, and carefully relieved him of the gun.

Stosh lurched painfully forward again, stumbling through the doors and gulping for breath, just as the two paramedics lifted their rolling stretcher up onto the sidewalk.

"Take woman!" Stosh gasped, exhausted. "Take! Goddamn, I no can carry more—"

"Grab her!" Keller screamed as Stosh started to topple under Betty Lundy's weight.

One of the paramedics leaped forward and slipped his arms deftly under her body, taking her from Stosh's arms just as the giant groaned in agonizing pain, clutched his hands to his bloody shirt, and fell forward.

In that instant, there was a blank in time. The Fairfax forest was strangely hushed as the huge tree fell to earth. Stanislaus Vlasic lay dead on the sidewalk in front of Citizens' Bank.

Minnie screamed and ran to him, dropping the two guns to the sidewalk and kneeling at his side as the paramedics wheeled Betty Lundy away. "*Gottenyu, Gottenyu.*" Minnie wailed, rocking back and forth. "Stoshele, Stoshele . . . God, forgive us!"

Abe was behind her, his trembling hands on her shoulders, and Vito was on the other side, on one knee, crossing himself in prayer, ". . . Spiritus Sanctus . . . son of a bitch."

"Oh, my God, Abe!" Minnie raised her tearstained face. "He was the baby—the baby of the whole bunch, you know it?"

Abe nodded slowly, in a daze, as the cops closed in, surrounding the four criminals.

"Where are the other two?" MacAdoo asked Vito. "The two men in the teller's booth?"

Vito shrugged, looking back into the bank. Then they all saw Louie come out from behind the counter, his left shirt sleeve soaked with blood, his right arm around Oscar's shoulder, leaning heavily on the little man as they both limped toward the front door.

"Stosh is dead!" Minnie cried out as soon as she saw them. "God will never forgive us—we killed Stosh!"

MacAdoo stepped into the bank to intercept the two ringleaders. "Where are your weapons?" he demanded.

"In the drawer of the booth," Oscar said. "Und here, take this also, please." He unhooked the hand grenade from his belt and handed it to the startled MacAdoo.

"Is this *live?*" MacAdoo asked him.

302

"Oh, yes," Oscar said. "It is only we who are dead."

"You're damn lucky you're *not* dead, Mister!" MacAdoo snapped. "Lopez! Where's Lopez!"

"Right here, Captain!" said Lopez, at his shoulder.

"Here, stow this," MacAdoo said, handing him the grenade. "And round up some handcuffs for these people."

"Handcuffs, Captain?" Lopez asked.

"You heard me. Move!"

Lopez ran to carry out his captain's order.

"All right, keep moving! Outside!" MacAdoo herded Louie and Vito toward the front door.

The two old men hobbled out to the sidewalk, trailing blood, to look down at the bloody body of the gentle giant from Cracow.

"Where are the hostages?" MacAdoo asked Vito.

"Conference room," Vito answered dully, jerking his head.

MacAdoo, Stryker, and two more cops ran back toward the conference room as Louie began to cry.

"Tsk-tsk-tsk-tsk," Oscar said, shaking his head. "So . . . good-bye, Polack . . . und good luck."

"Stupid big lummox!" Louie suddenly sobbed angrily. "Stubborn clumsy blockhead!"

"*Shhhh,* Levine! Und don't you yell at him—you make him feel bad!"

"I only wish to God the big dumbbell could hear me!" Louie cried out bitterly, then he broke into an uncontrollable exhausted weeping, his body racking with anguish as his friends gathered close around him and a big black police van backed to the curb. Lopez jumped out with a fistful of handcuffs.

The Benefit was over.

# 20

# AFTERMATH AND THE DEFENDER

The hostages were cut loose from the cable in the conference room, and those who required it were treated for wrist abrasions by the paramedics at the scene. Then, one by one, their statements were taken, and they were released.

The suspects were handcuffed behind their backs, read their rights, and transported by police van to Wilshire Division station, where they were fingerprinted and booked on a score of felony counts including murder, kidnapping, bank robbery, and illegal possession and use of firearms and explosives. Minnie was taken to the Sybil Brand Institute for Women; the four male felons to the Los Angeles County Jail. They were all held without bail, pending arraignment.

Louie had a slug removed from his left arm near the shoulder and was installed in a cell in the prison hospital section. The spent slug was stapled into a small manila envelope and sent down to ballistics for study, along with all the gang's guns, Oscar's pineapple, the Molotov cocktails, the thermite and dynamite, and Minnie's antique lamp base with the funny handle.

Police tow trucks promptly removed all the disabled vehicles from the embattled intersection. The street maintenance department dispatched a sweeper truck, which quickly swept up the debris, including all the guttered special issues of *The Voice of the Aged*—except one. Big Joe and his gas company crew set up overnight barriers and flasher lights around their open trench on time-and-a-half, and traffic was restored at the intersection of Fairfax and Beverly within forty minutes of the terrorist gang's surrender and their arrest by senior field commander Captain Michael MacAdoo. The citizens of Los Angeles could walk the streets again without fear.

Stosh's body lay in state on the sidewalk, with Gonzalo's white deli apron

304

covering his top half, for well over an hour before the meat wagon arrived to cart him to the county morgue, where Dr. Noguchi would perform the autopsy required by law in such homicide cases.

Patrick Xavier Lundy was born prematurely into a troubled world in the fire department's paramedic wagon parked in the emergency driveway of St. John's Hospital. Mother and child quickly recovered from the change in schedule for their blessed event, thanks to the Father, the Son, the Holy Ghost, and Stanislaus Vlasic.

The investigators from the district attorney's office went through the bank with a fine-toothed comb for most of the night, lifting fingerprints and seizing all the evidence, including the Morelli Detention System, the little old keymaker's hand-cranked machine, a raincoat hardware store full of tools, the Guardian Security Company's coverall uniforms, five Paul Muni wigs, a portfolio of primitive art works taped to the walls of Wilson's office— and the remainder of the entire printing of the April Fool's Day issue of *The Voice of the Aged* from the drawer in the drive-in teller's booth.

The mimeographed newsletters were stapled into a large manila envelope marked Evidence (Political).

The time of the arrest was too late on Thursday evening to arrange for the arraignment on the Superior Court's calendar for Friday, which meant the county would be obliged to house, clothe, and feed the five terrorists over the long weekend, at a cost of ninety dollars per head.

After consultation with each of the defendants on Friday, the young public defender assigned to the Superior Court for the month of April determined that, in order to avoid a conflict of interest—considering the differing nature of each defendant's participation in the commission of the crime—the canon of legal ethics dictated his defending only one of the individuals charged, whereupon he chose Minnie. Aside from his own considerations, the eager young man was informed in no uncertain terms by defendant and gangleader Levine that legal representation assigned by the court was absolutely *not* acceptable to him, and that he, Levine, planned to represent the legal interests of *all* the defendants before the bar, *period*.

"Let's face it," Louie explained to the young man. "How can five old people with one foot in the grave and the other on a banana peel be defended in a court of law by a snot-nose? Nothing personal, you understand."

Nobody knows to this day how it happened, or if anyone called him about the case, but early Sunday morning, an angry lawyer showed up, asking to interview Louie in his prison hospital bed—not just any lawyer, but Solomon A. Zorin himself, lawyer of lawyers. The venerable little immigrant lawyer had argued countless constitutional cases before the United States Supreme Court—and won most of them, too. Though he had retired from active practice several years ago at the age of seventy-two, he was still listed on the American Civil Liberties Union letterhead as General Counsel Emeritus.

His interview with Louie lasted exactly twelve stormy minutes. How could two tough old negotiators have a tranquil conversation on the subject of law and order in the county jailhouse?

"Who sent for you?" Louie asked belligerently. "Nobody sent for you, and nobody needs you here! So why don'tcha just take a walk for yourself?"

Zorin tried to explain that he was there to offer his help because a picture in the newspaper—showing the police handcuffing five old people standing in a gutter—had angered him. And when he learned that only Minnie had legal representation, that had upset him most of all—because every American citizen accused of a crime has the constitutional right of an able defense before a court of law.

"He's got rights only after the crime?" Louie growled. "How about before the crime? That's the question!"

Abe Zorin was no novice at the word games old men play. He had tested some of his own against the nine Supreme old men, finding his agile mind and tongue more than equal to the task.

"I made it a rule many years ago, Mr. Levine," he said dryly, "never to answer a question when somebody had to tell me what the question was. But here is the answer to another question entirely: The law must be respected—even after the law has been *dis*respected and a crime has been committed. It must be respected by the criminal, and by the judge. That is why I am here."

"So, what is the other question?" Louie wanted to know.

"That," Zorin said, "is a question I never answer—except in court."

Louie's head tilted quizzically to one side. His tongue clicked. And by that time, he had caught on. Solomon Abraham Zorin had Louie Levine's number, and he would have to be dealt with on equal terms.

"Mr. Zorin," Louie said, "you are a very irritating man, and I am prepared to *like* you, but I am not prepared to *hire* you for my lawyer, because I need no lawyer."

"And I put it to you, sir," Zorin retorted, "that an old fool in your position has so many needs, he doesn't even know what he needs! So I will answer that question for you . . . First thing tomorrow, at your arraignment, you will need an attorney to counsel you to an appropriate plea. Second, you will need an attorney to request that bail be set, so that you may arrange for release from custody while awaiting trial."

"Izzat so?" said Louie, wagging his head sarcastically from side to side. "Well, I will just question your answer, 'Mister Counselor'—how d'ya like that? First of all, between the whole bunch of us, we couldn't raise enough money to bail out a canoe! And in the second place, for your information, I already decided on an 'appropriate' plea."

"Is it a secret?" Zorin asked conspiratorily.

"Why should it be a secret?" Louie shrugged. "We are going to plead *nolo contendere*."

306

Zorin was impressed, both with the concept and with Louie's pronunciation of the little-used legal term. "I see," he said. "Very interesting. You understand, of course, that a plea of *nolo contendere*, technically, has the same legal effect as that of a guilty plea, don't you? And that all of you would stand convicted of all the charges at the very moment you so pleaded?"

"Do I look to you like a man who would order off a Chinese menu, if I didn't know what was gonna come outa the kitchen?"

Zorin ignored him. "—If, in fact, the judge would agree to *accept* such a plea in this case."

Louie suddenly had a sinking feeling, as if he had just been dealt a good poker hand in a pinochle game. "Whatta ya mean 'accept'? Doesn't he have to accept?"

"Not necessarily," Zorin said cryptically.

"Why not?" Louie asked angrily. "If the plea of *nolo contendere* was available for Spiro Agnew to use, why wouldn't it be available for us?"

"A-haa-hh!" Zorin paused a moment for the effect. "Now the dawn comes up like thunder! Now I think you are coming to understand that you do need the services of an attorney! Am I right?"

Louie sat staring at the wizened attorney, and Zorin stared calmly back. Two old gray lions, silently staring each other down. Neither blinking an eye, neither moving a give-away muscle. For a full twenty seconds, by the clock, they sat connected by their meaningful gaze.

"I'll make a deal with you," Louie said finally. "I don't know why—I guess maybe I just got a weak spot for people who volunteer to be heroes. Mosta them end up in the ash can—but if you wanna come around tomorrow to the whatta ya call it—the arrangement—just long enough to see that the judge accepts our plea, it's okay by me."

Zorin smiled. "It's very nice of you, Mr. Levine, to give me the opportunity to represent you."

"Just for tomorrow!" Louie said firmly. "That's the end of it—and no fee, you understand. Is it a deal?"

Zorin got up from the chair and looked down at Louie, holding his right hand out to bind the agreement. "Do I look like a man who wouldn't recognize a good deal when it comes right up and kicks me in the teeth? It's a deal. I'll see you in court. Tomorrow." And he shook Louie's hand with a wiry, firm grip.

"Yeah, yeah," Louie said, shifting his arm in his sling painfully, "if I live that long."

"Oh, we'll both live that long," said Zorin. "It's the day after tomorrow that you and I have to worry about."

With that he turned and strode out of the room.

Early Monday morning, two large bags of mail were loaded into the cargo hold of American Airlines nonstop Flight Number 76, departing Los

Angeles at nine A.M., due to arrive at Dulles International Airport at four forty-nine P.M. In one of those bags was a large manila business envelope containing the only nonconfiscated copy of the special April issue of *The Voice of the Aged* in existence, plus two Los Angeles newspaper clippings describing the April first siege at Citizens' Bank.

It was an airmail, special delivery communiqué, originating from the Fairfax substation, addressed in florid pink ink to

> The Honorable Gerald R. Ford
> President of These United States
> The White House
> Washington, D.C.
> For His Eyes Only

The return addressee was listed on the upper left-hand corner of the envelope: An Interested Party Who Might Vote For You.

The actual arraignment of the Fairfax Five took much less time than Judge J. Quentin Paine had spent on the telephone in his chambers that Monday morning regarding the case. He had been bombarded by phone calls from ordinary citizens, outraged that five harmless old people were being held in jail with hardened criminals, and by calls from men of political influence, deeply concerned about the effect Judge Paine's handling of this case might have on the outcome of his campaign for reelection in November. Then there was the call from the judge's mother, phoning from her luxury retirement condominium at the Laguna Niguel complex, to consult with him on the matter.

And finally, there was an urgent telephone call from Solomon A. Zorin requesting a private meeting in the judge's chambers with the public defender and the prosecutor assigned to the case by the district attorney, prior to the arraignment at eleven A.M., to discuss a rather unusual stand the defendants were taking with respect to their plea.

"Are you their attorney of record, Mr. Zorin?" the judge asked, over the phone.

"I think so, your Honor."

"I, uh, didn't realize that there was a constitutional issue involved in this case."

"I didn't either, Your Honor, until I met with their leader, the defendant Levine."

Judge Paine paused for a moment, tapping his pen on his desk calendar. "Come to my chambers at ten o'clock, counsellor. You can inform the others."

308

"I will. Thank you, Your Honor."

Paine hung up on Zorin quickly. He had another call waiting.


Zorin's arguments in the judge's chambers were brief and convincing. His clients were implacable. They insisted on pleading *nolo contendere* to the charges brought against them, and in fact would consider no other plea. This meant, Zorin pointed out, that if the court, in its wisdom, should refuse to accept that plea, the judge would be left facing two jurisprudential choices: A, to decree that the defendants be put through a full range of physical, psychiatric, neurological, and psychological examinations in order to determine whether they were physically and mentally competent to stand a public trial, which could take weeks; or B, to himself enter a Not Guilty plea on their behalf—which, of course, would result in a public jury trial, at great cost to the public.

Each time Zorin leaned on the word *public*, the judge winced inside. No judge in his right mind would want this case to come to public jury trial. The French toast Judge Paine had eaten for breakfast hardened in his stomach as he imagined hundreds of gray heads lining up in the corridors outside his courtroom each morning before such a trial.

"How is your client prepared to plea?" the judge asked the young public defender.

"She will enter only the plea entered by the defendant Levine, Your Honor."

"What would the district attorney's position be," the judge asked, "should the court decide in favor of accepting the plea requested?"

"Your Honor," the young lawyer said, "I would have to check it out with my superior before the arraignment, but I can't see any objection on our part to the plea of *nolo contendere*—it's tantamount to a plea of Guilty, in any case."

"This isn't just *any* case," Zorin interjected.

"All right, Mr. Zorin!" the judge said. "The court will take your request for plea under advisement. Thank you, gentlemen. Good morning."

"But, Your Honor," Zorin said, rising, "we are scheduled for our arraignment in just fifteen minutes."

"I have a watch, thank you, Counsellor," the judge said. "And you had better have a meaningful defense to support your clients' plea, in the event I agree to accept it."

"I assure you, Your Honor," Zorin said with a faint smile, "I will take particular pains to make my arguments concise and persuasive. After all, I will be defending my own contemporaries. These defendants are not juvenile delinquents. Their combined ages come to a total of three hundred and sixty-nine years."

And with that, Zorin swept out of the room, leaving the fifty-one-year-old judge to grapple with his decision.

Judge Paine did not enter the courtroom until 11:20 A.M. The "advisement" he had taken the plea request under had required some time, including two telephone calls, one to Orange County and one to Sacramento, each of which was logged at more than ten minutes' duration. He got very little help from Sacramento, but his backers in Orange County made it crystal clear, in dollars and cents, the exact manner in which Judge Paine, the incumbent candidate, must handle this case.

Campaigns cost money—lots of money—and nobody in his right mind bets on a sure loser.

The defendants sat in the almost empty courtroom without handcuffs, thus permitting Abe and Minnie, who had not seen each other for ninety-two and one-half hours, to hold hands across the wide lap of an understanding police matron, as the Judge read off the charges prepared by the district attorney's office, at a rate almost too fast to record.

He did slow down long enough, however, to make it understood that the two counts of murder had been deleted from the multiple charges against the defendants, following the official coroner's report concerning the two deaths involved in the event. That report, in coroner's medicalese, indicated that the nameless dead wino found memorialized under the funeral spray in Stosh's old truck had expired of diseased and corroded innards, caused by a thrown away lifetime of ingesting the cheap, poisonous nectars of bitterness and desolation . . . suicide on the installment plan—the only death style the poor bum could afford.

Further, the coroner placed the time of his timely death at some six to eight hours prior to the time of day the two suspected killers took him for a ride. On hearing this piece of news, Oscar looked reverently toward the ceiling of the courtroom and offered up a silent prayer for the dead man's pitiful, wine-soaked soul.

The second portion of the report found that the death of Stanislaus Vlasic was not caused by gunshot wounds, as most people at the scene had assumed by the sight of all the blood, but by a sudden massive paralytic stroke, coincident with a simultaneous coronary occlusion of his enlarged heart, which was made of mere mortal muscle after all, and not of indestructable iron, as were his loyalty and his will. The blood on Stosh's bank guard uniform was Betty Lundy's, issued forth in the pain and joy of early childbirth. Two other Lundy children had also been born during the eighth month of their mother's pregnancy.

Oscar shook his head sadly as the judge finished reading the brief medical descriptions of the double cause for Stosh's death.

"It would take this much," Oscar whispered to Louie, "to kill that man."

310

"Shut up, willya, Oscar?" Louie muttered.

"That's what I say," Vito said.

The judge asked the defendants and their attorneys to stand, then asked Minnie how she pleaded to the charges lodged against her.

"He goes first," Minnie said, pointing at Louie.

"All right," the judge said. "How do you plead, Mr., ah, Levine?"

"Your Honor, sir," said Louie, "this is the first time in my whole life that I ever *pleaded*."

"Yes, I understand, Mr. Levine," the judge said, not understanding. "Don't be nervous now, just tell me how you plead."

"Your Honor," Louie intoned, anything but nervous, "on behalf of myself and my associates here, and on behalf of every old person in this country who has been betrayed and forsaken, I wanna say—"

Judge Paine *rat-tat-tat*ted his ballpoint pen on the rostrum top. "Mr. Levine, I mean no disrespect, sir—I understand how upsetting this situation can be to a man of your age." He turned to Zorin. "But, Counsel, would you please explain to your client that I can accept only a plea from him this morning? I cannot accept a speech. He will have his chance to speak, but not today."

Zorin whispered the requested explanation to his client, for which he quickly earned a sharp response in a loud whisper that could be heard clearly all over the courtroom, to the effect that his client had understood the judge perfectly, and that he needed no interpreter so long as the language being spoken was one of four he proceeded to enumerate, *one* being English.

Zorin was not the least bit perturbed by Louie's quick show of grit. He was glad that Judge Paine had been exposed to this Levineian rebuff. To show an adversary a short fuse is to encourage him to keep his matches in his pocket.

Judge Paine tapped his ballpoint pen for Louie's attention. "May I have your plea, sir?"

"Certainly, Your Honor," Louie replied, as though there had been no interruption in the proceedings. "I wish to enter a plea of *nolo contendere*, because I got the *same right* to this plea as Spiro Agnew, and I—"

The judge was *tap-tap-tap*ping his ball-point like a woodpecker. "Mr. Levine! I have discussed this matter of your plea with your attorney, and with the district attorney, in chambers this morning. I have also taken your desired plea under advisement, as it is an unusual one in a case of this sort . . ."

Louie opened his mouth to speak.

"However," the judge continued, threatening Louie with another peck of his raised ball-point, "after due consideration, the court is willing to accept your plea as entered. All you had to do was state it in open court."

311

The ball-point tapped once.

"Izzat so?" Louie cast a new look of respect toward a modestly grinning Solomon Zorin.

One by one, the others entered the plea of *nolo contendere,* and one by one, Judge Paine accepted their pleas. Defense attorney Zorin then requested that the judge set bail for the defendants at a nominal figure which would allow them to be released pending the date yet to be set for their sentencing.

The judge agreed to set bail. He was quick to point out, however, that although the two counts of murder had been dropped, there remained the serious felony charges of kidnapping, grand theft (auto), assault with deadly weapons, and so on—none of which would encourage him to set what counsel for the defense had described as "nominal" bail.

It offended Zorin's impeccable sense of courtroom taste to employ a corny shaming tactic against a judge hearing one of his cases, but Judge Paine was begging for it.

"Look at these defendants, Your Honor," Zorin implored, with an imploring palm. "All over seventy years old, one with a severe bullet wound, one deaf, and crippled as a young man while escaping from a Nazi prison camp, another, in fairly acceptable condition considering his age— but frail, very frail, another suffering, he tells me, from a worsening case of arthritis—a man who used to dance on the stage, and the last, this woman, to whom Old Age Assistance pays an additional small stipend because she cannot even bend over to clean her tiny apartment . . ."

Zorin watched the judge slowly scanning the row of defendants in time to his narrative . . . from Louie, to Oscar, to Vito, to Abe, and then finally to Minnie, who coyly returned his kindly smile.

"Your Honor," Zorin pressed on, "As you know, this is the first arrest for each of these old people. They are aware of the seriousness of the crime they have committed, and all of them are contrite—contrite enough to plead *nolo contendere*—"no contest"—thereby throwing themselves on the mercy of one man with the power to punish them for their crime. Does the Court really fear that these five old people, these senior citizens, might represent a dangerous threat to society if they were to be released on bail while awaiting their hearing for sentencing?"

Judge Paine had not, in fact, taken Zorin's sympathy bait. Quick to detect the odor of schmaltz in his own courtroom, Judge J. Quentin Paine did not swing and sway on his bench to the music of emotion. He responded only to fact, legal precedent, and the political considerations bearing on his upcoming run for reelection.

Which was why, as he listened to Zorin emote and watched the only two reporters in the room scribbling in their notepads, he rejoiced inwardly at the heavenly hand of fate that brought Solomon A. Zorin out of retirement to lay down a courtroom appeal that would help him comply with his

312

Orange County "advice," which had been simple and direct: "That case is a hot potato. Get rid of it. Quick."

"Your honor?" Zorin prompted politely.

"Uh, yes, counsellor. You, ah, you present a very strong argument, which I must frankly admit the Court has not considered in just that light. Ye-es, it has great validity. . . ." Zorin watched the judge quietly tapping his pen on the rostrum, seemingly lost in concentration on his decision.

"Mr. Zorin, are you prepared at this time to suggest a specific amount at which you would like to see the Court set bail?"

Zorin had never in his life been asked that question by a judge at arraignment. Only as an appeal motion could the defense attorney request a bail amount.

"Well, Your Honor," Zorin began, with no change of expression, "as you know, all the defendants are on Social Security and Old Age Assistance. None of them even qualifies for food stamps, so they are on severely fixed incomes. Obviously they do not have the ability to secure bonding for anything but the most nominal amount of bail."

"That's not quite responsive to my question, Counsellor. You've used the word *nominal* several times. I'm sure you have some figure in mind, haven't you. . . ?"

When Zorin finally spoke, his tone was firm and righteous. "Your Honor, I would like to request, for the reasons already enumerated, that these defendants be released forthwith on their own recognizance."

The defendant's row buzzed as they whispered the unfamiliar legal expression to each other.

"Well, that *is* nominal bail, isn't it, Mr. Zorin?" the judge observed, as though such a release were the farthest thing from his mind.

"Well, really, Your Honor," Zorin reasoned, "what is the difference between, say, a thousand dollars bail for each, for which they'd each have to post at least one hundred dollars with a bailbondsman—money that they desperately need for food or lodging—and absolutely nothing at all? It's perfectly obvious that these defendants are not going to skip bail or fail to appear for sentencing. Where are they going to go? They are immobile— not a single vehicle among them. As you see by the report, only the dead man, Vlasic, owned a vehicle—an old broken-down truck which couldn't even make it the ten blocks to the scene of the crime."

Judge Paine permitted himself a slight smile. "I must say, Counsellor, that you have familiarized yourself very well with this case and these defendants in only twenty-four hours. They are ably represented."

"Thank you, Your Honor," Zorin said modestly.

"Tell me, Mr. Zorin," the judge wondered aloud, "I know I can't remand them to your custody, the way I could a gang of juvenile delinquents— although I dearly wish I could. But if the court were to grant them a release on their own recognizance, could the court also look to you to insure their

313

appearance at the hearing for sentencing, and also to see that they behave themselves in the interim?"

Zorin looked at Louie. How the hell could he insure the actions of Louie Levine? How could anyone? . . .

"Well, Your Honor . . ." Zorin grinned hesitantly.

Then, to his surprise, Louie cleared his throat and nodded—a steady, serious, sincere nod of absolute assurance.

"Yes, sir, Your Honor," said Zorin. "I feel certain that if these defendants are released on their own recognizance, they will appear on the appointed date for sentencing, and they will comport themselves as law-abiding citizens in the meantime. Furthermore, I will undertake to do everything in my power to see to it."

"Thank you, Mr. Zorin." The judge turned to address the other two attorneys. "Gentlemen, does either the district attorney or the public defender have any specific objection to such a release from custody of these defendants, pending sentencing?"

Both attorneys spoke at once, assuring the judge that they had no objection to such a release.

After a brief disruptive objection by Louie, who tried to insist on being sentenced at that very moment for some inexplicable reason, the judge quickly restored order, released the prisoners on their own recognizance, and set an early date for sentencing, one week from that day. Judge Paine's hot potato was, for the moment, on the back burner.

The prisoners were then returned to their respective jails to pick up their belongings, get checked out, and be delivered to their homes.

Actually, as it turned out, they were all dropped off three blocks away from the Senior Citizens' Center. Permit themselves to be delivered to their very own front doors in a black and white police car? Not on your life. That was only for criminals.

314

# 21

# *EARLY CELEBRATION*

The Fairfax Five enjoyed a week of celebrity at the Center as they awaited their day of sentencing. Back slapping and handclasping and hugging and kissing on both cheeks were the order of the week as they were welcomed warmly back to temporary freedom by their friends, and even by people they had stopped talking to years ago.

Henry Hoover became Louie's best friend and most ardent admirer, donating three whole dollars to *The Voice* all at one time. He insisted on pinning his World War II Purple Heart onto Louie's arm sling as though it were the Croix de Guerre.

Old Lady Kahn caught Vito unawares, in a corner, and pointing her three-legged aluminum cane at him, she hollered as though he were the one who was deaf, "Hey, you! I'm sorry I yelled at you the other day. You can help me up the steps any time you want, you understand?"

Jack Cantor cleared the bulletin board and put up a huge picture he had drawn, depicting the gang raising the American flag on the Iwo Jima of Citizens' Bank. Under it, in big letters, was Churchill's famous quote about how much how few had done for so many. Metaphors mixed are metaphors enshrined. It was an instant hit, and people gathered in the lobby in little knots to admire and applaud it all week long.

Meanwhile, the two probation officers assigned to the case by the Court worked furiously to finish their investigations in four short days, so that their reports, fully typed, could be delivered to Judge Paine and the three attorneys in the case before the end of the business day on Friday.

They questioned each of the five felons under oath, delving into their past lives far beyond their powers of recall. Birthplaces, parents' and grandparents' names, cities of residence throughout their lifetime, educational, medical, marital, military, religious, vocational, ethnic, immigrational—all the dark corners of their lives were investigated. Friends of the defendants, acquaintances, and even a few hard-to-find relatives were questioned as to character, integrity, loyalty, responsibility. All the unanswerable questions were asked and answered and entered into the probation report which Judge Paine would use on Monday to help him determine the sentence that the law would inflict on the radicals who had terrorized the city on April Fool's Day.

And while all this was going on, Solomon Zorin studied his law books, searching for precedent on pleas for clemency, for leniency, for mercy. Late into the night he paced his study, reaching deep in his mind for the thread of an idea that seemed to glimmer for an instant at a time and then to elude him over and over again as he agonized over the most important sentencing hearing of his life.

Then, on Sunday, Zorin awoke from his afternoon nap with a start. He pulled himself out of his big leather lounging chair and walked again to the Bible stand which held his huge dictionary in the very center of his study. Slowly he spun the big book around and around, trying to grasp the last dreaming image that had awakened him.

All at once, it struck him. He opened the book to a worn tab near the back, the section titled "Articles in Addition to, and Amendments of, the Constitution of the United States of America." For the hundred thousandth time, he read his old friend aloud:

Congress shall make no law respecting an establishment of religion, or prohibiting the free exercise thereof; or abridging the freedom of speech, or of the press; or the right of people peaceably to assemble, and to petition the Government for a redress of grievances.

He reread the last two lines, and his eye suddenly underlined the word "redress." Redress, redress . . . an uncommon word, not used in everyday language. What was the true and full meaning of that word? And why had he never in his life actually looked it up?

He turned the dictionary pages back to R. R-a, R-e—here it was, *Redress*. He read the definition aloud:

re dress (n.). . . .
1.) the *setting right* of what is wrong
2.) the *correction* or *reform* of abuses or evils
3.) *compensation* or *satisfaction* for a wrong or injury
4.) the *remedy* or *relief* of suffering, want, etc., and
5.) *reparations* for neglect.

There it was, plain as day. And it had been there all along. His clients had actually been denied a basic Constitutional right—and *that* was the mitigating circumstance on which he must base his plea to the court for mercy.

"These five old people can't be sent to prison, Your Honor—they mustn't

316

be. These old people are not a threat to society. Society is a threat to them."
Zorin was pacing the room and talking out loud, not realizing he was doing either.

"My God! Don't you see, Your Honor? They are not denied *the right to petition*. Oh, no! As a matter of fact—they are *encouraged* to petition. That is the most insidious, the most deceitful part of the fraud. Congress flies its committees all over the country, at a cost of millions, to hold their regional hearings on the problems of the aged. They sit there patiently behind their long tables while these old people shuffle up and cry out the degrading conditions of their lives. And the committee listens, and nods sympathetically, recording every word of every miserable story—insinuating the hope to these poor victims that, somehow, their lives will be bettered by their pathetic petition. But it's all just for a *show*. The committee then goes back to Washington, and these elderly supplicants are simply ignored—as though they were little children, babbling fanciful tales of imaginary monsters and ghosts in the night. I just can't believe that our founding fathers, the brilliant and sensitive men who wrote the most nearly perfect governing document in the world, would have meant to perpetrate such a hoax, can you? Let me put it brutally, Your Honor—what good is the right to petition, if the redress never takes place? Isn't that a denial of a Constitutional right? I say it is! These old people committed their crime because they finally boiled over from anger and frustration. Because they reached their limit, and didn't know what else to do to bring their desperate plight to the attention of their Government. They did it in self-defense. They were not claiming a Constitutional right—they were claiming their right to survive as human beings. Everybody seems to be so shocked because these law-breakers—these revolutionaries—are old people, and old people are supposed to be powerless and obedient. Well, they'd better start paying attention. We are old, but we are not impotent!"

Suddenly, Zorin's wife came running into the room from the garden, her pruning shears still in her hand, ready to use as a weapon if necessary. "What are you yelling about? You scared me half to death! I thought someone was in here trying to kill you, or something!"

Zorin just stood there like a grandfather clock that had run down. Then he sighed deeply and returned to his chair. "I'm sorry I frightened you," he mumbled. "But you know me—I was just winning my case in here for tomorrow."

His wife walked to the back of his chair, leaned over, and kissed the top of his head. "And did you find an argument to win with?"

"I don't know," he said. "We shall see. We shall just have to wait and see if I can convince the Court that in this case, two wrongs should make a right."

On Sunday night, the eve of the sentencing, Jack Cantor organized a hush-hush Freedom Party at the Center, postponing half the scheduled show to the following week. The big card room was festooned with red-white-and-blue balloons and bunting, and a complex plan was made to delay the entrance of the five criminal honorees until the proper moment, so that everybody could holler "Sur-pri-i-ise!!! Sur-pri-i-ise!!!"

A secret collection had been taken up during the week to pay for the party. Jack Cantor almost dropped dead when Ida Katz put up a hundred dollars to pay for a spread from Dave's Deli. Her hundred wasn't quite enough, so Dave himself popped for the rest, and the long table of assorted food was administered by none other than Gonzalo Díaz and Dave's newest busboy, Jesse Williams, happily working on their own time as they tried their best to keep up with the assault on the buffet table.

When the heaping trays of food were almost leveled, and most of the people had paper cups of coffee or tea in their hands, Joe Glass hopped up on the stage and started the show. After a flowery welcome and three hip-hip-hoorays for the conquering heroes, he asked for a moment of silence for Stosh, which really wasn't silent, because people were sniffling, and one woman broke out crying so loud that somebody had to walk her out of the room.

The entertainment following the moment of silence turned out to be pretty mediocre—a teenage brother-and-sister dance team, who kept kicking each other; and a twelve-year-old, red-headed cantor's son with a fierce falsetto, who will never be able to make it in his father's business. His father, who accompanied his kid on the piano, would be well advised to stick to his specialty, too.

But the highlight of the evening was the giving of the gifts, which each recipient had to open on stage when Ida Katz, chairperson of the gift committee, handed them out.

Everybody knew immediately what Minnie's gift was, because the wrapping paper didn't quite cover the rubber wheels of her fancy collapsible shopping basket. Giggling like a little girl with a new baby buggy, Minnie wheeled the basket back and forth across the stage, then came to the microphone. "You think maybe they got a supermarket at San Quentin?" she asked, and the crowd roared.

Oscar's big red alarm clock with the two large metal chimers sticking out had a cartoon of Pluto on the clockface to point out the time. He managed a forced grin and a grunt of thanks, and sat down.

Abe tore open his package to find two flashy paisley neck scarves, one red and one electric blue, both of which he proceeded to put on at once, and model for the crowd, turning profile left and right, like John Barrymore. Then he stepped to the microphone and said, "Listen, going to jail for a while won't be so bad—three squares a day, and nobody's gonna raise the rent on us, either!" He didn't get much of a laugh.

Next, Ida handed Louie his gift parcel, which he promptly stuck into his

318

sling, muttering what everyone assumed was thank you, and started to sit down.

"Oh, no!" Ida said into the mike. "You gotta open your present! Everybody's gotta open—right, folks?"

The crowd applauded and shouted their agreement, and Louie was forced to unwrap and exhibit a horizontally striped black and white long-sleeved T-shirt. He grimaced and started back to his chair.

"Wait just a minute!" Ida insisted. "Say something on the microphone!" And the crowd hooted and hollered and applauded again.

Louie walked scowling to the mike. "It's a very nice, uh, pajama-top," he said, "—just my size. Maybe the state of California will save a few dollars on me—ha-ha." And Ida let him sit down.

Vito's stomach had been tied in knots and turning over ever since Glass called his name out to come up and sit in one of the five seats of honor on the stage. And each time Ida Katz had called a name out and it wasn't his name, Vito knew more and more surely that she was saving him for last.

"And last, but not least," Ida announced, "I give you *Signore* Vito Morelli, who comes to us from Salerno, Italy, where the sun and the men are *both* burning hot, and the women lo-ove it!"

The crowd laughed and applauded, and Vito shuffled forward, hoping that a trap-door would open up and swallow him before he reached Ida, smiling at him like a black widow spider and holding her little box out to him. This time, it was an offer he could *not* refuse.

Vito snatched the carton and headed back toward his chair. "Open! Open it up! Make him open it," people yelled from out front, and Vito turned back to the mike.

"It's okay," he said. "I know what it is—it's cigars! Thanks a lot!"

"How about it folks?" Ida grabbed him by the sleeve. "Everybody else opened, right?"

Vito was still trying to pull away from Ida's talons when a woman in the front row screeched, "No-oo! Don't let him open them—he'll *smoke* one, for God's sake!"

Vito stopped pulling away. "If you please, Missus Katz," he murmured, gently removing her hand from his coat sleeve, "I would be very happy to open my present for you."

Then, with great ceremony, Vito deftly opened the same wooden cigar box he had opened before, quickly palmed and pocketed the folded card with the pink writing, selected one of the individually wrapped cigars, unwrapped it, carefully crumpled the wrapper, and flipped it off the stage in the direction of the screeching cigar hater. He delicately bit off the end of the cigar, rolled it sensuously between his fingers, smelled it, lifted his eyes to the ceiling in ecstasy . . . and finally—after wetting the end of the cigar with his tongue as he ogled a molten Ida Katz—he swished a wooden match expertly against his trouser leg, and slowly lit his cigar. . . .

319

As they all watched, either with pleasure or in horror, Vito blew the first gray plume of smoke luxuriously upward, as though he were an Arabian potentate inhaling nirvana from his hookah. Then, completing his act of glorious revenge, he smiled all over the carping woman out front, and blew her a perfect smoke ring. *Capish?*

And Ida Katz stood next to him, mesmerized by his performance, her heart palpitating, and her thighs trembling, as she turned over in her mind the bus connections necessary to make the trip to Dunhill's. *Farshtaist?*

320

# 22

# PUNISHMENT TO FIT THE CRIME

On April 12, 1976, at 12:30 P.M., attorney Solomon Zorin called for his four clients and Minnie at the Senior Citizens' Center, for the twenty-minute ride downtown to Superior Court.

It was unusually quiet in Zorin's Lincoln sedan, each of his old passengers thinking silent thoughts, fearing secret fears, as the moment of sentencing drew close and real.

Louie seemed particularly glum. For one thing, he had awakened with a bad spring cold, and his throat hurt when he talked. For another thing, the Center had been nearly deserted—no cronies had shown up to see them off, to wish them luck. Cantor wasn't even there behind the counter to make some dumb crack about how the judge was going to make it possible for them all to save up a few Social Security checks while they were room-and-boarding with the State.

But most of all, Louie was sorely disappointed with the news coverage of The Benefit. The media had certainly attended the event in force, but they had not really told the story—not the story Louie wanted told—not the story *The Voice of the Aged* had raised its voice to tell.

The newspaper and TV people were interested only in the violence—the armed standoff, the danger to life and property, the cops-and-robbers aspect of the event. They all but ignored the real reasons for the awful happening, as if the six old people driven to this act of violence were simply irresponsible rebels without a cause.

The papers and the TV carried pictures of the police ducking behind squad cars with their guns; of Keller, stripped to the waist and walking fearfully across the street with his hands up; of the injured Brubaker being lifted into the ambulance; of the SWAT team hunched on the rooftops, bristling with their snubnosed M-16s as they exposed themselves to armed terrorists in the perilous performance of their duty.

But nobody ran any pictures of Whitehead being interviewed, nobody ran any quotes from Louie's vital questions or any of Whitehead's nonanswers. Nor had even one news outlet gotten hold of Louie's newsletter with the hundred questions and the letter to the President.

Zorin pulled his car around the corner onto Hill Street toward the front of the Criminal Courts Building—and almost swerved into a mail truck.

There must have been seventy or eighty old people lined up on the sidewalk in front of the Courthouse, sitting in two neat rows on little canvas camp stools, almost all of them holding large double-faced protest signs which they turned slowly, so that people on both sides of the street and in passing cars could read the messages on both sides. Four uniformed policemen calmly patrolled the orderly picketing.

Zorin hit his brakes, slowing the car to a crawl.

FREE THE FAIRFAX FIVE—LET OUR PEOPLE GO!

DON'T THROW MOM AND DAD AWAY—
IT'S NOT NICE!

SOCIAL SECURITY—IS THE PITS!!

STOP AND TAKE A GOOD LOOK—IS THIS *YOU* A FEW YEARS
FROM NOW?

GRAY IS NOT GONE—ONLY FORGOTTEN!

DON'T STAY IN SHAPE—
YOU MIGHT LIVE TO BE A SENIOR CITIZEN!

SEND US *ALL* TO JAIL—
IT'S ROTTEN OUT HERE!

"My God, look at all the people!" Minnie cried out.

"No wonder nobody was at the Center," Louie said, "How do ya like that?"

"I like it! I like it!" said Vito, clapping his hands.

"That Cantor is a genius!" Oscar said.

"I don't like it at all!" Zorin said, pulling his car to a complete stop a half-block short of the front entrance.

"Whatta ya doing?" Louie shouted hoarsely. "Pull up in front!"

"I don't know . . ." Zorin hesitated. "This is not a good thing for us. . . ."

All five of his passengers started to talk at once.

"Whatta ya talk about?" said Vito. "It's terrific!"

"Yeah, look at all those people on our side!" Abe said.

322

"What a turnout!" said Minnie.

"Just a minute, just a minute!" Zorin shouted. "What is it they're chanting?"

They all shut up to listen. There, halfway up the front steps to the Criminal Courts Building, stood Ida Katz, semaphoring her arms like a cheerleader, as her senior rooting section chanted. "FREE THE FAIRFAX FIVE!—THEN HELP THEM STAY ALIVE! . . . FREE THE FAIRFAX FIVE!—THEN HELP THEM STAY ALIVE!"

There were cheers and applause from across the street, too, from a straggling lunchtime crowd, who had gathered to gawk and to egg the protestors on, no matter what their cause.

"It's bad," said Zorin, shaking his head, "very bad."

"Whatta ya mean, *bad?*" Vito said. "If ya ask me, she's a terrific yell-leader—terrific!"

"I'm afraid you don't understand. This kind of demonstration can be very upsetting to a judge sitting on a case."

"I don't get it," said Louie. "What could be better than this kinda public opinion, right out in the open?"

"Mr. Levine," Zorin pointed out, "we are here today to get the opinion of one man, and one man alone—Judge Paine—not the opinion of a mob in the street. And his opinion will be a legal opinion . . . a judgment and a sentence that will be handed down based on his concept of justice in this case after giving proper weight, I trust, to some arguments I have prepared on your behalf. A disruption of the kind your friends are heating themselves up for can only serve to intimidate a judge, to make him angry, at the very time when we don't *want* him angry, do you understand?"

Louie was thinking it over, and so were the others.

"There's no telling what these people might do when they see you arrive," Zorin continued. "I'd better drive you around to the rear entrance of the building, and then come out here and try to quiet them down before the hearing."

Zorin started away from the curb, but Louie grabbed his arm. "Oh, no you don't! Louie Levine never went in by the back door in his life!"

Zorin looked hard at Louie for a moment, studying his pride, gauging his resolve. Then he reached down, turned the ignition off, and crossed his arms.

Louie stared back tensely at Zorin for a moment. The Buddha did not budge.

"We can get out and walk from here, you know," Louie said.

"Yes," Zorin said quietly. "I have no doubt that you can. But before you do, if I were you I would decide which one of your friends there can best defend you before Judge Paine, so that you do not spend too long a time in prison to pay for your crimes."

It was the moment of truth, and Louie knew it.

"Okay, okay, Mr. Counsellor," he said, "I been right all my life, and I'm sick and tired of being right—so I'll take a rest for myself. Today, it's *your* turn to be right! I'll tell you whatcha do. . . . Drive up to the front. They'll see us, they'll make a little noise. We'll get outa the car, I'll make them shut up to listen to you, and you can tell them anything you wanna tell them. You satisfied?"

"Satisfied," Zorin said, starting the car.

"But I'm telling you," Louie warned, "you better be right, today!"

The Lincoln pulled up to the front entrance, and the crowd went crazy when they recognized the Fairfax Five—yelling, hollering, jumping up and down, rape whistles screeching, signs whacking into one another, even a couple of hats tossed up in the air.

Louie and the others had to force their way out of the car. "Quiet, quiet!" Louie tried to shout, but hardly anything came out. "Abe, please!" he begged.

"Okay, okay, folks!" Abe yelled above the noise. "Louie has got an announcement to make, you wouldn't wanna miss it! So shut up a minute, please!"

The crowd quieted down immediately, gathering close to listen as they realized that Louie had very little voice.

"You're a nice buncha people, ya know that?" Louie said. "Please excuse me, with my voice . . . but I want you should listen to our lawyer here, he's got something important to say to you. . . . This is Mr. Zorin, our lawyer."

The crowd started to applaud, but Zorin cut them off.

"Ladies and gentlemen! My name is Solomon A. Zorin, and I am representing the four men in this case. Mrs. Gold is being represented by the public defender, a very able young lawyer. I am very pleased that you have all come here today to support your friends. They are about to face a very critical hearing, and they can use your support. It is your right, and their right, for you to be here—the right of public trial. But I want to make sure that you all understand what is going on here today, so that you can be helpful . . . because if you do not understand, you can be very harmful to them, and I'm sure you don't want to do that. As you know, your five friends have broken the law. They have committed a crime—"

Some people in the crowd reacted noisily.

"Wait, wait, hear me out, please! There is no question that they committed these crimes. I understand that some of you were actually there at the bank, during the event. I have also been told, as a matter of fact, that many of you contributed money to finance these crimes—"

There were prompt cries of objection to that accusation.

"Unwittingly, innocently—I know!" Zorin shouted, quieting them once more. "What's more, your friends have confessed to their crime, tacitly, by the plea they entered before they were released. They were found guilty and will stand convicted. So today, they come to be sentenced—"

"No! No!" "No sentence!" "Free them!" People cried out.

324

"Please, Please! That's what today is all about. They will be sentenced. That's the *law*."

"That's crazy!" yelled Henry Hoover. "Send a bunch of old people to jail?"

"No, sir!" Zorin snapped at him sharply. "The law is *not* crazy! Don't you ever say that! I've spent my life in the law, and I can tell you that justice and the law, properly respected and administered, are far more desirable than mobs in the streets!"

The unruly group of elders suddenly became a respectful church congregation intent on their minister.

"Now," Zorin continued, "You are all welcome in the courtroom for these proceedings. The Constitution of the United States invites you in. But I warn you, as the judge will warn you, there must be no disruption—no demonstration of any kind inside that room! I have come today with arguments of mitigation, and other arguments, to plead for leniency in the sentencing of these five people, to pray to the Court for mercy. The judge will come into that room to listen to and consider those arguments before he passes sentence. If you disturb that process in any way—in any way at all—you will be passing a harsh sentence on your friends. Not the judge, not the law—but you!"

The members of the congregation shuffled contritely, nodding their understanding to Zorin and to each other.

"All right, then," Zorin said. "The signs you are carrying, of course, will not be permitted inside the building. So, rather than have the guards take them away from you at the door, I want each of you to stick your sign, handle down, into this basket, here—"

"Aw-w, that's a trash basket," Jack Cantor moaned.

"You are wrong, sir," Zorin said. "Today, this is a 'legal protest' basket. People passing will read them while you are inside, taking part in a well-ordered legal process, and they will be here for you when you come out, should you want them."

No one moved toward the basket with a sign. There was a certain hesitation, a mass indecision, as some of the crowd looked at Louie for direction.

"Do like the man told you to do!" Louie rasped at them. "I think he knows what he's doing. So no talking inside, you understand? And no applause, either. This ain't a show here today!"

Cantor took a step forward and stuck his sign into the big wire basket. Then, one by one, the demonstrators filed forward, each sticking a sign into the basket as though it were a bouquet. Then, they all folded up their camp stools and slowly mounted the wide stairs to the court, hushed and respectful, as though they were entering a house of God to hear a new voice of the aged pray to the blindfolded lady with the scales, for the freedom of the Fairfax Five.

# 23

# THE REST IS EPILOGUE

President Ford didn't answer Louie's letter in *The Voice of the Aged* before he left his Oval Office, so it's a good bet that Ernest P. Whitehead did not carry out his solemn oath to deliver it before *he* left office.

And nobody has heard directly from the new President on the subject of the letter, or on the hundred questions, either. But come to think of it, he did make some very strong and sincere-sounding promises to the elders of this country during his swearing-in speech, so maybe. . . . It's possible, after all. Not likely, but just possible. Maybe he read Louie's letter?

Maybe so, and maybe no. In any case, nobody knows what he is doing about it.

The gang's all gone now—all except Minnie—all gone to be served their pie in the sky on their great come-and-get-it day.

Abe was the first. Two months after the Fairfax Five had their day in court, he was killed in a freak accident while acting in a movie. Not exactly acting, really. He got one day's work as a nonunion extra in a cheap independent movie about these two turn-of-the-century flyers. They had these two red and yellow biplanes, and they would fly all over the Midwest, hitting the hick towns and putting on their sky circus for the folks, doing their bloodcurdling skyrobatics in these two old planes over some empty field, see?

And Abe, he was part of the grandstand crowd, supposed to be one of the town's aldermen or something, sitting right in the first row, dressed in his ice cream flannel suit, high collar, blue polka dot bowtie, and straw boater, watching these crazy stuntmen doing reverse loop-the-loops and other idiotic tricks in their flimsy canvas airplanes—when one of them simply disintegrated, while trying to pull out of a steep dive, and plummeted directly down toward the grandstand. The stunt pilot, Abe, and three other extras were killed instantly, and a couple of dozen other people were seriously injured.

They had all signed the standard releases, of course, protecting the motion picture company against damage suits in case of just such an accident, and since Abe Silver had no life insurance policy, the only thing that Minnie received at the end of her lover's life was a twenty-dollar bill, which was Abe's pay for the one day's work. The alert cameraman got the whole shot of the crash, too, and it was actually used in the movie when it came out, though not too many people ever went to see it.

Everyone around the Senior Citizens' Center went around saying that was just the way Abe would have wanted to go—in show business, and quick. Minnie knew better, of course. She knew exactly how he wanted to go—he had certainly *told* her enough times.

"I know exactly how I wanna go," Abe would say. "I wanna go exactly like John Garfield, sweetheart—coming and going at the same time!"

But then, we very rarely get exactly what we want in this life. Or in this death, either.

Vito Morelli just dropped dead in the hall of the Center, coming out of the men's room. He had an excellent cigar in his hand at the time, freshly lit—a Monte Cristo Especiale Deluxe. The people who saw him fall to the floor said he didn't cry out or whimper or anything, and the expression on his face was serene enough. As a matter of fact, he was sporting a faint smile.

Dirty Harry Haledman said afterward that Vito had a premonition of the precise time of his own death and had just gone into the john to take a last proud look.

Oscar died at Los Angeles County General Hospital, following four painful weeks of exploratory surgery by the young doctors there, getting their carving practice in while trying to find the source of the sudden terrible abdominal pains that had felled the little watchmaker from Hamburg. Oscar never did get over the fact that *he* had shot Louie in the arm when Stosh broke down the door of the drive-in teller's booth.

Luckily, Oscar still had his Medicare card, with all the labels intact for the month, when the ambulance came to rush him to the hospital. So the county broke even on his surgery and blood transfusions and tests and even his unclaimed burial, as soon as they attached the labels to their report, and HEW paid off by return mail.

Jack Cantor came from the Senior Citizens' Center to County Hospital, carrying a notarized letter of authorization from Oscar, to claim his antique gold watch which he had willed to be auctioned off for the benefit of *The Voice of the Aged,* but the hospital employees in charge of such things claimed that Oscar Stein had no such watch on his person when he was admitted, and showed Cantor an inventory list to prove it.

Louie was found dead in his bed on the morning of April 1, 1977, one year to the day after The Benefit at Citizens' Bank, cheating his probation officer out of two years' worth of visits and a lot of salty philosophy.

His body was discovered by his landlord, who came to his room to collect the rent. The bedclothes had been badly thrashed around, and the landlord told the police who were called in that he thought he had heard Louie cry out loudly several times during the night. His body was still warm when he was found, and his pajamas were still wringing wet with sweat. The County Medical Examiner, who came for his body, theorized that Louie had died of a heart seizure while in the middle of a frightening nightmare—not an uncommon way, he said, for old people to go.

Nobody knows how it happened, because Louie never signed up for it, but his body was claimed from the county by the Neptune Society, all required papers in order, and Louie Levine made his last earthly journey, ashes to ashes, in a handsome pink marble urn aboard a graceful white yacht, the ship's bell tolling softly as it sailed serenely west into the smog-bound orange sunset.


Minnie has long ago given up yoga, and from the day Abe was killed, she stopped being a redhead. She moved into a small furnished room, much farther away from the Center, and they don't see her there very often anymore. Every once in a while, on a Sunday, somebody will stop by and pick her up and take her to see one of Cantor's shows, but that's about it.

She has never missed a single visit to her probation officer, precisely at the appointed time, and she always insists on signing Abe's name, as well as her own, to the probation report, just as though he is fulfilling his decreed sentence with her. And each time the big probation officer permits her to do this, Minnie pats him on the cheek and tells him he's a nice boy.

There is only one picture on the wall in her new room, the one of her and Abe cutting their wedding cake. And beside it there hangs another frame, with a letter from Abe in it.

On the night of their divorce, halfway through a bottle of wine, they had made a pact. Each of them was to compose a farewell letter to the other, so that even on the sad occasion of parting, the one remaining would have a message from the other on that special day. After all, they had never missed celebrating an Occasion in their lives together—never missed a birthday, anniversary, Valentine's Day, Mother's Day, Father's Day, Fourth of July, New Year's Eve, Arbor Day. Name it, and they celebrated it with each other, with gifts and flowers and poems and fancy greeting cards and hugs and kisses and whatnot. Every day that had a name was a reason for celebration for these two—so why not a parting, like death? It was only temporary anyway, wasn't it?

So, his letter hangs in a frame next to their wedding picture, and Minnie

328

Gold reads Abe Silver's last love letter aloud every day of the rest of her
life . . .

> I've got to go now,
> So Goodbye, Minnie.
> You're the greatest!
> In the bed, and out of the bed—the greatest!
> On the stage, and off the stage—the greatest!
> When you were younger, when you were older,
> When you were older yet, and got even younger yet,
> The greatest!
> As my sweetheart, as my wife, as my ex-wife—oh, boy!
> When you were skinny, when you got chubby,
> And then, when you got plump—
> Which was really as fat as you ever got!
> What can I say?
> You're the number-one greatest, that's all!
> Who can hold a candle to you?
> Nobody—that's who!
> So all I can say is a nice goodbye, now.
> It was a pleasure, doing this life with you.
> Olly-olly-oxen-free!
>
> Your Abe.

All Saint's Eve, that year, was not so hot for the angels. Two smartass
teenage kids, making their after-dark extortion rounds of Louie's old
neighborhood with their Halloween sack loaded with trick-or-treat goodies,
rang the front doorbell of the house that Louie had called home for the last
five years of his life.

Bathtub Florence answered the door with a nobody-home, get-away-
from-here-before-I-call-the-police-on-you—monsters. One of the boys,
positive she wasn't even going to open the door to them, yelled back at her,
calling her a fat ugly whore, whereupon she tore the door open, screaming
furious bloody murder, and threw a brass fireplace poker after them as they
took off down the block.

Later that night, after all the lights were out in the house, the two boys
returned for their revenge, sneaking silently down the driveway into the
backyard to throw a couple of hefty rocks crashing right through Louie's
beloved Sophia, smashing her into a million shards of colored glass, so that
she will never again reflect the heavenly rays of the shining sun as it arches
its way across the southland sky to the old and peaceful open sea of Louie
Levine.